Last Dance of the Lochkray

By
Brian M. H. Goodwin

Damnation Books, LLC.
P.O. Box 3931
Santa Rosa, CA 95402-9998
www.damnationbooks.com

Last Dance of the Lochkray
by Brian M. H. Goodwin

Digital ISBN: 978-1-61572-889-3
Print ISBN: 978-1-61572-890-9

Cover art by: Dawné Dominique
Edited by: Kim Richards

Copyright 2013 Brian M. H. Goodwin

Printed in the United States of America
Worldwide Electronic & Digital Rights
Worldwide English Language Print Rights

All rights reserved. No part of this book may be reproduced, scanned or distributed in any form, including digital and electronic or mechanical, including photocopying, recording, or by any information storage and retrieval system, without the prior written consent of the Publisher, except for brief quotes for use in reviews.

This book is a work of fiction. Characters, names, places and incidents either are the product of the author's imagination or are used fictitiously, and any resemblance to any actual persons, living or dead, events, or locales is entirely coincidental.

Greg—Just Imagine

*And God made two great lights;
the greater light to rule day, and the
lesser light to rule night.*
—Genesis 1:16 *The Holy Bible* King James Version

Introduction

The pulsating rhythms vibrated their way through the brick walls of the building, pounding their way out into the street where they quashed the sound of passing traffic. Like a violent heartbeat, the bass sound throbbed its way out to the people who walked those streets, enticing the young as it repelled the more seasoned. The name of the song being played was unimportant to any. Just another act mimicking those before them, ready to make great amounts of money before fading away into obscurity, prepared to feed on those who bought into their sounds and then discarded by the fickle audience when their clamor became passé. For now, at this moment, they were played loud enough to lure many young into the den of vice.

The access to this den sat guarded by two large men, victims of their own vanity, standing beneath a neon sign which read, The Paddock, in bright red letters. Along the wall of the building, the patrons stood in line, kept in order by velvet wrapped cord, lazily strung between brass posts. Some waited an hour to enter into the establishment, still others wait longer before they could gain entrance to this place of vogue—but such was the price of being amongst the trendy.

Yet one managed to walk through the doors without being noticed by any outside. Not by the drunken youths eagerly awaiting their admission, nor by the stoic bouncers holding back the crowd with their exaggerated proportions. He did not steal or sneak his way in, he did not avoid causing attention. Although he was clad entirely in clothing as dark as shadow and covered by a pitch overcoat, it could not be said he made his way through by camouflage. He simply walked past the crowd, hovered for a moment outside of the doorway, and then walked in—and none gave him any mind. None even saw him, as if he walked between each person's line of sight, dodging glimpses like raindrops, avoiding notice like air. Inside, the girl within the cage did not ask him for admission, nor did the bouncer, duplicate to his peers outside, take notice of the new arrival. He walked past these and into the large vestibule where people lined up, awkwardly waiting their turn to enter the lavatories. He surveyed these with only the slightest of interest, and then continued into the main bar.

Here the music became deafening, crushing all other sounds. The clink of billiard balls was inaudible, the hum of yelled conversation was taciturn, the clashing of bottles and glasses unable to be heard by any. The music—the pounding, pounding music—dominated. With the giant room seemingly lit by an eclipse, covered in a smoke that denied any other smells, the senses became muted and numb–and what the lighting, music and smoke did not diminish, the inebriating effects of alcohol did.

For the one who just entered the room, his senses were not quelled or overrun. He looked about with clear eyes that penetrated the darkness, listened carefully beneath the music, and sniffed the air for a scent no amount of smoke refused to yield.

He lazily waded into the crowd, his huge build allowing him to see above the heads of the rest, to view all about. Like so many of the bar's male patrons, he was only looking at the females of the place. His requirements were far more strict than the rest here. Where libation and resignation allowed the others to approach those otherwise felt to be below standard, this hunter refused to surrender his criteria. His was the beholder's eye, demanding beauty, and the consort he sought had to beyond beauty in all respects—of the right age, of the right heart, and at the right moment by the moon's count. The feed had to be strong, for a long journey was at hand.

The hunter looked about, scanning left to right with his pale blue eyes, walking with a determined pace through the crowd. Occasionally he turned to take a more detailed look at one of the patrons, but none measured up to what he wanted. Too old or too young, less virtuous than originally believed to be, just not of the right scent. It was a difficult hunt for him, although to look at him one would never know it. He walked so calmly, so casually. He stalked the bar as any other might amble across a sunny park.

Then he located his prey.

His head jerked suddenly towards the dance floor, his eyes became determined slits, his nostrils flared and inhaled deeply. He found what he wanted, through a break in the crowd, a momentary alleyway that let him see his target. He changed his direction and headed for the circular dance floor, recessed three steps below the rest of the room. There, the giant speakers took a moment to relax and the song slowed down for a few bars, a sedated bridge before exploding into its rapid throbbing beat again, and it was then that he got a clear look at her.

She danced with two friends, both female, her hands held high above her head, slowly grinding down as if she were the euphony itself. Then, as the tempo raised again, her hands came down and her body joined in the wild dance of the song.

He locked on her. Twenty-one revolutions around the sun, twelve days from her last time, her virtue unknown. In an age of loose ethics, this quality of prey was a rare find and upon seeing it, the hunter's dark heart pounded as hard as the music. He immediately found her scent amongst the others and inhaled it deeply, feeding his appetite, turning its smoldering into a blaze. He forced his way to the dance floor and watched his quarry carefully. He looked into her as best he could, and cautiously devised his attack. He would do it right there, he decided, within the establishment. Right there. On the dance floor.

As for the young lady, she was unaware that she was hunted. Though she often found herself pursued by men, she knew how to obstruct their advances. While many in the bar went there with the thought of finding some kind of partner, her only real desire was to dance and have a few drinks with her friends. Both of her dancing companions had boyfriends that were off somewhere else that night. They would all meet up later, probably go out for coffee and listen as the boys made up stories about not having gone to see the strippers, but for now it was just the three of them, enjoying the evening together with laughter and revelry, relishing the simplest bounds of sisterhood.

So, as the pounding song came to a close, the three laughed at one another and prepared to exit the dance floor to go to a table. A brief moment of silence came from the speakers, a sure sign that a slower tune was about to start up. The prey's friends turned away and made towards the stairs off the floor just as the soft melody began. The prey never followed her friends. She paused. A faint hand brushed across her back with a touch like a breeze.

Her body followed her head's turn as she looked to see who touched her. Upon seeing nobody behind, her eyes darted about in a moment of confusion. Her gaze scanned left and then right, before deciding it was simply imagination causing her to pivot. A shrug of the shoulders indicated this was explanation enough, and she prepared to return to her company. Then something caught her attention. Standing just on the edge of the dance floor, staring at her. A man. A handsome young man. His head dipped casually forwards, his hands shoved deep into his stylishly dark pants, soft brown eyes shyly looking out at her above a pleasant thin smile. She returned the soft smile, an odd swell of familiarity washing over her as she studied the handsome stranger's face. Everybody else on the dance floor had matched up, and only these two stood alone staring at one another. For the girl it was a bizarre moment, as if suddenly locked into a dream, looking at a stranger and still feeling comfortable with him. The young man looked about, as if searching for objectors, before extending his hand with an inviting nod. The girl's slight smile widened as the faintest feelings of anxiety were pushed away. She softly floated over to him and took his hand, his warm soft hand, and let his other arm stretch around her as they swayed to the delicate beat of the song.

As his other arm went around her, she closed her eyes. He let go of her hand, abandoning the etiquette of formal dance. He held her as a lover might, and still she did not feel the need to retreat. A warm sensation started in her chest, as her breathing became deeper. She never danced with strangers, never, and yet it seemed so right to go to him, to let him take her into his arms. No salutation, no introduction, just the dance. She squeezed herself tightly into him, closer than she ever danced with anyone. It just seemed right, the way it was supposed to be. In her mind's eye she saw herself pressed into the young man as he gently caressed her back and pulled her into him. She saw him close his eyes as well, feeding off of her warmth. She saw herself swaying, dancing softly, falling in love.

What she could not see was the Lochkray. For she was not in the arms of any handsome dark-eyed young man, she was in the arms of a killer who stared forward indifferently with pale eyes, touching his prey, feeling its worth, drawing its mind toward his in preparation to feed. Yet, when the prey let her eyes flutter open for a moment, all she saw was the handsome young man, not the hulking form who held her now. When she closed her eyes again, praying that the song would never end, she slipped closer and closer to the Lochkray.

Soon, she could only see them dancing, all the others of the bar faded away into darkness. They were alone in a black room, dancing on a black floor, flickering flames above black candles illuminating only them. They were alone, dancing as if they were making love, their bodies wavering with the melody. No longer was she wearing the tight jeans and short top she had chosen for the bar—now she was wearing a beautiful evening dress, adorned with jewelry, dancing so close to the man that they seemed as one. Then she was as one. Alone. Alone on the black dance floor, her eyes closed, dancing contentedly, alone with the thoughts of the man in her heart.

Yet though her mind's eye could not see him, the Lochkray was still in there. He hid, out of sight of her imagination's regard. She continued to dance, her skin becoming warm and a quivering sensation started below her stomach, burning hard within her. She caressed herself and searched her body within her mind. She felt on fire and her body quaked. She saw herself dancing alone there. She saw herself quiver as the lascivious sensation ignited deep within her, pulsating throughout. This feeling grew stronger, turning her breathing into a panting, her chest rising and falling rapidly while she continued to caress her body. Still the Lochkray watched from the outside, his thoughts directing her actions, exciting the young innocent within the imagined ring of candles. She rocked her head back and forth, shoulder to shoulder as her passion grew stronger and stronger within. Her hands clasped together between her breasts and pressed painfully hard against her swelling chest. Her head was thrown back, her mouth opening wide towards the black ceiling, her lungs releasing a powerful burst of passion as she cried out into the darkness above.

But no sound came.

Her eyes snapped open. She stared upward at the colored lights throbbing along the bar's ceiling, her head locked back, able to see others dancing on the floor in her peripheral vision. There, right at her side, was the Lochkray, looking down at her with apathy, his own mouth open, as if ready to kiss.

The girl tried to cry out again, and again no sound emerged. The Lochkray gently brought his head above hers, until his view of the floor was blocked by her panicked face, framing wide white eyes that helplessly darted back and forth. Then he inhaled through his own open mouth, drawing in the girl's mute scream. A scream she could no longer stop.

Utter terror, unlike any fear she ever felt before, rushed through her as she realized she was unable to halt the silent cry. With her mouth agape and her scream escaping, she felt herself drain. Her very being felt pulled outwards where it became entangled within his inhaling breath. Her panic became heavy, her body felt drawn to the ground. The dark room darkened, and the colorful lights dancing above the killer's head faded.

Nobody noticed as life's basic impetus departed from the prey, escaped out of her mouth, and into the Lochkray. Nobody noticed as she grasped at his body feebly, clawing at him, trying to make him stop. Nobody noticed as the Lochkray stepped away. Nobody noticed the Lochkray leave the bar. Nobody noticed the girl crumple to the floor. Nobody noticed that she had died. Until it was too late.

Until nothing could be done.

While friends and family mourned, the Lochkray continued on without remorse. Just another feeding. Just another daylight who stayed out too long after the setting sun. Just another sacrifice. Just another hunt.

Just night.

Part One
Preparation

Chapter One

Panic.

Sheer panic.

Running was next to impossible on the uneven rock surface, making the breakaway more of a stumbling spurt of speed and floundering than a full sprint. The panic running through the man caused his judgment to fail miserably and his direction became frenzied, his steps awkwardly landing on the rough ground. The forest was dark underneath the moonless sky, making the race hopeless for him. Yet even though he could barely manage to have his feet hit the ground without sending him tumbling, the thing that was following him could be heard moving fluidly around him, circling through the brush, an eerie rustling that sped around in all directions, behind him, then instantly in front.

He was alone, crazily stumbling through the dark woods, fear making his heart pound so hard he could barely distinguish between it and the sound of the predator. Ego had told him to go on this expedition alone, and now he found himself cursing that pride. He stopped beside a tree and leaned on it, attempting to regain his control. He shut his eyes tight, making little difference to what he saw before. He breathed as deeply as he could, fighting back the urge to release those breaths as shrill shrieks. He ran the word *calm* over and over in his mind, hoping its meaning would impress on him. Slowly he brought his eyes open again and he listened into the night.

Not long before, he was someplace else, off in a dream. Or a hallucination. Or the beginning of this nightmare. The woods where he was working had melted away to become somewhere pleasant, some place nice. He was warm, he remembered that. It was daytime, and he remembered seeing a cold bottle of golden liquid sitting on a table, the condensation on the outside running along the bottle invitingly.

It hadn't seemed like a dream then, it seemed right that he should be there, as if that were the only place he should ever be. It was there, in that dream, the feeling he was being watched started. Ignoring the feelings at first, he instead chose to concentrate on the cool bottle, preparing to reach out and grab hold of it and bring it to his achingly dry mouth. Then he heard the predator, and knew that he was hunted. Then, he realized he was still in the dark woods and the warm setting that was around him shattered. Once brought out from the dream, he saw he had wandered away from his camp and his supplies. Then he heard the snapping of branches and brush as the predator advanced toward him and the hunt was on.

Without any direction he started to run, blindly stumbling through the brush and trees. He had not seen his hunter yet, but he could tell It was large, far too large to move with the speed and agility It did. Now he was listening intently to the woods, hoping to find some sound of this hunter, wishing that he had never wandered away from his camp, and wishing even more that he was back in that warm place with the cold bottle back in front of him.

He cocked his head to the side, trying to relocate the sounds of whatever was out there—or perhaps even a hint as to the direction of his camp. Because there, in his tent, lying parallel to his sleeping bag, wrapped in a burgundy nylon carrying case, was a twenty-two caliber rifle. Not a powerful weapon, but a weapon nonetheless. Perhaps just the sound of it firing would be enough to scare the animal off, or the sting of a bullet would make it search out easier prey, or, better yet, it would kill the animal. Even the ax which sat beside the smoldering campfire would be comforting in his hands, for now he felt naked and helpless, and his eyes would not reveal where he should go.

The sound of the animal in the woods had subsided, but this did not bring the man any comfort, for he sensed It had not gone away. It had simply stopped running when he had. The man stood perfectly still, frantically trying to form a plan. Caught within the terrifying silence around him, deep instincts buried within his psyche knew that the animal was coming closer. Slower now, maybe, but approaching still. He tried to find out what direction it was coming from, but nothing suggested that. Black sounds and silent sights were all that was offered to him. He smelled the smoke of his campfire wafting through the woods, teasing him, but he could not tell what direction it came from. Tears swelling into his eyes, blurring the black, the man quaked.

Out within the night, the animal watched the man cautiously. Despite their size, its clawed hands paced on the uneven ground gently. Its massive head tilted back and forth, catching all possible scents, seeing all possible sights. Its eyes pierced through the darkness, having none of the trouble that the prey was having. It knew which way the quarry needed to go in order to return to its camp. The animal could never get lost. It flicked its tongue out past the rows of spiny teeth, like a snake, tasting the air. It opened its mouth and inhaled a great gulp, revealing the inside of its fierce maw, drenched in saliva.

The hunter's dark skin undulated with every step, but the darkness of its hide absorbed the movement, making it look like a torpid shadow. Through its perfect eyes it saw the path of attack that allowed the cleanest kill. It already missed its first chance, clumsily awakening the quarry out of the dream state it had fallen into. Then the quarry ran, making the hunter more cautious, not wanting to effect its attack unless it made a flawless slay. Softly the hunter pawed and slithered forward. Just four more steps until the clearest path, just three more until the most direct kill, just two more until it pounced, just one more until the hunt was over.

The man spun toward the explosion of movement from behind him, a futile yell rising up from his lungs. The animal rushed past him in a blur, a giant force that knocked him to the ground with a violent blow, and then sped off. With the warm feeling of blood running over his body and a throbbing wound crying out from his side, the man released a guttural scream to the black sky.

The sound of the rushing hunter went back out into the woods like a rocket flying past him, but no sooner had the sound begun to subdue than he heard it start to return for another pass. The man flipped himself over onto his stomach and tried to claw away from the approaching sound. He reached out to take hold of a rock to pull forward.

His fingers brushed the stone just as he felt the animal lock itself onto his leg and pull him back, tearing open the wound along his side, and sending a rush of horror through him like none he ever experienced. With a firm grip on the man's leg, the hunter yanked him from the ground with a flick of its neck, tossing him into the air like a rag doll, and then caught him again in its mouth, clamping around his torso with a violent crunch.

The man looked down, screaming as the huge creature locked its impossibly immense jaws around him. He hit feebly at its vile head, trying to make it let go, but it would not relent. It just stared at him with a black eye, watching him scream into the remorseless night as the grip around him became tighter and tighter.

John Hadden listened to the sound of his body being crushed within the animal's massive jaws, blood flowing out of his mouth like a fountain. He felt the tears from his eyes run down the side of his face, back to his ears and down to the ground. For a fraction of a moment, he remembered the drops on the side of that golden liquid-filled bottle in his dream, running down to the table.

Chapter Two

The priest looked about his office, realizing how old it had become. Although the rest of the great building around him had changed over time with the outer world, this office had not. Outside of the giant oak doors were computers, phones, and fax machines. Within that room there was only simplicity—some would say obsolescence. Lit only by sunlight stabbing through the dust-filled air in long golden streams, the room was a mix of shadow black and wooden browns, furnished with objects beyond antiquity. The priest had long felt a part of that room. He felt just as ancient and untouched by the changing world as the setting he sat in. He felt locked away. He felt old. Most of all, he felt forgotten. Like the texts sitting on shelves in the walls: forgotten, yellowed, worn with age—despite a lack of use.

Today the books were remembered, though, as was he. He heard in his mind what they would have said in Rome. *"Is this not familiar?"* they would mutter to one another, and *"Were there not stories of this?"* and *"I'm sure I remember hearing tales,"* whispered between words, spoken in hushes. Then they would think. Then they would remember. They would remember the office. They would remember the books. They would remember the old man. They would remember the stories. *"An unholy place,"* would have been said cautiously. *"An unholy people."*

"Lochkray," the old priest whispered to himself, listening to the word as it echoed softly about the room. The word felt odd on his lips. So often he had read it, so often he had studied it, and yet he could not remember ever having said it. "Lochkray," he repeated, this time louder. He found the strength within to smile at himself, at his bravery. "Lochkray," he said one last time, his smile fading. His fingers drummed softly across a red file-folder that sat on his desk beside a torn manila envelope. He thought back to a time when that word, Lochkray, had first been heard by him, and he contemplated its meaning. He remembered having suggested the Lochkray were a test of faith rather than a reality. He also remembered his teacher becoming angry with him, the only time he ever seen the man provoked.

"The Lord requires faith alone," the teacher had chastised him. "The Lochkray do not. Man's ignorance of them is their advantage. They exist because man demands evidence, and they hide from scrutiny. You are needed in action, not conviction."

Action, not conviction.

He was now the age his teacher had been then, and he only remembered that man as ancient. So much he saw since then, so much he had done. Conviction and faith were the extent of his knowledge then. Only now was true action being requested. Only now, when he was far too old to do anything to help. If only they had asked before,. He closed his eyes and thought back to another time, another man. A younger man. The man he used to be. He could have helped. He could have done it himself. He would have been prepared. Yet back then, all that young man did was ask, "What do they look like?"

What do they look like?

Are they beautiful?

Nobody answered his questions then, and how he wished he could go back and talk to that young man. To tell himself what he knew. To teach lessons that only dark and bleak experience had taught him. To place his hands on the shoulders of Innocent fool, squeeze firmly and make the point clear. *They are not beautiful*, he desperately wanted to tell his younger self, *but when you see them, you will think they are.*

There was a knock at the door that brought the old priest back to the reality of the room around him. "Enter," he called in heavily accented Russian. The giant oak door, clamped beneath an elaborate stone frame, opened up, the robust iron hinges protesting loudly at being moved. The head of a young man stuck into the office; an earnest face under a mop of reddish hair that made him look even younger than he actually was.

"You wanted to see me, Father?" the young man asked, also in accented Russian.

"Yes, my son," the priest's gruff voice replied. "I have a task for you."

Chapter Three

Elisha King walked through the hallways of McGuinness University, her mind unfocused, awkwardly drifting from one thought to another. The slapping sound of her shoes hitting the hard floor echoed loudly through the halls, and yet she was listening to something else. Something in memory.
"It'll be fun," she just been told. "It'll be fun."
Just keep telling yourself that.
Occasionally she saw one of the doors that spotted the hallways slightly ajar, and within she made out the shape or shadow of a person working, hunched over a desk or lab table with a pencil wagging rapidly above sheets of paper, but no one gave her any attention. Anybody so devoted as to still be working this late in the afternoon would not be distracted by something as simple as a postgraduate wandering the empty halls. Within another hour, security would come by and tell all that the building was locked up, and whatever projects were not completed at that time would have to wait until the next day.

Elisha made her way to the grand foyer where she descended the sweeping staircase to the main level. The grand foyer and staircase in this part of McGuinness University were quite different than the rest of the school. Here, the painfully "modern" 1970's architecture was forgone by a more classic design.

In her six years at the school, Elisha had noted that every time a picture of some significant school event occurred, such as graduation photos and donated checks, it was the classic oak railing and dark carpeting of the grand foyer that was visible in the background. This, despite the students and staffs' constant vocal pride in the way the artistic and unconventional designs of the school's buildings mimicked the liberal approach to the institute's academic pursuits.

Sometimes, Elisha thought, *you just gotta stick with what you know works. Newer isn't always better.*

Elisha came to the bottom of the stairs, then turned one-hundred-and-eighty degrees, looped around past the stairs and went to another door, papers advertising rooms for rent posted on the cork board beside it fluttering up as she passed by. Through this door, beneath the great staircase, there was another stairway, this one made of cement, modest in design and smelling of the urine of a drunken student who took advantage of the privacy the usually idle stairwell offered. That smell would subside eventually, until the next drunkard was unwilling or unable to find a proper lavatory—and with the regular session of fall classes about to commence, this smell would soon be a permanent and regularly replenished odor until the following May.

Ignoring the reek, Elisha descended the stairs and went through the doorway at the bottom, into a hallway that was only slightly more decorated than the stairway that led to it. Long and narrow, a brown and yellow carpet ran along the hall into the dim lights that failed to properly illuminate the passage. The lighting was effective enough in showing her destination though, for the only inhabited office along this dark place had a ring of light in front of it, brightly puncturing the dimness.

On the open door of this room, letters were stuck on the middle, spelling out the words: J. HADDEN PHD, ARCHAEOLOGY DEPT. Elisha walked over to the door and looked at the printed title for a moment, and then shook her head at it. Even the sight of his name made her cringe. If that man was within the office, she would never have let herself come down there. She had no need for the harassment that routinely flowed from J. Hadden's mouth.

She reached forward and pushed the door open a little farther, revealing the sole occupant of the small room sitting behind a desk, intently reading from a thick tome, apparently oblivious to her arrival. The book drawing all of the young man's attention was one of many scattered on the desk, all open to different sections, and all lying atop a blanket of maps that completely covered the desktop and flopped over the edges like a paper tablecloth.

While one of the male's fingers guided his reading through the book, his other hand hovered in the air, holding a collection of papers that apparently could not find a place on the desk among the stained coffee mugs, lamp, and other articles and artifacts occupying spots between the strewn books.

Framing the entire room were books—piles and piles of books—all on shelves built into the walls, some upright, others laying awkwardly on their sides atop the more properly placed volumes, and others tipped forwards as a reminder to review some piece of information within. On the floor of the room there were boxes scattered about, as if somebody were moving in or out, and on the side of these were dates written thickly in black marker. Some of these had their tops open and within could be seen stacks of poorly organized papers, untouched and unreturned to their authors from the previous year.

Elisha long suspected that Doctor Hadden had a practice of avoiding the marking of term papers and instead gave marks to his students based solely on his personal opinion of them. That explained why Allen Therrien obtained marks high enough to qualify him to be hired as Hadden's assistant. A look into those boxes, she was sure, would confirm her suspicion, but her disdain for Hadden resulted in indifference over his procedures.

"Hey, Allen," Elisha called out. She was hoping to startle him, but he was so engrossed that he barely noticed.

"You have to look at this," Allen replied in a hushed, dry voice. "He's on to something. Doctor Hadden's...on...to...some...thi..."

Allen drifted away into his reading once again. Elisha shook her head and stepped into the office. Allen Therrien was a good-looking guy, twenty-four years old with dark hair and eyes.

Elisha found him mildly attractive, but every time she tried to flirt with him, it went over his head. She knew he found her appealing, but was way too socially awkward to catch on to her playful advances, so she stopped trying. She wasn't really interested but in her mind a little flirting couldn't hurt. For Allen, he was so busy being polite and convinced of his social ineptitude that he never understood what was going on. She knew he had long given up his befuddled attempts at expressing any interest in her.

"Is thatden's work?"

"Yes," Allen replied, still failing to look up from the book. "The university is being stupid. He's on to something here. This site he found is a complete paradox. He has to be right. I mean, look at this: Selkirk pottery, bone awls of Saint Lawrence Iroquoian style, and Huron-Petun pipes all lying on the same stratified layer together. And where? The middle of nowhere. He was on to something. He was on...." His voice trailed off again as he brought his nose closer to the pages in front of him.

"Allen, Professor Fellows wants me to talk with you about—"

"Look at this," he interrupted without realizing, his finger sharply pointing at the central book on the desk. "These burials are best described as Western Basin Woodland, a thousand kilometers north of where they should be, and nowhere near any evidence of settlement. Why? This isn't the result of long distance marriage practices, no way. The university can say what it wants about contaminated samples, but they can't argue that somebody went through a lot of trouble to bury these items in a very specific way. Doctor Hadden's right. There was something going on there, and these people thought it was awfully important."

"A late Woodland Canterbury cathedral, up near James Bay?" Elisha asked with acid tones. Allen finally looked up from his book, quick enough to catch Elisha wincing at the sharpness she just used. He could tell she regretted speaking in the disparaging manner.

Allen brought his lips together tightly and dropped his brow. It had been weeks since he last saw his mentor, leaving him to endure the comments and ridicule of Hadden's peers. Weeks of smart-ass remarks and cynical criticism from people with no interest in listening to the facts. None of the others at the university possessed Hadden's imagination or foresight. Always having been an academic, Allen found Hadden's personality impressive. Here was a man that stood up for what he discovered, stood in the face of critics and told them that they could believe in him or just plain go to hell. Throughout his schooling, Allen had seldom ever seen an academic so brazen and aggressive. It had impressed him when he had first met Hadden, and continued to impress him, all the way up to this latest find.

This latest find, however, left Allen alone. While Hadden was off proving how right he was, Allen was left to hold down the fort. Certainly not the first time he was left to keep things together while his mentor pursued some tangent—which had to be allowed, as a genius like Doctor Hadden needed room to pursue his unconventional intellect. This time, though, it wasn't just a matter of keeping his mail in order or coming up with excuses for missed appointments.

This time, he had to defend his mentor. Defend the determined intellectual. Defend against the sarcasm, ridicule, and shortsightedness. Without guidance and encouragement, Allen became lost. Working off of his belief in the man, he was alone against the rest of the establishment. Without knowing for himself, with only limited evidence and data to back him up, he had to defend Hadden—and himself. Allen pulled himself up in his seat. The scramble of papers in his hand dropped to the desk, and he left his search among the jumbled writings and collections to once again do his duty and stand up for his mentor.

"Just because there's no previous archaeological evidence of such a place doesn't mean It didn't exist," Allen said sharply to her.

"There's no historical evidence either," Elisha started to rebut, her words overlapping Allen's. "If what Hadden says were true, then the time period in which this site was active should have been mentioned in the historical record, from any one of a number of groups."

"Perhaps the locals were a little more cautious of the Europeans than we've been giving them credit for. Or perhaps nobody took it seriously enough to write down. Any which way, you can't deny that there is a site in Northern Ontario Is a complete enigma. It is well worth studying, and this university has missed out on a fantastic opportunity to research it. It would rather pass the site off as a fraud, or a fluke, or an error, just because it fails to fit neatly into the present model of Eastern Woodland Archaeology." Allen sat back in the chair, suddenly realizing that he had raised his voice.

After a heavy moment of silence, Elisha spoke softly. "No it hasn't," she said.

"What hasn't what?"

"The university hasn't missed out on its chance."

"Yes it has," he said. "I tell you, Elisha, he knows what he's talking about."

"They believe him," Elisha replied, all previous skepticism being forced away. "At least, they're willing to listen. That's what I've come to tell you. The department wants to meet with you to discuss locating Doctor Hadden. They want to bring him back here, so that they can make arrangements to sponsor his expedition." Elisha closed her eyes, hardly believing that she had vocalized such a pointless plan.

"Why now?" a much softer voice asked.

"The last time the university refused to support one of Hadden's expeditions, he ended up finding that site on Lake Huron."

"The Manitoulin Island Amikwa?"

"Right. Then, that archaic pottery-making clan that he believed existed in New York State. When he turned up evidence, every journal in the world reported how he went out on his own, made a fantastic find, and restructured how the archaeological community viewed prehistory. That made the university look cowardly for failing to back him when he asked.

Nobody cared when it turned out to be a mistake—that didn't get printed anywhere. Still, the university suffered the embarrassment and he got all the glory. This time, they decided to change their decision, and jump on board with his theories, before they end up looking...stupid." Again, Elisha closed her eyes.

"Why do they want to talk to me?"

"The department heads want to hear what you have to say on the matter," she said coolly. "They're talking about sending you after him to bring him back. They're going to listen to what you have to say in fifteen minutes in the anthropology lecture hall."

"Me?"

"If you can convince them that his theories are reasonable, they will support him. As it is, they figure you are the only one that has ever really listened to what he has to say on the matter. So, as it is, you are the closest thing to an expert on the subject. At hand, anyway."

"Fifteen minutes?" Allen frantically searched the piles of papers before him. "That's not enough time to put together a presentation...I mean...I need maps, and data. I don't have anything to show them...I mean..."

"Just tell them what you know. Just the facts. Don't get passionate or agitated. That's what they hate about Hadden's presentations. Stay calm." She turned out of the office and walked back toward the stairs. "I'll see you up there," she called to him, listening to the frantic rustling of papers behind her. She walked down the hall, and came to the bottom of the stairs. There she paused and took hold of the railing, and her head dipping towards the ground. A deep breath was inhaled.

"It'll be fun," she said softly to herself.

* * * *

In grade eleven, Allen Therrien had to make a speech for English class. However, that particular spring, the timing of the speech happened to fall at the same time that he had to complete his major research reports for biology and geography. Those being far more important and interesting to him, he took on larger projects than he probably should have. On top of these, he finally obtained his first steady girlfriend. Although the grand relationship barely lasted three months, the second of these landed when he should have spent time working on the speech instead of fumbling about with the girl in the hours between the end of school and when his mother got home from work.

So, when the day came for Allen to give his English speech, it was nonexistent. For the rest of his life, he recalled that weekend as the great one where he lost his virginity, rather than recalling the following Monday, standing empty handed before Mister Stafford's English class. Seven years later, as he stood before the Anthropology department of McGuinness University, his clumsy lustfulness was forgotten, and the fluttering uneasiness in his stomach was relived with vivid clarity. Back then, an ad-libbed monologue about a family car trip—half-true story, half stolen from a stand-up comedian he saw on TV the night before—garnered him a B minus, and more than a few laughs from his classmates. Now, he could not ad-lib or fake his way through this one. He had to give facts. *Don't get passionate or agitated,* he repeated Elisha's advice to himself.

That day in grade eleven was probably the closest Allen ever come to realizing his own talent for public speaking. He always felt that the strong marks for speeches and presentations he received during his schooling years were due to his excellent research skills on his chosen subjects—always oblivious to his talent and the quietly charismatic presence he had when speaking to groups. Standing unprepared in front of the Anthropology department lecture hall, Allen only found comfort in that he followed Hadden's work religiously. Once Hadden successfully turned the course of North Eastern archaeology around, Allen knew he would be in a perfect position to get his own PhD, and the groundwork of his thesis was already started. The study of Information made it easy for him to know where to start on that day:

"Eastern Woodland Prehistory is generally divided into two regions," Allen's presentation began. "The north and the south."

He stared down at the podium before him, as if he were reading information from the assortment of papers that he brought with him—he was in fact just taking a moment to divert his eyes from the group sitting in front of him.

This lecture hall was one of McGuinness University's smaller, seating just over eighty. six of these seats were empty. In the second row a half-dozen sullen-looking individuals sat, staring at the podium as Allen tried to hide behind it. With the lighting on him, Allen could not make out their faces or eyes—they were just silhouettes of black jutting out of the tiny hills of seats. Still, he sensed they were staring forward skeptically, and Allen found himself wishing he could just tell them about his dad losing his temper or his fight with his sister en route to the east coast, rather than this tough sell.

The only audience member he made out was Elisha, sitting off to the far right, and he already knew her opinion on this subject. Lecturing to the institution's most influential and educated on a subject they did not believe in was enough to make Allen want to vomit.

With a deep breath and a silent curse, he continued. "The south has always been known as the more progressed of the two groups, going right back to the time when humans first entered the area and the north was covered by glacier. All the way through to the historic period where it has been recorded that the south was primarily populated by groups who spoke Iroquoian languages, whereas the northern populations spoke Algonkian based languages.

"Throughout the archaeological record we can see that the northern peoples were a separate cultural entity from the south. They discovered how to make and utilize pottery later than the south, they were much less affected by the influential trends of the Hopewell culture, and when the south turned to agriculture as a means of food supply, the north still maintained the lifestyle better described as hunter-gatherer. While the south was progressing into a new age, the north was technologically behind. At first glance, the north had much it could gain from the south, but not vice versa."

Allen took a deep breath. The babbling introduction, partly borrowed from a third-year paper he wrote, was enough review, and it had served its purpose. He breathed more calmly, and focused on what he was there for.

"Doctor Hadden, however," he continued slowly, choosing his words more carefully now, "believes he has found evidence of a place far into the north, of special regard to all populations of the Eastern Woodlands. While camping deep in the forests of northern Ontario, Doctor Hadden discovered what he believes to be a burial mound. He did some preliminary digging into this mound and found what is nothing less than…" Allen paused. *Amazing? Astonishing?* Those were too dramatic. *Be professional*, he reminded himself.

"…enigmatic. Instead of a traditional Algonkian burial mound, he found specimens of Iroquoian pottery and tools, alongside the expected Selkirk shards. Of greater interest was the inclusion of evidence of maize and other cultivated agricultural products within the mound, over a thousand kilometers away from where they should have been. From his preliminary study, this was not a burial mound or ossuary as one might expect to find in the region. Doctor Hadden theorizes that this place had some kind meaning for the natives, not only of the area, but far reaching, right down to Hopewell. He believes that he has found…" Again Allen paused.

"North America's place of pilgrimage," a barbed male voice from the group finished, echoing around the empty lecture hall. "The Mecca of the subarctic." A snort of contempt followed.

"Let him finish, Stanley," hissed the woman beside him. "Please continue, Mister Therrien."

"I don't know what he found," Allen conceded. "Yes, Doctor Hadden believes that he has found a place of religious significance and people were willing to spend months, even years, traveling north to leave offerings there. And yes, Doctor Hadden stated that the behavior of the people suggests it was some kind of place of pilgrimage. I don't know if that's true. What I think is, he found suggestive evidence that the area is not as devoid of cultural merit as was originally believed. I know Doctor Hadden's research, and I can assure you there is a site of significant academic interest up there. I think he could be talked into sharing its worth with the university. If that's what you want—"

"The problem, Mister Therrien, is not one of worth." It was the woman speaking again. Susan Fellows. Allen liked her. Elisha worked as her lab assistant, and Fellows was just as much Elisha's mentor as John Hadden was his. Besides being the author of countless admired papers and books, Professor Fellows was also very talented at stepping on the toes of her peers—intentionally. She loved making declarations about how she viewed things in the most tactless way, but despite his equally unconventional and aggressive approach to academia,

Doctor Hadden was no fan of hers. Allen had listened to many heated arguments between the two. Despite his reverence for Doctor Hadden, Allen still thought of Doctor Fellows as one of the most brilliant in the institution.

"The value, both academically and financially, is not the primary issue," she said. "The problem is that this academy, and institutions across the continent, have shelves and shelves of artifacts and bones that have never been looked at before, never been studied. They're just collecting dust. Quite frankly, it's pissing the First Nation populations off. They view what we do as grave robbing, and they are right."

"Susan—" came from the row of sillouetted professors. Allen could not tell who had spoken.

"No, Carl. How many times in recent years have we gone to the reservations and asked for their assistance in examining an artifact, and all we receive is silence? The band councils are instructing their people not to talk to us, and the people are doing just that. Perhaps if we were more accommodating and understanding in previous years, we would have better communication now. Instead, all we get is dicked around." She turned her attention back to Allen, whose face momentarily held a smile. "If what Doctor Hadden found is of the magnitude he believes, then this university would happily back the exploration of his discovery. We're sure the native groups of the area also want to be involved in the discovery of any cultural location they have lost. We can't just tear into burial grounds and continue our cultural annihilation and genocide of this land's indigenous people."

"What Doctor Fellows is saying," Professor Carl Siouan's soothing words immediately started up when Susan took a breath, "is that caution is warranted. McGuinness University has a reputation of being both socially conscious, and academically innovative. It is possible that we were somewhat hasty in our decision not to endorse Doctor Hadden's find, but you must understand that he wanted to dive into it rashly, without proper consideration for all parties involved, and that simply caused us to feel...uncomfortable. What we want you to do, Allen, is to get him to return to the university, where we promise that we will support his expedition—providing that he will take the time with us to be methodical and solicitous. And out of that, a much better analysis."

"We haven't decided that," Stanley Azores snapped to the man on his right.

"Yes, we have," Susan Fellows returned in a voice so contemptuous it made Allen smile again. "We are going to send out a party to locate John and have him brought back here. If young Mister Therrien is confident that he can find him..."

Allen stared at her for a moment. The statement to Doctor Azores was in fact a question to him, and he knew it. It was the answer he was unable to identify.

"W-well," he stammered, "he showed me where he found the burial mound on a map. I know where that place is. That's not the problem. It's just that Doctor Hadden told me you can't drive or even fly into this place. It's not close enough to any big lake or river to land on. He said it takes a couple of days walking to get into it. It's over forty kilometers away from the nearest lake you can land on." Allen tried to smile a little. The idea of wandering two days into the bush sounded like one of the worst assignments he could possibly be given—the idea thatden thought of it as the best possible vacation was ridiculous, but certainly in character with the man.

"Are you capable of the expedition?" Carl Siouan asked.

"I could do it, I guess. It's just, I don't really know much about camping, or finding north on a map or anything. I mean, I know where he is *on* a map. Perhaps I could show one of you, or somebody from the university, and they could—'

"No," interrupted Susan, "we've already discussed that. Unfortunately John can be stubborn as an ass, and I don't think he would look upon it too kindly if any of us, who failed to support him when he originally asked, were to show up and start making demands on him. Is why we asked you. He likes you, Mister Therrien. You could talk him into returning. You're a reasonable young man, you know the survey of the site would best be funded and supervised by the university. You would be capable of showing him that. As for not knowing wilderness survival, don't worry. We will set you up with somebody to guide you. Besides, Elisha King will be going with you too."

Allen's gaze snapped to the female at the far right of the group.

"Elisha?"

"She is to ensure," Doctor Azores almost spat, "that you convince John Hadden, and not the other way around." Elisha gave Allen a feeble wave.

Susan stood up and spoke directly to Allen. "Preparations will start tomorrow and by Saturday the two of you will be flown to the lake closest to the site. Hopefully you will be able to find John and have him back before mid-week. If all goes well, we will have completed preliminary studies of the site by the end of September, before the snow starts. If the university likes what it sees from Doctor Hadden's findings, it's prepared to wave your next year's tuition." Allen returned his gaze to Susan.

"Wave my tuition? All of it?"

At this time, the other four PhDs got to their feet as well, collected their belongings and made their way out of the auditorium.

"Come to the anthropology office at ten tomorrow morning. There, we will get all of the crappy little details sorted out for you. Don't worry, we'll take care of everything. You just start coming up with a hell of a sales pitch to convince John that he has to come back. You have already convinced us that you are capable. Now all you have to do is prove us right." Susan Fellows turned around and walked up the sloped aisle to the back of the room where she exited, leaving Allen to once again stare at Elisha, alone in the lecture hall. She tried her best to give an encouraging smile.

"It'll be fun," she said to him.

Chapter Four

Elisha shared her apartment with another student who was working out of town for the summer. Because of the moderately high rent for the apartments, most of the students who lived in the complex were working as well as going to school, and subsequently there was very little of the bedlam normally associated with student residential areas. Most who lived in the building were either serious students or senior citizens, the building's other primary rental population—an unusual combination that oddly never clashed. Deborah, Elisha's roommate, was especially quiet and reserved. She was so quiet, Elisha barely noticed she was living alone during summer months. It always seemed like Deborah was just in the next room, studying, all day long. However, when the night came, the entire apartment was lonely.

Crawling into bed for the night, wearing her flannel red tartan nightshirt, she became all too aware of the places within the apartment that a person could be hiding, waiting until she went to sleep. Reason pushed these thoughts away, but still, they lurked on the periphery of imagination.

Eventually sleep quelled all reason and fears, and replaced them with dreams. Tonight it would take effort to ensure that these dreams were not about the latest situation she found herself in. She and Allen talked for a while after the meeting broke up. She felt the two of them had a healthy understanding of how this expedition should work. She made it clear to him that this was not her choice and the only reason she agreed to go find Hadden was that a similar offer was made regarding her final year's tuition. "We go in, we get Hadden, we come out." That's how she had summed it up. "Simple."

Like Allen, she also wasn't the most experienced camper, though she had done far more than him. Twice she went on digs in remote areas, requiring her to camp outdoors for extended periods. She also used to go fishing with her father in the summers of her youth, until she reached an age where such activities faded in appeal compared to more feminine pursuits. Her younger sister never lost joy for the outdoors though, and for the first time Elisha found herself wishing that she, too, continued to take part in the family camping trips.

As sleep washed away consciousness, Elisha fell away from the waking world, more quickly than she expected with a mind so full of thoughts. These thoughts were whittled apart swiftly, and rational thinking floated into nothing. She lay there on her back, oblivious to the feeling of her body becoming heavier and heavier and unaware that she was gently impelled into unconsciousness.

Then the dream began.

Still aware of herself within her sleep, Elisha realized she was not under her thick covers, snuggled into her soft flannel nightshirt. She was naked, lying limply on an unmade bed—but she was not cold. She was warm. Delightfully warm. The air caressed her nude body like an invisible blanket that engulfed her in comfort. She lay there heavily with her hands resting gently on her stomach. The thumb of her left hand gently drew circles around her navel, each circle spiraling her deeper into this dream—this dream of herself asleep.

Then she felt a hand caress her face. Without alarm or start, she smiled at the warm hand's touch. It was a man's hand, its strength unrecognizable beneath the gentle pet. Tender like a grandfather, soft like a breeze, the hand slid across her face at an excruciatingly slow rate, each untouched portion of skin desperate to be permitted the gentle caress of the hand.

Two hands.

Two hands cupped her face and chin. Two hands down her neck and over her shoulders, down the naked skin of her arms, past her own slackened hands, across her hips and down to her feet, where they started back up again, draining all the burdens that life placed on her. Her body became heavier with each passing of the fingers. These hands robbed stress and anxiety of any power. There was no shame, for there was no lust in the man's hands that rubbed her, not even when they caressed the inside of her legs or her breasts. They were there for her and her only. There to take all troubles away.

"Where are you going?"

The question was soft and hushed, spoken beside her ear. The hands still continued their relaxing strokes, up and down her entire body, and yet the lips that whispered the question stayed at her ear. A whisper asked without so much as a breath to cool her warm skin.

"North," she replied with a sigh. She turned her head to the side to better catch the passing of a hand across her cheek.

"What is it that you seek?" The question sounded like a dozen hushed voices echoing delicately in her ears.

"A man," she murmured back. "A man who says he has found a great place." The hands became stronger for a moment, and then they subsided to their gentle, moving embrace.

"Where is this man? Where is this place?"

"I don't know. Allen Therrien will take me there."

"The Therrien knows where this place is?"

"No," she whispered. Her brow furrowed. Too many questions, too much interruption to the relaxing strokes. Her head tilted slightly from side to side in agitation, but this quickly subsided when the questions stopped and the ethereal massage continued. She slowed her breathing down again, a soft hush soothing her back into relaxation.

Relax, it whispered without words. *Relax. Do not think about the questions, just allow the answers' release.*

"Allen can find him," she finally muttered. "I just have to follow him. We just... have to...follow...Allen."

Elisha pulled her hands up to her chest, and with them she also pulled up the covers, over her body. The movement of the blankets seemed to take the place of the moving hands, and her once warm, naked skin was again dressed again in the cozy red nightshirt that she crawled into bed with. She turned onto her side, snuggling into the covers all around her with a soft smile pressed on her lips. She adjusted her shoulders to best mold the pliable mattress to the shape of her body. Sleep deepened.

* * * *

The Lochkray opened its eyes.

Outside Elisha's apartment building, the Lochkray paused for a moment in the shadows, just outside a pool of light cast down from a streetlamp. He backed himself into a small alcove created by the meeting of two buildings, and took solace in the darkness. He stared back up at the apartment building ahead of him, into the chamber where Elisha was now sleeping. He had not learned what he wanted. He was told of potentials, not specifics. The Therrien, he was told, could find the place.

Laughter a few blocks away caused the Lochkray to snap his head in that direction. The sound of mirth in the night stabbed at him as if it were a blade. People laughing, daylights laughing, in his night.

Not for long, he promised himself. If all he could learn was of potentials, then he would nurture those until they grew into rewards. Those rewards, he seethed, they would stop the daylights' laughter. Stop the intrusion. No more streetlamps, no more nightclubs, no more invasion.

The Lochkray stepped out from the alcove and into the glow of artificial lights he hated. He walked away from the laughing fools playing in the streets. As he wandered, he saw two lovers walking down the road ahead of him, their bodies pressed together and arms locked over one another. "*Wait*", the Lochkray wanted to yell at them. "*Wait. A tomorrow will come, the sun shall set, and the Lochkray shall rise.*"

He wandered into the night.

Part Two
Embarkation

Chapter Five

"When the hell did you ever go to university, anyway?"

"Oh shit, that must have been over twenty years ago." The man stopped for a moment. *Had it been that long? Twenty years?* He looked down at the bottle of beer in front of him, his hand wrapped tightly around it. His hand still looked the same, still holding onto the same object it had been over two decades before. *Twenty years.* He quickly shook off these thoughts and looked back up at the young lady across the table from him.

"Fuck," she said, "I never would have thought of you as an educated man." She laughed at the insult, drawing on her own drink. "What did you study?"

"History, mostly. That's what I got my degree in, anyway. A Bachelor of Arts in history. What the hell, I figured. I got in on a sports scholarship, and as long as somebody else was paying the bills, I'd go anywhere. From what I remember, it was mostly just drinking beer and chasing tail." Now it was his turn to laugh at himself. *Twenty Years!* For a quick moment, he thought back to faces he hadn't recalled in most of that time.

"Beer and women. Fuck. And that qualifies you as alimony?"

"Alumni," he corrected, pushing the old faces away from his thoughts. "I got my degree out of it. It took me four years to get a three-year degree, but I got it. Besides, here it is, twenty years later, and they still remember me. You should be more respectful. If not for me, we'd be stuck cleaning up the cabin all week. Instead, we get a camping trip."

"Hmmm," she responded skeptically. "I'm in your debt." She looked up at the clock above the bar, its hands telling her it was just after lunch, and much too early to be emptying her third bottle. Still, the golden liquid vanished down her throat, and she found herself raising her hand to the bartender to tell her another round was in order.

Tyance Sachaney thought she would almost rather have stayed at the cabin than go on any camping trip. All the summer fishermen returned south again, and the hunting seasons were still a few weeks off, which left the lodge empty and ready for work—even better, since they had a large party cancel at the last minute, Rob and her with the deposit money and empty cabins. The perfect time to do the adjustments and repairs necessary to fix up the place. All these would be waiting for them when they got back.

She took some consolation in the fact that this time of year was perfect for camping. The mosquitoes would be long gone. The mornings would be a little cool, but the days would still be warm and pleasant. On top of that, where they were going would be exciting, way up past the logging roads and townships. True wilderness.

"Do you know this guy we're supposed to be looking for?" she asked, finally managing to get the attention of the bartender who was engrossed in a paperback novel with a colorful cover of a shirtless cowboy kissing an old-West whore.

"John Hadden? Oh yeah. I'm the one who told him about Willie Cheechoo's old cabin up there. John used to come up to the lodge back when your father was alive. He said he wanted something even more remote, and I told him about Willie's place. As far as I know, he uses it as a kind of base camp and goes fishing and camping from there. I don't think he catches too much though. He never brings anything back I know of. I think he just likes the solitude."

"Hmmm." Tyance got up and retrieved her drink from the bar, dropping her money in payment. While she was up there, her partner, Robert Madoc, found himself staring at his beer bottle again, thinking about those Twenty years. He vaguely remembered graduation day, and then coming back home. He remembered working for Tom Blais' hunting camp up on the Abatibi River. *How long did I work for him? Three years? Four? Not more than four, surely.* Then Tyance's father, Ray, came to him with an idea about starting their own place—they would cater only to the richest people who knew nothing about hunting.

That was Ray's plan. "Rich citiots," he say, using his own combination of 'city' and 'idiots'. "We'll bring them up, let them spend all day looking for a calf or fish, feed them at night and charge them a fortune. All we have to do is look classy."

He was right. All they had to do was look and act like they were civilized, like they ran the most civilized outfitting camp in the north—which mostly meant having a satellite dish and single malt scotches in the bar. They advertised in more urban business and society magazines, rather than the usual hunting and fishing mags, and pushed themselves as the classiest option for any hunter. The rich citiots went for it. The first couple of years were tough, but soon they gained a reputation for being the only place where any dignified hunter in all of Eastern North America ever went to spend a week looking to shoot a moose or bear.

Tyance's father died six years previous, leaving his part of the business to his only daughter—which had really made her brothers mad. As she was the only one that Madoc met in all the years he knew Ray, he figured justice had been done. A short court battle, which Madoc had helped Tyance through, and the camp was hers. Half hers, anyway. Ever since—although Madoc would never admit it to her—the lodge only improved. Nobody ever guessed it to speak with her, but Tyance had a knack for style and finesse.

Somewhere between hunting, fishing, and skidooing with the roughest and toughest, she learned the skills for being a lady…or perhaps it was instinct. Madoc didn't know. Just when Madoc and Ray figured that they reached a comfortable plateau in the hunting lodge business, along came Tyance to improve, not only the standards, but the revenue as well. While Madoc sometimes missed his old friend, Tyance turned out to be just as good a confidant. With his mind half set in the past, Madoc stared at his beer bottle again. Tyance sat back down in front of him, and his eyes darted back up, almost expecting to see Ray sitting there in front of him.

"What time did you say these two were supposed to be arriving?" she asked.

"They were supposed to have caught the overnight train up to Cochrane and taken the bus. The train was supposed to be in at nine, and then the hour bus ride to here. You have to think—how often is it on time?"

"Hmmm. Not usually this late though."

"Speak of the devil," Madoc interrupted, pointing out the bar's window and getting to his feet, "there it is." Tyance let out a brief curse, trying to down as much of her new beer as she could. Figuring that a third of the bottle was all that was going to get finished, she, too, got to her feet and quickly made toward the door. Outside, the two saw the bus turn the corner off Main Street, down to the stop. They followed on foot, a fairly short walk, and by the time they made it around the corner, the bus driver already dropped off the two passengers and their luggage, and mounted the stairs back into the coach, preparing to return to his route. Madoc and Tyance saw their charges standing by the curb, looking around in a state of moderate confusion.

The male stared at the street directly beneath his shoes, apparently shocked to see that the roadway wasn't paved. The female took a full survey of all about her, sniffing the air and trying to locate the origins of the slight aroma left over from the morning shift at the town's pulp mill. To Madoc's satisfaction, he saw the two stood beside tall backpacks, quelling his concern they might show up with suitcases at their sides. They were fit enough for the task they were supposed to perform, too. The male was fairly tall, somewhere in his early twenties, a little thin, but overall looked healthy enough to take into the woods. The female appeared quite athletic, somewhere around the same age or perhaps a little older, her long sandy-blonde hair tightly pinned to the back of her head.

Easy to look at too, Madoc thought. Too many times the borderline obese showed up at the lodge looking to go on heroic adventures in the wilderness, while Madoc was left to worry about the impending heart attack—and on two occasions those fears were realized. Considering the destination the university had told him they were seeking, it was especially good that all were in acceptable physical condition.

"Allen Therrien?" Madoc called out once close enough. The two students turned toward the voice, relieved to see that they had not gotten off at the wrong stop.

"Yes," Allen answered, extending his hand. "Are you Robert Madoc?" Madoc took his hand and gave it a shake. *A little weak*, he assessed. *What can you expect from a professional student?*

"Yep. People usually just call me Madoc. This is Tyance Sachaney. She's going to accompany us on the trip. You must be Alice."

"Elisha," she corrected, taking his hand.

"I was close. I have the two of you reserved in rooms at the Moose Motel for tonight. Did the university go over your travel plans?"

"Actually, no," Elisha answered, wondering whether the Moose Motel was just the name or a description. "The university only told us how to get to here. They said everything else would be taken care of."

Tyance nodded. "It is. We made reservations with Bush-Land Air to pick us up in Fraserdale tomorrow morning. It's a community about a hundred kilometers north of here. From there, we're going to be flying north of Dunsmore Township. We'll be landing on a lake off of the Kwataboahegan River. There's an old hunting camp there that your missing professor goes to—"

"Then we'll be walking to this site he found," Madoc finished off. "What I'd like to see is exactly where this archaeological site is. The university was a little sketchy about that part. They said you would have the exact location."

Allen stared at the two blankly. The wear and tear of fifteen hours of travel blurring his mind, he found himself only taking in half of what was said. The moment of silence that was left by his staring shook Allen back into the real world.

"Show you? Yeah, sure. Sorry, I'm a little tired."

"Don't worry about it." Madoc laughed lightly. "There's a pub just around the corner from here. Why don't we all go over there, and you can show us where we're going. Then we'll get you checked into the motel, and you can go and get some rest."

Before Madoc had finished his suggestion, Tyance was already picking up Allen's backpack and taking the weight of one of the straps onto her shoulder. Without giving either of them an opportunity to protest, Madoc did the same for Elisha's pack and the guides were instantly heading back toward the pub. Elisha and Allen gave each other a surprised look before they followed after. Their first few steps were quick to catch up to the guides—or possible luggage thieves—, and then they fell in behind, allowing Tyance and Rob to lead the way.

"So you're graduate students, eh?" Madoc called over his shoulder when he sensed the two were close enough.

"Yeah," Allen replied, half wanting to reach out to take his heavy pack from Tyance. "We're both studying for our master's degrees." He shook his head quickly, deciding that chivalry turned one hundred and eighty degrees.

"Fuck," Tyance muttered. "I couldn't wait until I could get out of school. I can't imagine sticking around that long." Allen turned to Elisha with an unsure glance, wondering if he had actually heard the word "fuck" or not. Elisha returned half a shrug.

"Yeah," Elisha replied before an awkward silence could fill in, "it gets to be a little much after a while. And expensive."

"Fuck, I can imagine." Still walking a step behind, Allen mimicked Elisha's shrug, now sure of what he heard. The sight of the York Tavern coming closer to them with each step of their walk reminded Allen of an old West bar. It perfectly completed the image of the small town they had arrived in. The square cedar-sided building with an upper balcony required nothing more than a prostitute making catcalls to the pedestrians below in order to make the image surreal. In less than ten minutes from meeting each other, they were all back at the booth where the two guides had sat alone for the late morning, drinking their brunch beers. More modern inside than the facade suggested, it looked to Allen and Elisha like just about every other roadhouse they visited.

Tyance was annoyed to see her fresh beer had been taken from the table, forcing her to order another. Allen decided that perhaps a drink was not a bad idea, though Elisha declined. Despite their exhaustion, the opportunity to plan came as a relief to both Elisha and Allen. Sitting down at the booth and bringing out the map made the two feel like they had some kind of hold on the situation for the first moment since the powers at McGuinness University came up with the plan. They were discussing action, not being ordered or bribed into doing something. They were asked for information, not simply responding to direction.

Elisha looked at their guides with just the slightest trace of skepticism. From their first approach she could smell beer off of the two. However, as both were polite and pleasant, she tried to ignore her uncertainty. Besides, it became evident to her that Madoc had an instant charm about him. An easygoing-ness that Elisha had forgotten existed in some people.

Six years of postsecondary education surrounded her with people resigned to pomposity and haughtiness. Her peers of late pontificated rather than just talked. Madoc's lack of *savoir faire* was a pleasant change, as he "shot-the-shit" instead of giving grand statements. Yet it was clear he was intelligent and articulate.

Tyance, too, seemed agreeable, although Elisha found it tougher to get a read off of her. Despite her inclination for cursing, she was quieter than Madoc, staring at the map as Allen went over their approximate destination, listening carefully to everybody speak. Elisha recognized what she was doing, for she was doing the same thing. While Madoc was happy with just about anybody around him, and Allen was too absorbed in their task to notice anything, Elisha knew Tyance judged them.

"Wow," Madoc blurted out at Allen's finger as it pointed at the map. "John really buried himself deep this time."

"You know Doctor Hadden?" Allen asked, looking up.

"He used to frequent my lodge. He was a teaching assistant at the university when I went there. I didn't have any of his classes, but I recognized him when he first started hunting up here." Madoc returned his attention to the map. "I told him to use this old hunting camp. It used to belong to a guy named Cheechoo, but he's been dead for some time now, so it doesn't really belong to anybody now. I haven't heard from John in years. According to the lady I spoke with at the university, they called me because of John's mention of our lodge. It'll be nice to see him again."

"If we can find him," Elisha commented.

"You're not joking." Tyance nodded. "We don't have a really specific location, and the area where we're going isn't exactly hospitable. It's rough country up there." She gave a slight smile. "It will make for an interesting week or more."

"Or less," Madoc said optimistically. Tyance looked at him, then down at the map where Allen had circled the approximate location, then back at Madoc. "Okay, not less," he conceded.

"More than a week?" Allen's eyes went wide.

"Hopefully not too much more," Madoc replied. "But there's a lot of land to cover, no way to know exactly where to look, and John doesn't know we're looking for him. Once we find him, we have to get back to where we'll be dropped off, to call for the plane."

"Call from the cabin? Can't we get him to some kind of settlement, or somewhere people could help us get back quicker?"

"No," Tyance answered first, with a laugh. "There's nobody else up there. No people, no communication, no radio, no cell phones, no landlines. We'll have a satellite phone with us."

"It'll keep us in contact with the outside world while we're out there," Madoc finished off, "Otherwise, once we leave, we're pretty much alone. Nobody around for three hundred miles in every direction and no way to get picked up until we return to the cabin."

Elisha and Allen looked at each other.

"Maybe I should have a drink," Elisha said.

"I don't mean to drive you to alcohol." Madoc smiled. "Listen, don't get too worked up. It's going to be some tough hiking, but I promise you, you'll have a great time."

"If you don't," Tyance piped in, "you'll be stuck out there anyway." Madoc flicked Tyance a disapproving look, to which she shrugged and mouthed back the question, "What?"

It took Madoc fifteen minutes of patient, soothing talking before he decided he had imparted confidence, if not happiness. Once he was sure they were not going to get panicky on him, he suggested they head over to the motel and get checked in. Although Allen tried to move quicker this time, he still failed to grab his backpack before Tyance could, and again he and Elisha found themselves following after their guides, this time walking the short distance to the Moose Motel.

With Madoc's preparation, checking into the motel was a quick process. He and Allen went into the motel's office, and within seconds of pressing the converted doorbell taped to the front desk, a short man with a European sounding accent emerged from the residence attached to the front office. The friendly man instantly produced a piece of paper from underneath his desk, and slid it across to Allen, an *X* highlighted to show where to sign. He barely even said the words "All I need is your signature," before he handed two sets of keys over to Allen. With only the requirement of his name scribbled across the form, Allen and Madoc rejoined the girls outside, and the students were shown to the rooms, Tyance and Madoc once again carrying the luggage. They dropped the bags in front of the doors with numbers matching those on the oversized tags attached to the keys. With no other information from Madoc and Tyance than, "We'll see you at six in the morning," their guides departed.

Standing outside his room, immediately beside Elisha's, Allen watched as the two guides walked across the courtyard of the motel to their own rooms. Allen made a comment about meeting up with Elisha later for dinner, to which she replied, "Sure," before disappearing inside. Then Allen stepped into his own room and practically collapsed onto his bed. He was asleep within a minute.

Elisha, however, took a little longer to relax. Happy to find her room at the Moose Motel was a clean and pleasant place to sleep, she immediately stripped out of her rumpled clothes and jumped into the shower, allowing the hot water to pour over her.

She hoped this might wash away the stress of the day but it didn't work. Staring at the water as it circled its way down the drain, she tried to comfort herself. Her reassurance call of "it will be fun," or Madoc's "you'll have a great time," was no consolation. Tyance's words "it will be an interesting week" also held little solace. Something in her mind told her that there was more than just fun and excitement involved. Much more. Something important. Something...dark.

A shiver ran up her spine.

Nerves, she told herself. *As if you don't have enough to worry about, without this stupidity. When we find Hadden, I swear I'm going to punch him in the back of the head. I've got too much to do. I have a thesis to complete, and class lists to review, and lesson plans to write. The last thing I need is to be here panicking over finding that jack-ass.*

She turned the shower off and listened as the water gurgled its way into the sewer system. The cold air wrapped around her skin as the shower's warmth faded. Grabbing one of the miniature motel towels, she dried herself off and exited the bedroom. Again a shiver ran up her spine—something more than the cool air. She sat down on the bed and tried to subdue the apprehension in her stomach.

Relax, she said to herself. *This will all be over shortly.*

Chapter Six

"Yes, sir?" Matthew Fanning politely asked the man walking into his office. Situated beneath a bare bulb hanging down on a chord from the ceiling, the cluttered counter Matt stood behind served as the customer service desk of his business. Outside, above the rachitic doorway, hung a rough sign that read *North Bush Air* in red letters. The paint had chipped away and the rotten wood beneath showed through, but since so few people came into the office Matt had little inspiration to replace it. Its main purpose was for people making deliveries, not for advertisement. As the business sat way out on the back roads, the office was a difficult place to find. Matt knew all he needed was a phone on that counter, and the business continued to roll in. Nobody speaking to him on the phone could observe his negligible organizational skills.

"You have a charter tomorrow," the man told Matt, rather than asked.

"Yes, sir, we do." Matt closed the file he was looking at and stood up straight. In the dim light of the Quonset hut, all he made out of the man was a silhouette against the bright day showing through the open door. The shadow stayed near that door, not wandering too far in. Matt knew the person was a stranger, not just by the odd, growling accent, but rather by the shape of the shadow before him. A large man, he could tell, his head apparently shaved clean. Matt could also make out the outline of an overcoat, which must have been stifling on such a warm day. This person was obviously not a local. Matt had lived in the area all his life and knew just about every person around—and all the shapes, sizes, voices, and life stories that went with each individual. Even those he did not socialize with or meet formally, he knew—just as they all knew him. This man was new. *Late season tourist,* Matt decided immediately.

"Who are the passengers on tomorrow's voyage?" the shadow asked.

That's my business, buddy, Matt thought to himself, defensively pulling himself up to his full height. *I don't divulge the information of my customers to just anybody who walks through the door. I don't mean to be rude, but the answer is "I can't tell you." I hope you can live with that.*

"It's Rob Madoc's charter," he answered faintly.

"Is the one called Therrien going with him?"

What right do you have to ask?

"Yes. Allen Therrien. He's a student from some university."

"What is their destination?"

Matt's thoughts were clear: *Customers' personal information, destination, and amount of payment are all private and confidential subjects, not to be disclosed to anybody. Don't ask. I can't tell.*

"A lake north of the Kwataboahegan River."

"When do you leave?"

Private information.

"By eight o'clock tomorrow morning."

"From where?"
Confidential.
"Abatibi Canyon, by Fraserdale."

Matthew Fanning looked up from the file he was reading, blinking hard as he did, the words "Yes sir?" ready to be spoken. His eyes scanned the office, confused, as if searching an unfamiliar bedroom immediately following first wake. He was sure that he heard somebody come in. He stared about the empty building, realizing he was alone. He smiled to himself, at how easily he had allowed himself to become startled. He was alone, as he had been for the past few hours.

But wasn't there just…?

He returned his attention to the desk, shaking away muddled thoughts.

What was I thinking? he asked himself, looking about the counter in front of him. He found the file he was reviewing and picked it up again. For some reason, he thought that he was going over tomorrow's charter, Rob Madoc's run up past the Kwataboahegan to Willie Cheechoo's old camp. This wasn't Rob's charter. This was yesterday's file. He shook his head, amused by his own confusion. *Of course you've got them mixed up*, he thought. *Yesterday's charter went to the same place. The same lake that college professor gets flown to every year. There must be good fishing up there. Maybe I should have mentioned yesterday's charter to—*

Who?

Again Matt looked up at the emptiness around him, before shaking off his muddled thoughts. It was late in the season, and he had been working too much. That was it. Too many charters, too many runs, too many people. It was becoming too difficult to think straight.

* * * *

The Lochkray wandered back into the forest.

Chapter Seven

"Well, what do you think?"

Tyance looked up from the newspaper she was reading and stared for a moment at Madoc standing outside the doorway of her motel room. Returning her attention to the paper, she absently asked, "About what?" and rustled the pages. Madoc opened up the screen door and stepped in.

"About our two customers," he replied over the shriek of the door shutting behind him.

"Hmmm. They didn't seem to be suffering from leprosy, syphilis, or any other diseases." The paper rustled again. Madoc smiled at Tyance's dry absurdity.

"That's not what I meant," he said, ignoring her obvious desire to be left alone.

"Sorry."

"I should have been more specific."

"Not at all. My fault entirely." While Tyance continued to feign interest in the conversation, Madoc went over to her bed and flopped down on top of the covers.

"The university equipped them well. They look like they know what they're doing."

"Yeah, that Therrien kid almost unfolded the map by himself."

"Do I detect a concern?"

"Fuck," she said, finally putting her newspaper down with a sigh, "the university may have equipped them well, but I think that was just to fool us into thinking this would be easy. That kid doesn't know anything about going into the bush. Did you see the way he looked at the mounted deer heads in the bar? Like they were talking. His high-quality gear was all brand-new, not anything he owned before coming up here. If he had money instead of being a student, we'd probably see him at the lodge looking to shoot a polar bear, paying us twenty-five hundred a week to baby-sit him."

"You noticed?"

"Fuck. The girl at least seemed to know a little. She had a camper's first aid kit in her back pouch, and that wasn't new. It must be her own. Her backpack has a Hunters and Anglers Association patch on it, so either she's been out before or she borrowed the pack from her father or brother. Her hiking boots were right out of the box though, nothing she's used before, so the pack probably wasn't hers."

Madoc smiled again. After years of dealing with guests at the lodge, Tyance had it all figured out. She could spot a rube. Trying to make her think that the situation was better than it was wouldn't work.

"You don't think they have syphilis, right?"

"Going on a manhunt is difficult. Looking in that area while dragging those two behind is going to be damn near impossible." She picked up her newspaper, rustled it into position, and began to read again.

"Okay, I admit," Madoc said after a moment's hesitation, "they aren't exactly expert woodsmen. That's why they hired us. This is easy money. A little camping, a little hiking, and a little hunting—only this time we're after a person rather than a moose."

"Fuck. Unless you can roast this professor, I'd rather be hunting the moose."

"Pessimist," Madoc snorted, getting to his feet and making his way toward the door. He hoped Tyance would be a little more playful rather than surly. His hopes quashed, he decided to go to Main Street and get a magazine and head back to his own room. As he placed his hand on the screen door, he heard the paper rustling again from behind.

"Something else bugs me," Tyance stated slowly. "While you were getting them checked in, the girl asked me if I knew anything about the area. I asked her in what way, and she asked if anything unusual ever happened up there. She was kind of spooked for some reason. I told her 'no'." Madoc turned back and stared at his partner for a moment before realizing that she was done speaking.

"So?" he asked with a shrug. "What bugs you about that?" Tyance laid the paper flat on the table and leaned over it, her voice becoming lower.

"Well, afterward I was thinking—do you remember what happened to Willie Cheechoo? I wonder if maybe she's heard about that."

Madoc's heart beat heavy for a moment. An image flashed in his mind's eye quickly, an image burned there from years before, one that he had tried hard to erase. He blinked hard to remove the recalled sight.

"Willie Cheechoo was killed by a bear," he stated dryly, trying to hide the crushing feeling suddenly taking residence in his chest. The image found another crack in Madoc's mind and it flashed into memory again, and the crushing became stronger.

"Yeah, but you remember how they said—"

"Killed by a bear. That's not unusual, just unfortunate. Don't worry about it. She's probably just talking about a bigfoot or something. I'll be back in my room. I'll get cleaned up and we can go out for some dinner later." He quickly turned to the screen door and stepped outside before Tyance said anything else, happy to be in the open air and late afternoon light. He took a deep breath and walked back to his own room, his legs moving swiftly, thoughts of going to get a magazine gone. He tried hard to focus on the setting around him—the motel, the parked cars, the sounds of the lumber trucks thundering down the highway—attempted to keep his mind cluttered and busy.

As he stepped back into his own room and shut the door, the image returned. The image of something unwillingly remembered. His shoulders gave a shudder as the image sparked a chill through his back. He leaned onto the shut door and closed his eyes as if relenting to the image, the memory.

He remembered that time, years ago, while Tyance's father was still alive. He remembered Cheechoo's cabin. He couldn't remember agreeing to go up to the camp with the police to help look for the old man. He couldn't remember who the two cops were who went with him. He couldn't remember who the pilot was and he couldn't remember flying on the plane. He couldn't remember the landing on the lake or getting out onto the dock. He couldn't remember walking up to the cabin.

He remembered seeing the trail of blood going into the cabin, though. That he remembered. The thick, stinking, coagulated pools, covered in flies like rotting meat in the sun. Smeared and blotted all the way around the cabin, up to and through the door. That he remembered clearly. Most of all, though, no matter how hard he tried to forget, he remembered the awful image—the sight laying beyond the door.

Willie Cheechoo, sitting naked on the floor of his cabin, with his mouth agape in a silent scream. His eyes wide in the middle of his rotting yellow face, which melted off of his skull. For the rest of his life Madoc clearly saw Willie sitting on that floor—his bloated body propped up against a toppled over chair and clutching the vicious wound across his stomach.

Five bears in the area would be killed, but it could never be proved if any were the culprit—their deaths served as little more than revenge for Cheechoo's family. No explanation was ever given for why he was naked in the cabin, and why none of his clothes were ever found. Nor was anybody able to figure out where the attack had occurred, for the blood trail that could be followed went deep into the trees, and became impossible to follow—even the police dog brought up from Timmins couldn't follow the trail.

Nobody could ever explain why Willie Cheechoo decided to spend the last moments of life, through the pain and shock from his wounds, while all consciousness drained away, to write the words—DON'T DREAM—in huge letters, in his own blood, on the wall of the cabin.

Those huge words and their author's rotting body sitting in front of them, would find themselves secure forever in Madoc's mind.

Chapter Eight

Allen Therrien sat on the edge of his bed eagerly waiting for the others to come get him. After his nap the day before, he woke up long enough to go to one of the hotel's adjacent restaurants to grab dinner, return to his room, watch an hour of television, and fall asleep again. Elisha joined him for the meal, but seemed distant the entire time. Allen was hyper and excited, but his partner's lack of enthusiasm had quickly calmed him down. Ever since they picked up the train in Toronto he noticed that something was wrong with her. At first he blamed it on nerves, but it eventually became evident that there was more to it. When he spoke of the upcoming year, or books, or anthropology, everything seemed fine. Whenever he tried to talk to her about the journey, she became...

What's the word? Fidgety? No...Something else. Nervous, maybe, or alarmed or...scared?

He released a sigh. *No, not scared. Not Elisha*. She had less to be concerned about than he did. She was the one who always knew what she was doing. Always in control.

There's something wrong.

He heard her speaking to Tyance about where they were going. Asking her if anything strange ever happened up there. Allen thought maybe she knew of some kind of local tradition associated with the area, something Susan Fellows might have told her. God knew Doctor Fellows could recite the facts surrounding just about every tradition between Mexico and the North Pole. He went over it in his mind again and again, but could not come up with anything—which was why Doctor Hadden's find was so interesting. The area was supposed to be a cultural void. He tried to broach the subject at dinner without any success.

"I'm just tired," she said.

No...there's something else, Allen told himself then too.

The sound of the horn going off snapped his attention to the outside. He stood up and went to the door, lugging the heavy backpack over one shoulder. He left the key to the room on the desk as instructed in a note written by the hotel's manager—which clearly requested not to be awoken before eight a.m.. Allen paused for a moment at the door to do a quick survey of the room to ensure all of his belongings were on his person. Satisfied with this, he stepped outside and closed the door behind him, listening to it lock. Parked directly in front of his room was an extended-cab pickup truck, looking far older than it actually was, the red paint blending awkwardly with the bondo and rust. In the bed of the vehicle, the rest of the group already had their belongings packed. Tyance was standing beside the open passenger-side door, her front seat folded forward. He saw Elisha through open door, already sitting in the vehicle's rear looking out the other window. "Good morning," Tyance said pleasantly.

"Good morning," Allen replied, shading his eyes from the early morning sun. He saw the smoke coming out of the local paper mill billowing upward in a huge cloud. As it caught the sun's early light, it was turned into shades of gold and red, making the vile pollution a magnificent sight. *Not quite as famed as the Northern Lights.* Allen smirked to himself. He was warned that paper mills created a smell that was a cross between an outhouse and rotting meat. However, and thankfully, the winds had saved him this particular experience by shoving the huge cloud west, and away from the town. "The smell of money," the locals all said, for the mill was the town's one main employer. It could be tolerated in such context.

"Ready to go?" Madoc called across the front seat. Allen returned his attention to the truck, advised his guide that he was, and threw his bag into the back with the rest of the packs. He climbed past the front seat awkwardly and settled into the small rear area. Tyance threw her seat back, snapping it into place a mere inch from Allen's knee, and once she was settled, the trip was underway.

The drive to Fraserdale took a little bit over an hour, Madoc advised over the sound of the radio, which he apparently set to 'blaring' once Allen got in. He advised they should enjoy the music, because they would miss such luxuries once they got into the bush. As a result, little was spoken amongst the group. Allen called out the question, "Excited?" to Elisha early on, who returned a smile and a nod.

She seems to have relaxed a little, he thought to himself.

With very little being discussed by anybody, Allen tried to amuse himself by looking out the windows, but it soon became apparent that there was nothing to see on this drive.

Two giant walls of trees reached up from either side of the vehicle and the rows stretched off to the horizon as an endless trench. Every northward stretch of roadway was a duplicate to the stretch before—trees, trees, and more trees. They were like tall green spears, pointing to the sky, standing so close to one another It was difficult to see the forest beyond the dual bulwark of trees. Every so often the boredom of watching this repetitive view overtook Allen and he called up to either Tyance or Madoc-asking mindless questions about the land, or weather, or people who lived in the area, or anything to initiate some conversation.

Every time he regretted doing so, for the twangy sound of guitars and forlorn singers made the replies inaudible. All he heard were the sputters of sentences in response: "…if the…you see up to…find…how long we…depends…" to which he always replied in earnest, "Oh yeah?" before settling back into his seat and deciding it would be too frustrating to ask for clarification. Eventually boredom would overtake him again and he would lean forward and ask another mindless question.

This long highway, with no turnoffs, forks, or extended conversation for Allen the entire way, cut its way through the forest seemingly forever. It bounced the truck roughly with its scores of potholes, making the vehicle rattle with each strike, shaking the passengers within. The closest thing to entertainment that Allen found, besides praying for deafness to save him from listening to any more of Madoc's music, was turning around to peak through the rear window, to see if any of their bags had jumped out of the back with the last hole in the road.

To make matters worse, the more they advanced towards their destination, the worse the radio reception became. The loathsome music became loathsome with crackling static. Then loathsome music with constant static over top. Then it was static, with patches of loathsome music and rattling truck interspersed.

A hundred mind-numbing kilometers from the town they left, the endless boredom mercifully came to an end at an intersection. Here the paved road became an option of four gravel trails. Two went north into the bush, the other two went east and west. A sign indicated that west would go to Fraserdale, and to Allen's surprise, the car turned the opposite direction. The radio signal Madoc coveted was now little more than the odd straining sound, and it was at this point that he relented and turned the radio off.

"We're here," Madoc declared over the clattering of the vehicle as it bounded along the rough road. "Matt Fanning is going to be meeting us on the river with a plane."

"How long should the flight take?" Elisha called back.

"Shouldn't be too much longer than an hour. Matt is the one who flies John up every year, so he knows where he's going." The truck made its short ride through the bush and emerged at a tiny clearing beside a wide river. The gravel road continued along, disappearing around a corner, back into the trees. Extending into the river from the clearing was a T shaped wooden dock.

Secured to this, bobbing gently in the waves, was a small single propeller seaplane-the meaning of the beaver painted on its front was unknown to Allen and quickly ignored, but he did take notice of the way the lettering of the words North Bush Air were peeling off of the side of the craft. Its pontoons rubbed against the dock with a high-pitched squeak as the softly undulating river lifted and dropped the aircraft repeatedly.

Sure that the craft was nowhere near big enough to carry all four of them, Allen started to ask a question, but decided against it. Mostly because he was sure that he was mistaken-that couldn't be the plane they were taking to their destination.

Standing on the edge of this dock, just off of the clearing, was Matthew Fanning, who waved to Madoc as he climbed out of the truck. Tyance opened her door and gave her own little wave back.

"How-are-ya-now?" Fanning ran the words together.

"Matt," Madoc called over the top of his truck, "this is Elisha and Allen."

"Hi," Elisha said as she followed out behind Madoc.

"Hey," Allen said as he awkwardly attempted to free himself from the cab's rear.

"Nice to meet you folks." Fanning grinned. "We're all gassed up and ready to fly when you are. Just grab your luggage and we'll be on our way." With that he turned around and walked back towards his plane at the dock, and it was then that Allen realized that he was wrong. It *was* the plane they were supposed to be taking.

Reminded of how unsure of everything he was, Allen joined his group as they quickly set about loading their belongings into the plane—four large backpacks, and what looked to Allen to be a metal briefcase, which he didn't even bother to question. Madoc and Tyance's packs were similar to the other two, but far more worn, with a musty smell of fish, smoke and a butcher's shop.

The bags were pushed forcibly into the rear portion of the plane, and once all belongings were crammed inside, the four travelers boarded. To Allen's surprise, they all fit in-although it wasn't a comfortable fit. There was nothing comfortable about it.

Matt Fanning untied his craft and climbed over Madoc and into the pilot's chair. The single front propeller sprang to life, and the plane began to taxi across the river. Unsure of what he expected, Allen shook his head at the entire informality of the loading and flight preparation. They parked the vehicle, loaded their bags, and were on their way. That was it. No official procedure, no conventions. Load, and go.

"I hope you remembered to turn the lights off on the truck," the pilot yelled over the sound of the engine. Madoc just laughed, but Allen found himself looking back at the dock to check.

"He was just kidding," Tyance clarified.

The engine screamed louder and the plane pulled itself along the river, faster and faster. Elisha grabbed onto the sides of her small chair, her knuckles going white as the plane sped along. Allen's stomach fluttered with a moment of sudden excitement, and the plane stopped its rough advance along the water and lifted into the air.

Suddenly the forest, which only appeared as walls of trees before, spread outward in a sudden wave of changed perception. Allen's eyes went wide as they flew over and past the river, and the expanse of trees went on forever. Green. Rolling, rolling green as far as the horizon showed, stopping only when the curve of the planet allowed no more. *Wilderness,* was the only description he thought of, completely forgetting he ever had any anxiety before. *True wilderness.*

Driving along the ground, with the walls of trees hiding any view, a town or even a city could easily hide around the next corner. When so far up in the air, it became clear that they went to the middle of nowhere, surrounded by nothing, tree atop tree in a land of empty. At first there were a couple of breaks in the forest to dispel the impression of pristine nature. They passed over train tracks going north, and evidence of logging having found its way into the area.

Soon there was nothing but the trees, broken only by thin wandering rivers and tiny lakes that sparkled blue, as if tiny segments of the sky had been cut out and dropped to the wild ground.

Allen had not been in a plane for some time, and that one was huge compared to this tiny aircraft. On that plane to Cuba, and the few other times he flew in the air, there were stewardesses, small meals, movies, peanuts, and washrooms. This was different, this was really flying. He felt the wind outside pushing, undulating, and shifting the craft. This did not scare him, instead it exhilarated. He felt like he was *really* flying, not just imitating flight like the major airlines . He soared through the air, overtop some of the most untouched land on the planet.

They went farther north, and the show of wilderness did not relent. Past the logging lands with their segments of cutout plains, past the rivers that housed huge cement damns, past the invisible lines of townships. Past man's invasion, and into the mouth of wilderness.

Chapter Nine

From the sky, Allen missed it entirely. Despite the repetition of what he was looking at, he couldn't pry his eyes away from the wilderness below him, speeding by. The complete opposite from the truck ride. He was looking for as much detail as he could from above, and yet when they flew over, he entirely missed the first distinct visual in almost an hour of the trip. So, when the plane suddenly turned around and made its way back toward the long lake, it took him by surprise. When they started to drop, he scanned the area to see why. Just on the shore of the blue waters, a cabin sat comfortably away from the tree line within its own clearing.

Both Allen and Elisha were impressed by what they saw. Elisha expected a shack, the kind her father used to go hunting in, made up of little more than two-by-fours and plywood, with a wood stove—and fire hazard—sitting in one corner. A place for men to sit around, play cards, and discuss the one that got away.

Allen wasn't sure what he expected, but it was certainly not what he saw. It looked more like a cottage than a bush camp. The cabin had a deck built all the way around it, which extended down a few stairs at the front and became a long dock. The wood had long before gone gray and cracked, and the railing around the deck was warped, lifting, or missing. The windows were filthy, a brownish-gray in color, many of them with thin cracks. Still, the cabin was impressive. Large and stylish, it was two stories tall.

Madoc didn't look at the building. His eyes remained on the map resting on his lap, which he had been studying the entire flight. As the plane descended, he allowed his view to flicker to water as it rushed up to meet them, then quickly back down at the map.

Don't dream.

"Not too bad, eh?" Tyance called over the sound of the engine, after they had softly touched down onto the water. The plane taxied toward the dock, sliding smoothly across the calm lake and sending two large columns of wake to the shore.

"Nobody uses this?" Allen asked, still impressed with the cabin before them.

"Just your professor. The guy who built it died here quite a while ago. None of his family wanted it, and not too many other people know about it. It's just been—"

"Died?" Elisha interrupted. "Died how?"

"Killed by a bear," The pilot called over his shoulder, maneuvering the plane's nose toward the dock. "Old Willie liked to go bear hunting with his bow. They figure he let one get too close."

"We're going to have a look around the camp first," Madoc told Fanning, still looking at the map. "Just give us a minute to make sure our friend isn't in the cabin. If he is, then we can leave with you."

"I thought you were all going into the bush."

"Probably. There's an off chance that we might not have to." Madoc's response brought a slight frown to Fanning. He was told that this charter was to have a repeat return. If their friend were local, it would put a quick end to the extra job.

"He'll be in the bush, trust me," Allen assured. "Doctor Hadden always has to be difficult. Right, Elisha?"

"Did they ever find the bear?" Elisha asked Tyance, taking the moment to ignore Allen's question.

"They don't know for sure, but they think so. A bunch were killed by his two sons. Nobody knows for sure." Elisha felt a now familiar sick feeling in her stomach. She didn't know why she was getting the feeling again.

Nerves, she tried to tell herself once more. *Just nerves.* The words held little comfort. Apprehension begot anxiety rapidly, and she couldn't find the source. Intuition, perhaps, or maybe even premonition, but definitely more than *"just nerves."* She knew it, and that only brought her more fear. Something was wrong, something she couldn't identify—and yet it was familiar just the same. Something... *close.*

The plane pulled up along the front edge of the dock, and slowed itself to a halt. Taking a deep breath, Madoc finally brought himself to look up at the cabin. To his surprise it did not hit him the way he thought it would. The image of Willie did not flash in his mind.

Years had not been kind to the cabin. Once a rich golden color, it went faded. The small, simple flower gardens Willie used to keep in good condition was now all wild plants, invisible to anybody who didn't know they used to be there. The windows were empty, the place was dead—perhaps to another, it might make the building more haunting, but to Madoc, it was the proud, fresh cabin that haunted him, not the tired construction before him. He released a contented sigh. Time had ravaged his nightmare, making it weak.

Madoc hopped out of his seat, Fanning following quickly after, before the propeller had time to stop spinning completely. Fanning secured the plane to the dock, then turned toward the cabin.

"Doesn't look like anybody is here," he said with some satisfaction. "Nobody seems to have heard us landing."

"Doesn't look like it," Madoc agreed distantly. The rest jumped out of the plane and onto the dock. Tyance frowned at the building. It had also been many years since she saw it, but whereas Madoc was happy to see the building undermined, Tyance was disappointed. She had visited Willie—'Uncle Bill' she used to call him—at the cabin when it was in its glory, with her father. That building housed many memories for her, and she could not think of any that were not happy.

"John?" Madoc called to the cabin. He reached back into the plane and pulled out his small gray briefcase. Allen saw It pulled down hard on Madoc's arm, apparently being heavier than it looked. Madoc walked down the dock, his other hand cupped to his mouth. "John Hadden?" Fanning followed after him, strolling along with his hands shoved deep into his pockets. Allen helped Elisha onto the dock with a steadying hand, then looked up at the cabin.

"I'm going to go have a look too," he said as soon as her feet were firmly on the dock. He turned after the other two men, and jogged along the dock eager to see inside the building. Elisha shook her head at his exuberance.

"Come on," Tyance said with a mock slap to Elisha's shoulder. "You can help me unload the equipment. If your professor didn't hear us landing, you can bet he's not in the area." Elisha smiled politely, and began the task of removing all of the provisions onto the dock.

Madoc went to the door of the cabin calmly. His breaths were deep though, and deliberate. He was oblivious of the other two behind him. Walking up the stairs he searched for evidence of the blood he saw trailing through the door a decade before, but there was nothing, not even a discoloration to the faded wood. A steady hand reached out and took hold of the knob, gripping it slowly. A moment to wish that the door might be locked, and Madoc turned the rusty orb and listened to the latch release. He paused.

Allen and Fanning were not aware of the pause, but Madoc knew he was waiting. This was a different place now, but not so different as to strike away what he saw all those years before.

Don't dream.

With his eyes shut, he pushed the door open, listening to it strain through the hinges' rust. One last deep breath and his eyes forced themselves open.

"Doctor Hadden?" Allen yelled out from behind him. Though he had not noticed Madoc's deliberate actions or subtle pauses, he did notice the man jump and spin defensively when the name was called out. Madoc shot a dirty look at the young man behind. "Sorry," Allen sheepishly said, bowing his head a little. "I didn't mean to scare you."

"I wasn't scared," Madoc replied sternly. He turned back to the open door and peered through. The room within was as different to memory as the shell that housed it. Those words, those simple words written in blood, were gone from the wall.

The furniture Cheechoo owned had been removed and replaced by Hadden. The cabin was one large open concept cottage, in essence divided into four sections. Willie Cheechoo had the room set up with his bedroom furnishings over by the wood stove to the right of the front door.

Hadden made that area into his living room, with a wood frame couch and a couple of folding chairs with dark red cushions. In the far right corner was Hadden's bed made up of two thin mattresses, piled one on top of the other. To the left of the door was the kitchen. In the far left of the room was a table and four chairs. Madoc gently placed the heavy briefcase onto the counter in the kitchen area.

Allen instantly recognized Doctor Hadden's sense of order, or lack thereof. In the living room area clothes were strung over the furniture, books across the cushions. The wood stove was surrounded by the gray dust of ash, pouring out of its open mouth. The bed was naked, a sleeping bag crumpled at its side. Two of the kitchen cupboard doors stood open, one revealing an unopened can of apple juice, the other an empty shelf. A string of fly paper hung down from the ceiling, long overdue for a replacement. The table in the back corner had a covering of notebooks and loose paper. Allen smiled at the familiarity.

"No professor," Fanning said. "Looks like I'll be seeing you when you get back." Oblivious to the comment, Madoc walked into the cabin.

Allen politely pressed by Fanning, and went in too. He turned back toward the doorway, and looked up at the loft. Although the cabin looked as though it should have had a second story from the outside, it simply had a high ceiling with a small storage area along the front of the building. It was empty now, a support beam for countless cobwebs and dust. The sun stabbed its way through the circular gray window above, in a bright streak of light that cut into the cabin's thick air.

Allen turned back to the room, oblivious to Fanning waiting at the door for official word to leave, and to his guide inspecting the rear wall with a cautious hand. Allen went over to the far table and looked at the papers lying there. There were six wire-bound notebooks, three open and facedown, the other half closed. Allen picked up one of the open books and flipped to the end, casually surveying the information there. It was in a kind of shorthand that he didn't immediately recognize. He then picked up one of the many pieces of paper on the table.

Doodling, Allen thought as he studied the meaningless lines that meandered all over the sheet. He put it down, then picked up another. More lines and shapes, this time covered with a grid. On another, more lines covered by another grid. Allen furrowed his brow. He had long become used to Doctor Hadden's shorthand, but none of this looked familiar.

He found another paper, this one without the lines or grid. It had writing on it—more doodling to the untrained eye. Allen knew what it was. He immediately recognized Doctor Hadden's chicken scratch.

"I've got something here," Allen yelled to Madoc. "Doctor Hadden was making notes about his departure."

"Yeah?" Madoc absently replied. Satisfied there was nothing left to read on the wall, he turned his attention to Allen. "What does he say?"

Allen read out loud. "'Thirty July. Despite yesterday's weather, I shall start my return to site today.'"

"Three weeks ago," Madoc mumbled. The rest was much more puzzling. Allen continued to try to read, attempting to make sense of Hadden's shorthand:

> Carb-dat strat org. Ret, 29AUG, atpt search whr mx nos. Appr arach sug = define...Will try make reason of glyp, by means of cpprarach. Will try weave by point of holes marked theory as E/W. If Th E/W = +, then return Mc w/ cppr arach. N/L air p/u on 02 SEP...

"Zero-Two, Sep: The second of September," Fanning said pointing at the date over Allen's shoulder. "That was the date I was supposed to pick up John."

"That makes sense." Allen nodded. "I know Doctor Hadden uses 'Mc' as shorthand for McGuinness University, so he was planning to go back to the school on the second. See, it says 'Return Mc' before the date. I think he's saying If he's right about his theory, he's going to go back to the site later."

"What's the 'E/W theory'? And 'arach'?"

"You got me," Allen replied. "East-west maybe. And...'arach'...maybe...uh...I haven't got a clue...I don't really understand any of this." Allen flipped through a few more pages. "No, I don't know what he's writing about."

"Don't worry about it," Madoc interrupted. "He's in the woods and we have to go get him. He can explain it to you when we find him. Well, Matt, it looks like you have your return charter." Fanning finally walked fully into the cabin, a relieved smile hidden as best it could be. Allen threw the book back down on the table.

* * * *

"When was the last time you were out?"

Elisha stopped for a moment. They were the first words Tyance spoke since they unloaded the plane—and Elisha's first reaction to the question was a defensive *None of your business*. Then it occurred to her the question might not have the meaning she thought it did. Deciding to clarify rather than defend her social life, she asked, "What do you mean?"

"Out in the bush," Tyance answered, dropping Allen's backpack at the bottom of the cabin's stairs. The two were piling up the belongings there, figuring the men would arrive shortly to carry their own packs up to the cabin.

"Oh, not for some time," Elisha answered. *Same answer either way,* her mind chastised. "My father used to take me and my sister out quite often. Fishing trips, camping holidays, things like that. It's been over five years, anyway."

"This your father's stuff?" Tyance nudged Elisha's worn camping equipment with her toe.

"Sister's. She loves the outdoors. She and my father go camping every summer, like a tradition. This year they went to Killarney Provincial Park for a week of canoeing. They asked me to go along, but I had to work at the university. I guess I lost interest in camping in high school. What about you? Any siblings?"

"Three brothers. They all hate the outdoors. Actually, I shouldn't say that. My younger brother, Winston, he still goes moose hunting. I can't remember either of the other two ever liking the outdoors." *Sister,* Tyance thought. *She has a sister.* How often Tyance thought she would trade all of her brothers for one sister. Or mother.

"I bet your brother loves being able to use your lodge when he goes hunting." Tyance gave a thin smile back, without comment. "Sure is pretty out here," Elisha continued, unaware of Tyance's uncomfortable relationship with her siblings. While Tyance was quiet, Elisha turned toward the plane, staring out beyond it. She placed her hands on her hips, and bent backward to crack her spine. She surveyed the area all around, listening to the wind blowing across the lake.

"I'm going to go see what's going on. Maybe your guy is up in the cabin. You coming?"

"I'll be up in a second," Elisha replied, staring across the lake. Tyance grabbed onto one of the packs and went up the stairs.

Elisha took in a full breath, expanding her lungs to their maximum. The air felt beautiful, almost sweet in the mouth. As she exhaled, all the tension she brought with her went out with the smooth breath. She had forgotten how much she liked the wilderness. She watched the tall thin trees swaying gently in the breeze, stretching all around her. She heard the door to the cabin close, leaving her alone with the plane and the endless forest. *You're an idiot, Hadden,* she thought to herself, *but you do know how to get away from it all.*

She smiled. Susan Fellows told Elisha that she would be okay once she was out there. Susan was right. The bright blue sky, the sweet air, swaying trees, the birds singing—it all came together rather nicely. Things weren't that bad. The feelings of apprehension now seemed silly.

Just look around, she told herself. *Tuition is going to be covered for next year, and all you have to do is be here. Here. You used to love hiking, you used to love camping. Allen is fun to hang around with. Tyance is a little tense, but she and Madoc seem pretty good. This is great. Why did you ever give all this up?*

"Raun Belleford," she said aloud.

The smile on her lips grew wider. She could not remember how long it had been since that name came to her. In May of her grade ten year, Raun Belleford had asked her to be his steady girlfriend. A month later, it was the first time she said 'no' when her father asked if she was ready to go camping.

Thinking back now, she could see his face. She anticipated anger that day in June, but none came. Now, she recognized there had been another expression. Probably the same look he got when she told him in grade three that she could walk to school on her own, or the same look he got when in grade eight she won the argument over curfew. She never acknowledged the look at the time. It was only after, looking back on the moments, she realized the pained expression that crossed behind his eyes—a look of sadness and concession. When she called up her sister to request the use of her camping equipment, the response was a sarcastic grunt.

She later wished that she called her father to request his gear instead of her sibling's. Her sister would snort and laugh. Dad would smile. She knew he would have. If only she called him, then he would have been happy that his daughter hadn't lost her love of the wilderness, and he would have felt needed.

Elisha took in another deep breath, releasing this one as a sigh. She closed her eyes and turned her head to the sky, feeling the early afternoon sun beat down on her pale face. Summers of boyfriends, summers of working, summers of school—none of them could equal this moment's sudden feeling of peace. The soft breeze, the sweet air, the lapping sound of the lake endlessly licking the dock, birds in the distance making up the background music for the vocals of birds immediately around, the sky an endless blue, the trees hushing each other in the breeze, the warm sun on her face. The feeling of peace swelled in Elisha. *Next year,* she decided.

Next year I'll go out with Dad. At this thought all her tension slipped from her soul and pooled around her feet before straining through the dock into the water below. She smiled, her eyes still closed, tilting her head from side to side, letting all of her face catch the warming rays of the sun. She gently opened her eyes, and looked at the plane a few meters away from her. She looked at the window, to see her reflection, to see how beautiful her smile must be.

And saw the Lochkray.

A moment's vision, a second's lapse, the shooting of a chill like ice up her entire body. Immediately behind her, close enough to touch, she saw the form. Tall, much taller than Allen or even Madoc, he stood behind her in huge proportions, her frame entirely engulfed by his in the window. Her eyes went wide enough to see the white in the reflection.

The man's gaze, startled, locked on hers trough the glass reflection. She whirled around, her hands instinctively coming up to defend herself against the bald stranger behind her. She squinted as she strained to keep control of her bladder, which suddenly wanted to release at the sight behind her. Her stomach had dropped a foot and she felt faint, as if the peace she found would rather her body turn off than allow this man in a black cloak to steal it away. As she spun to face the form behind her, with a scream stuck in her throat, she forced her eyes to open wider, and tensed her arms in a preparation to defend. She didn't know if she would be able to hit the man, but she knew she had to be prepared.

She looked up, but only found empty air waiting behind her. Ahead of her, she saw the dock stretching to the stairs, which went up to the cabin, which sat in front of the forest wall, which pressed against the backdrop of blue sky. Elisha stood still for a moment, scanning with her eyes left to right, her hands still held up in readiness to strike out. She spun back to the plane and looked into the reflection in the window again. This time, she only saw herself, the vision of the cabin hovering behind her. Instead of feeling comforted, she felt her stomach drop again. Not only was there no strange man behind her, there was nothing that could have caused her to be mistaken.

She spun around to face the cabin again, her fists refusing to drop. She stared hard at the building and all of the woods around her. It wasn't just her imagination. There was nothing behind her, nothing to make her think that she saw the large man. A figure passed by one of the windows in the cabin, causing her bladder to flutter again and the chill to run up her spine once more. This time, even before the chill could complete the journey to the base of her neck, she realized it was just Allen walking around the cabin. She dropped her hands down to her sides, feeling foolish. Her eyes now exclusively scanned the cabin, to make sure that nobody saw her actions.

The feeling of peace that took so long to come to her was gone. Now the pressure was swelling up around her again, the feeling of foreboding. She felt naked and watched. She drew her now clasped hands up to her chest, and her eyes darted so fast that the images barely had time to imprint in her mind before they moved off again. Elisha took a step forward, toward the cabin, listening to the wood of the old dock squeak as she stepped. She stepped forward, slowly making sure again that nothing was around. Then she stepped again, this time more quickly, ignoring the noise of the straining wood. By the time she reached the stairs, she ran.

* * * *

The door to the cabin burst open, and Elisha stepped inside, closing it tight behind her. She took the briefest of moments to try and compose herself outside the door, but if anybody paid any attention whatsoever, they would have noticed how quickly she burst into the room, and how securely she slammed the door shut. As it was, they were all over in the far corner by a table filled with books, busy discussing the matter of Fanning's return schedule.

"Twenty-four to forty-eight hours after I get the call from you," Fanning told Madoc. "I can't promise you anything more. I do have other charters to fly."

"Yeah," Madoc said coyly. "We'll call you as soon as we find Hadden in the bush with the sat-phone. That way you can figure out how long it will take us to get back here and be waiting-"

"Not unless that school is willing to cover the costs for an express trip. It's either forty-eight hours or an extra four hundred."

"That's what I mean, Matt. You know I'd give you more if it was my charter, but I don't have any say in the matter. It's the university who's signing the checks. All I'm asking is If you have a pocket of time, you use it to come up here as soon as we give you the call. We don't want to have to wait here any longer than needed."

"Twenty-four to forty-eight hours. Standard on-call. That was the deal. Call me when you find him, but you might as well wait until you get back here and call me on that thing, and then I'll start my plans to return." Fanning indicated to the heavy grey briefcase on the kitchen counter with a jerk of his thumb.

Madoc made the purchase many years before, putting down a large quantity of money for the latest satellite phone system. The entire top of the heavy grey case was used as an antenna, and the phone receiver sat inside. It looked like a radio system James Bond would have used in the sixties. It wasn't the like the sleek, cell phone-like unit that Madoc took into the bush with him—but having spent several thousand dollars on the large, heavy case, Madoc wanted to get his money out of it, and continued to bring it with him to wherever he set up base camp, as a back-up.

"And," Fanning continued, "unless any of you have any further need of me, I'm heading back to Fraserdale." He turned to Elisha and asked, "Are all the bags off of the plane?"

"Huh?"

"Your stuff," Fanning said slowly. "Is it all off my plane?"

"Yesh," Elisha replied quickly, her head turning so she could look through the dusty glass of the windows at the plane. There it sat, bobbing in the gentle waves, the dock empty, the land calm. Allen looked at her for a moment through the corner of his eye. His mind hovered around the idea that something was wrong, but refused to land. The thought went on its way, chalked up to the overall odd behavior of Elisha, and Allen returned his focus to the table.

"Well then," Fanning said, "good luck. I hope to see you all in a week or so. Or, at least, twenty-four to forty-eight hours after a week or so."

"We get the idea," Tyance stated coldly. Fanning smiled and gave a wave to the room, stepping out the door. Tyance looked over at Madoc.

"I tried," he said to his partner

. "I told you to give him the money yourself." Before they heard Madoc's reply, Allen beckoned for Elisha to come over to the table, which she did. Tyance and Madoc argued with one another, words like "Can't afford it," and "You're just cheap," being thrown back and forth. Allen, trying to politely ignore them, passed Elisha one of the papers on the desk.

"What do you make of these?" he asked, shoving the sheet into her hands. Elisha studied the paper for a moment.

"Doodling?"

"Yeah, that's what I thought. Look at these." Again Allen shoved forward a pile of sheets. Elisha tilted her head to one side and studied the papers.

"What's this grid for?" she asked aloud, not meaning to.

"Exactly. I wonder if this is a map or something. You know, like those lines are rivers and things. Looks kinda like it." Elisha slowly turned the paper around three-hundred-and-sixty degrees, stopping at certain angles to study the shapes before continuing the spin.

"I don't think it looks like anywhere around here," she finally decided.

Outside, the sound of the plane's motor starting up caused everybody in the room to turn their heads. Starting with Madoc, the group went to the cabin's door and stepped out outside. Elisha was the last to exit, carrying two of Doctor Hadden's notebooks with her, still half-studying them. In the plane's cockpit they saw Matt Fanning turning knobs and pulling levers. The loud hum of the propellers echoed across the lake and shattered the pristine tranquility. The plane pulled away from the dock and taxied along the water. Elisha turned to Tyance and showed her one of the grid-covered doodles in her hand.

"Does this look like anywhere around here?" she asked. "Like a map of the rivers or something like that?"

Tyance drew her attention away from the departing plane for a moment to look at the papers. After a few tilts of her head and a couple of furrowed brows she shrugged. "Hmmm. It's not anywhere around here I can tell. Is it supposed to be a map?"

"It was Doctor Hadden's. I don't know what it is supposed to..." Elisha trailed off and watched as the plane lifted off of the water and pulled itself up into the air. It banked hard toward the south, then ascended into the sky. Madoc gave the plane a large wave and then turned back into the cabin.

"Well, Allen," he said, "we better make sure that there's enough wood for tonight." He descended the stairs with Allen following after him. Tyance gave the papers back to Elisha, again giving a shrug.

"I don't know what he was drawing," she said almost apologetically. Elisha returned an understanding smile. Tyance followed after the other two, leaving Elisha to watch the plane slowly disappear into the sky.

Once it was gone, she turned back toward the cabin and entered.

* * * *

"Oh, my God. We're going to the wrong place," Elisha blurted out, causing the rest in the room to turn their heads toward her. The plane left many hours before, and the sun was now dropping out of the western sky. After some discussion it was decided It would be best to wait until the next morning, right after breakfast, to depart for Doctor Hadden's location. It was suggested that leaving immediately might not be a bad idea, but departing the next morning left them the rest of the afternoon and evening to better prepare.

To Elisha's surprise, once the bags were all brought in, Tyance took a small pile of maps out of her backpack and unfolded them on the table with Hadden's notebooks. She compared different maps to the grid-covered lines that Doctor Hadden left for them. "I swear they look like maps," she had muttered.

However, the attempt to make meaning of the enigmatic lines had failed to offer any correlation to the local topography. Lunch was eaten, and Allen and Madoc were successful in making a nice fire in the wood stove in the building's corner. With Tyance's maps already out, the group gathered around the table to review their journey one more time.

A plan was hammered out on how the journey would go. A little over fifteen miles on day one, then the rest on day two, convince Doctor Hadden to come back on day three, and so on. Madoc and Tyance argued about meals, Allen asked about obstacles the maps showed they would have to traverse, and other details were nailed down. After all the particulars were decided on, everybody went about keeping amused.

Allen and Madoc swapped stories about McGuinness University, comparing tales. Madoc was updated on how much had changed since his years there, as well as being surprised by how many things remained the same. Tyance took a seat over by the wood stove and read a very dated *Reader's Digest* thatden left.

Elisha busily dug through all of her sister's camping supplies to see exactly what she was given. After a complete inventory was taken, she wandered back over to Hadden's paper-covered table. She picked up a binder thatden used as a journal, and read through the enigmatic scribbling, which meant even less to her than it had to Allen. A lot of abbreviations and code, none of which made much sense. She shook her head, reading through each line, trying to discern what it meant. She flipped it over roughly, scanning more of Hadden's chicken scratch. After a few seconds she realized the papers actually read back to front, rather than the usual way. She smiled to herself. How Hadden.

"What's that thing?" Allen was asking Madoc, noticing that he fiddled with a small black box that looked almost like an oversized calculator.

"GPS," Madoc answered back. "Handheld unit."

"Cool," Allen nodded. "I have one in my car, but almost never use it."

"Yeah, well out here, it's our best friend. It's going to be telling us the way to go. See?" Madoc held up the screen. "Tyance programmed in the waypoints, based on her maps."

"Waypoints?"

"It's a location point programmed into the GPS," Tyance answered from behind her magazine. "Based on latitudes and longitudes. There ain't no roads, so that machine is the only thing telling us which way to go, and how far it is."

"Cool," Allen repeated.

"We used to do it all by compass, landmarks, and maps." Madoc turned the machine back toward himself. "See, tomorrow we're going to try and cover twenty-seven-point-four kilometers. However, rather than just head in a straight direction, we'll follow the GPS to the next waypoint, a little over three kilometers away. Then the next one. Then the next one. That way we can bypass and avoid any challenging terrain."

Elisha, half-listening to Madoc, placed the binder on the table. She watched the room for a while until Tyance was once more engrossed in some article in the magazine, and Allen returned to discussion of McGuinness. She listened as Allen regaled Madoc with a story about trying to steal eight-ounce beer glasses out of a bar by stuffing them down his pants. Madoc was amazed to hear the news that the Swine's Elbow, the dirty little drinking hole that students frequented in his day, was still in operation. Elisha shuddered at the very thought of the establishment, which to her always smelled like a combination of stale beer and urine.

To most students, though, the Swine's Elbow meant fun, laughter, and cheap drinks. She debated for the briefest of moments whether or not to try and involve herself in Allen's conversation. However, hearing Madoc exclaim—in a youthful voice not used in many years—"I gotta go back now—just to see the Swiney!" made her decide her opinion would not be appreciated. So, she turned back to the table and looked one more time at Hadden's mess.

She decided to turn the binder over and flip through his entire collection of notes to see how many discernible words she could locate. She flicked to the last page, which was actually Hadden's first according to his backwards system, and to her utter amazement she found something she never would have guessed. The writing was clear. Still subject to Hadden's poor penmanship, what she found was not his unfathomable code at all. It was a clear collection of sentences and paragraphs, littered with punctuation, and legible. She looked over at Allen, but stopped short of calling out to him. He was already entertained, and she was not. If he knew his mentor left readable notes on his excursion, she would be left with nothing to do but watch Allen read the papers. So she kept her mouth shut and began to read:

> Today I feel the need to start a collection of my thoughts, for future reference into what events led up to my discovery. So here, good reader, begins a journey into the story of the man who found the Hadden site.

Elisha winced. Pompous, arrogant, self-important Doctor Hadden. To read him was to hear his voice. Only two sentences into the pile of pages, and already she wished that they were all filled with his code.

> Having discovered many years before that the seclusion of the wilds is a place that offers me comfort, I take my respite in nature's roughest spots in order to obtain tranquility. Know that, for it is how I stumbled across Hadden site. I do not deny that my site was uncovered not by my skill and knowledge as a renowned archaeologist, but rather by fortune. Of course, few others would have acknowledged the potential of that which I came across, but Is fortune too. For the first person to come to this site in, what I imagine to be, four hundred years, was none other than Doctor Jonathan L. Hadden PhD, MA, HBa.

Elisha rubbed her eyes with the thumb and index finger of her right hand, squeezing the ridge of her nose. How Hadden irritated her. Once convinced that she could handle more, she read on.

> I have arranged to be picked up by my transport for return to the university tomorrow. With me I shall be taking a dozen spectacular specimens, enough to satisfy that pontificating establishment of my tenure, that what I have found is going to be known as the greatest archaeological find in North America, In the past fifty years. Still, I find myself jittery with the excitement of what I know, which the rest of the world does not.
>
> It frustrates me to no end that everyone I will come across before reaching my home will not understand the magnitude of what I have found. So I will stifle my ire, and keep to myself my discovery until such time as I reach McGuinness University, and then I will release to the world all I know, suspect, and expect.
>
> So, let me begin by describing how luck and genius resulted in the discovery of Hadden site.
>
> Having gone to my camp to prepare for my yearly respite, as I do every late spring, my academic duties were placed on hold so I might take an inventory of all the supplies I require during my summer months, allowing me time to order those things needed for my return. However, this year's mild spring tempted me into the woods before such a list could be drafted. I promised myself a few days of outdoor camping, coupled with a return to

my cabin and the continuation of my intended duties.

Three days into the bush, I found the site. The mound I found was approximately three meters in height, and six meters in diameter. To an untrained eye, it would be a hill or heap of earth. Perhaps a trapper or hunter has come by this place in past years, and Is all they saw, but as I have already pointed out, fortune allowed me access to this place, and I knew what I saw, and what it could be.

As I began my preliminary examination, it did not occur to me how out of place this mound was. I have done examinations of mounds all through the Saint Lawrence lowlands, and excavated many sites, so my first thoughts did not lean to the cultural habits of the Swampy Cree.

The first item I came across was simply a shard, one I presently suspect is Selkirk at first examination—and because of this, it is what I expected to find. It was the next object I located which caused me to remember that the Cree did not create mounds.

Dear Reader, it is difficult for me to describe the excitement that pounded in my heart when I unearthed the metal form, so clearly cast to look like a cob of maize. I pulled it out, at first thinking I had unearthed a long bone.

There it was, a thousand kilometers away from the nearest prehistoric agricultural population. I found it. Approximately a foot in length, and far more detailed than any other cold-pounded copper artifact I've ever seen. Clear knowledge of agricultural produce, from an area and time that should have been ignorant.

Why it was there, I do not know. The excitement pounds harder in my heart every moment I begin to think of what will be learned here.

Further preliminary digging revealed more evidence that the thick growth of vegetation atop the mound already had told me. This mound was created long, long before my arrival.

I turned up more pottery shards, and again they are either Selkirk, or so close to this as to be akin to it.

I found two more copper artifacts, one like an bird like shape, as well as what appears to be a spider, again far more detailed than any other Iroquois copper forms I have ever seen. Then I found a pipe. I believe at this point It is Huron in origin, and I look forward to seeing if this stands up to better examination.

I found several arrowheads, all different, and all suggesting an origin from thousands of miles around. All of these were pristine and in excellent condition, as was the pipe, and finding them convinced me that this mound was not a midden or dumping area.

What brought this theory further forward was the discovery of the skull. Only the cranium, I believed it to be that of a male, approximately 18-40 years old. Then the second one I unearthed, a cranium and mandible, belonging, I believe, to a female or young male.

    With this skull, close enough to cause my pounding heart further thrill, was a gorget. An Iroquoian gorget. I am sure that this was at one time worn around the neck of the individual I had found. It was here I stopped digging.

    I found myself standing, with a skull in each hand, looking for an explanation of what I found. It was then I realized that the mound I stood beside was not solitary in any way. Within moments, I realized there were three other mounds in the immediate vicinity. Further looking identified four more within a hundred meters.

    I have run theory after theory after theory over in my mind, and have only found only one acceptable conclusion. This is an important place. People came from far around to leave these offerings, and perhaps even to be buried. I look so forward to knowing why.

    Tomorrow I shall go south and report what I know. With evidence in hand, I will show my colleagues what I have found.

Elisha thought for a moment about the pile of artifacts that she saw on the desk in front of Allen when she went down to Hadden's office.

    I hope to begin a more detailed excavation within three weeks. These first few artifacts, these first few words written down, these first few thoughts, all of them excite me to no end. For what I have found will shake the archaeological community in this province, and it will all start with these small words and simple artifacts. I believe that what I have found is a prehistoric place of pilgrimage, if you will. A religious place, which people risked their lives to visit.

    Why did they do this? I do not know, but I expect the answer to this question will astound us, and make us rethink the religious nature of the Iroquoian people, and their northern Algonkian neighbors, and the way that they interacted.

    Doctor J. Hadden

Elisha shook her head. *He's already written the introduction to his book,* she thought to herself, flipping over the page. A slight sigh, and she looked down at the next page.

Elisha read again.

    June first.
    Damn bastards.

Elisha blinked hard. *An interesting way for Hadden to continue his magnum opus.* She looked around the room again, as if the reading the words caused the others to look up from their concerns.

> As I should have expected, my colleagues have denounced my find and left me without any support. So, to hell with them.
> I will return north on my own before the end of this month. All I need is a few weeks at the site and I'll produce enough evidence on my own to have every major journal publishing my paper: "Hadden Site: The Pilgrimage Place of the North, and Stan Azores Can Go Fuck Himself!"

Elisha released a brief laugh that came out like a snort. She wondered if Professor Azores would appreciate being included in the title. That was all that was written on the page. She put it down and turned to the next one. This page was starting to lean closer in style to Hadden's enigmatic shorthand, and Elisha almost dismissed it entirely. Instead, she read on.

> 24JUL—Hadden Site more than expected. Petroglyphs identified six clicks Est-Nrth-Est Hadden Site.
> Something more, much more. Will camp @ glyph site. The idiots don't know what they've given up. Returned to research possible meaning, however these glyphs are more like Peterborough than Cree.
> Brought back with me twenty-three new artifacts from original site. Will go back to glyph camp on 29JUL.

Again, most of this page had been left empty. Elisha read it, and reread it. She turned to the next page, but that one was where the writing deteriorated into complete nonsense. She turned to the next, and again, pages after pages with their meanings hidden beneath a stream of numbers and shorthand. She went back to the last page she understood.

She paused again. "'Petroglyphs…,'" she read to herself, "'…six clicks Est-Nrth-Est Hadden site…'"
Six kilometers east-northeast.
East-northeast.
Of the original site!
"Oh, my God. We're going to the wrong place."

* * * *

Allen read over everything Elisha found. Madoc scanned the last readable page, and simply chose to center in on the new information. Tyance got the maps out again and spread them over the table, attempting to figure out their new objective.

"Six kilometers east-northeast," Tyance muttered, running her fingers over the folds of the map.

"What does this word mean?" Madoc asked, holding his page out to Elisha.

"Petroglyphs. It's rock carvings, like etchings in stone. It looks like this new site is rock carvings. I'm surprised thatden's decided to center in on the glyphs though. Traditionally, more knowledge can be gained from middens and mounds than from artistic rock carvings—"

"Wait," Allen interrupted, grabbing the binder out of Madoc's hand. "Sorry," he said as he flipped through the booklet of Hadden's coded writing, "but Doctor Hadden believes that some glyphs may be a precursor to a writing form, used as a kind of written communication."

"That's classic pseudo-archaeology," Elisha responded with rolled eyes, "and typical of Hadden."

"Fine, you don't have to agree." Allen frantically flipped through the binder back to the front of the book. "It's what he believed. I'm sure I saw..." He trailed off. "Here it is." He put the binder onto the table and slid the open pages over to Elisha, his finger pointing to one of the lines in the center of the page:

Cuneiform theory—->on glyph

"See, he was testing his theories of the glyphs being like a cuneiform writing style." Allen turned to Madoc to continue his explanation, only to find that he went over to Tyance and was studying the maps, having lost interest immediately after Elisha had explained what petroglyphs were.

"You got a location?" Madoc asked.

"Fuck. It's pretty vague, but I'm guessing right about here." Tyance pointed to a spot on the map. "I can't say for sure, but I'm guessing If he wandered that far away from his camp, he would be going along this ridge, which pretty much goes in the right direction, towards this river. That's where I would get the GPS to point. That would be the easiest path for him to follow if he wanted to do any extra exploring. Along this way, and then, I'm guessing, parallel to this river to this spot."

"How does that affect our trip?" Madoc asked himself quietly.

"Not at all, really," she answered for him. "We might as well keep this river here to the south, all the way up to the ridge rather than crossing, but otherwise, it's still trekking through thick bush for over two days, looking for a needle in a haystack."

Madoc turned back to the other two. "Well, Elisha, it's a good thing you found this when you did, otherwise this trip would have been a complete disaster. I don't suppose this new information makes any of the rest of that scribbling sensible."

"Well, like I said," Allen answered, "these lines about cuneiform theory being linked to the—"

"Other than academically," Madoc interrupted. "I mean, does it have any further meaning in regards to how to find John?"

"No," came the meeker reply.

"Okay then," was said with a sharp nod. "Then tomorrow we go to this glyph site."

* * * *

The Lochkray sat, perched in a tall tree, scanning the cabin below him with eyes squinted so tight they looked shut. "The glyphs," the daylights were saying. *The carvings*, he thought to himself. *As done in the old ways*. He smiled as Lochkray smile—invisibly, across thin lips, a mere flutter across his visage.

The fact that the Hadden got closer meant little to him, for no daylight would get to the place of true worth. They already assumed the carvings were the works of the crimson daylights of this land. They would not look for the meaning within.

"A type of writing style," the Therrien said. *Close*, the Lochkray was tempted to reply aloud. *Very close*. What the carvings meant to the Lochkray was that he was right. The Hadden found the way to the valued place.

The Lochkray suddenly leaped from his perch, darting quickly from one branch to that of a tree beside him. His fist wrapped around the thin trunk of the second tree, and he used the momentum to pivot and fling himself into the air, where he flew for a split second before reaching a third tree, taking this one with two hands. He shifted his weight as he landed, his inertia suddenly disappearing, and came to a gentle halt, his body stretching up.

He stood on the new branch, the cabin still in his sight, and all came to rest as if he was always there. His shifting mass quelled the tree's reaction, and all was still in the forest—even the birds in the branches in the surrounding trees were unaware that this large male leapt through the forest, and now slithered down to the ground as if he were liquid.

The fluid motion of the Lochkray was like that of a snake but his huge human form made it strangely eerie to see. He twisted around and ran through branches far too weak to hold his mass, and yet they barely bent—spider's webs within the trees were not harmed, the leaves did not rustle. The Lochkray twisted and slid his way down, then dropped, ten feet from the ground. He came to a stop in a crouch, gently landing on the uneven terrain with a deep *whoof* that disappeared into the breeze.

The Lochkray smiled his Lochkray smile again. This setting was new to him and yet he felt content—even under the horrible, horrible burning sun. *The old ones were wise to have chosen this place*, he decided. *The trees are so thick, the terrain unforgiving. The daylights will not like this. Too dark, too dense. Yet the potential...*

The Lochkray came to his feet. The cabin was a hundred feet away, and the daylights' conversation was almost inaudible now. They had nothing more to offer him anyway.

He floated across the uneven ground and made his way to a tree that tipped over the year before. The upturned roots, encased in soil, stood vertical like a wall, and bent toward what had once been the tree's top, making it look like a giant's umbrella laying on the ground. The Lochkray crouched down low and ducked underneath the trunk, and made his way into the darkness created there by the roots.

He crouched within this cave of roots and soil and looked at the world around. He watched two spiders that also made their home within the plant's misfortune, sitting in the center of their traps. They were oblivious of him, the Lochkray decided. He followed the lines of each thread around and around, changing directions as the strands connected at intersections and went off in another way. *Very close*, the Lochkray's mind repeated.

The Lochkray closed his eyes. He decided to sleep the rest of this wretched day away, and then through the night as well. He felt no hunger—the virgin feast the week before would hold him well until he reached his destination.

"Kraell'Haatch," he said aloud in his guttural tones.

The Lochkray fell asleep, as Lochkray fall asleep.

Part Three
Journey

Chapter Ten

Dawn came.
The air warmed.
The birds sang.
The Lochkray awakened.
The journey began.

Allen heaved his backpack onto his shoulders, and strained under the unfamiliar weight. Through the corner of his eyes he caught Elisha staring at him, and he changed the expression on his face to a confident smile, which he turned upon his partner.

She returned the smile, adjusting her own load comfortably. Again she felt relaxed, as she had on the dock the previous day, before she— *There had been no one there*—before she joined the others in the cabin. Tyance and Madoc were also squirming and shifting the luggage attached to their backs. The sun shone down from a blue sky, allowing Elisha to wear shorts and a T-shirt comfortably. She looked at Allen's attire, and decided he would be boiling by lunch. He wore jeans and a dark blue golf shirt. Although it was nearly autumn, summer had no intention of relenting just yet. Madoc's tan pants and shirt or Tyance's shorts and top were a much better choice.

Poor Allen, Elisha thought.

Tyance, on the other hand, was impressed Allen wasn't wearing camouflage or maybe even designer slacks and a tie. Although not the choice of attire she recommended, the jeans and stylish shirt were by no means the worst hiking clothes she saw. She was more concerned about footwear, and the two chose that piece of equipment well, for the flexible low-cut boots both students wore were perfect for the upcoming terrain. Allen, though, was completely oblivious to what he or any of the others wore, as was Madoc.

Allen was more concerned about how uncomfortable the backpack was. Not too heavy, just uncomfortable. He tried to shift his shoulders as subtly as possible, attempting to adjust the weight to a better position. Madoc walked up to Allen and tapped a bulging pocket on the back of the pack.

"What's in there?" Madoc asked, nodding at the bulge as he walked around to Allen's front.

"Those are Doctor Hadden's notes. I thought we should take them with us in case we have trouble finding him. I mean, look at all the stuff Elisha found I missed. I figure if I just spend a bit of time in the evenings reading over his notes, maybe it can help us pinpoint where he is."

"Solid reasoning," Madoc said, smiling at his own response. It was the same sardonic statement one of his professors had used to make whenever a student offered a theory not completely thought out. "Although, you may be a little too tired to do much reading in the evenings."

Allen offered a weak grin. "It's gonna be that rough, eh?"

Madoc opened his mouth to reply to this, but instead looked around quickly, then held up his index finger to Allen."Are you ladies ready?" he called over.

"Ready when you are," Tyance said.

"Then let's get rolling." Madoc turned back to Allen, this time using his finger to indicate Allen follow. The four marched off in a line, walking straight into the woods. Madoc carried a long walking stick, one he found that morning. As he pressed forward into the bush, he held it in front of him to push back some branches. *A little less cliché than a machete,* Allen thought with a smirk when he saw his guide go forth, dividing the woods with his staff.

Tyance followed after the two men, noticing the direction they were going. They were heading up the slope behind the cabin, up toward the ridge standing over the lake as a long tree-covered guard. They weren't going along the water's shore, as she assumed Madoc would start out. Before she could call out to question this, Elisha was at her side.

"I figured the bugs would be worse," Elisha commented. "I heard that they were horrible in this area."

"It's been a warm summer," Tyance replied, forgetting about Madoc for a moment. "We might get more as we get in deeper, but the worst of them have been burnt off. Fuck, you should have seen it in July; the black flies were already gone, but there were clouds of moose flies, an inch long, I swear. Fuck, they would take a chunk out of you. They were thick enough to carry you off. Ha."

"I can imagine. When I was in Banff once with my father, and we were out on a hike—I don't know who did it, but one of us stepped on a hornet's nest. I still remember running, and looking back and seeing this huge cloud behind us. I didn't think there could ever be that many hornets in the whole park, never mind just one nest. When we finally got to the camp, we all dove into the water, even though we lost them..." Elisha stopped to laugh at the memory.

"Fuck," Tyance said casually, "they are bad. Like I said, we should be doing okay now. If this were June, I would have told you to go in on your own, 'cause I wouldn't be going with you." Tyance smiled to herself. "So, what about your friend there, he a great woodsman?"

"Allen? Oh, gawd no. Allen's not the outdoors type. More dissertation than field, you would say."

I might say if I knew what you were talking about, Tyance thought to herself. "Are you two seeing each other?" she asked, already knowing the answer—but more interested in Elisha's reaction to the question. To her surprise, Elisha released a brief snort of a laugh.

"Sorry," Elisha said, bringing her hand over her mouth sheepishly. "I don't mean it like that. It's just that...Allen's just a friend. Why, are you interested?"

"Hmmm. I think that our lifestyles would probably clash." Tyance smirked. "Oh, well. He's got a cute ass."

"What about you?" Elisha asked, a smile nearly splitting her face in half. "Married? Single? Divorced?"

"Single and not looking."

"You say that so resolved." The word *dyke* jumped to Elisha's brain, much to her embarrassment. She didn't like the word, and its sudden intrusion to her thoughts offended her. *Besides,* she thought, *would a lesbian take notice of Allen's ass?*

"Just careful."

Up ahead, Allen and Madoc reached the top of the ridge. With a strong push, the branches of one of the summit's trees fell aside, offering a window to the scene beyond.

"That's how rough it's going to be," Madoc informed Allen, motioning his head to the view beyond. Allen stepped forward and looked out. On the other side, the hill sloped away quickly and offered an impressive view of the scene beyond. Rolling and folding, the land spread out from the hill into an ocean of unending green. From above, in the plane, Allen saw how bleak and endless the terrain was. From here, just above the level of the trees, he was given yet another new perspective: that of his place within that wilderness—small and insignificant, expected to cross an eternity of wild. Yet, this did not deter him. Instead, unknown to its wearer, a smile crept across Allen's face, and an excited flutter danced across his chest. *A journey. A quest. A...*

The smile grew wider. Allen turned his eyes toward Elisha, who he just realized was standing at his side, also staring out at the infinite vision before them. Her face did not wear the same excited anticipation, but rather a forlorn weariness. Allen tried to look more energized, but this did not work to enthuse his partner. Instead, she shook her head, and walked back down the hill slightly, following after Madoc, who was already heading at an angle along the hill back toward the shore of the lake. Undaunted, Allen returned his eyes to the objective, and his smile returned. Maybe Madoc was right, maybe he wouldn't have a whole lot of energy to do reading at night—but that didn't matter.

An adventure.

* * * *

So, the troop of four went forth. Simple steps, one at a time, over dirt and leaves and wood and water. Each pace took them a tiny bit farther, each step drew them closer to Doctor J. Hadden. Puddles splashed, branches cracked, small animals scurried away at the sound of the approaching intruders, and the trees watched.

The trees listened. They listened to the two females talk and laugh—one with an easy sophistication, another with a pleasant roughness and penchant for cursing. Each tree saw a different pair, each successive trunk was walked by with a growing relaxation. The difference in styles between the two fell away, and although the trees close to the old Cheechoo cabin would have noticed an awkwardness, those surrounding them during lunch would not.

For the males, it was similar—although the older took pleasure in the occasional awkwardness felt by the younger. Still, they chatted, eventually finding common topics which they hammered on for hours, the younger surprised to learn that the older was quite up on the most recent topics of entertainment, politics, and sports. So, the trees and leaves watched the four go by, watching them bond in their own ways. The rustle and crackling of dried fallen flora slowly building in the distance until the warm bodies of the travelers were right beneath, the lead occasionally pushing hard with his walking stick, bending and snapping the lower branches to clear a path, the rest following behind. Then the rustles and cracklings died off into the distance and the trees continued their silent vigil.

Then they would be disturbed again. Not from below, but from within. This disturbance would come without warning. Not even the slightest suggestion of a mole approaching. The body would just be there, clamoring across the branches, sometimes allowing its massive weight to bend them until it found a new perch upon a neighboring tree.

This body was cold, not like the four before. He went from tree to tree, jumping between some, others he swung to through the plant's own bows under his mass, as if swinging from inverted vines through a jungle. He moved like liquid, not stomping along the ground, but sliding through the branches. His eyes were little more than thin slits, each one burning in agony in the light of day—still his movements stayed smooth and quick. His dark clothes hung off of his body loosely, but never got caught in any of the tree's needles. His direction was clear. Just seconds before, the four warm bonding bodies took the same route.

The first day's advance went without event or predicament. The group and their stalker went deeper and deeper into the bush, advancing with their steps, laughing at each other and with each other. Madoc was especially happy about the way the trip was going that first day. Years of guiding the arrogant and the obnoxiously wealthy usually inspired him to keep conversation to a minimum, but these two were different. They were filled with enthusiasm and eagerness rather than hubris and objections. In fact, the only complaint of the day came from Madoc himself, when he looked up from the device in his hand and turned his head toward Tyance and said, "I thought we would make better time today."

"Are we going to cover the full distance?"

"We'll be at least one waypoint behind."

"Are we going too slow?" Allen called forward, deciding if the group were lagging behind their schedule, it must be his fault.

"No," Madoc said, louder now. "The bush is a little tougher than I expected. We'll either have to make up for it today or tomorrow, or just take the extra day to get to John."

"Take the extra day," Tyance decided aloud for the group. "There's no point in exhausting ourselves."

"I thought you were in a hurry to get back home," Madoc said snidely, more quietly. "You're not enjoying yourself, are you?"

"Bite me."

So, four kilometers shy of their intended resting place, the group came to a finish that first day within a clearing. The Lochkray arrived within the branches above them, unnoticed. He watched them pitch their tents and secure their nourishment before building a fire to huddle around and heat victuals over. That night, after their simple feeding, they talked and laughed, a bottle of liquor emerging to cautious delight, at one point even singing, making the Lochkray cringe at the sound. Eventually, one of the group mentioned their need for rest, and they all disappeared into their tents, each one into their own tiny canvas fortress.

The Lochkray hung above them. Although his heart demanded that he run out into the beautifully dark night, he forced himself to rest. To sleep. While other nocturnals could scamper and perform as they were designed, the Lochkray forced himself to ignore their joyous sounds and sleep. To rest his burned eyes.

Chapter Eleven

"Good morning."

The words startled Elisha, as she thought that she was the only one down by the river. When the morning rose over the distant horizon, Elisha stuck her head out of her tent and searched the camp, the cool, damp woodland air a welcome feeling as it invaded her lungs. She believed all the other tents' flaps had not been lifted since they had all retreated the night before.

With a pasty feeling in her mouth, she stretched out all of the major pains in her body, inflicted by the rocks below her thin air mattress, without making any noise. She was extra careful to be quiet as she crept into the woods to have a quick pee.

The night before, Madoc produced a bottle of sambuca to celebrate their journey. Although the alcohol had melted away any remaining inhibitions within the group—just shortly before an awful rendition of *"California Dreaming"*—, it had also caused Elisha to drink an unusual amount of water in fear of a morning hangover. This in turn had created a very full bladder in the morning.

So, after her brief squat among the bushes, she took her toothbrush and a tube of paste down to the river to remove the night's painting of her mouth. The river was only a few meters wide, and only a few feet deep, but Tyance found a deeper pocket in which to actually swim. Her morning salutation caused Elisha to jump, as she was unaware of the head sticking out of the gentle current.

"You scared me."

"Sorry," Tyance apologized, swimming over to the edge of the pool. "I got up early so I could get in the water before the guys. I know Rob won't be up for a bit yet." She stood up and walked toward the shore, naked. Elisha hid her initial surprise, quickly darting her eyes down at the water once she realized that the water ran off of immodest skin.

"The water's not too cold once you get used to it. You going in?"

"No." She smiled sheepishly. "Just here to brush my teeth."

Out of the water, down the river from Elisha, Tyance picked up a towel, and made her way back, drying herself off and wrapping the towel around her. "For a second there, I thought maybe you were your friend."

"Allen will be a little while waking up yet too. I think he took a few extra swigs off of the bottle to impress Madoc." Elisha smiled, while Tyance laughed at the comment.

"Fuck, yeah. The two of them weren't feeling no pain last night. If we weren't on such a tight schedule, I'd bet we could leave the two of them until noon before we'd see them."

"The way those two were, you shouldn't have been too worried I was Allen."

Tyance laughed again. "Yeah. Well, I startled myself there a couple of minutes ago. I thought I saw a guy standing by the water and it caused me to jump. I really should invest in a bathing suit. It—"

"Saw a guy?" Elisha broke in sharply, looking up from the water, her mouth foamy from the tooth paste. "Saw a guy where?"

"Right here." Tyance nodded at the spot where Elisha was. "Don't worry, it was just my imagination. Just paranoid, 'cause of my bath, I guess. There wasn't anybody here." Tyance raised her eyebrows, looking down at Elisha whose eyes showed a genuine concern. These quickly went sheepish again, as she turned back to the river and brought a cupped hand of water up to wash out her mouth.

"Sorry," Elisha said. "It's just that…" She thought for a moment of the vision on the dock. "Well, I thought I saw a guy down by the cabin yesterday, and it gave me a scare. Same thing though. It was just my imagination."

"Oh yeah? What did he look like?"

Elisha looked back at Tyance with distant eyes. "A big guy," she said, remembering. "Really big. His head was bald, like shaved. It looked like he wore a cape or overcoat or something. He was all in black."

"Fuck," Tyance exclaimed. "You've got a better imagination than I have. All I thought I saw was a guy." Tyance laughed, making Elisha feel silly for the apprehension that came back to her. Tyance turned back toward the camp and walked away. Then she stopped, looked back for a moment, almost prepared to say something to Elisha, shook her head and continued on.

After brushing her teeth and dropping her modesty enough to remove her shirt so as to wash under her arms, Elisha returned to camp to assist Tyance with the preparation for breakfast. Once the fire was going and the food was retrieved from its tree perch away from camp, Madoc and Allen were rudely awakened. In pain, Allen crawled out of his tent, looking as green as the foliage all around. Madoc bounded out with far more energy.

Elisha heard Allen retch in the bushes a short distance away from the camp after he came out. Once he choked down breakfast, he was able to handle himself all right. A little more human color returned to his cheeks. Although the thought of putting food on top of a hangover personally revolted Elisha, it worked for poor Allen. Tyance made a few unkind comments at Allen's expense, to which he returned a good-humored, if somewhat weak, smile.

Camp was broken down, folded, and compacted as much as possible and placed into the packs. The direction of travel was determined by the GPS and they struck forward. It was a quick job to dismantle the camp, much quicker than the time it took the night before to set up—an experience Madoc enjoyed watching, at the expense of Allen.

Again, Madoc took the lead, Allen close behind. Tyance stayed closer to the two men this time, or perhaps it was that Elisha held back more. In either case Elisha was the last of the group, attempting to enjoy the walk, but failing. The rest did not see her regular checks, the repeated turning her head every few moments to look at the way they came. Every time she turned, all she saw was the forest closing tightly behind them, nothing but the branches folding back over each other. Still, she looked, waiting to catch sight of an unknown something. Every time, she shook her head at herself and her stupidity, and then try to just enjoy the walk.

The group went through more of the forest and crossed more streams, climbed more hills and forced their way through more thickets. The sun sauntered across the morning sky, peeking at them through the spiked canopy above. Despite Elisha's anxiety, like the day before, the morning was uneventful. When they reached the clearing where they stopped for lunch, Elisha felt relieved to finally step out from the relentless forest, and commented on her relief to the others.

"Y'know, some of these trees are well over a hundred years old," Madoc said, pouring boiling water from the char-blackened kettle into his cup, where brown crystals had sparkled in the sunlight, waiting to be turned into coffee. Allen looked around him to study that which he was relentlessly subjected to for two days.

"Where?" Allen asked, looking at all the standing timber, none of them reaching more than forty feet.

"Any of these." Tyance nodded with her head to the woods around. Allen furrowed his brow. In California he saw centuries old trees, and they were massive. Madoc smiled at the flash of doubt that crossed Allen's face.

"It's true. The drainage of the ground is so poor around here that they never get to grow very tall. The ground is saturated, and as a result the plants are almost drowned within their own soil. Most of the area surrounding us right now is technically swamp land. If you look at a lot of the rivers around here, they look like they're brown with pollution. In fact, it's tannic acid. The acid comes from the rotting vegetation that's trapped in the wet ground. When that moisture eventually gets drained into the waters, it turns the water brown. The rotting vegetation sits in the ground for so long It rots away and releases the acid and turns the waters around the same color as a cup of tea—because tea is turned its color by the same tannic acid. What's interesting about that—"

"What's that smell?" Tyance interrupted. She heard Madoc's speech about trees a hundred times, and wasn't even aware that she had spoken over him—the words were as familiar to her as silence. Tyance put down her cup of coffee, and sniffed the air.

"I smell it too," Allen said, glad that somebody else had caught the odor. He was afraid It was just another one of those outdoor things that he didn't know about, augmented by his heightened sensitivity to the world around from the previous nights imbibing. The wrenching of his stomach had subsided until this rest stop, but had returned when the rank smell wafted by him in this place.

Elisha cocked her head, trying to catch a sniff of what it was they were talking about. She saw Madoc looking around as if trying to see the smell. Elisha was sure that he could not detect it either, until a soft wave of stench found its way to her nose. It was then that Madoc pointed to the west with his chin and said simply, "Over there."

Tyance got to her feet and wandered over to the edge of the clearing and pushed back the branches. Madoc put his steaming cup of coffee down onto the uneven ground, slapped his hands together, and got to his feet. Curiosity got the better of the other two and they left the small fire to follow. Tyance had pushed through the bush and into the woods beyond. The other three followed after, all catching a definite scent from the woods ahead. At first Tyance missed it, mistaking the black shapeless form for a shadow or rock. Then, as she got closer, the smell became more obvious and she realized that the shape was an animal, and a familiar animal at that. Ironically, her first contact with the creature was accompanied by the same rotten smell. As a girl, she was taken out to the dump one evening with her family, to see the bears clamoring all over the garbage piles, searching for edible refuse. That same rotting smell accompanied the sight of the animal this time—the dead animal. Lying on its side and surrounded by a cloud of flies and other insects, was the still body of a bear.

Upon her approach, Tyance could only see the animal's back. Had chance landed the animal facing the other way, she would have seen the dark red atop the black and a detailed look into the hollowed-out cavity of the animal. A female, Tyance immediately recognized, dumped onto the ground gracelessly, its hollowed-out innards nowhere to be seen.

"Fuck," Tyance muttered, squatting down to look within the voided abdomen. While Elisha and Madoc looked on with a little more prudence, Allen took a moment a few trees away to empty out his own stomach in a different way.

"Black bear," Madoc said to the two students when Allen crept back up to them.

"What would do that to a bear?" Elisha asked, tilting her head so that she could better see how empty the inside was. Along the back edge, through the broad opening, the spine covered in red stickiness and bugs could clearly be seen.

"Another bear, probably," Tyance said, standing up. "Black bears eat carrion. That's why they tell you not to play dead if you see a black bear. Supposedly a grizzly will lose interest in you if you don't move, but blacks are different. They just look at you like an easy meal. I've never seen anything like this though. Look at this, Rob. There's not so much as a scrap of…Fuck!" Tyance's sudden exclamation startled Allen, who had become transfixed with the gore. He looked at Tyance and noticed that she was looking beyond the animal. He followed her line of sight, focused through the repetitive background of trees, and then saw the object that caused the curse. Another dead bear.

The second animal lay just like the first—on its side and torn apart through the chest and stomach. Like the first, the tear was broad and gaping, showing off the hollow carcass's missing viscera.

"Fuck," Tyance repeated as the group made their way over to the second bear. Madoc did a quick look around the area, wishing for a moment that he had his rifle. It was in pieces right now, carefully secured to his backpack in an olive-drab canvas carrying case. The rotting smell of the meat made it obvious that this happened some time ago—so presumably the culprit had long before departed the area. Still, Madoc's eyes darted about the landscape with a cautious glare.

"Two?" was all Allen said of the discovery.

"Maybe they killed each other fighting," Tyance said, none too convincingly. She joined Madoc in searching the immediate surroundings.

"Then what did this?"

"Black bear," Madoc repeated. "Another one. These two must have killed each other…maybe fighting or something…I've never seen one do this to another bear though…Maybe a third came along when…This is…" his voice finally trailed off. The smell was starting to remind him of something. Something from years before. The smell of another bear attack.

"Poachers?" Tyance offered when it became clear that Madoc wasn't going to finish his sentence.

"Why eviscerate them…?" Madoc whispered, too quietly for it to be an actual answer.

"Poachers do this?" Allen asked.

"No…" Madoc whispered to himself again. He glanced at Allen. "I mean, a hunter *did* this. Why would he kill two bears, yet leave the hide and meat? I mean, why…?" Madoc's voice faded.

"Let's go back to the fire," Elisha said, already walking in that direction. Allen was quick to take this suggestion, as eager to get away from the animals as he was to drink some water to remove the taste in his mouth. Tyance left quickly too. Madoc, though, lingered for a moment, tilting his head and squinting his eyes.

Finally he stood straight and scanned the surroundings. He pushed his way back through the branches, toward the clearing. When the rustling subsided, the sound of clanging tin pots, rustling canvas, and the hiss of an extinguished fire could be heard in the near distance, along with the sound of metallic tubes being connected together.

When the human sounds stopped, the fire was out, the camp was broken, and the tromping of feet subsided into the distance, the pleasant silence of the wilderness took over again. The Lochkray slid down from his perch above the rotting beasts. He landed softly on the ground and padded his way over to the bears.

The smell did not deter him in any way—just another smell, no more pleasant or disgusting than any other. He reached out and touched one of the vile heaps, picking up a flap of skin and studying the tear. His brow arched sharply above his squinted eyes. Long tears, more like broad slits. If the four saw a zebra torn apart by a lion, lying on the African savanna, they would have felt the kill looked familiar to that. But they never had.

The Lochkray recognized this type of death. He knew no other bear had done this. The rips were too violent, not the work of a seeker of carrion. These wounds came from a fight. A fight with a creature whose claws were like razors, not spears.

He stepped away from that one and approached the other, again studying the results of the attack. Then he did what the rest never knew to do—he walked a few meters away to the third bear, hidden from the group by only the slightest of hills. There it lay, victim number three of an unseen predator.

Like Madoc had before, the Lochkray scanned the woods around, only he did so with desire and expectation. There was nothing to be seen, as he knew there would not be. The creature that took on two bears, subdued them, and then gutted them hollow would not allow itself to be seen so easily. Whatever animal might have been able to kill the two, surely did not have the ability to kill the third bear. Not the way this one had died.

What would the group think if they found this one lying on the ground with its insides untouched and its skin unbroken? What animal would they think could have caused this death? Have caused a bear to ram its head repeatedly, over and over, against the trunk of a tree, until it crushed its own skull. What animal could cause such madness in an animal, and then devour the prey's family?

The Lochkray reached out and felt the head, the indent where the animal had pounded its cerebral matter into pulp. He felt the edges of the shattered skull pressing up against the decaying flesh. The Lochkray knew a few other dead animals would probably be in the surrounding area.

The Lochkray smiled.

If he were a daylight, perhaps he would cry tears of joy. As a Lochkray, he smiled. His thin unrecognizable smile. He was close. This proved it. He was hunting the right mark, he finally had a tangible indication that he was heading toward Kraell'Haatch. The great Kraell'Haatch. A place guarded by a nightmare. A nightmare that could drive an animal mad, then slaughter its herd. A nightmare that could infiltrate a mind and fester there until its tangible claws could take hold of flesh. Then feed.

The Lochkray stepped away from the animals and walked down to the clearing where the group had originally intended to have their lunch. He could still hear them, a good distance away. They were quieter now than before, not chattering as much. The Lochkray liked that. Right now, the Lochkray liked everything. Even out from the shadowy shelter of the forest, his eyes did not sting as badly as before. The hateful sun did not have the same burn right now. For that was the same sun that sat over Kraell'Haatch.

Chapter Twelve

"What kind of gun is that?"

Madoc turned his head back toward Allen quickly. "A Ruger Mini-Fourteen," he answered, shifting his shoulder within the weapon's strap.

"Oh." Any answer would have been alien to Allen. He just liked to hear somebody say something, and the formidable rifle certainly was a starting point. Even if he knew nothing about guns.

"Should have brought the shotgun," Tyance said quietly in an *I-told-you-so* voice, with a singsong quality.

"I hate using buckshot in this bush," Madoc returned in an equally sarcastic singing voice.

"What about the slugs?" the tune continued.

"I hate firing slugs. They make my shoulder sore, and half the time it almost knocks my arm back out of the socket. You have a hard time staying on your feet. So, who's going to fire them?"

"Fuck, it's not even legal," Tyance said to Elisha, stopping the tuneful retorts. "The government made them prohibited weapons."

"Restricted weapon," Madoc interrupted, without even looking back. "I'm not turning in my old man's rifle just because the law changed. I'll get the paperwork done when we go back."

"The new firearm laws came into effect years ago. You've been saying that for—"

"Besides," Madoc interrupted again, "this is better for distance. If I see an irate bear, I want to keep it as far away as possible." The group stopped for lunch a few kilometers farther along from where they found the bears. Following their quiet meal, they packed up while Madoc took a reading on his GPS, and then they all went back into the bush, pushing their way to natural paths through the trees. Tyance, for the first time in her life, felt claustrophobic.

The silence that got to Allen was, to her of some comfort. At least she could listen to the forest, and all the sounds she knew so well. She would be able to hear something coming. Better than with her and Madoc yammering, anyway, but Allen sparked an argument she wasn't going to let drop.

She hated that rifle. It was no good to her. She was right-handed, but had to shoot with her left because her left eye focused better. The Ruger wasn't very forgiving to the lower coordination. Not like a pump-action shotgun. She could shoot southpaw with that and always manage to grab some of the target. Now she felt naked—and though she might trust her partner, she would have liked access to a more comfortable weapon.

Tyance and Madoc bickered on for a while. For Allan, listening to them jab back and forth was better than just thinking about keeping his lunch down. Elisha kind of liked the sound too. Everybody knew something was wrong with those animals, something wrong with the way they were just lying there, ripped apart. Reasons were given. They would have to do.

What Allen unknowingly started was a debate not unlike one between married couples. Starting with the topic of the rifle, Tyance and Madoc fought back and forth on every topic from their business to their personal habits. What Elisha and Allen did not know was that the two partners often fought like this, intermingling personal jabs with less-than-constructive criticism.

The two guides didn't really think anything of it, and nothing said between the two, no matter how slanderous or vicious, was ever taken to heart. Not knowing this, Elisha and Allen backed off from the others so as not to be dragged into the verbal duel. The bush thinned out for a while, and the tall thin evergreens became spaced at more moderate intervals. Had Madoc not been preoccupied, he would have told Allen and Elisha about the fire that swept through this area decades before, and how the trees still had a hard time reclaiming the saturated soil. He didn't.

Really, Elisha and Allen didn't care. They listened to the other two bickering, tried not to laugh at the more witty digs, tried not to pay attention when it got too personal. With the brush becoming less dense, they were able to fall back more, take their pace, and still never lose track of the others and their never ending audible beacon of argument.

Eventually Elisha and Allen walked along their own paths, away from one another. Elisha wanted to be away from the others now, so that she could better listen to the world around, and continue to make her glances behind without question.

Allen would have been quite happy to talk with Elisha, but she was acting strange again. The dead bears hadn't helped. It was clear she wasn't in the mood for talking—the reasons for which Allen projected back on himself rather than considering more logical reasons.

Probably pissed off at me for bringing up the gun, and getting those two fighting, he thought to himself. *How was I supposed to know? She's probably also less than impressed with your puking, stud. I told you—you should have quit about six drinks back. What the hell do you think sometimes?*

"Allen?"

He turned his head to the side, to where the voice came from, but instantly ignored it. Only the passing trees there. *And sambuca?* He was thinking. *My gawd, Allen, you know you can't handle that stuff. I'm sure Madoc thought you were cool, making an ass out of yourself, banging that back. You're an academic, not a barfly.*

"Allen?"

Allen turned to see the bearded man sitting in the chair, behind the desk. *You should have tried to be a little more controlled. Who were you trying to impress? Elisha? Forget it. That Tyance?...She is really hot. I'd love it if she were interested, but you can forget it with the way you were acting.*

"Allen, what's wrong? You seem preoccupied."

"Sorry," Allen said to the man. He sat down in the chair opposite the desk. The forest was gone—it had never been there. Allen sat down in the padded blue chair opposite the gray metal desk, where the man with the beard sat. On the desk in front of the man was a file folder, a cup of coffee, a couple of pens, and a framed picture that faced away from Allen.

"Is there something wrong?" The man asked.

"No." Allen smiled. "I was just thinking about somebody I know." Allen didn't recognize who the man sitting in front of him was, and yet it didn't seem to be an issue. To Allen, he felt as though he was supposed to be in this office. It looked like the professors' offices back at the university, except this one was much neater than Doctor Hadden's. There were no boxes of unmarked exams, and the shelves were neatly arranged. It was clean and orderly. Almost...*sterile*.

"How's your dissertation coming? Is it going to be ready by May?" The man talked easily, comfortably. His small dark eyes, above a reddish-brown beard, stared forward openly.

"No problems so far," Allen replied.

"Good. How's everything going otherwise?"

"Really good. I've got a new roommate moving in with me in September. He's one of my mother's friend's sons, and he's going into first year. I'm not really too keen on moving in with him, I only know him a bit. Sheldon moved out in June, and it kind of left me in a lurch. So, anyway, this new guy came up last month to have a look around, and we hung out for a while. He seems pretty cool. I don't spend much time at the apartment anyway, so as long as his half of the rent's on time, all should be okay."

"What's his name?"

A thin sheepish smile spread on Allen's lips. "That's the bad part. I know his last name is Yaretz, but for the life of me I can't remember his first. He goes by the nickname Red, but that's not his real name. I'm terrible for names. Thank God we never ran into anybody I knew when we were out. I'd hate to have to introduce him. I don't want to ask him, because then I'd look stupid. I've tried to get my mother to tell me without asking, but haven't had any luck."

The man laughed a facile laugh. "I'm sure it'll work out. So, what're your plans after you finish school?"

"Well, I thought I'd go out into the field a little. I haven't had any real field experience. My thesis is based entirely on quantifying data from finds all across the northwest, and I don't get out from the computer screen much. I never really liked the idea before, doing field work, but I went out on a camping trip recently and found it a lot of fun..." Allen's voice trailed off for a moment, as he stared away from the man. *Camping recently...*He furrowed his brow for a second. *What was I supposed to remember about that?*

"Yes?" the man inquired, bringing Allen back to the room. Allen looked back at him, but already the room was faltering. His focus on the man blurred, but he tried to continue.

"Yeah, so I figured it would be fun to mix that with my academic interests. Y'know, go on a dig and..." Allen shut his eyes. He couldn't focus.

"Allen?" the man asked.

"Fuck, like that was my fault," a woman said in the distance.

Going camping.

Allen opened his eyes again and blinked them hard. The trees around him seemed closer than before. Nearby, Tyance bellowed the word, "Bullshit!"

Allen looked back and forth. He wasn't too sure for how long his feet stopped moving, but the banter between the guides sounded farther off now. If not for Tyance's loud exclamations, he would not have been able to locate the rest of the group within the forest. His head tilted around in an effort to pinpoint the sounds. Then his feet moved toward them, running back to the others. He darted and dodged trees and stumps until he came upon his guides, with Elisha just off in the distance. She gave Allen a confused look when he jogged past, which he smiled sheepishly back at.

"Daydreaming," he said. "Thought I lost you for a second."

"Be careful, Al," Madoc called over his shoulder, happy to pull away from his debate. "If you get lost out here, it could be a permanent thing." Madoc fell back a few paces, just dodging the words "Don't be fucking stupid."

He slapped his hand on Allen's back and laughed, and then told him a story about the time he got lost during a fishing trip on the Little Abitibi River. Tyance rolled her eyes, unsatisfied with the conclusion of their argument, fed up of hearing that story, but content that she sent Madoc into retreat.

A hundred meters away the Lochkray walked up to where Allen came to a stop earlier. At first, he had not understood why the Therrien just stood there, staring blankly into the trees. Then he realized there was something more. He realized the Therrien was not in the woods anymore. The Lochkray followed the Therrien to that place. The Lochkray followed the Therrien into the dream. While he only had enough time to see a room and the fantasy of a balding daylight sitting behind a desk before the Therrien awoke, the fact he went there, had fallen into his mind, was proof enough.

The Lochkray listened carefully to the woods around, listened with every hair on his body, hoping to catch the sound of that which sent the Therrien into the dream. But it didn't come. Only the softest of tingling at the base of his spine indicated that something was close—and yet too far away to take a proper hold. That was why the Therrien got away.

* * * *

Off in the woods, outside of the reach of the Lochkray's listening body, another hunter coiled backward with a push of massive claws. Black lifeless eyes blinked apathetically and watched the Lochkray.   Even from a great distance away and through the thickest branches, it saw the Lochkray listening for it. The hunter slithered back farther, silently. The Lochkray was following the others and knew it was there.

The hunter backed away. Not in fear, but in disinterest.

Chapter Thirteen

"Would you look at this," Madoc whispered to the rest of the group. Hours passed since Allen's drop out of reality. Things had returned to normal between Tyance and Madoc, and the bears were quickly being pushed away from their thoughts—dark holes in the journey, best left ignored. Allen saw what Madoc was looking at a few paces back, but didn't think anything of it. To him, it simply looked as if the forest's branches rose higher than before, and disregarded the clearing as natural.

"Fuck, it's like I always said," Tyance muttered, "no matter how far in the bush you go, you'll always find somebody's been there before you."

"Alas, no land is virgin," Madoc said softly, "no ground so hidden as to be uncompressed by fallen foot."

"What's that mean?"

"It means that no matter how far in the woods you go, you'll always find somebody has been there before you."

"That's what I said."

"I said it better."

"Fuck you, Rob."

Elisha caught up with the rest and surveyed what they came across. A clearing within the woods sat before them—a very large clearing. The ground was devoid of all small plants, the trees were trimmed of branches, ten feet into the air. Many of those branches had been stripped and turned into small platforms clumsily nailed back into the trees, reaching between trunks that served as the legs. Many stumps stuck out of the ground and dotted the clearing, or existed as moss-covered patches with roots stretching out from their center. Somebody even took the time to fashion a crude picnic table within the clearing, turning the fallen trees into useful lumber.

About where the center of the clearing would be, just off to one side of the picnic table, sat the charred remains of a fire pit, with benches made of logs existing as a perimeter around the blackened ground. The ground sparkled red and green all around this area, as beams of sunlight fought their way through the high canopy of branches and reflected off of broken glass. So much broken glass, that to Elisha it looked dangerous. Here, a few years of drinking parties left the ground a mess of broken wine, beer, and liquor bottles, spotted throughout by bottle caps and rusting cans. The sun danced off of these playfully, making the environmental abuse seem alive with color and sparkle. To the west of the clearing, the group saw what happened to the branches and trees that not been converted into seating or firewood. A pile of faded brush sat drying and rotting.

"Kind of remote for a drinking pit," Madoc said. Tyance nodded and then held up her hand to her friend to request silence.

"Mmm," she replied, "You can hear a river nearby. They probably follow the rivers from Moose River Crossing, or one of the other communities over that way."

Allen already wandered over to a beaten trail that shot away from the clearing and looked down the gentle hill It followed.

"Yeah, here it is," he called back. "You can see the river through here."

"People come all the way out here just to drink?" Elisha asked in dismay.

Madoc smiled. "No, this is probably a hunting base camp. Doesn't look that old, either."

"It's probably used all year long," Tyance added. "They'll boat down in the summer, and use skidoos in the winter."

"There's a lot of broken glass."

Madoc released a brief bark of laughter. "Not much to do when nightfall comes." Madoc looked around at the camp with a cautious eye. "I was hoping we would go for another couple of miles or so before calling it quits but this is a pretty good place to break out camp. What do you think?"

Tyance looked about for a minute, making estimates and figuring out numbers in her head. "We're already running behind from yesterday," she finally responded. "If we call it early tonight we can get a jump on the morning, and make up for it tomorrow. This place is a good stopping point. Close to water, level, clear, sheltered, all that good stuff. We're not going to make it to where this professor is supposed to be today, anyway. It just means we'll have to find him after lunch, rather than before."

Before the words finished coming out of her mouth, a deep thud sounded over by Allen as his backpack fell to the ground in relief. He went over to the picnic table and sat down on the rough seat, leaning backward onto the uneven table. A sound—half-groan, half-sigh—came out of him as he stretched his arms upward, allowing his contracted spine to crackle and snap. Madoc turned to Elisha.

"Care to make it unanimous?" he asked.

She just laughed, dropping her own heavy pack down to the ground. She turned around and looked back the way they came, a smile still present on her face. She looked back into the seemingly impenetrable thicket.

The woods stared back. Despite her continued glances behind, and her search for anything following them, Elisha didn't see the woods watching her now. The eyes hid among the shadows, and behind them was a mind frustrated by the group.

The hunter out there could seduce most herds without effort, but not these two-legs. They must be taken one at a time. Separate. Now they clustered down for the night, leaving no further chance for attack.

So the eyes looked elsewhere.

* * * *

It was just before dusk.

Tents went up quickly, the practice from the day before being enough for Allen, who put his structure up more quickly and efficiently than before. Of course, he still made a few errors, placing pegs in the wrong holes, and putting the over-tarp upside down, but these difficulties were quickly corrected. Tyance smiled as she watched him strip down the mistakes and quickly fix them.

He's getting the hang of it, she thought. *I figured we'd have to drag his body back to the cabin by now.*

"Looks like you got it," she called over, once the shape of the structure looked a little better.

"Almost." He smiled back.

Madoc went over to the pile of cut-down trees and collected logs and branches for kindling. A fire was created in the pit, and Elisha took it upon herself to try and clean up the mess around the clearing. Using an impressively effective makeshift broom fashioned out of an evergreen bough, she swept a good deal of the scrap metal and jagged glass away, depositing the garbage into some bushes along the perimeter of the camp. Lots of glass was imbedded in the dirt and that which could be pulled out found its way to the bush as well, while those too deep were decided to be no threat to booted feet.

Tyance went through the supplies of dried and vacuum-sealed food and came up with the best possible meal option. Although Allen had sneered at the sight of the foil freeze-dried food packages and canned milk she had set aside, Tyance knew she would be able to impress him—just as she did the rest of the rich southerners whom she guided. "Haute cuisine from crap," Madoc called her creations.

Just a little extra effort and pepper, she thought. *That's all it takes.*

Allen filled the collapsible water jugs down by the river, dragging up the night's supply, one jug at a time, enjoying the ebbing warmth of the day and the cool of the river as it rushed through his fingers as he filled the jugs. They all happily busied themselves, enjoying the break after the long day of walking. The dead bears seemed like a lie, Allen's daydream was forgotten by him. They worked in contentment until that moment just before dusk.

Madoc recognized the moment, knowing It lasted for just a few minutes, but lingered longer in the days of late summer. Not yet evening, not yet twilight. A special calm came with that summer's moment. Like the last minute before five on a punch clock on a Friday—comfortable and easy, awaiting the tranquility of night.

It was the calm of that moment that caused Madoc to realize something was wrong. He just put down a bundle of wood, dropping it beside the fire. Tyance muttered to herself, still working out the details of her culinary combinations. Madoc stood upright, turning his body to the north. Tyance caught the suddenness of his action and raised an eyebrow at him. This gone unnoticed, she, too, got to her feet and looked into the distance.

"What is it?" she asked, and was immediately shushed. Elisha was close by, humming happily to herself like a small girl, tidying the camp's supplies. She heard Madoc's sudden hush, and turned to the guides, figuring the request for silence had been directed at her. She saw the two standing tall, their eyes sharp and straight. To her they looked like startled deer. She, too, looked to the north but saw nothing.

"What's going on?" Allen asked her, dropping a heavy jug of water at Elisha's feet.

"I think something's wrong," she whispered back.

"I thought I—" Madoc started, but stopped to scan the scene ahead again. Like a herd of animals, the group all sat still, their senses pushed to the limits, searching the wall of trees before them. There, the forest stood motionless, yielding no reason for their caution. In the branches, a bird released a contented chirp, mocking the group's paranoid stance. The bird's sound stopped and all was still again. The group still maintained their hold. Then a rustling of leaves stirred in the distance, abruptly and violently, followed by a wet snort that made Allen's heart sink down to his stomach. He could not see where the sounds came from, they were outside of the group's view, but too close to dispel the panic that swelled forward. The sound stopped, the trees were silent again.

"Is that a bear?" Allen asked in deep pants, trying to get his feet to go backward.

"No," Madoc replied calmly. He darted his eyes, just beyond Elisha and Allen. "Hey, Al," he nodded to his tent, "go inside and get my gun."

"What is it?" Elisha whispered, too quiet for Madoc to hear. Allen took two steps toward the canvas structure but the sound returned. The rustling of branches and leaves with the incongruous snorting growl, made Allen stop. This time he saw the source. Twenty or thirty meters out into the bush he saw the dense wall of flora convulse, flutter, and then stop. Allen looked over at Madoc, whose brow was deeply furrowed.

Allen looked over at the tent, five meters away. He could even see the end of the nylon carrying case for the rifle just peeking out through the tent's upturned flap. He slid his left foot just a few inches, then followed with his right. He did this again, and again. When the unseen "it" failed to react to the movements, Allen grew braver, and dared to take a full step toward the tent. This angered what was out there, and the sounds grew loud again. Allen stopped his movement, but it did not halt the commotion, and instead the gnarling excitement became more agitated.

Seeing that Allen stopped and the "it" had not, Madoc made a move, darting toward his tent, fearing what was about to come. He rushed past Elisha and Allen, aiming for his tent, but before he even came between Allen's view and the shaken forest, the noise made its move.

To Allen it was as if two giant hands had exploded out of the wall of branches, rushing out to grab the group. Giant didn't quite describe them either. They were massive, each three feet long, with pointed claws that curved forward like they wanted to wrap around a gigantic neck. It was absurd how he saw it, and he knew it, but there they were nonetheless, two giant hands that rushed out of the forest on unseen arms. The woods burst as the clawed hands broke forward, shattering through everything in their way. Allen watched, frozen, as they rushed up to him. He felt his chest compress as the hands suddenly dipped forward and backhanded him, lifting him off of the ground.

Allen flew through the air—the massive surreal hands sent him aloft with an explosion of pain. The ground came up fast, and as immediately as he took off, he landed hard on his back, his legs continuing their momentum, flipping him over onto his stomach.

Madoc didn't see hands. Madoc saw what they really were. He knew what the animal was from its snorting, before he even saw it. The look of total shock on Allen's face made it clear to Madoc that his young friend never knew what hit him.

The bull moose came to an abrupt halt after knocking Allen to the ground with its full rack of antlers. It was at least seven years old, possibly more, as big a moose as Madoc ever seen. The full rack on its head, the hands Allen saw from the woods, reached up almost ten feet into the air. The animal came to a stop, then danced on its hind legs, quickly turning back the way It came. The hindquarter of the animal caught Madoc as he tried to advance to his tent, making him back away from his rifle to try to avoid the clomping hooves of the beast.

"It's a moose!" Allen yelled from the ground. "It's a moose!" The animal turned toward him, as if confirming the title, and Allen scrambled back from it as the eyes burned forward at him. The giant animal shook its head violently, a spray of snot and saliva exploding out of its mouth in a guttural wail. It stomped its feet twice at Allen, causing him to retreat again. Then it turned its attention to Tyance.

"The fucking gun, Rob!" she yelled.

"I'm trying!" the frustrated response came as he danced backward from the stomping hooves again, this time the animal backing right over the tent where the gun lay, knocking the structure down like a house of cards. It looked at Tyance, starting to move toward her with threatening clomps. Madoc tried to take advantage of the movement and stepped forward, reaching down to the mangled collection of canvas, prepared to dig to find his firearm.

The moose sensed the move and turned back to Madoc, practically rearing up on its hind legs in an attempt to kick him. Madoc, already off balance, allowed himself to roll out of the way, barely missing the crushing stomp of the animal. He rolled right over the crushed tent—he swore he felt the outline of the gun-case beneath him as he did—and managed to get to his feet. Now the animal was right on top of the tent, turning its body in circles, trotting on the spot with the tent tangled about its feet, surveying the bipeds around.

Allen was still on the ground, his scrambling retreat finally halted by a tree. Tyance had backed off considerably, herself using a tree as a shield. Madoc hovered like a football player waiting to make a play, hunched over, his feet dancing nimbly for his age and waiting for the moment he would either rapidly run away or attempt to regain his weapon. The animal looked at all these, then over at the fourth individual.

The other female stood just on the edge of the clearing. Unlike Allen and Tyance's speedy retreat, she was slowly backing up in disbelief, and the animal had almost missed her entirely, less than thirty meters away. Now their eyes met, and for a brief moment in its muddled mind the animal made a decision. It decided that the thin female standing at the edge of the clearing was responsible for the burning that recently invaded its mind. The female standing at the edge of the clearing had caused the waking nightmares that kept coming. All four stood still in their positions as the big animal made its choice.

It turned its head down toward Elisha, released another deep explosion of sound and mucus, and ran. As if a starter's pistol went off, movement exploded from nearly everyone. The animal galloped at full speed toward Elisha, and Madoc made his move toward the tent. Tyance stepped out from behind her shielding tree, and also dove for the tent with the gun.

Allen scrambled to his feet, an unorganized thought sending him toward Elisha, perhaps to push her out of the way, perhaps to stand in front of her, but a futile plan in any case as the animal was closer than he, and much faster. Madoc dove into the scattered tent. His hands clawed and dug into the pile in a scramble through poles and canvas. In his peripheral vision he saw the moose's target, and his heart sank as he realized he would not be able to find the rifle in time.

The only one who didn't move was Elisha. She stayed frozen, her mind not fully comprehending what was going on. Like Allen before her, she saw the giant hands coming. The animal's rack of antlers became like giant claws reaching out for her, and held her frozen.

Boom!

The explosion of sound caused Madoc to stop his digging and look out into the woods. Twenty meters away, the running animal's front legs gave way while the rear ones continued on, driving it down hard into the ground, an eruption of dirt all around. The animal almost immediately tried to get back up again, pushing on its suddenly weak front legs to become erect once more. The animal's efforts looked almost ludicrous, like its front legs went soft.

Boom!

The animal's efforts halted, and its front legs buckled underneath its weight. This time the hindquarters of the animal joined the anterior, and it toppled to the ground. Madoc got to his feet just as Tyance got to his side. He stared in disbelief at Elisha, still frozen, and the giant animal's last deep, heaved breath through the haze of dust and dirt filling the air. With a wet release of death's breath from it lungs, the animal went still. Allen also became frozen, his feebly heroic motion stopped at the realization that two shots went off. He stood still, trying to figure out what happened.

A quick dart of the eyes made it clear It was not Madoc who had downed the animal. He looked at Elisha, who finally looked away from the giant antlers that were just barreling down on her, and matched Allen's confused glare.

"Is everybody all right?" The shout through the woods startled Allen as much as the shot had. His tingling head turned toward the origin of the sound. Behind him, coming out of the thick bush at a rapid pace, he saw the form of a man, his red hair and pale skin standing out against the foliage behind him, brighter than the tan outfit he was wearing. As he came into the clearing, he leaned the shotgun in his hands against a tree. He came to a halt and looked at the four, who in turn stared back gaping in confusion and shock.

"I'm okay," Elisha was the first to respond with a gasp.

"I'm okay." Allen darted his gaze over at her for a moment before returning it to the new arrival. "I think we're okay," he said to the stranger. Tyance and Madoc moved off of the tent.

"You've got good timing, buddy," Madoc called over. The man came to a stop, the five people making a large circle around the site.

Tyance finally went over to the still animal and looked at the two wounds, then over at the newcomer's shotgun.

"Slugs," she said to Madoc. "I told you."

Chapter Fourteen

"Vance Halverson," the man said his name when he properly introduced himself. The fire that they sat around crackled and sent an upward shower of sparks toward the dark sky. He had helped Madoc and Allen drag the dead moose toward the slope to the river, then roll the corpse into the water to prevent any large scavengers from coming to the camp to feed on the carcass. It took them a great deal of time as the massive weight of the animal only allowed for tiny movements with each drag the three worked at.

Once the animal had been disposed of, everybody took turns with introductions. Before all of this, relieved thank-yous were repeated over and over to Vance, throughout the chore of the moose removal, as they rebuilt camp, and sat down around the fire that Tyance built. An invitation to dinner was offered and accepted, and Tyance went forth to create the final meal for the day, with a surprising amount of help from Allen, who was trying to preoccupy himself and get his heart back to its proper place.

In the warm glow of the fire, the group laughed nervously about what happened, uneasily referring to the event. Forks scraped across tin plates filled with Tyance's culinary creation, as the dinner was gratefully consumed. Elisha took part in the conversation, but the rest noticed how much the bull moose's attack had affected her. She looked almost ill. Her plate of food failed to entice her at all.

Madoc's own plate of dinner was sitting on the ground beside him, but he was making regular efforts to pick away at the food. For the most part, though, his hands were preoccupied with the remains of his satellite phone, which had fallen victim to the stomping hooves of the animal. He was trying to coerce the guts of the device back into its cracked casing, as if getting the tangled mess of wires back within the confines might somehow be enough to get it to power up again. Yet, with every try, they awkwardly fell out again, dangling out of the smashed covering.

"I think it's safe to say," Madoc finally sighed in defeat, putting the destroyed device down, "that my phone if officially…"

"Fucked," Tyance finished off, more preoccupied with her food than Madoc's efforts. She gave up trying to convince him that his attempts to fix it were futile.

"Yeah."

"That's a problem, isn't it?" Allen asked.

"No," Madoc shook his head calmly. "We still have the sat-phone case back at the cabin. When we get back we can still call in for pick-up. This is exactly why I always bring the second phone with me." The last words were obviously directed at Tyance, who just rolled her eyes.

"What about checking in? I thought you had to call in regularly to report our progress."

"Ha," Tyance snorted with amusement at Allen's genuine concern. "How many times have you seen him call in so far? Rob Madoc doesn't check in," she continued, her voice going suddenly deeper. "He's been running these woods since before they put satellite's in the sky. He doesn't need no phone to call in."

"That's right," Madoc tried not to laugh at his partner's impression.

"Yeah, and especially not at two dollars a minute to use the phone."

"You can use my GPS tracker," Vance Halverson offered, apparently not quite sure how to take Madoc and Tyance's bickering. "It can alert 9-1-1 with a reading of where you are. I'll use it to alert my flight when it comes time for to go back home."

"Not necessary," Madoc waved his hand politely. He was familiar with the type of orange box that Vance was now holding out in his hand. In fact, he had planned to get one of the beacon devices himself, but always just relied on the, now dead, portable sat-phone. "Thank you, though. We still have a ways to go, and we're not quitting yet."

"So, what brings you out here, Vance?" Tyance asked, the last slops of gravy being sopped up off her plate with a heavily buttered piece of bread. "Hunting out of season?"

Madoc winced a little at his partner's bluntness—for he already assumed that the answer Tyance gave was the correct one—and if a few out-of-season geese were the price of his help, Madoc was fine with that.

A smirk went across Vance's mouth as he brought a mug of coffee up to his lips, as if to hide his amusement. The question of what he was doing there regularly went through his own mind over and over the past few days. It had an answer, but not one that made sense to him. Revealing the answer to somebody else seemed all the more absurd.

"No, I'm not hunting," he said before a short pause. "I've been assigned here by my employers." He took a quick sip from the mug, the sharp heat stealing away the thin smile.

"You work for the MNR?" Tyance continued, unaware that she was less than tactful.

Allen looked up from his plate. "MNR?"

"Ministry of Natural Resources," Madoc answered. "Are you a conservation officer?"

"No, no." Vance shook his head quickly. Tyance caught a quick glance from Madoc, knowing it was a recommendation to drop the subject. She decided to take the suggestion, but Vance continued. "I work for a monastery in Eastern Europe," he said, "and they requested I come here to do some…surveying for them."

"Eastern Europe?" Madoc said with a bark of laughter. "You don't sound like you're from overseas."

The smile the hot coffee momentarily stole away returned. Elisha liked this smile instantly, just as she had the man whom it was attached to. Not just because he had saved her life less than an hour before, but simply because he was…*likable*. Not a handsome man, nor strapping or tough-looking. Quite the opposite really. He had a mop of red hair atop his fair face that made him look younger than his mannerisms suggested. His features were boyish but sharp, and his build was bordering on being too thin. However, there was a peaceful charm that Elisha saw, and she quickly decided that she liked him.

"I'm from Charleston, originally," Vance clarified. "South Carolina."

"Are you some kind of missionary?"

"No." His meek smile widened. "I'm not a priest. I just work for them. I originally had intentions of joining the priesthood, however, after a couple of years in the seminary, I decided It was not my calling." Allen looked up, with a question on his lips, but decided not to ask it, for fear of being impolite.

"Well, that explains your timing," Madoc laughed again. "God must have sent you, 'cause if you had showed up a few seconds later..." He trailed off as the thought made his stomach sink.

"I've never seen a moose act like that before," Tyance said. "I've seen them chased out into traffic by flies, and I've seen a mother charge a guy that got too close to her calf, but I've never seen anything like that. Fuck, it was like it was attacking our camp."

"Perhaps we got into its territory?" Allen offered.

"Moose aren't like that," Madoc said. "They get brain parasites quite often though. They get goofy when they get them, running in circles and stuff, but that one was...violent."

"Maybe she had a calf in the area?"

"It was a male, but maybe," Madoc answered, unsatisfied. A momentary hush fell on the camp.

"So," Vance broke the silence, looking over at Allen, "what about all of you? Why are you out here?"

"We're work for McGuinness University," Allen answered proudly. "We're searching for an archaeological site." Again a silence fell, this one more awkward than before. Allen waited for a reaction, but was met with a blank and confused stare from the newcomer. "We have reason to believe," he continued on slowly, "that there's a site of academic worth—"

"Are you Doctor Hadden?" Vance suddenly interrupted, his eyes turning toward Madoc.

Elisha quickly looked between Allen and Vance. "What?"

"No," Allen responded for Madoc. "That's who we're looking for. I'm his assistant. The university wanted us to come out here to find him. How do you know Doctor Hadden?"

"I am also looking for him. In fact, I thought I was following him when I came across you. I was advised I might find him near a hunting cabin south of here. I was searching the area trying to find him, but had no success. When I was returning I saw the smoke from your campfire from a ridge. I thought I would follow it to see if it was Doctor Hadden. I understood him to be alone out here."

"Doctor Hadden left his old site," Allen explained. "He found another one."

"What do you want to see Hadden for?" Elisha asked. "I mean, why would a monastery want you to locate an archaeologist?" The four noted the oddest of moments as Vance sat silent with a thoughtful look upon his face. The thought that flashed through Vance's mind was fairly simple: *Do I tell them?*

"It's complex," he said. He considered leaving it at that, then made a decision to answer the question. Perhaps it was the being in the same setting that motivated thousands of years of humans to gather around fires and relate tales of wonder and fancy, or perhaps he simply wanted to get the story out of his mind and put it into words. "I want to see Doctor Hadden because the monastery I work for is very interested in the site he claims to have found."

"How do you know about that?" Allen asked.

"Information flows freely around the world in this day and age. Your Doctor Hadden placed some pictures of artifacts he found on the internet. These pictures caught the attention of a brother who teaches at a university in Glasgow, Scotland. The information eventually made it to the attention of my…employers, who asked me to locate Doctor Hadden. However, when I went to the university to speak with Doctor Hadden, I was too late. He already returned here."

"Why would priests be interested in a Cree burial mound?" Elisha asked, very aware that her first question had not been answered yet.

"It's…complex," Vance repeated. He released a sigh. "The monastery where I work is home to an order of monks whose primary purpose is to assist with the arrangement and cataloging of the vast array of books from the church's libraries around the world."

"Monks in front of escritoires with long quills?" Madoc laughed. Tyance cast a look of astonishment at her partner, unaware he knew any word larger than marmalade.

"No." Vance returned the laugh. "In this day and age it's Packard Bell and Microsoft Word. The church went digital along with the rest of the world. It had to evolve. In fact, the electronic revolution is only the latest change in a long list of adjustments for the order in the last hundred years. You see…" He paused again, this time with a humorless chuckle. "The order was originally put in place to protect humanity from a vampire-like race of people who feed on the human soul."

The group stared at him as Vance raised his right thumb and index finger to rub the spot between his eyes. Putting it into words didn't help.

"A what?" Allen finally laughed. Vance joined him.

"Ever hear of the Lochkray?" Vance laughed and watched the group as they all shook their heads. "I guess almost nobody has. Not anymore. The few books that exist on the subject are located at the Daugava Monastery in northern Belarus. That's where I live and work as an aide to the monsignor."

"What's a Low-thing?" Tyance asked.

"Loe'ck-kray," Vance pronounced slowly. "It's a fascinating mythology, if you're into that kind of thing. It is believed that they have existed for the entire history of man. So the story goes, anyway. They are supposed to be a kind of…cousin of human beings. Actually, there's a good origin myth on the subject. Supposedly when God created man, he also created the Lochkray." Vance licked his lips, oddly excited.

"One theologian in the eleventh century wrote that when Adam and Eve were sleeping pure in Eden, it was the Lochkray that conspired with the serpent to motivate the two to sin. When they were banished from paradise, the Lochkray took to the night to hide from God's punishment for the trickery. The Lochkray became the people of the night. When God could not locate the Lochkray in the dark, He drove them from paradise by taking away their souls, making them starve for life.

"They found satisfaction feeding on no animal but man. Forced by starvation, the Lochkray left paradise to hunt, to become parasites, reliant upon those that they had tried to damn. It's just a story, but it is one of a complex mythology surrounding them. There is a whole parallel series of stories about them throughout Christian legend.

"They are said to be an incredibly intelligent, complicated society of nocturnal beings. Somehow, it is said they learned how to draw out a living creature's…life force. Soul. Essence. They feed on human beings." Vance looked about the group and studied their expressions. "Just about every society has stories of undead night people that feed on us," he said. "The Lochkray are the Church's."

"That's true." Allen nodded. "Most people are only aware of the European version of the vampire myth popularized in the eighteenth century. There's a really good article written by Paul Barber about the origins of the vampire myth..." Allen trailed off. "Sorry," he said.

"No problem," Vance said, actually relieved that somebody was interested in hearing the story as much as he wanted to tell it. "In fact, I have read that article. It is an interesting look at vampires and how much people believed in their myths. People within the Catholic Church believed in the existence of the Lochkray so much that they created an order to study, locate, and annihilate them. It was put together by Pope Stephen VII in the late eight hundreds. Is how far back the Lochkray mythology predates the European vampire myth. Interestingly enough, the only reason the order existed without the attention from outsiders, or even from the highest levels of the church, is that Pope Stephen was assassinated shortly after having the order created. He was insane."

"Apparently," Madoc muttered.

"The order of vampire hunters was about the sanest thing he ever did," Vance laughed. "He actually conducted, what was called, the Cadaveric Synod, where he had the corpse of Pope Formosus dug up and placed on trial for—" Vance stopped and shook his head.

It's another story, he told himself. Years of mythological and historical study, and nobody to share the stories with left him with a brain full of anecdotes.

"I'll tell you that one later," he said to himself more than the rest of the group. "So, the pope created the Order of the Cimmerian Quest and was killed before anybody knew he had done so. Rather than disband because their originator was a lunatic, the order went forth in their assigned duty. Lo and behold, what did they find?"

"Low-kray?" from Madoc.

"Supposedly." Vance nodded. "There's one book written by one of the original members of the order in the early nine hundreds. This man was the first to record firsthand contact with the Lochkray, in what is now southern France. He claims to have found them living in a series of caves..." Vance made quotation marks with his fingers. "'Not like animals, but as a city within the caverns.' Supposedly, the Lochkray took five of the brothers hostage, and killed Brother Kiever Lestivius, the one who wrote the book. He claims to have escaped from them after watching the four others be killed by the Lochkray. According to him, he describes them as having an advanced body of knowledge based on plants, minerals, and even the mind.

"I read a paper written by my mentor who described it as an organic-cerebral technology. Brother Lestivius describes the Lochkray as being able to make moving paintings appear on rocks, make plants able to talk, and fog the mind into seeing what they want you to see. He said that the other four who were taken with him all walked to their own deaths willingly, deceived by the Lochkray into giving up their souls freely. He said that the Lochkray can climb inside your mind and twist your thoughts.

"He further described other captives being held by the Lochkray. Like his partners, he stated that all of the other captives were kept calm and blithe by the Lochkray's ability to deceive with their minds. He even describes how he fell into fantasies and delusions, the only thing which kept his mind from succumbing to their illusions was what he called his faith in God.

"After he escaped and returned to the order, the brothers worked towards the annihilation of the Lochkray. A small army was sent out to locate the caves and destroy the underground city. That first group was lost, no survivors were ever heard of. That started the unknown war. The war between the Lochkray and man: battles without names, armies without countries. There are stories that run parallel to the war between the Church and the Lochkray, from the Battle of Hastings to the French Revolution.

"As with every war, technology advances. The Lochkray, however, had a starting point more advanced than man. While it was believed their knowledge was previously used simply for the advancement of their own luxury, they turned their science toward the genocide of mankind. They were not satisfied with anything but the extermination of all humans. So, rather than create a series of weapons to fight with, they set forth to create one perfect weapon. However, while they were preparing to wipe out all of mankind with one single blow, we were beating them down, fragmenting them, and winning the war.

"Unable to do what they wanted under the duress of attack, they decided to retreat. In the early thirteen hundreds, the Lochkray gathered their most intelligent, their most advanced, and all of their most radical systems of knowledge, then they set out across the Atlantic to follow the setting sun. Once away from the Church's attack, they planned to advance their weapon to a point where they could return and destroy all humans. They called their objective Kraell'Haatch, which has a meaning so complex, I can't even start to try to explain it.

"The long and short of it is: Place of New Beginning. The Order of the Cimmerian Quest followed the Lochkray's vessel into the ocean, and were never heard from again. The Lochkray were beaten down and scattered across Europe, Asia, and Africa. Their cities were found and destroyed, their population wiped out by the Order. Stories of human contact pop up from time to time throughout history, but very few and far between after the voyage west."

Vance took a deep breath, enjoying the attention of his audience, all of whom completely forgot why this story started. Now, Vance knew, the answer came. "It is assumed that both the Lochkray and the brothers' voyages ended in disaster. Two months ago, your Doctor Hadden posted a series of pictures and unorthodox theories on the internet regarding an Iroquoian/Cree burial mound he found in this area. One of the pictures he posted was of a metal artifact, in the shape of a spider."

"The copper spider," Allen said aloud. "I know the one. Doctor Hadden showed it to me. It's really amazing." Allen turned to the rest of the group. "Some of the natives in the Great Lakes area were known to cold-hammer copper pulled out of veins in the ground. Most of them are needles and other simple tools, but some were ornamental. All the ones I've ever seen before were flat. You know, two-dimensional. This one, though, was neat. It's about fifteen centimeters long, and the legs actually curve around like a real spider, and a thin handle extends from its body. Two of the legs are broken though."

"You've seen the spider?" Vance asked over a sudden crackle from the fire.

"Yeah."

"Did you see a marking on its back?" Vance leaned forward.

"Oh yeah, that was really cool. It was almost like a shamanistic figure, all along the body and head. Disjointed though. Usually the figures are almost like stick men, all continuous, but this one looked like it was pulled apart."

"That symbol," Vance said, "is why I am here. The Lochkray are said to have had a language base far more complex than any human language. That symbol on the back of that spider matches one supposedly written by the Lochkray. There are those in the church who believe that your Doctor Hadden has found the lost Lochkray. They believe that he may even have found Kraell'Haatch—the concentration of Lochkray knowledge and technology. They believe that, right now, we are all walking into a lost realm, where an evil people laid claim long ago, and where a malevolent knowledge sits, waiting to be released onto man." Another snap and shower of sparks emanated from the fire, sparkling upward to the stars.

"Do you believe that's what he found?" Tyance asked, her voice coming out more hushed than she had intended.

Vance surveyed the group about him, taking more joy in their intense looks than they could ever imagine. Then, taking even more joy in watching the looks shatter, he laughed out the answer. "No, I do not," he said. "I am afraid I have met no Lochkray in my life. I am a glorified librarian, and I love a good story, so I can say with confidence that the tale of the Lochkray definitely falls under fiction."

"So why are you here, friend?" Madoc smiled.

"Because that's what I'm being paid to do. That artifact, coupled with the death of a young girl near the university where Doctor Hadden works, caught the attention of the monsignor at my monastery. He asked me to look into it, so I go to look into—"

"What?" Elisha snapped out. It was the first sound she made since the tale of the Lochkray began. While the others were intrigued by the story, it was a growing splinter in her mind, bothering her and sounding somehow close.

"I'm sorry," Vance asked. "What's wrong?"

"The death of a girl?"

Vance felt his heart sink, realizing he may have let his mouth get ahead of his brain. With Allen and Elisha attending McGuinness, the girl could have been a friend of theirs.

"I'm so sorry," he said. "Did you know her?"

"Know who?" Allen asked.

"You mean Cynthia White," Elisha answered.

"You did know her." Vance's heart sank farther.

"No." Elisha shook her head, gently. "I just heard about her."

"That's the girl who had the heart attack on the dance floor of the Paddock," Allen said to Vance. "It's a dance bar in town. That was just a few weeks ago."

"Not a heart attack," Elisha said distantly, unaware why the mention of the girl bothered her so much. "Unconfirmed heart condition," the papers said. The flags at the university had been at half-mast for several days.

"I'm so sorry," Vance repeated. "I didn't mean to reduce her to part of a story. It's just they somehow managed to link the idea of the girl's death to the idea...you know...kind of like what a Lochkray was supposed to do. Consume you, and...it's stupid. I shouldn't have said anything about that." Elisha shook her head, looking down at her crossed legs on the ground.

"No, I didn't mean to...It's just that when I heard about her, it made me, you know." *Tyance saw a man by the water.* "It's just the story is kind of creepy, and..."

I thought I saw a man by the cabin yesterday. "When you mentioned her death, I found It was just kind of scary when I heard about it..." *Lochkray.* "So it, just made me..." *Climb inside your mind.* Elisha stopped. "I'm tired," she finally finished.

"What are you talking about?" Allen asked.

"I'm sorry," she muttered back.

"It's okay," Vance soothed. "I got carried away. I must admit I, too, am tired."

"Sorry we weren't the one you were looking for," Madoc said. "I'm sure glad you showed up when you did."

"Yes," Elisha agreed distantly.

"You're welcome to join us," Madoc continued. "We think we have an idea where John, uh, Doctor Hadden is. If we find him you can...do whatever it is that you want to do."

"Simply offer some ideas," Vance said. "The ideas are not even mine. The way I look at it, I'm paid to go into the woods and be laughed at."

Tyance was the first to get to her feet. "Fuck," she said before she could catch herself. "That's enough for me. I liked your story...uh..."

"Vance."

"Sorry." She gave a meek smile. "Vance. See you all at sun-up."

She made her way toward her tent. A subtle motion in her progress went unnoticed by one of the group. Madoc was the next to stand up, practically in unison with Allen.

"Well, that's enough for me. Like the lady said, friend, we'll be getting up with dawn, eating quick, and breaking camp. Do you want to come along or would you rather we just deliver a message to John? I mean, Doctor Hadden?"

"I will join you, if Is no inconvenience."

"None I can see." Madoc smiled. *Should charge him*, spat through his mind almost too quick to acknowledge. Vance got to his feet as well.

"Good night everybody." Allen smiled.

"Night, Allen," Elisha said mostly as reflex. "Good night, Madoc."

"Night," Madoc replied, wandering off, slightly away from his tent so that he might urinate before going to bed. Allen went directly to his own tent without such a pit stop—which he regretted three hours later. Vance got up to leave the fire but then stopped to look back. There, a person looked upset.

"Is everything okay, miss?" he asked, stepping back into the glow of the fire.

"Elisha," she replied, looking up from the fire with an apologetic smile. Vance returned the grin, all too aware of the length of time since his last physical contact with a woman. Though he never joined the priesthood, living within the walls of the monastery had not offered great amounts of opportunity for social activity. He almost married once but that was a narrowly avoided error. Still, despite the smile on this attractive young lady's lips, Vance detected her lingering around the fire had more to do with the trouble behind her eyes, rather than his presence.

"You look like something's bothering you."

"I just...what do you think the Lochkray are?" She looked up at Vance and saw the surprise. "I mean," she tried to clarify, "every myth has its origins."

"Like I said, just about all cultures have their tales of night people. Lochkray are just the Catholic Church's version. I imagine it has links back to pagan beliefs in night spirits, and such things. Perhaps you could write a paper on that." Vance's attempt to make light failed to raise another smile from Elisha.

"You did say you were studying anthropology, right?"

"It's just been a weird trip," she sighed. "I don't know why, but I seem determined to spook myself out."

"I didn't mean to scare you—"

"Don't apologize," she interrupted, waving her hands. "I really liked your Lochkray story." Vance beamed. "Actually, I think Doctor Hadden will too. He loves superstition and mythology."

"Well, next campfire, I'll tell a happy story. How does that sound?"

Elisha got to her feet. "That sounds good," she replied with a small wave. "Good night." Vance returned the words, content with the thought that the young lady was simply too tired. He went back to his tent and left Elisha to do the same. She walked away from the fire, uncomfortable with leaving the security and light it provided, and felt relieved when she looked at the canvas structure next to it, and heard rustling inside, the sound of somebody searching through a package.

"Good night, Allen," she called to it. The rustling stopped for a moment.

"What?"

"I'm just saying good night."

"Oh, good night, Elisha." The rustling resumed. She crawled into her tent, and similar sounds began as she dug through her pack, putting clothes away.

In the darkness, the Lochkray left his perch in a nearby tree and landed on the ground gently. He slid around the camp, careful to stay out of the pool of light made by the dying fire. He skulked his way over to the newcomer's shelter and hovered over it, listening to the final motions of the day as they were performed, and the body within became still.

Several meters away, the Lochkray sensed motion within one of the other tents, but the rest he suddenly became uninterested in. Before him, on the other side of the thin cover, was a Cimmerian Knight. Or, at least, one of their acolytes. The temptation to reach through and take a hold of this vile being and crush the life out of it was overwhelming. The Lochkray knew it was these that forced him and his kind to undertake such reclusiveness. It was these who had hunted his kind with a genocidal purpose. The rage within him swelled, a rage that built while he listened to the acolyte tell lies and half-truths about the Cimmerian Knight's attacks on his people.

The Lochkray moved away from the tent and backed into the darkness of the forest. He knew time for the acolyte was short. For another hunter was not far off, and he could hear it. He would make sure the hunter took this one. He would make sure the acolyte learned a lesson and then died screaming.

Chapter Fifteen

Madoc stepped out of his tent into the darkness of night. The fire around which they had all been sitting now only showed the faintest veins of glowing orange where embers hid beneath the crusty black on top. He shook his head, yet again reminding himself that he *must* take the time to put the fires out before he went to bed.

He took a few more steps away from the tent and produced a cigarette. Putting it into his mouth, he looked back and decided to take a few more steps away before lighting it up. Inside his tent was Tyance, she was waiting there when he returned from his bathroom break in the woods. She hated it when he smoked, so he did his best to hide it. No one noticed she didn't go to her own berth for the night

As with every trip with guests, Madoc figured it was just as well nobody knew about their activities. It saved for any awkward conversations, or requirements to explain the situation. For, although they occasionally did sleep together, their relationship was not an exclusive one. Rather, more so, one of convenience. When the other was involved with an outside person, they simply did not engage in such activities. There was no jealously, or hard feelings. They just didn't have sex. *Casual sex*, he called it. Better than her term of *Fuck Buddies*.

What brought her to his tent that night was beyond him, for they almost never got together when guiding groups. He figured she must have been more shook up about the animal attack than she was showing. She was happier now, curled up under the opened sleeping bag, wearing his shirt, her full lips slightly upturned. He was happier for it too, except he now had to get out of his tent for a smoke, rather than just stick his head out the flap.

He struck a match against the back of the book in his hand, then paused to listen, to make sure the rasp did not disturb his partner. *That's ridiculous,* he told himself, *such a little sound.* Then he brought the tiny flame up to the cigarette, and shared the match's glow with the roll in his mouth

The rewarding, subtle flavor of tobacco smoke entered his mouth, and burned its way down his throat to his lungs, where the delicate narcotic effect quickly caused his head to lighten. He held it and closed his eyes, then released the cloud with a deep sigh. With a smile for his filthy habit, he took a guilty look around the camp, then strolled across the clearing, moving parallel to the river. He would go for a quick walk, just until the end of the cigarette, he told himself. Then he would turn around and walk back. Seeing as the walk would take exactly the amount of time to have a smoke, he might as well have another on the return. It made sense.

* * * *

The Lochkray stirred from his awkward sleep and saw the Madoc walk away from its tent with the smoldering roll stuck in its mouth. He went to close his eyes again, to return to slumber, confident that Madoc was no threat, but he quickly caught that all was not right. There was something else close by. The Lochkray went to the ground and glided around the camp, following after the Madoc. He knew he was not the only one following. The Madoc was oblivious to it, but it was hunted. If the hunter did its job properly, the Madoc would never know it had been stalked until it was dying.

* * * *

Madoc strolled along, toward where he first heard the moose. That was as good a direction to go as any. As he got to the edge of the clearing, he immediately noticed the bush thickened again, and the ground became more difficult to walk over—not impossible, just more difficult. So, he simply modified his steps to accommodate whatever small obstacles there were. He took longer strides in some spots, slightly shorter than normal in others, stepped over a stump, walked around the fire hydrant, cocked his head to the side to avoid a branch, and twisted around...

Fire hydrant?

Madoc looked back the way he came. He was just a few meters into the woods, and could easily see the camp in the moonlight. He closed his eyes for a second, in an effort to clear them. *What did you just see?* He squinted into the darkness, knowing that something wasn't right. He peered hard, unsure of what it was he was supposed to be looking for. What he thought he saw, he wasn't sure, but he knew It was wrong. Looking back, he saw the wafting cloud of smoke from the near-dead campfire. He saw the tents, and the makeshift picnic table. He saw the mailbox. He saw the closed doors and the parked cars. He saw the lampposts, and he saw the...

Madoc turned back around and looked up the empty city street. He inhaled deeply on his cigarette, and found it more smooth and pleasant than the draw before. He studied the dark street, the closed shops all tightly packed together, doors locked and secured, the large front windows like mirrors as the darkness behind allowed the street to reflect back upon itself. The streetlamps sent down pools of light, illuminated circles of white dotting the street all the way along, showing the dark lumps that were cars, parked and silent. Madoc listened for the sound of traffic, but heard none. The town went to bed. He was the only sign of life for blocks all around.

Behind him an animal scurried across the street, ducking in from one alleyway to another. Madoc turned toward the movement, but only caught a shadow as it darted into hiding. He dismissed it with a shrug and turned around to walk back up the street, toward a shop on the right, where the window showed light rather than mirror.

He decided to investigate, seeing as he was out anyway. He strolled up the street, enjoying the sweetest of cigarettes as he went, absently flicking the ashes to the pavement. It was warm out tonight, but not unpleasant. A light, cool breeze moved across him occasionally, making the street seem perfect, removing any edge of heat the summer night might have. There was a smell in the air, and although the streetlights would not afford a view of the sky to see, Madoc could tell that rain was approaching.

* * * *

The Lochkray saw that the Madoc left. He took a safe perch and closed his eyes. Then followed after.

* * * *

Madoc stood outside of the storefront, looking at the lettering painted in fancy green on the large front window: Tam O'Shanter's. The front door to the establishment was open, allowing the cool breeze from outside to vent out the warm stale air from the business. Inside, he saw a simple bar. A long serving bar with ten stools sitting in front, all along the left side. Opposite that were tables, sitting empty, with a clean ashtray parked in the center of each. It was scantily decorated: a few promotional signs and lights, along with two huge flags on the walls. That was it. The pub was empty, except for the lone bartender who stood behind the bar, a rag in one hand endlessly wiping out a clear glass in the other, oblivious to Madoc's approach. Madoc flicked the butt of his disappearing smoke out into the street, then stepped in through the door, into the small pub. Suddenly, it made complete sense why he was out in the city that night. He was looking for a drink and, here one was.

"You still open?" Madoc called in a friendly tone to the tender. He was a big guy, really big. His head was shaved bald, but showed no evidence of stubble. He was wearing a white collared shirt with a black vest overtop, making him seem too refined for this simple drinking hole. He turned his pale blue eyes toward Madoc, and a smile—a rich, friendly smile—spread across his face.

"Yes sir," the Lochkray replied, forcing the simple grin onto his lips. "What can I get you?"

Madoc stepped into the establishment, and walked over to the bar, another cigarette produced and placed at his lips. He took the stool in front of the large man. He lit a match and, again, lit the paper between his lips. "Rum and coke, friend," Madoc instructed.

The Lochkray nodded and prepared a tumbler containing the requested concoction, his hands moving effortlessly to the bottle and mix, making the drink quickly. Outside the door, the Lochkray sensed the hunter coming closer, coming together.

"How are you doing this evening?"

"Fine now," Madoc replied, raising the glass in a mock toast. He drew back on the drink with a deep gulp. Then, just as the liquid completed its decent, he inhaled deeply on his smoke. Two of life's guilty pleasures brought together. Madoc took another survey of the bar. "Quiet in here tonight."

"People are wise enough to stay in at night, around these parts."

"Except me," Madoc laughed, taking another swig. Outside the door, the hunter darted past, causing Madoc to look over. "Jesus, what was that?"

"A dog." The Lochkray looked over at the door sternly. The hunter was sloppy. Such clumsy motions would normally send the dreamer back into the real world but the Lochkray held on tight. He realized, however, that he was running out of time.

"Big dog," Madoc said, still looking out the open door. "I knew a guy who owned a Great Dane—the thing was as big as a horse. I have no idea why somebody would want a dog that big. Stupid thing chewed up his couch, and all of his CDs. It got hit by a car once, a perfect chance to have it put down, but this guy turns around and spends sixteen hundred dollars to get the damned thing fixed up. I tell you—"

"How does your journey go?" the Lochkray asked innocently.

My journey? Madoc furrowed his brow for a moment, then shook it off. It was, after all, a reasonable question.

"It's going pretty good," he replied. "We had some trouble with a moose today, that was a close call. Smashed my sat-phone. Otherwise, we're making good time. We should be at John's camp by tomorrow, no problem. We've been running behind a bit but nothing too bad. We picked up another person today. He's looking for John too." Madoc took a sip of his drink. Something seemed wrong but he couldn't quite put his finger on it.

"Another? Who is the other?"

"Vance Hal-something. I can't remember his last name."

"Why does he seek John?"

"Well, that's a good question." He took another drink. "He works for some kind of church. They seem to think John's site has some kind of mythological value or historical value. Or something." Madoc laughed. "To be honest with you, I really don't know what he's after. Seems like a good guy though. I don't think he knows what he's doing out here either. Kind of the way I feel."

"It is the Therrien who is leading you? He is the one who knows where to go?"

"Allen?" Madoc barked with laughter. "No, not exactly. Don't get me wrong. He's a good kid but he wouldn't be of much use except as bear food out here on his own. I have to practically bite through my lip every time I see him set up his tent, or else I'd end up rolling around on the ground laughing."

"So, you do not need him to reach your destination."

"Mm," Madoc mumbled through a sip. "No, we need him. He's the only one who understands John. They've been working together, and he knows John's work. Unfortunately we're kind of digging in the dark out here, trying to find this place, so we need whatever advantage we can get. The kid just doesn't understand living in the bush." The Lochkray looked outside the door, and observed the glimmering of two eyes looking back in.

"Without you, they would not make it. Is right?"

"I should guess not. They're bright kids, but the woods would eat them alive." The irony of the statement was noticed by the Lochkray, but ignored.

"Then you should go," the Lochkray stated coolly.

Madoc flicked the ash from his cigarette down to the ground, and looked about the dark forest in a mild confusion. He blinked hard twice, and then shook his head. There he was, standing amid the trees, the black of night illuminated only by the sliver of moon. Away from him, off to his right, he heard an explosion of movement. He turned quickly toward it, shaking off the daydream. His hands went out from his sides, ready to catch whatever might come at him. However, he realized the movement in the darkness was becoming quieter as it was going away from him. He listened intently as the crashing through branches diminished with distance.

Madoc looked toward the camp, could still smell the smoke, still see the darkened humps of the tents. He stood there for a time. Disorientated, he wasn't sure how long. It might have been three minutes, it might have been thirty. For the time he stood still, listening to the silent woods left by the departing animal.

Finally, his feet moved, and he edged toward the tents, startled by the sound of his own feet shuffling across the ground. With an excruciatingly slow pace, he made it back to his tent, all the while listening defensively for what was out there. Outside of the tent, he took comfort in the sound of Tyance's breathing. Already the moments in the bar were fading from his mind. The reality of the dark night all around quashed the dream world. All Madoc was left to wonder was whether the animal he heard running away was real, or simply an extension of his dissipating vision.

He lifted the tent's flap and slid in, settling down on his rear to shuffle off his pants, stopping every so often to think about what just happened, and with every stop, he had less to think about. When Tyance finally rolled over and asked if he had enjoyed his cigarette, reality removed all reminiscence of the dream.

"Sorry," Madoc muttered.

"Don't apologize to me," Tyance replied, rolling back over again. "Apologize to your heart, your lungs, your arteries, and your liver."

"Smoking doesn't affect your liver."

"Yeah, but you've also drank a lot lately, too."

Madoc smiled at his friend as he slipped into his sleeping bag. He rolled over and put his arm around her. He could tell from the way that she tensed her body she wasn't in a very snuggly mood, so he pulled his arm back. She hated the smell of the smoke, but he felt obliged to try anyway. He closed his eyes and went to sleep.

* * * *

In the woods, the hunter circled the camp. It had its prey in a firm grasp, but lost it. During the advance, it knew it should have lost its hold long before, but chose to just enjoy the approach. The *other* had helped the prey. It did not know why, and more confusing still, it did not know how the *other* entered into its prey's vision—but that was what happened.

In the hunter's tiny mind, it could not comprehend its own pondering. The considerations entered its blurry thoughts, and only added to the confusion there. Its mind worked best on instinct. Instinct told it to back away until the next day, and then to try again. Instinct told it to ignore the *other* for now. It was not affecting its hunt directly.

The hunter faded into the darkness and disappeared.

* * * *

The Lochkray smiled his thin smile.

Chapter Sixteen

The sun still sat close to the horizon when the group broke camp. Tyance was once again cooking. She had emerged from her tent earlier than the rest, taking advantage of the quiet, and gone for a cool swim in the nearby river. By the time the rest stuck their heads out into the new day, her tent was already folded up and secured to her backpack. She took care to make extra noise during her activities following her swim in the hope It might motivate the rest to get moving a little quicker. If they made good time today, they would be in the general vicinity of where Doctor Hadden was supposed to be after lunch.

Vance fit into the group with little effort. He was friendly and pleasant, helping Allen with his repacking—stealing from Madoc his morning entertainment—, offering some of his supplies to Tyance to add to her culinary creation, joking with a likeable easiness. After his story the night before, he quickly took to mocking himself and his purpose there. His darting glances at Elisha went unnoticed for the most part, except possibly by Allen.

"One last look." Madoc said after settling his pack onto his shoulders. He looked about as the rest were doing the same, reviewing the ground and making sure nothing was left behind.

"Fuck, that's everything."

"Okay," he nodded, "then let's get going. Is everybody ready?" The not entirely enthusiastic reply from the group was enough for Madoc and they were on their way out of the clearing and back into the relentless trees. The sun stepped higher as the group walked on, away from the camp, toward their destination. They made good time that morning, just as Tyance hoped they would.

The Lochkray slid through the trees behind them, springing between the branches silently. As he moved after them, making an effort to ignore their banal dialogue, he became aware of the other hunter with them again, also sliding through the branches, invisibly and equally as silent as he. The other hunter went with the group, being all at once beside them, in front, behind, and through. It wandered along with each one of the daylights, burrowing into their forgotten recollections, looking for a place to parasitize. Looking for a memory to hold, a dream to pervert. The Lochkray wished he could fully see the hunter, watch it's beautiful dance through the minds of its prey. Instead he only sensed it in the air and waited patiently until one of the group fell victim to its deceptions.

It was in Tyance where the hunter first found opportunity. An old dream, a mental shadow in which to hide and form. A memory from long before.

When Tyance was a young girl, on many nights she was awakened from her sleep by her dreams. Most of these momentary disruptions faded back into sleep without any lasting memory. Occasionally—like all children—she was pulled right out of her sleep by the dreams and a scattershot of remembrance existed with a deal of confused emotion. If these emotions resembled fear, she wound her way into the bedroom of her father, or her older brother Simeon—the only one of her brothers she actually liked, before he fell heavy into the bottle. There she took solace in the company until the fear faded like the memory of the dream.

When she was six, Tyance had a different kind of dream. Different because it kept coming back to her for years—and each time, the memory of what she saw stayed with her. She couldn't remember when the dream stopped occurring. Perhaps by the time she was nine or ten.

In the span of those few years, she had learned to hate Interruption to her sleep, because it had injected her with a fear that she could not relate to any emotion within the waking world. It had paralyzed her in her bed, making her unable to escape, to find comfort with her family. She had lain there, staring into the darkness, sweat and tears rolling down her face. She had never known why the vision brought her such terror, but every time it came, it affected her the same way. Paralyzed her with fear. Why her mind kept taking her back—over and over—to the same scene, she didn't know.

It was always night in the dream and at the front lawn of her father's old home, back in Cochrane. It was a nice place, with beautifully cut grass, where two well-groomed pine trees sat halfway down to the road. She would be out on the lawn, alone. Her parents were never there. It was always a warm night, the grass a bright green, even under the faded light of the moon. It would be a perfect night to be outside. A perfect night to be out playing with other neighborhood children, taking part in a game of hide and seek, or tag, or graveyard, or whatever other childhood game. It always felt like it should be a weekend, just after the start of school, a tiny bit of summer broken away from the rest of the week, the flavor of July recaptured slightly. A perfect night to be a playful child.

There were never any other children to be seen in her dreams. The rest of the neighborhood would be empty. Everybody would already be inside. They would already be hiding. Because the winds were blowing.

She heard the doors being shut all down the street as the sound of blowing wind started up. Leaves would suddenly bounce down the road—caught in the gusts of wind, scraping dryly across the cement. The hollow rumbling of a tin can bouncing down the street would be heard with the stronger gusts. Lights on the neighbors' porches were turned out with a horrible suddenness. Something in her stomach told Tyance what was coming, and that she should already be inside. When she turned toward the comfort of her own front door, she saw it already shut and locked. She knew her father was inside, shaking his head sadly.

"You're too late," she heard him saying. "Hide, before she comes. The winds are blowing."

She looked frantically around for one of her brothers, for some kind of support, but they were never around to protect her when the winds blew. She was so alone. The trees bent. Garbage flew down the street, bouncing along helplessly in the gusts. The season aged. The air became cold, the air went damp, filling with the smell of rot, and the green grass faded as she dropped to the suddenly wet ground, trying to make herself flat on the lawn. She lay there, watching as the last curtains across the road where drawn shut, sad shadowy faces stared at her helplessly before they disappeared behind shades.

Then *she* would come.

The lady walked down the center of the street slowly, painfully slowly. Her long white dress dragged along the ground, catching the leaves and empty plastic bags as she went. The veil over her face would be folded back, clumsily stuffed into a headdress, but it would be bunched around her face so Tyance could not see the profile. Tyance begged over and over in her mind, that the woman would not see her on the ground. Every time, her pleas were ignored. Every time, the woman stopped at the end of the lawn and turned toward Tyance. She would see the lady's awful visage. The empty eye sockets, the bloody dried skin, the dark wrinkles, the desperate begging on the cracking lips. Now, Tyance begged to awaken, become aware she was caught in her terrible dream. Awaken before the woman walked toward her.

Sometimes she would, sometimes she would not. It didn't matter, for when the woman in the white dress turned to her, pure abject terror would wash over her and freeze her. A terror that she never felt anywhere in the real world, and thought she would never feel again after growing out of the dreams, so many years before.

She did feel it again on that third day of the journey with Elisha and Allen. She felt it again, when she saw the woman standing among the trees as the group walked by. Tyance started the day walking behind Madoc, side by side with Elisha, chatting away, Madoc throwing in his opinion on a number of topics as they pressed forward.

Behind her, Allen and Vance were yapping happily to one another, rambling back and forth on topics Tyance had little or no interest in. For some reason, their conversation went to the topic of the city of Paris. Tyance fell back a few steps. Allen said he had visited there a few years before and absolutely loved it, Vance was going on about how crowded he found it. The closest Tyance came to Paris was at the France exhibit at the EPCOT theme park in Orlando. Listening to Allen's enthusiastic descriptions of the architecture, museums, and other things she associated with the great city validated her images. Vance said he had a love for the country of France, but found Paris itself somewhat disappointing.

Tyance thought about mentioning her Florida-based French experience, but decided to pass. She just enjoyed listening to the amiable banter between the others, and the thoughts that she definitely had to go to Paris herself became firm. She fell back some more, picturing herself in front of the Eiffel Tower, perhaps with Madoc in tow. He would want to go; he said so, before. He always wanted to do another European tour. Perhaps next summer. In fact,

Definitely next summer, she decided. *This time next year. We'll close up a week early, do all the fall maintenance, and then fuck everybody else! No hunters, no campers, no university students. I'm going to do what I want for a change.*

The lady standing off to the side of the trail startled Tyance so badly she stopped dead in her tracks, a broad gulp of air forcing its way down to her lungs. About twenty feet away, facing the other direction, half-hidden behind a tree. A woman. The woman, wearing the long white gown. She stood, the wind eerily blowing her dress, making it float about her like a cloud.

Tyance opened her mouth to call to the others but could not. What was more, there was nobody to scream to. There was only the woman. The woman and Tyance, standing at the edge of a beach. The tree was still there, one of a few that stood close to the white sand. The woman walked toward the surf, where the ocean lapped loudly against the darkened sand and pebbles. Tyance reached out to her, not knowing why. She watched her own trembling fingers grasped at the empty air. The woman continued her silent glide toward the surf. Tyance took a step forward, still grasping at the air, now calling out the single word: "Wait."

The woman paid no notice. She floated across the pale beach, her long white train dragging through the smooth undulations of the sand, sweeping it flat. Tyance followed after the woman. The crashing sound of the waves became deafening. The winds picked up. The dread in Tyance's chest was painful, but she could not stop herself from following after this woman from her childhood nightmares. Finally the woman stopped when the bottom of her gown touched the washing surf. Tyance walked along the woman's brushed trail, her footprints marking up the empty beach. Tyance was starting to cry now, as she always had in her dreams. She reached out to the woman, now repeating, "Wait!" over and over, in an emotional and strained voice.

Tyance was directly behind the woman when the latter finally turned away from the water. There was the face—the one Tyance knew and feared so much—gray and deformed and familiar, peering out from beneath the bunched up veil. Only now the face was angrier, much angrier. Its empty sockets arched in fury, the black lips poised in accusation. The skin of this hag cracked as she saw Tyance rushing up behind her. Tyance came to a stop, unsure why she followed after this horrible apparition.

"All hate in here," the voice shrieked at her.

Tyance stood rigid in the forest as the flat blue waters of the ocean quickly rose, and the pale sand fell away. Her hands were tight fists of pain as her nails cut into her like knives. The rustle of the surrounding leaves was no match for her own body's quaking.

* * * *

Nearby, the great hunter thrashed its head back and forth violently, its arms fell away, and it retreated.

Another hunt foiled. It watched from a distance as the prey walked in a circle in an odd panic. For a moment, the hunter expected the prey to run off. She stopped, took a moment to press her weight against a tree and allow water drops of sweat or tears to fall from her face. Then she stood up, her respiration rapid and hard. She turned her head back and forth, then headed toward the pack.

The hunter tried to placate its prey, but failed to do so, terribly.

Success was lacking lately, but this was different. Had the rest been farther along, the hunter would have disposed of its prey right there. The group was close and her screams would bring the rest, alerting them all.

Instead, the hunter followed the prey and watched as she scurried through the woods and caught up with its group. The hunter considered trying to lure her away again, but the sting of her vision was still too harsh.

The hunter faded away.

Chapter Seventeen

"You okay?" Madoc asked as Tyance hurried up to the rest of the group. At first he assumed she had gone off for a short squat in the woods, but as she drew closer, he detected concern on her face.

"I'm okay," she replied distantly. To Madoc, the reply was sufficient. The group was now undertaking a steep incline, preparing to cross the ridge framing the river they had camped beside the night before.

"So," Madoc turned his attention back to Vance, "how exactly did a monastery manage to exist in the Soviet Union during the communist era? I thought that religion was supposed to be an 'opiate of the masses.'"

Vance released a yap of laughter. "True enough." He grinned. "You would be surprised. Roman Catholics make up about thirty percent of the population. During the time of Soviet control many people believed that the Greek Orthodox Church was heavily infiltrated by the KGB, so we were actually treated with a great deal of respect. Still, it was a very long and dangerous period for the brothers and for me. If the authorities had known an American lived there, I don't think any of us would have lasted too long.

"The brothers were smart. Just after their revolution, in the brothers' territory, the local prefect's father was an orthodox minister, and he had a certain reverence for the brothers—and they were secluded enough not to be noticed by anybody for decades. All the local villagers just kept to themselves. As the years went on, the brothers got involved in actually working for the local authorities, cataloging information and such, working as an archive. Seeing as the brotherhood was a secret from Rome, they were quite adept at laying low and keeping to themselves."

"How did you end up there?" Allen asked from behind.

"Well, when I originally decided to leave the seminary, I decided to take on a pilgrimage. My degree was in Theology and Mythology, and I heard of the monastery in my studies. I hadn't heard of the Lochkray at that point. I just thought getting there would be a challenge to undertake—a little test for myself. I wasn't even sure if the place existed. When I got there, I stayed, and studied. As I said, I decided to abandon the priesthood, but stuck around with the brothers." Vance smiled to himself. "So many stories there, so much to learn. So, I stay on. However, when the chance came up to return to this side of the ocean, I jumped at it."

"Think you'll stick around after we find John?"

"Maybe. I don't know what my future plans are. I think I spend too much time studying the past."

"Don't you have any family back in South Carolina?" It was Elisha who asked this time.

"No," Vance replied simply. Something in his tone made her decide not to pursue the matter.

"What about you, Allen?" Madoc was asking. "What are your plans after all this is over?"

"I just want to finish off my Master's degree. After that, I don't know. I was thinking of doing my PhD but I'm getting a little tired of school. I was beginning to think that maybe I'd go out and find a job for a while, then maybe return to school."

"What about you, Elisha?"

"Definitely want to get my PhD. I'd really like to teach at a university. Be a professor." *If I ever get out of here,* she thought to herself.

"What a view," Allen suddenly interjected. The group was close to the edge of the ridge, and they saw out over the forest below. The ground beneath them was rockier now, and this hard surface rolled over the edge of the ridge, making a sheer cliff. The group paused to look through a break in the trees allowing them to see acres and acres of undulating green.

"Wow, Is nice," Madoc stated. "Tyance, come here and have a look at this view." Though he was oblivious to it, Tyance didn't even hear Madoc's request. Almost as reflex, she stopped with the rest of the group, but did not join them in their amazement. She stared off into the woods, listening to the words *"All hate in here"* quietly whispering in the back of her mind.

"This still goes up quite a bit," Allen said, leaning out to look up the direction of the ridge. "That'd be a fantastic view from up there."

"We'll know shortly," Madoc replied, starting to walk again. "That's where we're headed."

"You ever been this way before?" Vance asked.

"Nope," Madoc replied. "No real reason to. We're pretty lucky we have a limited selection of areas where we can look for John, because everything around here is so thick and wet. There aren't too many paths you can take. Still, while it may make this manhunt easier, it sure makes for shitty moose hunting. You'd spend half of your time trying to pull yourself out of the muck. Not a whole lot of fun."

"You do a lot of hunting?"

"Not as much as I'd like to. The camp keeps me pretty busy. I used to do it every chance I could get. I used to bow hunt too, but lately I have a tough time getting out even once a year, you know, for myself. When I'm out with the tourists, I just look after them. No real thrill in that."

"What about you, Allen? You a hunter?"

"No. I'm really not much of an outdoorsman."

Madoc looked over at Tyance to see if she found any humor in the understatement, but saw that she was off in her own little world. "Watch the edge there, Ty," he called over.

"What about you, Elisha?" Vance tried to keep the conversation going. "You hunt?"

"No," she laughed back. "I think there are better ways of showing one's respect for nature's most majestic animals than shooting them." She looked over at Madoc, her laughter suddenly stopping. "Sorry," she added.

"Not at all. What about you, Vance? I'm guessing the way you shot that moose, you can handle a gun okay."

"That was mostly luck. I do a little bit. I prefer fishing when I can. I didn't bring my rod on this trip. I wasn't even going to bring a gun, but one of the fathers in Timmins gave it to me. He said I might need it for bears. Whoa—" Vance stopped speaking as the ground quickly changed texture. The soft brown earth beneath their feet went gray and hard, as rolling rock pressed itself out of the ground. The clearing created was welcome, as the trees fell away and the rocky area became large. Small clusters of bush took root within crevices, and veins of moss crisscrossed over the natural paving, but otherwise the forest took a moment to step back. Suddenly the climb became steeper but still easier on the clearing. Beyond the drop of the ridge, the view below became more distant and magnificent.

"Watch the edge, Ty," Madoc repeated.

"I swear," Vance said, "you can almost see all the way back to civilization." His words were a little more panted, his breathing becoming deeper as he traversed the rolling incline.

"It's amazing." Elisha's breathing was heavy. A glance over at Allen revealed him using some of the small branches sticking out from the rock face to pull himself up, a reach at a time. "Does that make it any easier?"

"It works," he replied. As if to contradict him, the branch he was pulling gave way from its hold, and Allen stumbled backward, managing to rebalance himself before tipping all the way back.

Elisha laughed. "Sure looks like it does."

"Ty…" came from Madoc.

"I'm hoping down will be a little easier," Vance said.

"Tyance."

"We'll know in a minute," Elisha replied. "Looks like we're almost there."

"Tyance!" Madoc's panicked yell startled the group. They turned toward him in reflex, then followed his wide gaze to the cliff where Tyance stood balanced on the edge. She, too, turned toward Madoc, only she did so slowly, as if in a haze. The rest stood frozen, focused on how close her feet were to the lip of the land. Her feet were unbalanced on the edge, bizarrely placed half in the air. Elisha, noticed her face, rather than her feet. She saw the pale, confused stare and quivering lips.

"I—" was all Tyance squeaked past those lips. Then, her face disappeared. It slipped out of the air with speed, half-backward, half-downward. The rest watched her right foot slip behind the edge, pulling her body with it. There was a furious grasping at the air once she realized she was going over. With nothing to grab on to, she fell helplessly. Vance tried to reach out to her, but his hands only grabbed at the emptiness between them.

When Tyance finally heard Madoc yelling at her, rather than being startled back into reality, she emerged from her daydream slowly, bringing with her the sounds and sights of her nightmare. She saw Madoc and the rest of the group, but she could also still see the gray face and empty eye sockets. Then all of these fell away. At first she didn't realize she was falling. The world just continued its dreamlike contortions.

She didn't understand what was happening until a screaming pain shot through her back, and she realized that the cliff was moving by her side in a distorted blur.

The pain that shot through her was not caused by the ground far below, but by a slight outcropping on the cliff face—a spontaneous ledge, one that subtly jutted out from the rock, no more than the size of a grade-school desk. Growing there, almost in defiance of the location, was a small tamarack tree. Over decades, erosion had claimed the cliff top, and upon this smallest of ledges, soil had paused on its decent to the river below. There a seed had landed, submerging into the dark soil, and had slowly begun to take root. Over decades, the seed had become the small tamarack tree, much smaller than those of equal age either above or below it—perhaps a meter tall. However, despite the terrible conditions, the tree had survived. Positioned by fortune, five meters from where Tyance started her journey down, and far above where that journey would have ended.

Tyance's back crashed into that tree, the plant giving way easily beneath her. Its roots were torn loose, and the feisty tamarack left the ledge and made its own descent down. For Tyance, the brief respite from her fall gave enough time to scramble outward and take hold of the ledge where the plant had spent many seasons before. Her fingers clawed hard into the meager soil, grabbing onto a portion of root left behind. Her legs dangled down, her feet scrabbling at the rock face. She managed to get a slight footing on a sliver of ridge and was able to stop moving, her descent held in a precious pause. Her hands went firm on the rock, her feet holding on, pressed onto slight bumps on the cliff surface.

"Tyance," Madoc cried.

"Rob," she yelled back. The movement caused by the quick expression of air caused her to slide a bit. She dug her hands harder into the ledge.

"She's caught," Madoc called to the others over his shoulder.

"Hang on," Vance yelled. He shrugged his backpack off of his shoulders. "I have a rope in here," he muttered. "I have a rope. Hang on, I have a rope."

"Hang on, Tyance." Allen turned toward Vance and helped him frantically empty out his backpack. On the bottom of the pack, coiled up tightly and tied with itself, was a length of rope. Vance had packed it just in case...but this situation wasn't one he had imagined.

"That's good, that's good," Madoc said distantly, darting his attention back and forth between the two fighting to untangle the coil, and his friend below.

"You need to tie it to something," Elisha instructed Allen, without taking her eyes off of Tyance. Despite the precariousness of her perch, Tyance secured herself to the cliff wall effectively. Her feet were not dangling, and her hold was strong. "It's going to be okay," she told both Madoc and Tyance. "She's okay."

"Got it," Vance muttered, finally getting the bundle loose. "I'll tie this end off." He turned away from the ledge and looked about rapidly until he identified a rock of sufficient size. He ran to it, quickly tossing the rope around the small boulder. Allen looked back to where Vance went, then at the remainder of the length.

"This should be enough to get down to her," he said. Vance fumbled with his end, trying to remember the only knot he knew.

There's a hole by the tree, he repeated in his head out of habit. *Little brown rabbit comes out of his hole, runs around the tree, then goes back in his hole again.* He pulled tight. The knot didn't slip.

"I got it," he yelled over his shoulder. He looked up, his view crossing the woods, and stopped in shock, his heart skipping a beat. He froze hard at the eyes staring back at him.

The rest didn't notice Vance. Allen tossed the rope over the edge of the cliff, and let it dangle down. Thankfully, it made it all the way to Tyance. "Grab ahold," Madoc yelled, "and we'll pull you up."

"Okay," Tyance squeaked back.

She looked at the rope carefully, then released her right hand from the ledge to take hold. She pulled it taut. Her right hand wrapped itself in the cord, her left grabbed tightly on, and she began to climb with her feet. Her left hand let off the rope for moments to grab onto the rock face to steady herself. Then her feet pushed upward again. Up above Madoc and Allen also slowly pulled her closer to the edge, while Elisha assisted from behind.

Still, none noticed Vance staring in the other direction, out into the trees. Out there, where he saw the man in black standing fifty meters away, wearing a bizarre, taunting smile on his lips. At first startled by the appearance of the individual, Vance now felt faint, slightly unreal. A feeling came over him, a feeling he only read about in vague mythologies.

He felt an invasion throughout his mind. His own thoughts became cloudy and muddled. Then, one simple clear thought came through the haze, originating from outside his mind: *Lochkray*. It was like an outside voice, invading his mind not through his ears. It came from that man—the one who shook his head in mock sadness, with the taunting smile.

"Lochkray," Vance repeated the thought. His own thoughts fed from the spoken word, waving away the clouds.

It's a Lochkray! his mind screamed. He shook his head back and forth rapidly, retaking a hold on his thoughts.

The Lochkray shrugged, and walked off into the woods, satisfied with having shown himself to the acolyte. With just a few steps, Vance lost sight of the Lochkray. It disappeared behind a tree far too small to conceal the huge figure. Vance gave his head another shake, widened his eyes, and screamed *Go after it!* in his own thoughts. His foot finally stepped forward.

"Give me your hand," Allen yelled.

Vance turned his head back toward the edge of the cliff. There, Allen was bending to reach down to Tyance. Madoc and Elisha still strained to pull the rope upward. Vance withdrew his step, turned fully toward the group, then looked back to where the Lochkray just vanished.

After two hard blinks, he ran to the cliff's edge, and joined Allen in reaching down to where Tyance was straining her fingers upward. Slightly longer arms permitted Vance to take hold of her and pull her up far enough for Allen to take her right hand.

"Pull," Vance gasped as he and Allen lifted Tyance up to the edge. Madoc had now let go of the rope, and joined them in bringing his friend to safety. When her feet were firmly on the solid ground, the group huddled around Tyance and ushered her away from the edge, and then let her take a seat on the rolling ground.

"Fuck," Tyance gasped out over her heavy breathing. After a brief pause, this utterance caused Elisha to laugh. Tyance looked at her for a second, at first insulted, then amused. She joined Elisha's nervous laughing. Madoc just shook his head.

Fuck indeed, Vance thought to himself looking back at the woods.

Chapter Eighteen

"I guess I was daydreaming," Tyance said. The group decided to break for lunch, a considerable distance away from the edge of the cliff.

"I knew you were too close," Madoc muttered, shaking his head back and forth. "I knew you were too close."

"I didn't even notice." Allen smirked sheepishly. "I heard Madoc calling out to you, but I didn't really pay attention. I'm so sorry."

"You were lucky," Elisha said. "I think a tree stopped you on the way down. I thought I saw one falling beneath you when you were hanging there. I thought it was you."

"Fuck, I don't know what's wrong with me."

"We'll keep away from the edge," Madoc said sternly. "It won't take us long after we get back down into the valley. Then, if we're right, we should be in the area where John is supposed to be."

"What do you mean by daydreaming?" Vance asked. He was standing outside of the group, looking off into the woods silently. As each told their point of view over the incident, he said nothing. When he finally spoke, it caused Allen to jump. He looked back over his shoulder, and saw Vance still looking in the other direction.

"You know," Tyance replied, "daydreaming. I just let my mind wander. I'm not usually that distracted. I'm so sorry."

"What was the daydream about?" Vance turned back to the group.

"Fuck, I don't know. Uh…I don't think I was really thinking of anything. You know how you sometimes just start…you know, thinking things."

"Think for a minute. Can you remember what you were daydreaming about?"

"What difference does it make?" Madoc interrupted.

"It may be important. Tyance, I need you to tell me."

Madoc glanced at Tyance, who looked quite serious, trying to remember. She stared upward for a moment, then closed her eyes. She mouthed something Madoc couldn't follow. "It doesn't really matter," Madoc said to Tyance.

"All hate…" Tyance said very quietly. Madoc, who was sitting beside her, didn't even make the sounds out.

"What was that?" Vance asked, stepping closer, his voice more demanding than he intended.

"Hey, relax." Madoc stood up. "It doesn't matter what she was thinking about. It's over."

"I just want to know—"

"Drop it," Madoc demanded. Now Elisha and Allen got to their feet. A protective hand went out from Allen, between the two. He stared at Vance hard, hoping the look would help him decide to stop. It didn't.

"Look, I'm not trying to cause a problem. It's just I…" Vance trailed off. He scanned the group. "I don't think we're alone out here. After Tyance fell, I thought I saw somebody standing off in the woods."

A chill went up Elisha's spine.

"What?" Madoc asked, seeing her stiffen.

"I thought I saw somebody standing in the woods."

Madoc looked back, waiting for something more to come. When nothing did, he went for the obvious. "She wasn't pushed. She fell. We all saw her."

"I know." Vance turned away from the group and took two steps away.

"Wait," Tyance said, now standing up as well. "Elisha, you said that you thought you saw some guy out by Cheechoo's cabin."

"And you thought you saw somebody when you were swimming," Elisha replied gently.

"This is stupid," Madoc said sternly to Vance. "We're the only ones out here for five hundred kilometers in every direction, with the exception of John Hadden." He turned to face Elisha. "Was it John that you saw by the cabin?"

"No—"

"Okay then."

"Do you remember me telling you about Lochkray?" Vance asked.

"The church vampires?" Allen returned.

Vance smiled humorlessly at the response. "Yeah, the church vampires."

"Don't tell me that you think one of your Low-kray pushed Tyance over the edge of the cliff."

"Quiet for a minute." Tyance slapped Madoc's shoulder, coming up beside him.

"No," Vance replied, "I saw her fall off the edge by accident. I'm not saying it wasn't an accident. It's just...the Lochkray are supposed to be talented at clouding the human mind. Tyance said she was daydreaming. It was written—"

"I'm sorry," Madoc coughed out. "Are you suggesting that they're real? And that there's one out here right now?" He raised his arm up to block another assault on his shoulder from Tyance, but none came.

"I'm telling you I saw somebody standing in the woods," Vance snapped back. Immediately he knew that this wasn't going right. However, already in too deep, he continued. "You two say you saw somebody as well?"

"I thought I did," Elisha admitted. "By the plane when we landed. A bald man. Really big."

"Wearing all black," Vance finished.

"Fuck," Tyance blurted out. "That's what you said by the river. The guy you saw was wearing all black, and was bald. Rob, that's what she told me she saw before. That he was wearing all black."

"I thought you saw him too," Madoc snorted back.

"Yeah, when I was swimming, I thought I saw somebody. I don't remember what he looked like. It just kind of startled me—"

"You don't remember what he looked like? That's a big surprise."

"Don't you think it's weird that Vance and Elisha saw the same person? Don't you think—?"

"Oh, c'mon," Madoc snapped. He turned to Tyance and grabbed her by the shoulders. "Think for a minute, Ty. Just think."

"Calm down—" Vance started. Madoc barely turned his head.

"You be quiet," he said. "Tyance, think. I know going over the edge was scary, but just think for a second. Of course the guy's wearing black. He's a shadow. How many tours have we taken into the woods where they've seen a bigfoot or something else? It's shadow and imagination. Think about it."

"Yeah," Allen finally said. "Are you sure you saw somebody, Elisha? Couldn't it have just been a shadow and…y'know…imagination? Like Madoc says?"

"Yeah," was the unconvinced reply, "I guess."

"Wait, I know it sounds crazy. I'm telling you I saw somebody in the woods. Not a shadow, a person. Throughout the writings about the Lochkray, there are repeated stories about how they are able to confuse people into seeing things, distracting them so they can attack. What if it's true?" He paused for a second. "What if it's all true?" He stared at the group blankly, allowing an odd silence.

"Look, buddy—" Madoc started.

"We have to go back," Vance interrupted, still looking off into space. "We have to go back and get more help. It's all true."

"What?" Allen gasped.

"It's all true," Vance said excitedly. "All of it. We have to go back. We're in danger."

"Okay, calm down." Madoc again. Now he was rubbing his temples with his fingers. He took a deep breath, then released it, almost as a whistle. He turned around and walked away from the group, still cautious enough to avoid the edge of the cliff. The rest watched as he came to a halt, his frame rising and falling in a slow deep pattern. There, Madoc took a moment, repeating the words "Calm down," gently to himself. His frame expanded in one last deep breath before returning to the rest. "Calm down," he now said to the rest. "Calm down. Look, Vance. Okay, look. Stop. We're not going back. Let's not be stupid."

"I know this sounds crazy," Vance said again. "There was somebody out there. We're in danger."

"Okay, fine. I don't think so, but let's say I believe you, and maybe there is somebody out there. Okay. We're not going back. That's stupid. Maybe somebody is following us. I mean, you were out here too, why not another person looking for John Hadden? Hell, maybe it is John. There's no reason to turn back. We're almost there. In fact, we should be in the right area by this afternoon. I am not getting this close and then turning around because you think you saw the bogeymen. It's not happening." Madoc hadn't even finished speaking when Vance already picked up his bag and was securing it to his back.

"We have to go back," he said. "We have to go back and tell the fathers." He turned around and looked at the group, who all remained still. "Please, I have to go. I'm begging you. Come with me. It's all true. Don't you see? They haven't been keeping the monastery around for no reason. They know it's true. The Lochkray are real…" He stopped talking. The looks on the others' faces showed him how insane he sounded to them. However, before he began to doubt himself, he started talking again. "I have to go. Please, come with me."

"Vance, we can't go with you." Elisha was the one who answered this time. Vance stared at her hard. Then he nodded, slowly, in concession.

"Okay," he relented. "Look, if you're not going to come with me, just do me one favor." Vance reached around to his backpack and released two clasps on the side. Before Madoc knew what happened, Vance had his shotgun in his hand. Had it been any closer, Madoc would have jumped for his own gun. Instead, he froze.

Without even realizing the quick panic he had caused, Vance was already handing the gun over to Madoc. "Take this," he said, while Madoc gulped in relief. "I think it may be following you. I'm going to go back and get help. I'd feel a lot happier if I knew you had it."

You and me both, buddy, Madoc thought to himself, taking the weapon. "Uh, thanks."

Vance reached around the other side of his pack and produced a small red plastic box. Inside were six more shells for the shotgun. He passed those over to Madoc as well.

"Look," he said, "I know how it all sounds. I really do. If you want to think I'm nuts, then think I'm nuts. Please, just be careful. I'm telling you..." He trailed off once again. Both he and Madoc locked gazes. "Please, just promise me one thing," Vance finally said. "Pay attention. If things start to get out of control, turn around and get yourselves out of here. Get back to your pickup point, and get out. Do you hear me?" Again the two just glared at each other in silence.

"Yeah, we understand," Allen said when the silence became too much.

Vance nodded at Madoc, then turned back the way they came, and walked off. He stopped and turned around a few paces away but said nothing. He shook his head and then disappeared into the trees. The rustling of branches slowly dissipated, dying into the woods. Vance Halverson disappeared into the woods just as he had arrived. Less than eighteen hours after joining them, his sounds went back the way the group just traveled.

* * * *

By the time Madoc said the words "We made it," Allen and Elisha had long given up trying to come up with a reasonable explanation for Vance Halverson's behavior and concern. It had been five hours since he departed. Almost immediately after he left, Madoc got the rest of the group moving in the opposite direction. Instead of his usual position in the front of the group, pushing forward, he allowed Tyance to guide as point, while he took up the rear, stopping every so often to let the group get ahead so he could listen to what was behind. After a couple of hours, he was convinced they were not being followed, he joined the rest in their discussion of their previous ally.

"I know," Allen piped up. "Maybe he was from a rival university. You know, that's how he knew all about Doctor Hadden's research. Maybe he was trying to get us to back off so that some other institution stopped us and make the site their claim."

"Maybe," Madoc said, cocking his eyebrow upward at the suggestion. The river far below was now blocked out by the treetops as the group descended to the valley floor.

"Yeah," Allen went on. "Maybe he wasn't out here alone. That's who Tyance and Elisha think they saw. Vance too."

"Wait," Elisha spoke up. "Why would he claim to see his own partner if it was supposed to be a secret?"

"I...I don't know."

"Tell me again about the guy you saw," Madoc asked Elisha. "Out at Willie Cheechoo's old cabin."

"It was when you guys were up at the cabin. I was looking at the lake. I saw a man standing right behind me in the reflection of the plane's window."

"Standing right behind you?"

"Yes."

"What happened when you turned around?" Madoc's question was initially met by silence.

"There was nobody," Elisha finally said quietly.

"People don't just disappear."

"Maybe it was one of those Lochkray," Allen suggested. Madoc stopped walking and turned toward him.

"Whose side are you on?"

"I..."

"It wasn't a Low-kray," Madoc said coldly. "It wasn't a ghost. It wasn't a werewolf, or a vampire, or Frankenstein's monster. We need to stop this. The woods can get to people. I think Vance was exactly what he told us. I think he has been hanging around a library, reading stories for too long. He freaked himself out. He's told by his church to come out here and talk to John Hadden about monsters, he starts wandering around out here, runs into us, starts telling his little stories. When Ty goes over the edge, so does he."

Tyance shuddered.

"Sorry," Madoc said. "I'm just saying the stress was too much for him. He'll go back, advise his church that he needs help catching one of the Low-kray. They'll tell him to come home right away, and then he'll probably get some rest. Some much needed rest."

"Right," Tyance agreed, nodding hard.

Madoc looked back behind the group one last time, glancing back at the ridge they just climbed and descended. "Let's all focus on getting to where John is supposed to be." An unwritten rule was made clear in Madoc's tone. Vance Halverson was not to be mentioned again. He was to be pushed away. Just like the gutted bears. Just like the moose.

"Right." Elisha mimicked Tyance with a firm nod. Tyance let out a laugh. The sound made Madoc relax. It was a familiar happy laugh—perhaps a little forced, but still familiar and comfortable. Finding topics unrelated to Vance proved difficult at first—like Tyance's laugh their conversations started out forced, but the group talked and talked.

Four hours of walking and talking, nobody allowing for the long pauses between topics they had enjoyed before. No listening to the birds. No enjoying the sights. They went forward, parallel to the river they saw from up on the ridge. Forced talking, forced laughing, and forced effort to ignore tiny nagging doubts wanting to start with the words, *"Why is it that...?"*

"We made it," was said in surprise.

"What?" Tyance replied, smiling at some sardonic comment made by Allen.

"We made it," Madoc replied, his feet coming to a halt, a sigh rolling out his mouth. "We're here. Look." Allen came up to the front, and stared to where Madoc's finger was leading. About fifteen meters ahead, by the river's bend, the humped shape of a tent sat sandwiched between a steep incline of rock, and the river's edge. Other colors peaked through the branches: supplies scattered around the camp, signs of human presence standing out against the endless brown and green of the woods.

"Doctor Hadden?" Allen called out. He dashed quickly past Tyance and Madoc.

"We made it," Elisha repeated Madoc's words.

"Doctor Hadden?" Allen called out louder. Elisha came up behind, her steps a little less excited, but happily gaited nonetheless.

"We made it," Madoc repeated, stretching one arm around Tyance with a shaking hug.

"Thank Christ," Tyance sighed back. "I was beginning to wonder if we were going to make it before dinner."

"Doctor Hadden! It's Allen. Doctor Hadden?"

"John," Madoc called out, stepping into the clearing. His eyes scanned the woods, then the camp. "John Hadd..." He trailed off.

"Fuck," Tyance murmured, coming up to Madoc's side.

"Doctor Hadden!" Elisha joined Allen's yelling. "It's Allen and Elisha from the university. Doctor Hadden?"

"Jesus," Madoc said.

"Doctor Hadden!" Allen yelled out again.

"He's not here," Tyance called over to Allen.

"Doctor Hadden!" Allen continued, either not hearing or not detecting the seriousness in Tyance's voice.

"He's not here!" Madoc snapped, harshly. Allen and Elisha stopped their yelling and cast confused glances at Madoc. "He's not here," Madoc repeated, his voice under more control. "Look at this." Madoc squatted down in the area between the tent and a blackened fire pit. "When was the last time we had rain?" Madoc asked the ground.

"A week ago," Tyance answered. "I don't know about up here, but it's been over a week for us."

"What do you mean he's not here?" Allen came up to Madoc, disbelief in his eyes. "This has to be his camp—it's right where he wrote it would be."

"Look." Madoc straightened himself up. His finger pointed down, beside a canvas chair close to the fire pit, to a pile of papers sitting beside it, a rock placed on top, and a pen close by. The papers were stuck together, almost melted, the writing on the top sheet mixed with that which soaked up from below. The edges of the sheets were gnarled, bending up and down like a strip of burnt bacon. "And this." Madoc indicated the tent. One of its corners had slipped away from the peg and it sat unevenly on the ground. Debris and a puddle of water on the flattened edge of canvass, making something very clear to the two guides.

"He hasn't been here for some time."

* * * *

The fire crackled atop the darkened ash where John Hadden's fire had last burned out over a week before. The sun was still hovering over the horizon in the west, and everybody was thankful for the light. The groups' gazes darted around rapidly, continuously, watching the darkness. Theories as to what happened to Doctor Hadden passed between the group, the most popular involving Vance Halverson.

"Why give us his gun?" Madoc kept asking. Madoc even went so far as to fire a shot across the river to make sure the weapon worked. "If he's some insane guy, why give us an extra weapon?" Now the shotgun sat across Madoc's lap, the Ruger he brought with him close to Tyance's side. Hadden's slender .22 was also close to Tyance, a tiny round chambered. The burgundy carrying case had been tossed back into Doctor Hadden's lopsided tent.

"Perhaps we should get away from this camp," Allen offered. "I mean, if he comes back."

"We don't know it was Vance," Elisha said. She stood, staring about.

"Whoever then," Allen snapped. "Maybe we should find another place to camp."

"No," Madoc said distantly, his eyes also scanning the area. "I mean, we have the river to this side, and a cul-de-sac of cliff all the way up along the river. The river's moving too fast to swim across here. John found a nice sheltered little spot. There's only one easy way to this spot and that's coming from upriver. A guy could come around the other side," Madoc pointed down river, at the uneven pile of rock and rubble, "but we'd hear him a mile away. We'll see him the other way long before he gets close. This is a good spot to hold up until tomorrow."

Elisha recognized Madoc was right. The pile of rubble down river, along with the rather steep incline of rock running beside them and the river, made for a contained campsite. Elisha looked up and down the rock face, studying its wall, then walked over to it.

"Do you think maybe Doctor Hadden just took off?" Allen asked. "Maybe it had nothing to do with Vance, or anybody else."

"John didn't just take off without his camp gear."

"Fuck, maybe he got himself lost. Maybe he got himself turned around and, fuck, maybe he's out there hurt or something. Do you think we should look for him?"

"I don't think John got lost easily. He came out into these parts long before GPS was available. Besides, if he's lost, he's been missing at least seven days. I don't want to be morbid, but if he's out there on his own, without any supplies, there's no way he's lasted seven days."

"I don't know. Remember that guy down in Hastings County? He went into the woods and was gone for eight days. No food, no water, and they found him okay. He was legally blind, deaf, and slow."

"I don't know if you can be legally slow." Madoc smiled.

"You know what I mean—"

"And you know," Madoc said calmly but sternly, "we aren't a search party. Tomorrow we'll turn back, get back to the cabin, and alert the authorities. I don't think it's just a coincidence that John's missing and Vance Halverson's running around here, acting nuts. I swear to God, if he hadn't given us his gun, I would find us a cave to hide in. As it is, tonight, we're going to take turns staying up. Two of us at a time. We're going to be careful, but we can't get terrified. We need to get rest. There're only two directions he can come into here from. We'll have plenty of warning before he gets here. We know he has no gun, and I only saw a buck knife in his pack. We have the advantage."

"Maybe he had a pistol," suggested Allen.

"The guy dumped his entire kit," Madoc countered, "when he got out the rope for Tyance. If he had any other weapons, we would have seen them."

"So you think Doctor Hadden is…y'know…is…"

"I think we have to go back to the cabin, get on the satellite phone, and call the police."

"Hey, Allen, come see this," Elisha called over her shoulder. Allen stood up and went to the rock face where Elisha was gently running her hands over the surface. Allen stepped up to the wall of rock. It went up ten meters before an awning of roots and grass folded over the top where the incline became more gradual, and continued upward for another fifty meters. Where Allen and Elisha stood, the wall was flat, and went perpendicular from the ground. It ran, at various heights, parallel to the river, reaching around the river's bend away from the group's camp, and then gradually downward to where they had first seen Doctor Hadden's disused camp. As Allen got closer, he noticed what he thought were just dark veins of rock running over the pale wall of stone. Then he noticed a pattern to the dark lines. Tiny flowing valleys ran over the rock, some aimlessly, some with obvious pattern.

"Whoa," Allen muttered. "These must be the glyphs Doctor Hadden wrote about in his diary."

"He's filled in the carvings with crayon," Elisha said quietly, still running her hands over the stone. "Look at this." The area of carved rock stood like a five-meter wide wall that jutted out slightly from the rest of the long rock face, rising above Allen's head less than a meter. Around the top of the wall a darkened staining existed where Hadden had peeled back the overgrowing sod and roots to expose covered carvings. "Here, doesn't this look like the shaman symbol on that spider artifact? The one that Doctor Hadden brought back to the university."

"Yeah, it does," Allen replied in a hushed voice. "This one over here almost looks like a rabbit. This one's a lot like a moose. Look at these. They're all just squiggly lines."

"Maybe they're snakes," Madoc said from behind, his rifle in his hands.

"This is amazing," Elisha muttered. "Look at these. There are holes in the rocks, not just carvings. They go right into the rock, like they were drilled."

"I've never heard of holes being bored into any petroglyph site."

"Maybe Doctor Hadden drilled the holes?"

"Why would he scar up the site? And with what? You can tell by the coloring that these were drilled a long time ago—"

"You know, all this is very exciting," Madoc lied, "but we need to keep on our toes. You guys can tell the university all about this site when we get back, and then drill holes into the rock all you want. I think we should settle down and get some sleep. First light comes up, we're heading back."

"I've never seen glyphs quite like these," Elisha whispered, not quite ignoring Madoc, but not acknowledging him either. "The figures are disjointed, much more abstract than I've seen. These holes..."

"Odd," Allen agreed.

"Yeah, odd, great. You know what else is odd? The missing doctor and the nutty Methodist vampire hunter. Could you two please come back to the fire? I need everybody to under—"

"Hold on a minute." Elisha rushed away from the rock face to her backpack, where she searched through the pockets.

"Catholic, not Methodist," Tyance said to Madoc. Madoc turned to her, at first annoyed, then suddenly happy at the realization it was the first time she took the time to correct him since going over the cliff.

"Sorry," he smiled.

"Here." Elisha stood up and went back to the group. "Move out of the way." In her hand was a small camera. She had packed it before she departed the university, but never thought to bring it out. She wasn't much of a picture person. The white flash lit up the rock face in a sudden strobe.

"Okay, now you've got a picture. Can we all focus on—"

"Hold on a minute," Elisha repeated. She took a few steps closer and framed one of the figures. Again a strobe of light pulsed against the rock. Before Madoc said anything, she was already getting ready to shoot another one of the figures, one that Allen thought looked like a moose.

"And the holes," Allen said, digging into his pocket. He pulled out a long tent peg he had in his pocket and stuck it into one of the holes bored into the rock. "To show scale," he called over his shoulder to Tyance and Madoc. Elisha snapped off another picture, showing the hole with the tent peg sticking out of the tiny shaft just over an inch.

"I want to get these squiggly snakes," Elisha said. Again the light pounded off against the rock. Again; and again; and again.

"You've recorded where we are on the GPS thing, right?" she asked Madoc.

"Yeah." He nodded. "I know where we are."

"Good," she said, turning the camera off. "Good," she repeated, not taking her eyes off of the wall.

"If you're done," Madoc said, "I think you and Tyance should set up for a sleep. Allen and I will take the first watch. Then you and Ty will take over for a few hours. First light, we're getting the hell out of here."

* * * *

Vance Halverson first heard music just after he thought, *I need to take a break*. The sun was low in the sky. Vance moved fast, his legs flying as he travelled back to Willie Cheechoo's camp. As fast as his feet could carry him, they were slow compared to how quickly his mind was racing. He went through every single myth and tale he ever heard or read about the Lochkray…over and over. He had been out in the woods before, alone, through dark nights and lonely days, but this was the first time he felt nervous. His mind racing, his feet flying, his eyes darting across the trees around him, he progressed in a flurry of thoughts and worry.

He knew he would have to rest soon. Not only due to the enclosing darkness, but also to rest his fevered mind. Although it was the Lochkray's existence running foremost in his mind, he was not ignorant to what happened. From high school, he recalled the word "freaked." Not one with a perfect Russian translation, nor one the generally impassive priests and monks ever needed to use, so not a word he ever recalled using in the past decades. Now, however, he knew that he had "freaked" the four travelers with his abrupt shift in conviction. He felt badly for the alarm he caused them. He knew exactly what they thought of him, and he was sorry. He knew how he sounded. If nothing else, the Doctor Hadden search party was a perfect prelude to how he would be treated when he contacted the monastery.

Unless they already know they are real…

He knew he had to stop, and think—think carefully—about what was going on. Myths, stories, and legend were all well and good, but he needed to think about how he would present himself. How he would convince the brothers to send help.

And think carefully about what kind of help they needed to send.

"Let's not be stupid," Madoc said. Obviously that's how he came off. Stupid. *I need to think,* Vance told himself. *I need to go over everything. I need to think this through carefully.* The music, a thumping rhythm from up ahead, came on suddenly, but without surprise. *I need to take a break,* barely passed through his mind before *I know this song* came along to replace it.

The dark oak double doors in the middle of a brick wall were just as matter-of-fact. No transition of perception, just trees, rocks, woods, and doorway set amid snapping branches, chirping birds, and sultry rock and roll. Vance's rapid footsteps slowed down as he approached the doorway.

Relax, he told himself. *No need to rush.* Vance reached forward and opened the heavy door, pulling one side away by the large brass handle. He stepped into the establishment, the music becoming clear. The heavy beat, a bass plucking out a deep thumping tune, boomed through the giant room, and a sultry voice slowly sang along, masking the sound of the door closing door behind him.

The room was dark and long, with circular tables all across the floor, chairs at each. A long bar, dark oak, ran along the left-hand side of the room. A pathway led through the tables, down the middle of the room, stretching out from the doorway, leading to the stage, where brass posts rose upward to the ceiling.

The establishment was empty. No other patrons sat at the tables, nor were there any tenders behind the bar. The room was dark except for a few colored lights flicking on and off across the stage in time to the throbbing music. Vance closed his eyes. *Familiar,* his mind muttered to itself. *I've been here.* He rescanned the large room. He continued to advance down the path between the tables, toward the stage. *Strip club,* he recalled. *This is a strip club.*

The thought came along with the proof. Amid the darkness of the stage, Vance caught movement. A figure, barely a silhouette against the gloom, was on the stage, toward the back, swaying back and forth in time to the music. Vance stopped his advance, and watched as the figure allowed its torpid undulation to move it forward into the meager lighting. Flashes of blue, red, yellow, and green bounced across the stage, duskily illuminating the figure. The naked figure.

Her nakedness startled Vance, despite the realization of where he was—*where he was supposed to be*—in his clouded mind. The dancer waved her hips back and forth, her long thin legs gliding her up to the front of the stage. Her hands were held above her head, reminding Vance of a belly dancer. Then they came downward, touching her body and naked breasts, then stroking her belly, then lower, then up again, caressing her body. Her long hair flowed heavily down her back, perfectly framing her beautiful face around her closed eyes. Her pivoting hips twisted around in time to the music, allowing Vance to view her thin torso and perfectly formed behind. Then she pivoted on her long legs again, stroking herself up and down, causing Vance to breathe deeply.

He remembered this place. It could have been a club anywhere, but this one, he knew, was in London, England. It was a stopover on his way to Belarus. He was making a statement to himself and to his faith that he was *not* going to enter the priesthood. The dancer, the stripper, like all the girls in this type of place, could have been anyone's daughter. Her identity did not matter. All she needed to be was beautiful, alone, sensuous, and bare. And all these things she was.

Alone.

In the shadows, where he had first seen this beautiful naked thing moving, he caught movement again. As quickly as the stirrings of his carnal appetite came when he saw the young dancer, trepidation took over when he saw the movement in the back. As lucid as this surreal strip club was, he knew that he was supposed to be alone with the girl. For no fleeting moment did he consider the other might be the next dancer, or a stagehand, or the person working the music or lighting. There was supposed to be nobody, *nobody*, there with them. Yet the movement was obvious.

Vance went to move forward, to warn the girl. He took a few steps before he hit the glass. A wall of glass, invisible but solid, stopped Vance from getting any closer to the naked young dancer, as she continued her cadenced public masturbation. The dark movement drew closer to her. Vance put his hands out—if he saw himself he would be reminded of a mime feeling an invisible wall. This wall was more than any annoying street act. It was real, solid. He felt the barrier, looking for a break. Then he banged on it—slaps at first, then full-fisted hits.

"Hey," he screamed at the dancer. "Get off of the stage! There's somebody behind you!" He smashed his hands against the wall, his own words deafening in his ears. "Get out of there! He's behind you!"

The dark movement moved closer to the oblivious dancer. Closer. Its human form was clear now. A man stood behind the dancer, just out of the lights, a huge man. Before he even allowed the colored lights to hit him, Vance knew who it was.

"Behind you," Vance screamed at the dancer. "Get away! Run!"

The Lochkray stepped into the light and grabbed onto the dancer as she raised her hands above her head once more. He wrapped around her, his arms enveloping her like tentacles. The dancer did not seem to mind. Her head tilted back onto the Lochkray's shoulder, her eyes still closed. Vance screamed, shrieked at the girl to run. She relaxed into the Lochkray's hold as the colored lights pulsed themselves out, one by one, color by color, leaving the room in darkness.

Vance stood with his hands clawing at the invisible wall. He closed his eyes and rested his head against the wall, enveloped in blackness. He stood there, ready to weep and not knowing why he felt for the girl on the stage, why he felt so horrified and sorrowful at her consumption by the Lochkray.

Then the lights came on throughout the establishment, illuminating all corners of the bar. Even the pulsing lights above the stage came on but they were muted in the strength of the bright whites. The tables revealed themselves to be cheap and cracked in the light, the dark oak bar was clearly panel board. The carpet underneath was stained and tacky in color. Vance's fingers fell forward against the invisible wall as its denseness vanished. The stage was empty. The dancer was gone but Vance knew the Lochkray was not.

He turned around, facing away from the stage. Toward the center of the room, near the central pathway to the stage, sitting at one of the tables with outstretched legs, the Lochkray sipped on a dark drink, ice clinking against the sides of the glass.

Rum and coke, the Lochkray thought, sipping on the drink. The Madoc had brought it with him to his fantasy. The Lochkray was unfamiliar with the beverage, borrowed it from the Madoc's dream, and brought it here. Now he took the time to sip on it, to give the libation a judge. Unlike some of his other brethren, this Lochkray enjoyed exploring human interests and creations when the opportunity arose. At that moment, this Lochkray was simply wasting time—no better an opportunity to try the drink.

"Lochkray," Vance whispered at the form. The Lochkray barely lifted his eyes to look back in acknowledgement. Vance looked around the empty bar.

Where am I? he finally asked himself. Vance took a few steps toward the table.

The Lochkray put his black drink down on the table. *Sweet*, he decided was the best description.

"Where am I?" Vance demanded of the Lochkray. This time the Lochkray raised his eyes to meet Vance's. The Lochkray lifted its hand, two fingers extended in a point.

"Inside," the Lochkray said, lazily tapping the side of his head before pointing at Vance. Unlike with Madoc and other humans he came in contact with, the Lochkray did not bother to disguise his speech with perfect English. His deep, accented, mumbled voice growled out the words to Vance. It was vile enough that he had to speak in one of the daylights' many convoluted languages—he made no effort to suit a Cimmerian Knight with linguistic convenience.

"What?"

"This," the Lochkray motioned around the bar with a casual sweep of his hand, "is dream." The Lochkray picked up the drink again, deciding to give it another try.

"I don't understand."

The Lochkray smiled. "You are hunted," he explained over the rim of the glass. "By sanok." The Lochkray looked at Vance to see if it was knowledgeable. It was not. "Do you know not of sanok?"

"How do you know who I—"

"Sanok," the Lochkray interrupted, "is animal. Lochkray made and subdued, during time of glory. Like much of our knowing, they were forfeit when the Cimmerian Knights endeavored our genocide. Sanok were taken to Kraell'Haatch and lost."

"You *are* looking for Kraell'Haatch," Vance hissed at the Lochkray.

"Sanok," the Lochkray went on, repeating himself, "is animal. Hunts in minds of the simple. It is not incarnate...until it is. A dream on the wind, it waits for prey to come. Prey causes sanok. Real in mind, is as real as sanok needs be. Prey dreams, sanok forms. Dream continues, sanok advances."

As if to prove the point, a crashing sound came from outside the walls of the club. Vance turned from side to side, frantically looking for the source. The Lochkray shook its head in disgust.

"This one," the Lochkray continued, "has become remiss. Wakes prey from reverie, allows them to become aware. Sanok is cautious and wary; Once prey is aware, it is apt to depart, as will the dream." Another crashing sound from around caused Vance to jump.

"Aware?" he repeated, trying to understand what he was being told. "Then I'm aware. This is a dream. Okay? I am in a dream, and there is an animal coming toward me." He looked around the club again. "Why am I still dreaming? Why won't I wake?"

The Lochkray drew on the sweet black drink again.

"I won't let you."

* * * *

For whatever reason, the hunter, the sanok, had not awakened the prey as it stood in its illusion. The sanok padded its clawed forearms slowly forward. The *other* had done this for it before. Only now, the prey was far away from its pack. It was alone out here in the woods, alone with the *other*. The sanok knew it would get close enough this time. Close enough to strike. The *other* would not care if this prey screamed.

* * * *

"Kraell'Haatch is of the Lochkray," was half heard by Vance, "guarded by sanok for them. Why do Cimmerian Knights believe they have right to Kraell'Haatch?"

"I only work for them," Vance said, spinning around in all directions, looking for the source of the clumsy animal advance. He considered for a moment running out the door of the club, but he knew this was pointless. There was no door. There was no club. What the Lochkray had described, he heard of, and he knew he could not run from his own thoughts.

An animal that lives in nightmares, he read before in a foreign language, *is the Lochkray's creation. The Lochkray control it only by margin. It arrives in a dream but does exist in reality. Only it must form in the hunted man's mind. Still, it is as real as any predator. Real in the dream, and real outside of it.*

Sanok. He now knew its name. "Call it off," Vance demanded.

"I cannot."

The clumsy tripping of the animal, now much closer, caused Vance to turn about frantically.

"Let me wake," he pleaded.

"No."

Vance felt about in his pockets, but found nothing. He tried reaching around his back, but could not feel the backpack that he knew was actually there. He closed his eyes and tried to concentrate, feeling around his back again, but still nothing.

"Why do the Cimmerian Knights believe they have right to Kraell'Haatch?" the Lochkray asked again, still not getting to his feet. He looked calm and almost disinterested to Vance—despite the effort it was taking to hold this dream. While the sanok made its ungainly advance, the Lochkray was struggling to hold his own form in Vance's mind—to keep him there, in the dream, as well as standing perfectly still in the woods.

"You kill," Vance said. "It is written that Kraell'Haatch has all the knowledge of the Lochkray. Enough to let you to conquer all people. They can't let you do that." A table at the back of the bar moved on its own. Then another, closer to the two, tipped over.

"All knowledge of Lochkray," was repeated with a slow nod. "Why do Cimmerian Knights have right to withhold knowledge of our own?"

"You kill people," Vance said again. Another table tipped over, its chairs also crashing to the ground.

"It is our knowledge, for us to have."

"You kill people!"

"I kill you." The Lochkray solemnly nodded again.

The sanok pounced, tearing through the prey's dream like paper. Vance's scream poured out from his lungs.

The huge skull came at Vance in a blur of teeth and saliva. The claws knocked him over in a violent push that sent him to the ground, but never released. In the same moment Vance felt the ground smack up at him from behind, he felt the stabbing pressure from the animal pushing down on him from above. Then the teeth, wet and needlelike, coming back at him with a rotting smell, enveloping his head. The points grasped all about his face, causing red, then black.

Vance recognized the horrid sensation of the tearing claws through his abdomen, the weight on his chest and the wetness about his head as the teeth stabbed into his skull in a death grip.

Somehow, through the pain and terror, he realized that he was no longer in the strip bar. He could tell that he was lying on the ground in the woods, damp and cold, struggling helplessly. He sensed the debris of the forest shifting underneath his bloody body as he struggled. He allowed one of his hands to leave its feckless blows against the gory mouth to scramble across the ground in a vain effort to find some kind of bludgeon or weapon.

Eventually, the enveloping death was a comforting release for Vance, taking him away from the horrid pain of being torn apart. The Lochkray opened its eyes and looked down on the giant animal from his perch in a nearby tree. He tilted his head back and forth, trying to calm down and relax. Much effort was required to hold the daylight in the sanok's dream. There was much satisfaction in watching the acolyte's fear, as it knew death was coming. The sanok tore apart the acolyte's body, fully real and tangible in the woods, even after the acolyte was dead.

Soon the sanok decided its work was done and faded away again, continuing on to find the rest making their way toward its lair. Waiting for them to be alone and vulnerable, and attempt to slip into their dreams for another hunt.

The Lochkray left the site of the sanok's feeding, slipping from tree to tree, to return to the group. To see if they were getting closer to finding Kraell'Haatch for him.

Chapter Nineteen

Allen watched Madoc's relentless stare as he scanned the woods, the river, and the water's edge where they sat. By Madoc's side sat his rifle, and beside Allen was the shotgun, unloaded. Madoc gave a brief tutorial on how to operate the weapon, but knew it was of little more value loaded in Allen's hand than it was unloaded by his side. He would never be able to fire off a shot at Vance, never mind actually hit him. Only the threat was required.

Allen turned his attention to his side, watching as the white rapids stood out in the faint firelight against the darker waters. Then he looked at the woods, dark and empty. Then his watch. Then Madoc again. Then the river. Then his watch.

Forty-five more minutes until Tyance and Elisha took over, and Allen would have an opportunity to get some sleep. Only forty-five more minutes of the awkward silence. He looked at the river, then the woods, then his watch. Then back at Madoc.

"Do you believe in ghosts?" Madoc's question startled Allen. It came out of nowhere, timed perfectly to his innocent stare's return.

"Uh," Allen squeaked out, "no. Well, I guess not. No."

"I saw a ghost once," Madoc said quietly, turning toward Allen. "When I was about twenty. There were four of us renting the upper floor of an old house. Downstairs there was this Laundromat the landlord owned but he kept the upstairs as an apartment. Cheap rent. There was a door in the apartment—it went up to this huge attic space. It wasn't like most old attics, where you have to go through a trap door in the ceiling or anything like that. This was a set of proper stairs that went up to this huge unfinished area. You could have put a whole other apartment up there—just put insulation and walls up. For us, it was just an empty space where we stored crap, like our bikes, empty suitcases, boxes of books—stuff like that.

"One night, when I was home alone, I went up there to get something for the kitchen—I had a box up there with some utensils I hadn't unpacked. I went up to get this spoon, it's this spaghetti spoon, for dishing out pasta, the kind with little prongs along the sides. I was making dinner for myself and got it in my mind I wanted to use this stupid spoon. Anyway, I went up there and started going through a couple of the old boxes, and that's when I saw the ghost."

Madoc reached behind and picked up a log and threw it onto the fire. "I swear to God, Allen," he continued, "I saw a man standing at the other end of that attic. I was looking in the box. I looked up and there he was. He looked young but thin and pale. His face was so thin he almost looked like a skull. I saw him looking at me, and I nearly screamed. I just froze, though. I don't think there was any air in my lungs to scream, because I just froze. Then he walked, without making a sound, almost like his feet weren't hitting the floor. I finally looked down into the box to find something, anything I could protect myself with. I grabbed onto this wooden meat tenderizer, like a small square hammer, and picked it up out of the box.

"When I looked up, the guy wasn't there. I was alone. I stood there for ten minutes, with this stupid meat tenderizer held above my head. I breathed so hard I'm surprised I didn't pass out. I finally ran down the stairs and slammed the door shut. I never went up there alone again."

"Whoa," Allen breathed.

"Yeah. You know what, Allen? You know what the strangest thing about it all is?"

"What?" Allen asked. His skin felt cold and tingly.

"I don't believe in ghosts." Madoc smiled. "I never have and I never will. I'm telling you—and I'm not lying—I saw a guy, looking thin and sickly in that attic, a man who floated across the room and disappeared into thin air. I saw him, just like I see you right now. Despite that, I don't believe in ghosts. Do you know why?"

"Why?" Allen's dry voice asked.

"Because it's not rational. It's not rational at all. Why, if there were a ghost in that house, would he decide to live in the dirty, dark attic? You'd think a ghost hang out in the living room or kitchen. Where did he buy the clothes he wore? Did he get them at an otherworldly shopping mall, or did he pick them up on sale at an undead tailor?" Madoc laughed at himself, though Allen didn't join in. "If he could disappear, why reappear in the first place? Just to scare the shit out of me? Why was I so scared? For the most part, I don't react to seeing new people by hitting them in the head with a kitchen hammer—but he scared me to death. I reacted in total terror, but I've never actually heard of a ghost hurting anybody."

"I don't get it."

"That's just it. There's nothing to get. We're told that seeing is believing, but that's just not the way it is. People say they've seen fantastical things all the time, and I don't think they're all lying. I just think we get...confused. Like I said, I'm telling you, I saw that guy up there. And yet, he wasn't there. Just like there're no hairy ape people living in the Rocky Mountains. Just like there's no dinosaur living in any Scottish lake. Our minds sometimes see things wrong—see mistakes, shadows. If we pick it up a certain way, it's a ghost, or monster, or UFO. Otherwise, we dismiss it."

"That's really what you think?" Allen asked.

"That's what I know. Firsthand. So, don't let Halverson's story get you worked up. We'll be cautious but there's no need to freak yourself out over this."

"So, you think everybody that's ever seen a ghost or anything supernatural is just mistaken?"

"Or lying or crazy. Most of the time, though, I think we just get tangled up in the web of our own mind."

Allen smiled. He wanted to interject with his own comments, but decided against it. It was nice to think Vance Halverson just became tangled up in the web of his own mind, and only saw something in his imagination.

The only problem was Doctor Hadden's disappearance was too much to ignore. There was no way to explain why the man just vanished from his own campsite. Allen thought about bringing this up again but then decided better of it. He just nodded at Madoc's theories.

Madoc went silent again, resuming his vigilant watch of the area, and Allen started his circle of staring again too. This time he decided to widen his visual repetition, and his gaze fell onto the white petroglyph covered wall on the other side of their collection of tents. In the darkness of the night, its shape was barely visible. His eyes went to resume their circuit of stares, back to the woods, to the river, to Madoc, to the fire—but as quickly as his eyes darted away from the wall of rock, they darted back. Allen scrambled at his side until he located his flashlight, and made the dark rock wall alive in light.

"Whoa," Allen said. Madoc looked lazily back at the petroglyphs.

"What?" he asked, half-interested. Allen didn't answer, but instead stood up and walked over to the carvings. He shone his light all over the surface, again examining the figures.

"Whoa," Allen repeated. "Wait a minute. Wait a minute." Madoc reluctantly stood up to go over to join him, placing the rifle's strap across his shoulder and putting it behind him. He brought his own flashlight and pointed the light at the wall. Just as he reached Allen, the suddenly excited student turned around and darted back over to his tent.

"What? What is it?"

"Wait a minute," Allen said again. Madoc listened to rustling and zippers from inside Allen's tent, a ball of white dancing across the canvas dome from within. Then Madoc heard scuffling coming from Elisha's tent, beside Allen's, his frantic digging obviously disturbing her sleep. Finally Allen emerged, carrying in one hand the flashlight, in the other a pile of papers, his head not even turning toward the movement in the tent beside his. "Look," he said frantically. "Look here. Look. Look."

"Look at what?" Madoc asked, pointing his own light at the papers. Allen dropped to his knees and put the papers on the ground. Madoc recognized them as Doctor Hadden's doodles from Cheechoo's cabin. The ones Hadden had drawn grids over.

"He almost had it," Allen enthusiastically sputtered. He pulled out one of the sheets with the doodles on it. He stood up and went over to the rock wall. "See," Allen said. "The doodles are like the lines. Not the glyphs with the animal shapes. The ones you called the snakes. He drew all the snakes."

"Okay," Madoc said with a sigh. Allen took the piece of paper and held it up against the wall. Elisha had now emerged from her tent. She lay awake in there, listening to the sound of Allen and Madoc talking. She couldn't make out the exact words, but she could tell that they chatted with one another. She had been awake for almost an hour before hearing the muddled sound of the two conversing, and she had actually found the talking comforting. Before they spoke, all she heard was the occasional snap or crackle from the fire. When they talked, she known that they were out there, and she could tell they were calm. That was gently comforting. The one word she finally made out from their conversation was Allen's sudden, "whoa."

She looked over at Madoc with a *what's-going-on* expression, and Madoc shrugged back at her. He could also hear movement now coming from Tyance's tent. Madoc took the time to do a quick survey of the land, out of habit, to ensure it was still just the four of them.

"Look at this," Allen said. "It is the lines. It's all the lines on this rock face. He was drawing the grids over them. He almost had it."

"Who almost had what?" Elisha asked Madoc, now shining her own flashlight onto the rock. Again Madoc shrugged. Allen turned toward the two, just as Tyance poked her head out of her tent. "It wasn't grids," he said excitedly. "It was webbed.

That's why the glyph matches the one on the copper spider. It was a spool. That's why it had that point coming off of the end of it."

"Uh, yeah...Allen," Madoc said, "I have no idea what you're talking about."

"What's he talking about?" Tyance asked, joining the group.

"Exactly," Madoc replied.

"I need rope," Allen told the group. "String, thread, anything. And sticks." He scanned the ground and found a small branch. He picked it up. "Like this, I need sticks."

"I have twine in my backpack," Tyance said.

"That's it," Madoc said with quiet sarcasm. "Encourage him."

"And sticks," Allen said as he broke off a piece of the branch in his hands. "About...I don't know, like...six inches long." He broke the branch again and returned his attention to the rock wall. Tyance looked at Madoc.

"Okay, go ahead," Madoc answered before Tyance even asked her question. She departed to get the spool of twine she carried in her backpack. Elisha spotted a long stick, retrieved it, and passed it over to Allen.

"What's going on, Allen?" she asked. "What do you want the sticks and string for?"

"Remember the copper spider? The one Doctor Hadden found at the midden?"

"Yeah."

"It had this shamanistic figure on it. Remember? It looked like it had a short stick coming out of its abdomen. Almost made it look like it was used as a puppet. But it wasn't a puppet; it was a spool. A spool."

Allen broke the stick that Elisha gave him into six-inch pieces, like the others. "Look," he said. He took one of the pieces and placed it into one of the holes drilled into the rock. Then he took another stick and did the same thing in another of the drilled holes. Madoc walked over and picked up a stick and placed it into another of the many holes drilled into the surface of the rock.

"Like this?" Madoc asked.

"Exactly," Allen said, filling another hole. "Doctor Hadden didn't drill these. They've always been here." Madoc and Allen continued to fill in the holes while Elisha went off and located another substantial branch. Tyance emerged from her tent with the spool of twine and passed it over to Allen. "Thanks," he said.

"Why do you have that?" Madoc asked absently.

"A world without string is chaos," Tyance stated. Madoc looked over his shoulder at her. "Fuck, you never know," she explained, "when you're going to have to build something in the bush. A hammer and nails are too heavy to carry—"

"A world without string is chaos?"

"I heard In a movie once."

"There, that's all of them," Allen said, pulling out the end of the twine. Madoc stepped back and looked at the wall again, now covered with sticks pointing out of it. Allen reached up to the stick that pointed out of the top left and tied the string around it. "Like a spider," Allen said. He pulled down on the tied twig and made a tight line to the stick below, and off to the left of it. He twirled the twine around the stick, then continued to pull until he came to the next one down, and again off to the left.

"I see what he's doing," Madoc suddenly whispered. "Like a spider. Like a spider's web."

"Tangled up in the web of our own minds," Allen said, smiling to himself. Madoc let out a quick uncomfortable laugh. Tyance and Elisha looked at each other and shrugged.

"You tie all the sticks together like a spider's web," Madoc explained to the two girls. "You can already see the pattern in the sticks. You tie them all together, and you make a web over the pictures."

"Each glyph is within the grid made by the web," Elisha finished.

"It *is* a map," Allen said. "Doctor Hadden was right. It is a map. You can't grid it like you normally would. You have to build a web over it."

"A map?" Madoc blurted out. "That's quite a jump."

"No, it's not. Look at this." Allen dropped the spool of twine. He raised his finger to point at an engraving already sectioned off by the string. "Look at this line. What was the name of the river that we're north of? The one with the really big long name."

"The Moose River?" Madoc asked.

"Yeah," Tyance snorted. "Moose is a real big name." She turned to Allen. "You mean the Kwataboahegan." She turned back to Madoc and added, "Besides, the Moose River is to our west."

"East," he corrected.

"Fuck you, Rob."

"Right," Allen said. "Imagine that this is the Kwata—Kataboakwata—whatever. Then this long part down here is like the Moose River…See? It runs over to this part, which is the shape of a U with, like, this symbol that could be like a fish or a whale. Look, look. Imagine the U with the whale was James Bay. Then this is the Moose River and this is the Kwat-thing River."

"Yeah," Madoc interjected, "but the Kwataboahegan runs east to west. Not north to south."

"No, no, no," Allen said, picking back up the twine. "It's not like a regular map. You can't think of it as north-south-east-west. It's not like that. It's the web, with the figures. You have to read the web." Allen continued his connecting of the sticks with twine. "That's why the copper spool was shaped like a spider." Tyance suddenly darted away from the group and went back to her tent. Madoc and Elisha barely noticed.

"What do you think?"

"Pretty far-fetched," Elisha said. Madoc noticed that her voice was lacking its usual confidence in dismissing one of Allen or John Hadden's theories.

"That does look like a fish in James Bay," Tyance said, coming up behind them.

"Maybe." Elisha turned back to see Tyance clumsily unfolding a map with her flashlight in her hand. Madoc again took the time to scan the environment all around, then he readjusted the rifle strung across his back.

"He might be on to something," Tyance said. "Look at that line there. It does follow the same basic pattern of the Kwataboahegan. You can see this here, this lake. Look at the rock. That looks like the shape in that grid."

"It's off to the east. That lake is to the north."

"Not like a map," Allen stressed over his shoulder. "You have to follow the pattern of the web." He strung a few more sticks together.

"Look at that one," Tyance said, pointing past Allen. "Imagine the Missinabi River."

"Wouldn't it connect with the Moose?" Madoc asked, getting a little frustrated. "And it's three times as long."

"No," Elisha said, her voice suddenly low. "It does touch—by the grid. Not by the actual carving," she spoke louder, "but by the quadrat. The bay goes to the Moose; that goes to the Kwat-river which is fed by the lake."

"There," Tyance pointed to a newly formed grid. "Look at the little jut out on that drawing with the bird. Just like the jut on the ridge we crossed yesterday. It had a sharp jut near its highest point. Each carving is not in scale to the other carvings—"

"It is in scale to itself in the grid," Elisha finished.

"Wait," Allen stated. "I'm almost done. Don't do it without me." Allen let the rest of the spool of twine fall to the ground and stepped back. There, on the rock wall of carvings, a huge web was strung. Each carving fell into one of the grids created, the smaller ones housing the smaller carvings. The only carving which didn't have a grid all to itself was the one in the center, where all of the grids met. The lines of twine all intersected at the carving's center—the one carving that matched the symbol on the back of Doctor Hadden's artifact, the one that Allen called shamanistic.

"Wow," Tyance said.

"Pretty good, Allen," Madoc stated.

"Unbelievable," added Elisha.

Excellent, thought the Lochkray, from the shadows.

"I get it," Tyance stated. "There we are. See—the grid with the arch shape. Under it is the river. Along the long grid. See it?"

"You think that's where we are?" Elisha asked.

"Sure. Even the shape of the carving is a little like this wall. The line," she pointed to the wall, then brought her finger down to the map, "is the same shape as this river here. The one we're camping beside right now."

"So, what's this one? The one in the middle, where all the strings meet?" asked Madoc. Tyance looked at her map, running her fingers along it.

"I don't know," she said. "Look. If that's supposed to be here...and this is the river...and this is that river..." She fell silent again, mumbling to herself. The group huddled around her, staring at Tyance as she moved her fingers across the map in her hands, looking back and forth between the map and the rock wall. "Look at this," she said. "If I'm reading this right, that grid with the thing which looks like a rabbit...That one..." She pointed. Allen walked up to the wall and pointed at the shape.

"This one?"

"Right," she said. "That one is where we were originally going to go look for Hadden, before Elisha found that letter. Where his midden things were supposed to be. See, up here. So, if that's there and we're here..." She trailed off again. "Then..." She stopped. "The middle is..." Another pause. "Here," she finally pointed at the map.

"Where is there?" Allen asked, almost pushing his way past Madoc to get to the map.

"Abso-fucking-lutely nowhere," Tyance said. "There's nothing there. According to the map, just trees and swamp."

"Are you sure that's the spot?" Madoc asked.

"Get me the GPS," Tyance said without even dignifying Madoc's question with a response. Madoc moved somewhat lazily to his tent and returned with the tiny computer. Tyance took it from him and looked at the map, then punched numbers into the GPS receiver. She then held it back toward Madoc. "There are the coordinates. All punched in. Just follow the arrow."

"That's nice," Madoc replied, "but we aren't going."

"What if Doctor Hadden is there?" Allen asked loudly. "What if he figured out the map and went off to the site?"

"Without his gear?"

"It's possible," Elisha said. Madoc turned toward her in surprise. "Well, it is," she defended herself. "Hadden's an idiot. If he thought he figured this map system out, it is possible he left everything and went off to this place, whatever it is. If he liked what he found, he could just as easily stayed there, not bothering to come back and get his stuff. Or maybe he got hurt along the way, and is waiting for somebody to come get him. It's worth looking into."

"Actually, Rob," Tyance interjected, "we could be there by late tomorrow afternoon."

"What about Halverson?" Madoc asked.

"We don't have to worry about him," Allen said. "There's no way he could follow us there. There's no way he knew about this map. C'mon. If Doctor Hadden figured it out, we owe it to him to go look. And to the university."

Madoc looked at the group in silence for a long time, without so much as making a movement. Finally he shook his head. "Elisha and Tyance, you two take over the watch. Allen and I will get some sleep. Tomorrow we head back to Cheechoo's cabin." The group ahead of him deflated. Then he added, "By way of whatever this place is. We go to this new site, look for John, then we start heading south again." Allen almost clapped in excitement but held off. Tyance and Elisha let out a short, "Yay."

Madoc shook his head some more and walked back to his tent.

Part Four
Destination

Chapter Twenty

Allen poked his head through the flaps of his tent and saw Tyance and Elisha were already in the midst of preparing breakfast. To his surprise, he had slept rather heavily. He figured the tension and excitement of the previous day's events would have left him completely unable to sleep, but instead he was exhausted and remembered almost nothing after crawling into his sleeping bag. He paused for a moment to study Elisha as she bent over by the morning fire, her shorts riding up slightly to give him an ample view of her long tanned legs. A twitch of a smile cracked on his face.

Would you just ask her out? a familiar voice goaded him.

"Good morning," Tyance called over. Allen jerked his head toward her. She was already looking back at the cooking pot in her hands, a smirk on her own lips.

"M-morning," he stuttered back, stepping out of the tent with his towel and toiletry kit. He saw Elisha turn toward him and give him a smile. "I just was…river to wash…uh…" He finished by giving half a wave, and then walked down the rocky surface to the river's edge. Tyance watched out of the corner of her eye until she was sure Allen was out of earshot.

"I think he likes you," she said with a girlish giggle.

"Who?" Elisha looked at her. "Allen?"

"He was checking you out."

"He was not."

"Yep," she laughed. "I saw him."

Elisha tried to suppress the rush of blood going to her face. "He was not… really?"

Tyance laughed at her again. "You said 'just friends', right?" she reminded Elisha.

"Right."

"Have you ever thought about…y'know?"

"Dating Allen?"

"Dating. Sure, whatever."

"I…" Elisha shook her head. "I'll consider it when we get back home. Right now isn't the best time to be thinking about that."

"It's always time to think about that," Tyance said in a deep, satirically sexy voice.

"I can't stand Doctor Hadden, but he is Allen's mentor. Maybe we should stay focused on him."

"Well." Tyance looked up at Allen again. He was crouched over the river's edge, his shirt off, rubbing a bar of soap over his soaked hair in an attempt to lather. "What is it about John Hadden you don't like?"

"It's just that he's…" Elisha stopped, not wanting to say anything bad about the man right then.

"He's an idiot," Tyance finished for her. "That's what you said before, right?"

"Uh, yeah," Elisha coughed back.

"I mean, I read Introduction thing he wrote. He seems like an asshole. The way he says he's going to look at one site, then suddenly decides to go wandering and find another site—it sounds exactly like you said last night. I was thinking about it—if this guy is such an idiot to go wandering around the bush on his own all summer, then go jumping around from place to place without telling anybody, I'll bet he's just the type of person who figured out Allen's spider web thing, then just grabbed some supplies, left his tent, and ran off to the new site."

Elisha looked at Tyance silently. It was exactly what she had proposed the night before, but coming out of somebody else's mouth made it seem even more likely.

"Yeah." Elisha nodded. "He's taken off to this new place, made a shelter, and is now digging around there."

"By tonight we will be at his new camp."

"Yeah." She nodded again, smiling.

"Allen will be happy, and we'll all be heading back by tomorrow morning."

"Yeah."

"Then you," Tyance said, suddenly stern, "should go over there and ask that boy if he wants to go on a road trip before you head back. Stop in Timmins or North Bay or Sudbury on your way home. Get a hotel, see a movie, go out for dinner, fuck him—"

"*Ty*-ance!" Elisha squirmed. "Besides, I'm not supposed to ask him out. He's supposed to ask me out. He's the guy."

Tyance stared back silently. "Maybe he'll ask you between lunch and afternoon recess," she finally muttered. "You know, we are adults here. There's nothing wrong with asking the guy out. Puts you in control."

"It's not un-adult." Elisha laughed at herself. "I just think that, y'know, if the guy doesn't ask you out, it's…y'know…he's wimpy."

"Hey, it's your life." Tyance shrugged. "Go back to school on the bus with the idiot professor and read books. Just 'cause the guy's a little shy." Tyance resumed her concentration on the fire in front of her and spread the embers to make an even cooking surface.

"Besides, he probably wouldn't like being asked."

"Hey, it's your life."

"It's not my job."

"I guess."

"Good morning," Allen repeated. He still had his shirt off, and a towel strung across his shoulders. Tyance looked over and gave a smile. "What's not your job?" Allen asked.

"Uh…," Elisha started, still startled by Allen's sudden appearance.

"To spend her summer looking for lost people," Tyance answered for her. "Hey, Elisha was just saying that she wanted to see the big Science North museum in Sudbury. I told her the two of you should stop there overnight on the way back south. Let your Professor Hadden go back to school on his own, and take a little road trip." Tyance stood up and wiped her hands on her shorts, not even looking at Elisha. "I'm just going to check on Rob." As she walked behind Allen, she ogled Allen's butt so Elisha would notice. Oblivious, Allen looked around.

"That sounds like a good idea," he said. "Do you really want to do that?"

* * * *

"So, you really think he's going to be there?" Madoc asked Tyance.

"Yep."

Madoc looked back at her skeptically. She was scheming, he could tell. When he came out of his tent that morning, Elisha and Allen were talking about going to Sudbury together to spend a night and see some science museum. Madoc could smell Tyance's hand in the matter. Everyone was happy today, and the idea that John went to this new site turned out quite a popular thought. Madoc, however, wasn't so sure. Seeing as Tyance shook off her fall from the day before, the two students were in good spirits, and there was no way for Vance to be following them, Madoc figured *What the hell?*

If John was at the new site, then everything was great. If he wasn't, then they would just head back and get the police and have them start up a search party. They could bring a helicopter in and cover the area easily.

Today's walk went far better than Madoc could have hoped for. The brush and bush were fairly spread out and the ground was hard and dry. They made good time, not having to burst through thick branches or pull their feet from marshy ground. It appeared they might make it to their new destination quickly. When they first left, Madoc took time to look over his shoulder again. Now, a few hours into the woods, he only bothered to look up, for above them, through breaks in the trees, he saw the clouds were coming together, and the brief patches of blue were becoming less and less frequent. The clouds still had a white fluffy quality, but he saw streaks of gray in them. He just hoped what was coming held off until mid-afternoon.

Behind the group of four, the Lochkray still followed. At first he kept his distance. Now, he allowed himself to get fairly close to them, still out of sight, far enough back to ensure nobody glimpsed him, but close enough that he heard their chatter. From the way the Madoc talked, the group was headed toward Kraell'Haatch. Still, the Lochkray decided to let the group go on. They were no threat, and as long as their vulgar electronic technology was guiding them to the destination, there was no need to take it from them. Beyond their conveniences, he had grown used to their presence ahead of him.

Certainly, he could make better time by being done with them, and pressing forward on his own—in fact he could easily have disposed of them and already have arrived at Kraell'Haatch. Despite his burning desire to return his people to their rightful glory, and be done with daylights forever, he also wanted to see just how far the four advanced. They had done so well. The one they were looking for was dead, there was no doubt about that. Yet they pressed on with tragic confidence and beguiling hope. Somehow, despite their ignorance, and with only hints and suggestions, the four managed to do what the Lochkray's people failed to do in five hundred years.

To the Lochkray they were...*amusing*. They were intelligent and amusing. For that, the Lochkray let them live. More precisely, he would not be the one to kill them.

The Lochkray knew, despite the subtle entertainment they provided, they would soon all be dead. He knew the invisible hunter, the sanok, was close now, and staying close. He sensed when it was near to them, coming close and breaking away, pushing out at the perimeters of its territory. Now, though, it was staying with them. He felt it near, watching them and felt it was growing taut with concern.

When in its corporeal form, it was twenty feet from the tip of its snout to the end of its longest tail—one of three that stemmed out from its thick trunk like tentacles. Four feet wide at its shoulders, it had arms but no legs, a body like that of a snake with the trifurcated tail that worked simultaneously with the powerful arms to propel it forward with unnatural speed.

The sanok was a giant nightmare, a combination of predators, formed together in the mind of ancient Lochkray and released into the world, waiting, guarding. Its age was not measurable in years, for it rarely spent any of its existence in time. Without ever touching the ground, it pawed its way across the landscape. Never bending a branch, it went from tree to tree. Seldom taking form, it was seldom hungry. The nightmare moved through space, but did not take up any.

The sanok knew the four were close to its charge. They had been around for days now, and the failures to secure a hold on their dreams was frustrating it. It recognized the failure to hold onto them was of little consequence. It wanted the hunt; it enjoyed the hunt; it enjoyed being animal rather than ethereal. It savored the taste of human blood and the feeling of the forest's temperatures on its hide. The lost hunts were not of any significance. Is, they had not been before.

Now, the four were headed for the center. A line, clear in purpose, was drawn and was followed. They headed for the heart of its territory. It did not know what they advanced upon but it did know it could not let them get there. The closer they progressed, the clearer the sanok's thoughts became. They could not be allowed to continue. They must be stopped. Whether in reverie or in actual, they had to be stopped.

The sanok, neither in the trees above the group, nor anywhere else, watched without eyes as the four pierced into its domain. The two males and two females were oblivious to its existence, which made them easy to hunt. The sanok found great difficulty in sliding into the mind of a prey that knew it was hunted. Then, if it did drop the prey into dream, it was easy for the prey to become aware and awaken—either before the sanok could take form, or, even more dangerous, when it was formed but not in advantage to strike. In tangible form, it knew it was vulnerable. A knowledgeable mind could step out of deception and take action against the sanok. The danger that a prey might know of the sanok's purpose and method always held the greatest threat. For that reason, it needed to hunt them one at a time, away from the rest. Concern and frustration washed over the sanok again and again, as its instinct for cautious advance clashed with its need to eliminate them quickly as they pressed too close.

The sanok advanced along with the prey, carefully stalking as they went forward, snapping branches under their feet and clambering over rock and brush. They stayed as a group, always as a quartet. Sometimes the units broke into two groups of two but both stayed close. Two females and two males, then mixed, then a group of four again. Their spirits were light, the sanok could fixate on their minds and see that clearly. They laughed and teased, but none ever broke away. The sanok continued its hunt, sliding lightly into their thoughts and out again. If it knew what frivolity was, the sanok would grow even more frustrated with how trivial they treated their advance into its layer.

Then the sanok caught a need within one of the four. A base, simple, and natural requirement. The nightmare animal recognized it coming on before the female did. Always leaving its physical form behind, the need was never one the sanok felt itself, but it recognized the basic requirement to allow what was taken in for nourishment to pass through. That, it knew, would take the female away from the group. It would break away for modesty. The female would not wander as far away as the sanok would like, but the need to strike was too great. It backed away from the group, satisfied to make its move.

"I have to pee," Elisha said quietly to Tyance with half an embarrassed laugh.

"Elisha needs to take a piss," Tyance yelled up to Madoc and Allen.

"Thanks." Elisha rolled her eyes.

"No problem."

"Well," Madoc said, looking back over his shoulder, "looks like there's a clearing at the bottom of the hill. Why don't we stop for lunch up there?"

"Sounds good," Tyance said. "We've covered more than half the ground we have to today. We're ahead of schedule for a change. I don't think we should be too far now. We break for lunch, and we should be at your missing teacher's site within a few hours." Madoc glimpsed a satisfied look go over Allen's face, and he found himself thinking everybody really believed John Hadden was going to be there.

"I'll be down in a second," Elisha said, stopping on the ridge of the hill. The other three kept on going down the slight slope toward the brightness of the clearing, which peeked out between the leaves and branches. She paused by a tree, dropping her backpack and waited for the others to descend out of sight. She dug into her pack for a moment, then scouted for an area suitable to her needs.

Although she had never considered herself an overly prissy person, Elisha couldn't stand sitting on public toilet seats, and instead would "hover" when using public washrooms. Thankfully, this habit made her a little more practiced at urinating in the woods. Finding a tree close by for balance, and positioning herself to take advantage of the slope of the hill, she managed to get fairly well poised for the task at hand. She could faintly hear the group in the distance, circling their temporary rest point, settling down for lunch.

Elisha closed her eyes for a moment, and had she known what was about to happen, she might have noticed a slightly fanciful feeling starting to come over her. It was there, but not immediately recognizable—no more different a change in cognizance than a person might feel before a morning cup of coffee and after. Just a slight alteration, a subtle change in perception. Elisha opened her eyes, unaware that the change happened, unaware of where she was about to go. She stared ahead, blinking slightly harder than usual. She could have been looking right at the sanok, were it discernible. But it was not, and all she saw were spots of light that pierced through the flora above.

The sanok fell back and prepared to form. It watched without eyes as the female went back to its feet, pulling its garments up to its waist, fiddling with the clasps and buckles. Elisha took a step away from where the stream had been formed. She then went over to her backpack and retrieved a small plastic bottle from within. She squeezed out an amount of a thick clear liquid and rubbed it between her hands, a strong antiseptic smell of alcohol coming off of it. She then put the bottle back.

"Do you want the receipt in the bag?" the girl asked.

"Yes, that's fine," Elisha replied. The girl behind the counter placed the narrow piece of paper into the plastic bag sitting on the counter. Elisha noticed as it went in, the receipt showed a stripe of red along its edge—meaning the register's tape feed needed changed. After six years of working as a cashier at a grocery store, she knew what the red stripe meant. She thought of saying something to the cashier but decided not to. She picked up her bag, and had a quick peek inside. Along with the receipt were a pair of pants and two tank tops.

That's right, Elisha thought. *How could I forget so quickly what I just bought?*

She thanked the girl behind the counter and stepped out into the mall. People bustled by and the full noise of the busy mall was all about her: the background hum of swarms of people talking, the occasional crying child, the laughter of teenage girls teasing one another, the rustle of bags, and the very faint hint of music being pumped through speakers hidden in the ceilings. The overpowering white and cleanliness of the mall struck Elisha as she wandered through the hallway, absently looking at the display windows. Clothes on mannequins dominated the displays, presenting the latest fashions to buyers. Within other windows, household decorations, music posters, trinkets, and toys beckoned to shoppers to come have a look and deposit their money.

Elisha stopped her lazy advance through the mall for a moment, just a moment, and took a quick look about. There was a feeling she had. There was something she was supposed to...*see*. She looked all about the people and stores around her, searching for...

All her scan revealed was the usual mall activities.

She started to walk again but then something caught her eye in a store window. It was a luggage store. Elisha saw a man standing behind a counter at the back of the store, apparently reading a newspaper. Otherwise the business was empty.

It wasn't the inside of the store that caught her eye. It was the front display window. Not as flashy or trendy as the other windows attempted to be, it was simply laid out with several suitcases and three racks of purses lining the back. There were also some school bags and backpacks, and it was one of these backpacks that drew her over to the window. Sitting awkwardly out of place among the shiny leather suitcases and purses and the brand-new vinyl bags, was an old khaki-green backpack. Dirty and worn, it stood out despite being tucked away in the corner of the display window. It looked faded and blotchy, like it was left out in the sun and had become bleached. Elisha made out a patch peeking around the side of the pack—a hunters and anglers association patch. Elisha tilted her head to the side. The pack was familiar.

Elisha heard a quick curse from behind her, causing her to turn her head. A short distance away, a woman dropped a box onto the ground. Now the woman, dressed neatly in a dress suit, was stooped awkwardly with her purse falling down to her wrist. Her legs gaped and cocked in a less than graceful pose as she attempted to pick the box up without losing control of the collection of other shopping bags she had looped over her arm. Behind the woman, Elisha saw a man running up behind her to assist.

"I didn't think you were getting that much," he called over to her. The woman, both frustrated and relieved to see her mate, stood back up, leaving the box on the ground.

"I didn't think I was going to either. I thought you would meet me at the store."

The man apologized humbly as he retrieved the box, and Elisha turned back to look in the display window, pretending to study the items again, but still listening to the two.

"I waited for you, but felt stupid just standing at the register."

"Sorry," the man repeated.

Elisha smiled to herself thinking, *Boy, he's whipped.*

"Here, take these." The rustling of bags followed the sharp instruction.

"Do you want to take these to the car first, before we go pick up dinner, or—"

"You take them to the car, and I'll meet you at the grocery store. Don't leave me waiting this time."

"I won't."

"Where were you anyway?"

Why would you come back is a better question, Elisha thought to herself. She continued to look in the window, at the floor of the display, while she listened.

No reply came from the man. No answer. Elisha furrowed her brow, then subtly, trying to make it appear that she was still looking at the window, she turned her head back toward the couple. She turned her head, bit by bit, still trying to make it look like she was examining the purses. When she tried to steal a glimpse of the two, she still couldn't see them. So she turned some more and tried to glimpse them again. Again, with no results. She turned her head some more. Then subtlety dropped, and Elisha turned around completely.

The couple was not there.

Nobody was there.

Somehow, while focused on the two's conversation, the hum of the mall had died. The faint music, the constant talking, the crying children, the laughing teenagers, the couple—all were gone. Elisha looked about, realizing she was alone in the giant mall.

Elisha turned back to the store, looking now through the doorway. The man she saw standing behind the counter was gone too. His paper still sat beside the cash register, lying open, but the man was gone. Elisha stepped back, looking again to where the woman had dropped the box, but nothing was there.

Elisha dropped her bag of purchases and went over to the railed balcony that let her look down to the lower level of the mall. She peered over the edge slowly, hopeful that somebody would be down there, yet knowing that nobody would. She glanced over the railing, and found nobody to meet her gaze. Empty. She turned around and ran over to another store, one of the endless selection of dress shops, and saw nobody within. She looked in the next store, and the next. She realized how quiet the mall was—so silent that her ears felt swollen and popped. The sound of her breathing hissed in her ears.

"Hello?" she called out feebly. Her voice echoed in the cavernous corridor, reaching to the giant domed skylights, and bouncing back along the tall white walls. "Is anybody here?" She went back to the railing and looked down into the lower mall. "Hello?"

"Will you amuse me?" The question came from the other side of the pit showing the lower level. Elisha looked up and saw a large bald man standing still, looking at her.

The Lochkray looked about, surprised at himself for coming to this place. Lochkray do not cozen themselves and the question he called across the chasm to the female's mind was the reason he was there. To be amused. He assessed the setting, and was impressed—the sanok was getting better. Wide open spaces, little obstruction imagined, and clear route to the prey. A kill was likely.

"I'm sorry," Elisha started, "I was just..." Her speech slipped away.

I know that voice.

"Will you amuse me?" the Lochkray repeated. In her dream, the voice was at her side—and yet she knew it was the man talking. His lips did not move, and yet the familiar voice whispered in its relaxing deep tones right to her—*Just like it had...*

When?

"Who are you?" Elisha called across to the Lochkray.

"You are hunted," he hissed faintly. "Lastingness is wanting. You are little purpose, pardon diversion. So I wish to know...will you divert? Will you amuse?"

"I don't understand. Who are you?"

"I am of the Lochkray." He was at her side. He had not moved, he had not walked, but the ten meters between them vanished. Elisha took a step back, but it didn't make any difference.

"Lochkray," she whispered back. *That word*, she thought. *Where do you know that word from?*

"Understanding is not of your capability," the Lochkray went on. "For amusement will not be drawn by intentional action. Pitiably, last recourse for survival is I might observe something within you to find inadvertently beguiling. A question not for you to answer, but I to rule. So to my determination I ask: will you amuse? If I think no, event shall proceed without interruption. If yes, then conceivably I may respite the inevitable."

"Lochkray," Elisha repeated to herself, looking down at the tiled floor. "That's what Vance talked about..." A muddled realization struck and she looked back up at the Lochkray. "You kill people," she said, taking a step back. "You drink people's blood."

The Lochkray smiled imperceptibly. *Not drawn by intentional action*, he repeated to himself. "Blood, no," he said. He took a step away and turned to examine the setting about him. "Blood is feral. Empathy, cognizance, passion, edification, anima...Is of value. Is consumed. All separating daylight from bestial is taken. Drained. Maximized."

"I don't understand."

"You have not means to." The Lochkray turned back to Elisha. "Is of little significance." He tilted his head to one side and stared at her thoughtfully. Reaching down to her side, Elisha took a hold of the railing and squeezed it tight. A heavy silence sat between the two of them, as the Lochkray contemplated and Elisha became anxious. "I anticipate," the Lochkray eventually said, "I might take indulgence in watching you continue. I like you foremost."

Elisha reached down to the waist of her pants, and realized she had not zipped up her fly after peeing. She looked down, pulled the zipper up, and then scanned the trees about her. She blinked hard. *What was I just thinking?*

She looked down at her backpack and saw that the pouch where her hand sanitizer was kept was also still open. She fastened that up too and positioned the pack again. *No, that wasn't it*, she thought to herself. *What was it?* In the distance, she heard Tyance laughing, and she looked down the hill to where the group had disappeared. *Oh well*. She shrugged. *You'll remember later*. She made sure the pack was comfortable enough for the short trip, then scanned the ground, wondering where her shopping bag went to.

What shopping bag?

Elisha's heart gave a hard beat—not at the thought of a nonexistent shopping bag, but at the answer. *The one with a pair of pants and two tank tops.* She continued to scan the ground, unsure why she thought she should have these items. She almost stumbled over her own feet as she moved quickly toward the sound of her companions.

* * * *

The Lochkray watched Elisha stumble her way back toward the rest. *Most frivolous*, the Lochkray said to himself, both critical of allowing her to wake up, and glad that he had done it, if only to watch her lurch and blunder her way out of the dream and down the hill to the other daylights. Perched in the branches of a tree, he waited until the last snapping of brush underfoot was heard, then turned to descend.

The drooling teeth of the sanok sat perfectly at his eye level. For the first time in his long existence, the Lochkray knew what it meant to be startled. The sanok, in its full heinous physical form, came up behind, completely in silence, completely without his knowing. Its mouth opened wide, a disturbing smell coming from within. The Lochkray steadied himself on the trunk of the tree, staring at the monster.

One of its huge claw-like hands snapped a hold of the trunk of the tree where the Lochkray stood, the other taking hold of a branch above the Lochkray's head, and the sanok drew its head in closer. It closed its gaping mouth and brought its nose up to him, and nudged him. The Lochkray stood silent, watching the nostril slits expand and contract with heavy whiffs and blows. A low growl came from above as the hanging creature fumbled through its simple mind, attempting to figure out the next course of action.

Instinct told the sanok it could approach this male, this other, and instinct also said it should not consume him—not It *could* not...just It *should* not. It opened its mouth again, its teeth exposed, as if ready to bite. The jaws hovered for a moment, then were covered by black mouth again. The sanok pulled backward, and drew itself back by its huge tails into another tree. It then coiled down to the ground, and disappeared into the thick brush.

The Lochkray remained still for a while after the sanok went. He listened to the faint sounds of it moving through the woods, until he could tell it had departed physical form. He was unharmed—even the sharp emotion of first sight of the sanok was already a memory—but the message was clear. Games and amusement were over. There were to be no more interruptions.

The sanok had bared its teeth for a reason. It had, in its simple way, communicated. The Lochkray descended from his tree and smoothly made his way to the edge of the clearing where the others made their camp.

Chapter Twenty-One

Allen stared at Elisha, slightly confused. That morning, after Tyance's suggestion for a side-trip to Sudbury, Elisha was unusually friendly. He found himself trying to act somewhere between responsive and composed. He had kept repeating the word "aloof" in his head, but it didn't seem to help. *Play it cool*, he kept saying to himself. *Don't be overly excited. She'll hate that. Make sure she knows you want to spend time with her but not that you're desperate. Be aloof. Be aloof.*

At first it worked. Elisha was really interested in the trip. Now something was different. Ever since she rejoined the group for lunch, she acted strange again. Allen was sure this strangeness was caused by something about their trip. He attempted to bring the topic up but when she seemed less than focused on the idea, he tried to act like he didn't care if they went either.

He decided to give up. He looked back down at the tinfoil package that used to hold his meal and picked it up. He folded the pack into a tight little tube and shoved it deep into his backpack. In there, a good little collection of garbage collected from the other meals he had enjoyed. He half-wanted to just dump the garbage on the ground, but ultimately he was quite proud of the way his group kept all of their garbage in hand, for proper disposal upon return to civilization.

The clearing where they were was a perfect picnic spot—a wide open field nestled at the bottom of the wooded hill they just descended. Tyance had kept saying they were really close to where Doctor Hadden was going to be, and that was generally enough to keep Allen's mind off of Elisha's sudden change in attitude.

Tyance had also noticed Elisha's mood shift. She had become concerned, as Elisha periodically stared at the ground for extended periods, almost appearing to mutter to herself. Tyance even thought she heard Elisha say the word, "...amuse..." quietly. Normally, Tyance would have decided to be blunt and ask outright what was the matter. Something was wrong with the way Elisha behaved—wrong and something *familiar*.

"Everything okay?" Tyance asked after their meals were done. Allen was over by Madoc, talking to him about drainage and tree growth again.

"Hmm?" Elisha looked up from her feet.

"Everything okay?"

"I'm sorry." Elisha smiled. "I'm just a little tired."

"Look, if you don't want to go with Allen, just tell me. I got you into it, I can come up with something to get you out. It's no trouble. I just thought that maybe you two would want—"

"No, no," Elisha interrupted, "that's not it. I just…" She looked at Tyance silently. "Remember when Vance was asking you about your daydream?"

"Vance?"

"After you fell off of the cliff. Do you remember? You said you were daydreaming, and Vance asked you about your dream."

"Fuck, yeah." Tyance nodded. "That's when he started going nutty. Said I got hypnotized."

"Yeah." Elisha looked down at the ground again. "I mean, I don't want to sound stupid, but…I was just daydreaming. But not like…It was like when you're asleep. It seemed real…" She looked back up. "Was that what your daydream was like? Did it seem real?"

"I don't remember," Tyance replied. "I walked through the forest with you guys…and I was thinking about…I can't remember."

"Me neither." Elisha gave a laugh with no exuberance in it. "I know I was dreaming. I can remember holding a bag and putting it down. I even remember there were clothes in the bag. I remember being asked if I was amusing. I remember…"

"All hate in here," Tyance said in a whisper.

"What?"

"Something I was thinking about," she answered. "Just before I tripped over the cliff. Something that was said to me…" Tyance shook her head. "It's weird. I don't remember. I know what you mean; I felt like I was out of it."

"Doesn't that seem strange to you? I mean, have you ever felt like that before?"

"No."

"I'm not trying to sound crazy. I just think something may be wrong."

"You don't sound crazy," Tyance said, almost to herself. "I know what you mean. There's something…" Tyance trailed off, closing her eyes, trying to remember.

"Where's Allen?" Elisha blurted out, coming to her feet. She was looking over at Madoc who was now alone, kneeling beside his backpack, tying it up.

"He went to take a piss," Madoc said, nodding with his head toward the wall of trees.

"I think we should stay together," Elisha said.

Madoc looked over at her, his eyebrows frowning downward sharply. "I'm pretty sure he can manage on his own."

"No, that's not what I mean." Elisha went over to the edge of the woods and called out Allen's name. When he didn't respond, she left the edge of the clearing and went into the forest.

"Wow," Madoc snorted, "I've never seen a girl want to watch a guy take a leak so bad."

Tyance looked back up from the ground and went over to Madoc. "Rob, you know how I said that we should find the professor within a few hours?"

"Yeah."

"I want to start heading back after that."

"That's the idea," Madoc laughed, returning his attention to securing his backpack.

"No," Tyance said sharply. "I mean, if we don't find him in three hours, I want to start heading back to the cabin. Immediately. As soon as three hours are up, we turn around and go. We keep walking until we run out of light, regardless of the weather."

"Jesus," Madoc said, shaking his head. "What's gotten into you?"

"Fuck, I'm serious, Rob. I don't know what it is, but I'm getting a bad feeling about this trip again. Three hours."

"You're the one who wanted to follow the map on the stone wall."

"I don't care. If I didn't think Allen would freak, I'd insist we go right now."

"Fine. You know, if it was left up to me, we'd already be heading back—"

"Don't start blaming."

"Now," he continued, "you want to leave? One minute you're happy to go deeper in, the next you want to get serious about leaving." He bent back over and reached into his pack, bringing out a package of cigarettes. "Fine," he said, removing one of the sticks and putting it in his mouth. "Don't start, Tyance, I swear, don't start," he mumbled through the cigarette as he lit it. "I get to have a smoke, and you get to change the itinerary however the mood hits you. When the other two get back, we'll get going." He looked up and scanned the tree line. "Where *did* he go?"

* * * *

Allen lowered himself into the pool's cool water, easing himself in by bracing his arms on the tiled side. The water was a bit chilly, but he knew he would get used to it quickly. The strong smell of chlorine wafted up to his nostrils and caused his eyes to burn. That didn't matter though, for it wasn't often he could have the whole university swimming pool to himself.

Although it was housed in the school's recreation center, the pool was shared with the rest of the town, and it was usually filled with people. Even during public swim time, the facility had classes of children on top of the large numbers of people there for exercise and relaxation. Allen heard If you got in the pool in the morning, before eight o'clock, you would often find it quiet. This was even better than quiet—this was empty. He had the facility to himself. As he dropped into the water up to his neck, he felt calm.

He grabbed onto the side of the pool and scanned the giant room, looking up at the high ceiling. This gave him the idea that, seeing as there were no lineups of kids or teenagers showing off, he should take the opportunity to take a few jumps off of the high board. He had been on his high school swim team, and they often goofed off on the high dive after practice. That was years before. Since coming to university, the few occasions he found for swimming did not allow him juvenile entertainment. Today though, just a few laps for exercise, then fun.

A few meters below the surface of the imaginary water the sanok took form. It watched Allen leave the group, and now it watched him break his way across the water. His arm cut through the undulating surface in a torrent of bubbles and muted splashes, pushing his body forward. Behind him, a trail of white and waves was left. The sanok took form—its black eyes, its head, its arms and body, its endlessly long tails. It took shape, then moved through the new medium. In the dream, under water was the safest approach.

With a gyration of its tails, it slid through the water beneath Allen without notice. The prey moved swiftly for a human but not as swiftly as the sanok. It was able to move through water even quicker than on land. As each tail propelled it forward, its arms reached out to guide itself along the bottom of the pool. This setting was perfect for the sanok. That other, the one who held the prey in their dreams, or pulled them out at its whim, was nowhere in this reverie. Within the water, the approach could be silent and invisible.

Allen reached the other end of the pool and turned around, pushing off with his legs, propelling himself through the water at a quickened pace. Below, the sanok changed direction, playfully enjoying this hunt. Allen drew a breath with each reach of his right arm, pulling himself along, oblivious to the stalker beneath. His feet paddled behind, kicking faster, in a classic front crawl. The sanok fell back behind the prey, just behind, and made its way toward the surface of the water. It came up closer to Allen, drawing itself into the froth behind the swimmer. Its nose silently broke through the surface and breathed in the imaginary air little more than a meter away from the kicking feet.

"Allen!" a female voice echoed in the giant chamber. The sanok went back down beneath the surface of the water, behind a tree in the woods.

Allen stopped swimming, making his feet come to rest on the bottom of the pool. For a split second, Allen found himself wondering why he could stand upright, so far from the shallow end. He turned around and saw Elisha coming toward him through the trees.

"Allen," she screamed out, from fifty meters away. "Behind you!"

Still not quite sure what was happening, Allen turned around, half in a daze, to barely catch the explosion of brush as an animal, obviously huge, made a sudden break away from him. This sudden flurry snapped Allen back into reality, and he took a step backward, tumbling over his own feet. With a sharp thud to his backside, Allen landed hard. He scrambled away from the movement in front of him, a clear memory of the attacking moose foremost in his mind.

"What the hell was that?" he yelled as Elisha came running to his side "Was it another moose? Don't tell me it was another moose!"

"Where were you?" Elisha said, out of breath and kneeling down beside him. She scanned the still moving flora in front of them. "Do you remember? Where were you?"

"I was right here," Allen said, confused.

"Before that." She tried not to yell. "Think! Where were you right before that?"

"I was right here," he said, equally as loudly. "I was right here. I was...swim..."

"Yes?"

"...Swimming...What?" Allen shook his head, becoming very quiet. "I was daydreaming I was swimming. That's odd. It was..."

"Like it was really happening?"

Allen looked hard at Elisha, her face less than a meter from his. She had a look of panic, with more sweat on her brow than there was on his. With his mouth agape, he let his eyes go from her face, to the brush, and back to her again.

"Like it was really happening," Allen finally repeated. He shook his head hard. "Did you see what the animal was? Was it a moose? A bear?"

"I have no idea," Elisha said, getting to her feet, dragging Allen up with her. "I couldn't make it out, but it was right behind you. It wasn't a moose, I know that. If you hadn't been hallucinating, you would have heard it."

"Hallucinating?"

"I can't explain it, but I had it happen to me too, when I was alone. It was like I was actually away from myself. I don't remember the details...it's just weird."

"Just because I got a little distracted doesn't mean I was hallucinating."

"No, Allen. You were more than a little distracted. Remember when Tyance fell over the cliff? She said that she was daydreaming too. Then I was daydreaming. Then I see you standing off on your own—in a daze—and there was some animal coming up behind you."

"I don't get it."

"Like Vance said," she hissed at him, frustrated. "He talked about Lochkray distracting people so they can attack them."

"I thought they look like a bald man dressed in a black coat. You said it was an animal."

"Maybe they have pets," she almost yelled. "It doesn't matter. I want to go back now. Now! Forget Doctor Hadden. If he did go to the other site, I don't care. The university can wait until he comes out on his own. I want to go, Allen. Now!"

"What about Madoc and Tyance?"

"I don't think they'll argue." Elisha started pulling Allen back toward the camp. He wanted to mention he still had to urinate but thought it had better wait. While still bewildered, the memory of his dream was gone. Elisha guided Allen through the trees and down the hill toward the camp. Despite the suddenly strange behavior from Elisha, Allen did take a brief moment of pleasure in having his hand held in hers.

The sanok followed after them from a safe distance, choosing to remain in corporeal form. It slithered and crawled its way through the woods, violently grabbing onto the trunks of trees to pull itself forward. It hissed in aggravation, spitting out onto the ground. It continued toward the two, then pulled back in the other direction, then again started to follow. A deep, gnarling noise resonated in its chest as it gnashed at the air.

Then it stopped.

Then it decided.

* * * *

"We have to go," Elisha called to Madoc, breaking through the trees. "We have to go right now. Forget John Hadden. If he wants to come out to this fucking place, he can find his own fucking way home."

"Well, that saved three hours," Madoc said, drawing on the cigarette at his lips. He was seated on his backpack, enjoying being able to indulge in his filthy habit in public. Whatever the excuse, he would happily take advantage of it to get a shot of nicotine.

"I didn't know you smoked," said Allen.

"I didn't know she said the word 'fuck'."

"I'm serious," Elisha said.

"What is it today?" Madoc shook his head. "Fine. Let's go now—I don't care. Like I said, I wanted to head back from the river, it was you guys that wanted to keep going. So let's go." He took another drag on the cigarette. "You have to tell me," he said with the gray cloud emerging out his lips. "What is with you all today? What's gotten into you?"

"There's something out here with us," Elisha said in the most matter-of-fact voice she could muster. "I don't care if you believe in Vance's story or not; there is something out here with us. I saw it going after Allen."

"It's true, she did," Allen confirmed.

"What?" Madoc continued to shake his head. "One of Vance's Low-kers?"

"Lochkray."

"No!" Elisha shouted. "I don't think so. Something else. I couldn't make it out, but it was an animal, and it was big. It caused Allen to daydream. Like what Tyance said to us before she fell yesterday. She said she was in a daydream."

"There was an animal behind me," Allen offered. "I didn't see it but I heard it running away from me."

"How do animals make you daydream?"

"Elisha said maybe it was the Lochkray who makes you dream, and this animal eats you," Allen tried to explain.

"That's not what I said."

"You said that's what Vance said."

"Damn it!" Elisha screamed out. "It doesn't matter what I said, or what you said or what Vance said, or how demented you think I am. I don't care. Things are insane. First there were those bears, then that freaked-out moose, then Vance and his Lochkray stories, then Tyance pretty much jumps off a cliff, Vance says he sees a Lochkray, gives you his gun, and runs off into the woods, and I see Allen almost attacked. We're starting to hallucinate. I mean, come on. Hasn't anything weird happened to you since we've been out here?"

"No," Madoc said, quietly and seriously, thinking about the question.

"Look, the university is going to pay you—"

"*Don't dream*," Madoc recited, interrupting Elisha. She stopped talking, suddenly frozen by the distant words. Madoc stared down at the ground, not saying anything else. The other two took pause.

"What?" Allen felt dread sweep over him with the cold way Madoc had spoken.

"Willie Cheechoo," Madoc said absently. "The guy who built the cabin we stayed at."

"The guy who was killed by a bear?"

"After he was attacked," Madoc's now raspy voice said, "he crawled back to his cabin." Madoc looked at Elisha. "He wrote the words *'Don't dream'* on the wall of his cabin in his own blood." Madoc drew on his cigarette, deeply, the red and orange nearly burning all the way back to the filter.

"Don't dream?" Elisha repeated. "Oh, Christ."

"Maybe we should go," Allen said weakly.

"Fine, we'll get our stuff and—" Elisha stopped. "Where's Tyance?"

Madoc got off the backpack and looked around the field. "She was here just a second ago."

* * * *

Tyance was lost. She wandered through downtown streets, watching the cars from the sidewalk drive past, splashing old puddles over the curb. It was late now, very late, she could tell. She had looked at her wrist and found no watch, but even a small-town girl like Tyance knew that cities had a different feel once the hours got deep into the night. Anonymity surrounded each person walking the streets with her, each person unique, each person a stranger.

Occasionally they appeared out of the darkness, abruptly illuminated by the streetlamps, then fade into the black of night, their clomping feet fading away into silence until replaced by another passerby. Tyance advanced along the streets, watching the traffic and the people. She looked at the street signs but none of them were familiar. It was difficult to recall what brought her here to this place at this time of night. Tyance went along the streets, cautiously watching the traffic and the people.

All of the shops along the streets were long closed, and their blackened insides were as impossible to see as the interiors of the cars that went by. Tyance stopped and looked into the shops, only to be greeted by blackness.

A restaurant up ahead caught her attention. Green canvas awnings stuck out over the sidewalk, sheltering long windows and flower boxes that held graying dirt and shriveled flowers. A railing encircled a small patio area where empty chairs leaned against vacant tables.

As Tyance approached, she noticed that the patio area was not completely empty. Within the little courtyard, between the flower boxes, there stood a little girl. No more than eight years old, the small girl leaned against the wall, her head tilted down, her eyes looking at her feet. Tyance took a moment to check behind her and across the street to see if anybody else was around. The street was empty and she was alone except for this girl.

"Hello," Tyance said in her kindest voice as she got closer. The little girl looked up from her feet. She gave Tyance a tiny smile with thin pink lips that stood out from her pale skin. Tyance walked up to the railing, trying to look as nonthreatening as possible. She could remember being told to be wary of strangers, and knew that this little one had probably been told the same. She also knew what it was like to be lost. She knew how scary it could be, and while she was capable to wander this strange city's streets alone, one so small would not be.

"Are you lost?"

The little girl stared forward at her silently, her adorably pathetic eyes looking out from beneath her thin dark hair. *Like a doll,* Tyance thought. *Even dressed like a doll.*

"Is your daddy here?" Tyance asked.

The little girl shook her head slowly. Her little smile never left her face for a second.

"Are your brothers here?" Tyance asked.

Again the little girl shook her head slowly. She stopped and tilted her head. Her tiny smile widened ever so slightly.

"Is your mommy here?" Tyance asked.

The girl just smiled.

"Where's your mommy?"

The little girl's hand rose up, her diminutive index finger extended outward, indicating somewhere behind Tyance. She stood up straight, and turned to follow the point. Across the shiny black street, opposite the little awning-decorated restaurant, there was another shop, its doorway as black as the other stores along the late night street. This store had no sign above it—just the skeletal remains of where a sign used to hang. The big display windows were covered in newspapers from the inside. Corners came away from where they were attached, and the papers bent back in places, revealing the darkness within the shop.

"Your mommy is in there?" Tyance asked, looking back at the girl.

The little girl smiled at Tyance. Then nodded, slowly.

"Okay honey, just stay here," Tyance said.

She turned around and looked up and down the street to make sure it was safe to cross. There were no cars in sight. Tyance stepped off the curb onto the wet asphalt roadway. She stepped over the streetcar rails running as endless trenches in the road. She made it to the other side, and went up to the store. Through the window she could tell the newspapers hung there were very old—they were dried and discolored from the sun pounding on them during the day.

She walked up to the window, to a place where the newspaper fell away, the sticky remains of the tape left in tiny rectangles on the blank spot, collecting dust. Tyance placed her hands on the window, cupped them, and brought her face up to the glass.

Peering into the shop she could only make out darkness. From what she could tell, the store was empty. Completely empty. The little light intruding in from the streetlamps showed a floor so covered in dust it appeared white. Tyance was about to call over to the little girl when she saw movement at the back of the darkness. It was unclear, though definitely a person, moving slowly along the back wall of the store.

Tyance moved over to the glass door of the closed shop. Again she brought her cupped hands to the glass to peer in, and again she made out the faintest whispers of motion near the back.

"Hello," she called out, knocking on the glass. "Is this your little girl out here?" The movement in the darkness stopped and the black became still. She adjusted her gaze, attempting to locate where the person had halted but could not.

"Hello?" she repeated.

For a moment there was nothing, then the subtle sense of movement, aimless and undefined. Tyance knew somebody was in there, yet they continued to stay away from the glass. She pulled back from the door and looked back across the street. There, the little girl was no longer leaning against the wall. She made her way to the edge of the curb, still across the street, where she stood with her hands at her side. "Are you sure your mother is in here?" Tyance yelled across.

The little girl stood perfectly still, her tiny smile gone from her face. Bending at the elbow she raised her hand, a finger pointing beyond Tyance. Arching her brow in bewilderment, Tyance decided to try again. She turned back to the door. Then she brought her fists up to her eyes and screamed.

The empty eye sockets of the old woman's face burned out at her, the blackened blood staining her gray cheeks like tears. Pressed up against the glass door, her hands wanted to grasp at Tyance.

"All hate in here," the woman howled pathetically, pleadingly. Tyance, her eyes still closed, stepped backward, away from the horrible face. Her back slammed into something hard behind her. Forcing herself to depart from the terrifying paralysis that threatened to take her over, she spun around to face the object behind her, forcing her eyes wide to see what it was.

It was a tree.

Tyance turned around again, and again, having difficulty focusing, seeing trees upon trees all about. Forest. Bush. All around. She brought her hands to her chest and pushed on herself hard, trying to stop her heart from pounding its way out. Again she closed her eyes, her breath going in and out of her lungs in heavy draws. She reached out and put her hand onto a trunk, bending nearly completely over as she tried to stop her body's frenzy.

Before she could calm herself down, she realized that there was something else. A bolt of instinct shot through her with a rush of adrenaline, and she thought, *Something's wrong.* She scanned the woods again, this time slowly. That was when she saw it. Twenty meters away, visible through the cracks in the endless weald.

An animal. An animal unlike any other. Its angular head shook back and forth violently, nearly smacking tree trunks on either side.

The sanok stopped its convulsions, though it wanted to continue shaking the sting of the prey's nightmare out of its mind. Its own sharper instinct told it had been seen. That was where instinct swayed, and frustration swelled. Despite instinct telling it to go to flight, to abate, to vanish, frustration was strong. Frustration wanted to confront. To hunt. To charge and attack. To feed. To kill.

Tyance looked at the monstrosity before her, its own black eyes obviously seeing her. Its long snake-like body slowly curled up underneath its torso, while its upper body and arms poised themselves aggressively. The sanok rose up like a cobra, its arms like its hood, arched downward and flexed, the sinewy muscles pressed up against its skin so harshly it looked like it would burst. Its mouth was shut tight, a thin black line against its dark skin. Its angular head tilted to one side, while a guttural rumble built up in the creature's throat.

Tyance lifted one foot, ever so subtly, the seal of ground to sole barely breaking. The sanok caught the slight twitch of her movement, and rose up. Its mouth opened and closed quickly in a sudden snap. Tyance relaxed her foot, allowed her weight back onto it.

Wait, she said to herself, still watching the ghastly animal sizing her up. *Don't panic. Whatever it is, don't panic.*

The two stood, staring at each other. The sanok's entire body undulated, away and toward the female at the same time. It made itself appear as large as possible, swelling out. The prey stayed still, not making a move, not making the hunter's decision for it. The dream was over, but the prey could still be within its grasp. Its inherent cautiousness was present, wanting the hunt to close. Now that the sting of the female's dream had abated, all that remained was frustration and anger.

The sound was distant when Madoc called Tyance's name, much more distant than she would have liked. A foreign sound to the sanok, it caused the creature to turn impulsively toward the man's voice. Their eyes unlocked, Tyance took her chance and made the sanok's decision for it. Had she waited, had she held still, the beast would have retreated at the knowledge that others were looking for her. Tyance darted, a quick and agile move laterally to the sanok's gaze, down the steep hill, and that set the sanok off. Heedless of the others, the frustration within the animal burst out wildly as it uncoiled and went into the charge.

The speed of her hunter was stunning to Tyance, even over the noise of her own running. The animal, twenty meters away before it saw her move and decided to take chase, was instantly behind her, the crashing of brush closing in on her within seconds of her move. Not allowing the surprising speed of the hunter to daunt her, she identified a steeper incline to the hill ahead and acted.

Half-jumping, half-falling, she slid along the hill toward the incline, just as the sanok sounded atop her. The slide prevented the animal from grasping her, as its horrid claws grasped at empty air where her head had been. Tyance went over the incline, pushing her feet downward, and retook her firm stride. The sanok, too focused on catching its prey, fumbled over the edge and lost its acceleration. A claw took a firm hold on a trunk, the animal twisted its body, and resumed the pursuit.

"Get the gun, Rob!" Tyance's voice carried into the clearing. "Get the gun! It's after me. For Christ's sake..."

"What the hell?" Madoc muttered, cocking his head to the side. He identified where the sound came from, and turned in that direction.

"What did she say?" Allen asked, scanning the wall of forest that rose up the hill ahead of him.

"Get the gun," Madoc snapped back, his hand already removing the rifle from his shoulder. Allen looked over, as Madoc trotted toward the forest's edge. The sound of the sanok could be heard bursting through branches and trees with Tyance's screams carrying over it.

"It's after me," she shrieked. "Get the gun. Fuck, it's after me!"

"What's going on?" Elisha came up to Allen's side.

"I don't... What the hell is up there? What if it's that animal..."

"Tyance," Madoc yelled into the trees, then looked over at Allen. "Get the gun," he repeated, nodding harshly at the weapon on the ground.

Allen looked down at Madoc's backpack. Opposite from the side where he had carried the Ruger was Doctor Hadden's .22 rifle. Allen grabbed it and ran over to Madoc. He scanned the side of the weapon, words like "slide," "safety," "clip," "firing pin," "magazine," and just about every other term he ever heard in movies running through his head. "I don't know how to shoot."

"What the hell is going on?"

Madoc ignored Allen's comment, but suddenly added, "It's chambered. Just pull the trigger. Wait until Tyance is past us and start pulling the trigger."

Elisha looked over at Tyance's bag where Vance's shotgun was secured, but thought better of taking it. Madoc went to take a step forward to enter the bush, but stopped. Up the hill, he saw the brush shaking and moving as something large forced its way through at great speed, and he realized it would soon be on top of them. He shouldered the stalk of the rifle and brought the sight into his view. Allen mimicked this as his own eyes darted back and forth between the focused Madoc and the sounds closing in.

The sanok took another rapid lunge at Tyance, but like a deer she darted to the side, finding a shield against the pounce behind a tree. The tactic worked, and the beast slammed into the trunk, splintering it over. Still wanting to maintain its momentum, it followed through with the movement, and took off perpendicular from Tyance for a moment, then matched her advance. Excited now, more than frustrated, the sanok was not capable of stopping the chase. With the pursuit now established, it did not have the faculty to bring it to any end other than an absolute close.

With the slightest list of her head, Tyance saw the animal speeding alongside her, the view interrupted by the trees, like frames slipping through an old projector. The whisk of branches stung at her face as she blasted through the brush, gravity now pulling her down the hill as hard as her own physical force. She focused ahead as the animal moved in again, closing the distance once more.

"Run!" Madoc yelled from below, his finger tight against the trigger.

The sanok removed the gap between it and the prey, coming down at her hard. Again, when it was within striking distance, the sanok forced out an extra push and lunged at her. This time Tyance, anticipated the surge, ducked into the beast and forced herself to move toward its outstretched claws. She moved in, her head going low, and rolled underneath the attack. Ahead she saw the light breaking through the forest from the clearing. She heard Madoc's panicked yell, and she knew she was capable of clearing the distance.

The sanok bounded past Tyance again, its hold passing over her as she ducked. It felt her hair wisp under its arms, and felt the scraps of debris pushed up from her feet against its tail. The missed opportunity only served to thrill the sanok more, as it again sped away from the missed attack only to bring itself back in line with the prey, and back toward it, this time taking a position behind.

"What the hell is that?" Elisha hissed, the sight of the giant pursuer closing in on Tyance faintly visible through the brush.

"Oh, Christ," Madoc said, dropping his eye from his sight for only a second. Then he retook his aim, waiting for the moment that Tyance was safely out of his line of fire. Allen dropped his barrel down, his mouth agape at the sight before him.

Tyance made out her party now, saw the three of them standing at the edge of the woods. She knew Madoc had his gun, believed it more than was able to see it. Her bursting lungs and swelling terror momentarily eased at the sight of her friends. Her feet pounded against the ground, and she forced herself forward, trying to break through the brush as fast as she could.

Elisha watched in horror, screaming, as little more than the top of Tyance's head was able to make it through the wall of forest. It came out, breaking into the clearing only by a margin, her hands high up in the air. With more suddenness than they'd emerged, they were pulled back again, her body drawn back into the woods. Like a rag doll, she was jerked into the branches again, her legs kicking into the clearing for the briefest of moments, before being sucked into the tree line.

Tyance felt her body snap back, and then darkness enveloped her head. For a flash, she thought she caught a glimpse of light as the animal repositioned its bite, but she wasn't even sure she saw it. She wasn't even sure she felt any pain, except for her aching legs and burning lungs, which now had trouble drawing anything in. The darkness was there. That and a voice. A voice spoke in her ears; "All hate in here."

The sanok moved away from where it sensed the others were, its prey hanging out of its mouth limply. It moved with its incredible speed back up the hill, back into the thick of the woods.

Madoc stood still, his barrel still raised, but his eye looking over it.

"What the...what...was that?" Allen asked faintly with a slackened jaw.

Madoc dropped the weapon down to the ground, staring silently at the trees before him, listening to the creature retreat. He heard Elisha, off to his side, crying. He took a step backward, and turned toward the rest of the clearing. "Tyance," he said so softly that the other two did not hear it. "No. That's not real."

"What was that?" Allen repeated.

"No," Madoc said, this time louder. "It's not real."

Elisha pulled her face out of her hands. She looked at Madoc as he stared blankly at the graying sky. He turned back toward the woods, then back to the clearing.

"No," he said.

"We have to go," Elisha managed to get out with a rasp.

"No," a determined reply came.

"Madoc...we have to go."

Madoc turned burning eyes to Elisha. "Take the GPS," he snapped. "Just turn it on to program number one. Follow the direction arrow. It will take you back to the cabin. Tyance..." He stopped for a fleeting moment. "Just follow the arrow. When you get there, use the satellite phone and call for the plane." Madoc ran over to the rifle he had dropped on the ground and picked it back up.

"We can't—" Elisha started.

"Follow the arrow," Madoc just short of yelled. "Take the shotgun and the rifle. Follow the GPS. Walk as far as you can. Don't stop. Go. Now!" Allen attempted to put up his arms to try and calm Madoc down, but he just forced past him, nearly knocking him over, and disappeared into the brush.

Elisha and Allen stood there, silently, listening to Madoc's violent push into the intertwining branches.

* * * *

The sanok dragged its prey, proudly, back to the top of the hill, its corporeal lungs drawing in and releasing air rapidly. Tyance fell to the ground, her now limp body landing with a dull *whomp*. She landed facedown, her body oddly askew with arms twisted around, under, and over her. Her head was cocked abnormally on a now malleable neck. The sanok slithered its way around her, as proud as it could ably be within its animal mind. It tilted its enormous cranium from side to side, studying the capture. Three it had caught, three bipeds this past season more in total than in so many years. This one was the best—this one gave the sanok a feeling, just short of an emotion, better than any other prey. It almost didn't want to feast on the capture.

The animal tilted its body forward, catching itself on its front claws, and took the prey into its mouth again, and gave its neck a mighty flick. Tyance's body flipped over, limbs and head wobbling oddly as the weight of the corpse shifted around. Again her dead body landed with a dull sound, and again the sanck circled the capture.

It leaned its weight forward again, looking down at the empty face of the prey as her head rolled softly to a halt. Already the face began to go gray in the jaundiced waxy look of death. Her eyes were blank—and yet a careful examination by another person could have revealed the emotion that was hiding beneath the death mask: surprise. Not a truly shocked look on the stagnant countenance, but a faint remainder of the last sensation her mind had registered before the snap of her neck.

The sanok stuck its long purple tongue past its needle teeth and stroked the prey across the face. Now the excitement of the chase, the high, was fading into memory—but what a chase this prey gave. So frustrated it had been, so agitated by the prey's fractured psyche. When the chase started, it all worth the effort. So fast it was for a biped. It anticipated lunges, dodged attacks.

The sanok bent its head forward to the ground, its nostrils grazing just above the earth. It nudged Tyance with its snout, then brought its head back up again to observe.

Then it repeated this action, this time tapping Tyance's corpse twice, more forcefully than before. Still, Tyance's body lay still, her blank eyes looking up into the canopy of leaves and branches. One last attempt by the sanok to regain its playmate, and then it decided it had nothing left to do but feed.

Crack!

No pain was felt, but the sudden snap of sound caused the sanok to dart away from its prize. It covered twenty-five meters in the blink of an eye, and stopped, turning back to look in the direction where the sound came.

Crack! Crack!

"Damn you!" Madoc screamed over the sound of his rifle. It was all he could manage to get through his mouth. Looking at the animal, that thing, leaning over his friend and lover's body caused a shrill cry in his heart that wanted to explode from his mouth. His body had wanted to freeze, to come to a complete standstill and await any kind of reasoning to explain what he saw. He knew he couldn't stop, knew he couldn't wait. Somehow, he managed to turn the horror into hate. He couldn't freeze, he couldn't wait, but he could take the disbelief and shock and make it hate.

"Damn you!" he repeated at the thing. No matter how hard he stared, he couldn't focus on the shapes. Like a snake, a giant snake, seven meters long—but with arms, and two tails...*no, three*...and a head like a shark...*no, a dragon*...a crown like a dragon, blood dripping down its teeth like...*a nightmare*. With Tyance's blood, dripping down its teeth. Tyance, all over its repulsive face. *Tyance...*

Madoc screamed his curse over the sound of the rifle "Damn you!"

Crack!

The animal bolted forward, the bark of a tree beside its head snapping under the blow of a bullet. It moved quickly away from Madoc, flashes of fire abruptly bursting from the rifle. The sanok quickly forgot about the fading excitement of its successful hunt, and realized something went wrong. Something went very wrong.

The possibility it was designed to avoid happened. It was injured. Irrelevant if it was from the very first shot, or from one that followed, the sanok knew it was hurt. A serious wound. The thrill of the venery made it ignore its overriding instinct to stay hidden, to stay in shadow and dream, to only hunt single prey when it was alone and vulnerable. There was no more clear a signal of its failure than the crush of pain and warmth of blood it felt on its side. It knew the hunt was over. A mortal wound. It could not go back to the intangible. It would not be able to focus and draw back now.

Crack!

Madoc burst through thatches of twigs, lowering his rifle at the creature ahead of him, his feet still moving, his vision blurred by the sting of salt. He was still swearing, quietly now, to himself, allowing for blind shots in the direction of the moving form ahead. He crashed across the uneven landscape, branches slicing tiny cuts across his reddened face.

Crack! Crack!

The burning hate of Madoc could be felt by the sanok. It felt the sorrow-filled stinging that emanated from his soul, even as it retreated from him. That emotion, that rancor, bound like a parasite to the sanok's own fractured feelings of regret and animosity. It bore into it, even as it darted away from the sound of attack.

Though wounded, the sanok was able to move away much faster than the other could take chase. Escape wasn't enough. Once sure it covered enough distance It was no longer an easy mark, it changed direction.

Crack!

Madoc came to halt, pivoting the rifle in the direction of his unnatural quarry. He dropped his left hand to the side pocket of his cargo pants, retrieving the other magazine there. He wasn't sure how many more shots were left in the clip, but he knew he would be ready when it ran out. Pulling the metal clip out, he brought his hand back to level the rifle, taking the time to brush the back of it across his cheek.

He retrained the rifle to a steady track across the forest, following the sound of the huge nightmare. The sound of movement was not getting farther away. With a clumsy grip he held the magazine and the front of the weapon. Still Madoc was sure he could get another shot in. He knew he hit it at least once. He saw the blood—black like tar—splatter against the trunk of a tree behind the animal on his first shot. He was sure he hit it at least once more. Surely twice.

The sights of the rifle followed the sound as it moved quickly through the trees, still not getting closer, still not going away. Occasionally the interlocking branches permitted an opening, an aperture for Madoc to glimpse the animal, a blur of unfocused movement when it broke past the natural gap.

Crack!

Unseen by Madoc, the sanok rolled at the sound of the shot, anticipating the bullet, lowering itself to the ground. It managed to get the biped to hold still, to create a stalemate. It could move around it, never advancing, never departing, and wait...wait...wait.

Crack! Crack!

Madoc was sure the animal had slowed at that last opportunity, had allowed him to take the shot. It actually paused for a moment, letting him see its dark, dead eyes staring at him. It stopped to look at him, to see him take aim, to watch him pull the trigger...*and miss*...and then start moving again, still circling. *I'll get you,* Madoc swore to himself. *Just keep moving around me, and I'll get you. Don't you go away. I'll get you. Don't you go. There you are! There you are!*

Crack!

Fifteen in the mag, one in the tube.

Crack!

Get ready.

Crack!

The sanok, having made several circles now, knew exactly when the thinning bush made it vulnerable, as well as where the best advances would be. The best attacks. Just when the moment was right, just when the hunter became prey, the injured would cause infliction.

Crack!

The rack on the rifle locked, failing to snap forward with the advance of another .223 round. The plastic ramp of the magazine sat exposed at the top of the weapon, empty. Without looking, Madoc felt the trigger hold down and knew the cycle had not completed. Still holding the second magazine in his hand, he pressed the rifle into his shoulder, putting the weapon in place as he let go of the trigger and went for the release ahead of the mag. He ripped the empty metal case out of the rifle, discarding it violently to the ground. Before it even stuck dirt, his hand went forward to the other rounds.

He could already tell the animal was coming closer. Coming closer from behind. His fingers stumbled slightly, positioning the second magazine, and pivoting his body to face the advancing hunter. At that sudden point, as the sanok pounced and Madoc reloaded, the odds were called upon to identify chance and deal out a fate.

Fifty-fifty.

Half and half.
Fifty percent chance.
One way or the other.

The magazine had a slight curve, to indicate to the shooter which way it was supposed to go into the rifle—curve facing forward. In a high stress situation it became impossible to identify the slight bend within a split second. Weakened fine motor skills, Madoc heard it called.

One way...

So, when Madoc grabbed the extra magazine, he had a fifty percent chance he would jam it in the right way, point the bullets forward, slide them into place, draw back on the rack, and send a shower of burning rounds into the advancing monster. A hail of projectiles accompanied by a percussion of bangs would pierce through the animal and bring it down. Its blood, black like night, would shower up behind and it would crash down to the ground. All fifteen would go in and out of it, ripping the animal to shreds, tearing it apart. It would fall dead. Revenge would be exacted...*or the other.*

Madoc didn't point the bullets the right way. He felt it as soon as he tried to put the magazine into place. It started to slide upward, but it was awkward. Now he felt the curve of the magazine, felt that he was trying to put a square peg into a round hole. His fingers squeezed hard on the metal clip and pulled it out, spinning it around to be reintroduced to the weapon.

The time it took for that was enough. Enough for the sanok to be upon Madoc. It stretched out its claws toward him and struck forward in a flash. Madoc, partly knowing that his chance to reload was gone, and partly out of reflex, abandoned the magazine and used the rifle to block the sanok.

He swung the butt of the rifle outward, toward the attack. He sidestepped, and pushed forward, catching the side of the animal with the rifle. The sanok rolled against the innocuous defense, abandoning its attack for a moment to readjust, but not retreat.

Ignoring the size of the animal that was before him, the impossibly horrid mien of it, Madoc did not try to run. Instead he went forward at it, his unloaded rifle firm in his grip, and brought the butt of the weapon hard against its skull. Surprised by this, the sanok reeled back on its tail like a rattler—a small recoil in shock. Madoc, still seething, advanced again, swinging out with the weapon, trying to strike at the sanok's head.

Madoc's eyes darted to the ground. He saw the magazine. The sanok struck forward with a snap, aiming to take hold of Madoc's head. Again Madoc lashed out with his rifle, smacking the gaping hole of the sanok's mouth, rattling across its pointed teeth.

Behind the animal, Madoc saw the way it moved constantly through its multi-forked tail. They reached back like tentacles and took hold of the tree trucks behind, steadying the creature, allowing it to take its stand. While the head and arms cautiously regarding him, the rest of it acted like a separate animal, one which fortified and strengthened. Even before a slash across his belly opened up from a blow from a mighty claw, Madoc realized the fight was not for him to win. His three attacks on the animal with the weapon were no true defense. The magazine—*that could have gone in one way or the other*—was only just out of reach—only centimeters away from his face after he was knocked to the ground.

Two swipes came at him from the giant arms. One opened him up and stole the Ruger out of his hands. The other sent him to the ground beside the clip of bullets.

The sanok placed one hand on Madoc's chest, pushing down on him with incredible weight. He turned his eyes away from the useless magazine, and looked up at the animal. With the remainder of all that was left in him, Madoc took a feeble swing at the sanok, striking the side of its head.

It didn't even recoil at this. It just continued its slow advance toward its prey. Like Tyance, the last light Madoc saw was glimpsed through the sanok's teeth, a moment before the bite and violent twist of his neck.

Sure Its assailant was dead, the sanok released its bite and recoiled. Exhaustion, unlike anything it ever felt, came over it, and it drew itself backward, away from the mangled body of Madoc.

This prey was not exciting like the last. The sanok did not wish to play with this one any longer. Punctures were drawn through it, three at least, wounds that tore into the animal and drained its strength. It knew it could no longer draw back into nothing. That was impossible. To fall into intangibility required focus, and that required an undiminished whole.

The weakened sanok cocked its body up with great effort, and tried to sense water. It was suddenly thirsty. It listened and it smelled. It identified a creek or tiny river a short distance away. It looked at the mess of red that was Madoc one more time. Then it slid into the woods to find the water so it could drink and not die thirsty.

Chapter Twenty-Two

Had they thought about it, they would have realized Tyance's program in the GPS wouldn't lead them back home.

Surely he's killed it, Allen thought after each distant bang. More shots rang through the air, snapping across the trees, until that scream. Far away, but clear enough to hear the horror and the pain that was in it. A scream echoed through the woods and turned Allen's spine to rubber.

"Get your bag and the guns," Elisha said after the long silence that followed, the two of them staring at the trees before them, the interlacing branches folding over each other as a wall, Tyance's blood still hanging on to the outermost limbs.

"What?" Allen squeaked out. Elisha went to Tyance's bag and knelt down beside it, pulling out the flattened freeze-dried packs of food and placing them into her own backpack. The rest of the assortment of camping items she discarded to the ground.

"Get the two guns ready," Elisha said, "and pick up your bag. I'm going to take enough food for the two of us to get back to the cabin. I just have to get the GPS."

"What about Madoc?" Allen replied in the faintest of voices. "We have to go help him."

"We'll follow the GPS," Elisha continued. "Remember what Madoc said—we just have to go to program number one and follow the arrow. The display screen shows an arrow, and Tyance programmed it to point the way back to the cabin..."

"Tyance...," Allen whispered.

"There's the satellite phone at the cabin. That big heavy briefcase. You use the lid of it like an antenna."

"What about Madoc?" Allen repeated.

Elisha looked up from the bag and stared back at Allen. Her mouth opened and closed a few times, but nothing came out. Allen didn't need an answer to his question, he knew it already. He knew it when he heard that awful shriek pierce the air, suspected it when Madoc had run off into the woods after that thing.

"No," Allen finally said gently to his own question. "Aww no, no, no...this can't be happening."

"Get the guns," Elisha said, returning to her search. "Get the guns. We'll follow the arrow on the GPS. Maybe we're just in its territory or something. Maybe if we start to go back, it'll leave us alone."

Having emptied out the entire contents of Tyance's bag without finding the GPS, she turned to the pockets on its side. It was located in the first one she checked. She opened up the cover and looked at the display screen on its front, sitting above a series of buttons. It looked like an oversized calculator.

Elisha pressed the power button, and the display sprung to life. A menu appeared, and on top of this was a tiny picture of a battery. Four digital bars were lined up inside the battery diagram, and to Elisha it looked like it could have held five. Encouraged by this, she experimented with the menu, and eventually managed to bring up "Program 1" on the screen. Somewhere up above, circling the Earth, satellites picked up on the tiny box, and told it where it was.

On the bottom left of the screen, the numbers one through twelve were piled up. In the top right, a small arrow beside the letter *N* showed true north. In the middle of the screen, a larger arrow appeared, pointing to the right of the screen. Elisha pivoted on her feet with the unit, and the arrow turned with it, until she faced the direction that allowed the arrow to point to the top of the unit.

"I've got it." She felt a wave of relief that passed quickly. "There's twelve landmarks Tyance programmed in here. The GPS will take us to them. They will take us back. We just follow the twelve waypoints back."

"I'm ready," Allen said. Elisha looked up at him, his pack already secured on his shoulders, with Vance's shotgun in one hand and Doctor Hadden's .22 rifle in the other. She picked up her own pack, the weight of the extra food unnoticeable. She secured the belt, then walked over to Allen, taking the shotgun from him.

"Do you know how to shoot?" Elisha asked.

"Madoc said it was already loaded, and all I had to do was pull the trigger."

"There should be half a dozen bullets in it, I think," Elisha said, trying hard to recall what her father had shown her about his guns. She gently pulled back on the rack of the shotgun and looked inside the chamber. She took it back far enough to see the top of the red tube inside.

Loaded, she thought to herself. *Just like Dad said you should never, ever, carry a gun.* Ignoring the lesson, she brought the slide forward again, the chambered round securely in place. *Squeeze the trigger, don't pull,* she remembered. *Tight into your shoulder. Don't anticipate the kick. Just squeeze the trigger. Once it goes off, bring the rack back, and chamber the next round.* "Ready," Elisha said, taking the shotgun into her left hand, her right pointing a finger forward. "We have to go this way. We'll go all day, until we can't walk any further. We'll try to find a place with shelter. We'll take turns, like last night. One of us will watch."

"Elisha?"

"One of us will watch, and the other will sleep. First thing in the morning, we'll start moving again. By then we should know if that thing is following us."

"Elisha?"

"We'll go all day…"

"Elisha, what about Rob and Tyance? Do we just leave them here?" Allen asked, once again already knowing the answer.

Elisha's silence was her own reply.

* * * *

Thunder rocked across the sky, pounding off the hills in mighty echoes. The rain was streaming down on the two before they noticed. Instead of thinking, *what next?* they barely even took note of the rain. It just made sense. It fit the mood. They pressed forward as the sky opened up in roars of thunder and streams of rain, pulses of lightning fanning across the sky, but not penetrating the canopy of trees above.

Trudging steps took the two forward. Glances backward were regular at first, just as they were when Vance disappeared. As a couple of hours slid past, they just went on, occasionally glancing at the GPS to make sure they went in the right direction—going home.

Elisha maintained that focus almost completely. *Follow the arrow,* she thought. *Follow the arrow. Get to the cabin. Call for help. Follow the arrow.* The rain flattened her hair to her head, turning her sandy blonde into a dark tangle. She pushed her hair back until the matted tresses were hooked behind her ears. The thin rivers that ran off her head and down her cheeks occasionally became salty but her resolve to follow the arrow kept away most emotions.

Allen had a tougher time focusing. He could keep his mind on the trek only for so long before something else would slip in. *Vance was right,* occurred to him. *They distract so they can attack. The thing that got Tyance was a Lochkray; it must have been. That's what Elisha saw behind me. It's a Lochkray. Vance said it looked like a person, but maybe it can change. Or maybe it has nothing to do with Lochkray. Or maybe...*He shook his head sending drops of water scattering, and returned his focus to the matter at hand. *Walking. Walking. Walking. It moved so fast...Walking. Walking. I wonder if Madoc managed to shoot it. Walking. Walking.*

As they grew more tired, the guns found their way to the shoulders of the two. Like the constant looks over their shoulders for pursuers, the guns that seemed so needed at first became more cumbersome. A distant roar of thunder might make them look back and place a hand to the straps on their sides, but eventually the only focus was forward.

Without Madoc's talent for traveling through the woods—his ability to predict and take the path of least resistance—their advance was retarded. Still they did not relent in any way. Eventually, after a few hours, the terrain relaxed a little. The trees, which stood so close to one another and tangled together within their branches, stepped back from each another. The land was less even now, and rocks pushed through from beneath the pine needle covered ground. With the woods less thick, they advanced better.

Elisha studied the uneven terrain as it dipped down for a few feet and then back up again, making her think the land was a levee, and a river had once run through here. Her mind, so focused on the advance, finally let go for a moment, a tune coming to her head. A great tune, one she remembered as a constant favorite at the campus bars, no matter how old it was. Some songs just kept their popularity, bypassing the usual expiration date stamped on popular music.

"Drove my Chevy to the levee, but the levee was dry," she recalled the words. "Them good ol' boys were drinking whiskey and rye, singing this will be the day I—" Elisha abruptly ended the tune. Her feet faltered for a step, but she quickly shook off the misstep. *Stupid song. How can you drink whiskey* and *rye? Rye is whiskey. Should be, "good ol' boys drinking bourbon and rye," or scotch and rye, or something. Stupid "American Pie" song. Just follow the arrow. Just follow the arrow to the cabin. Let the arrow take you home. Sweet home.* "Sweet Home Alabama; where the skies are so blue. Sweet Home Alabama; Lord I'm coming home to you."

So, another tune kept Elisha focused for a few moments. As she progressed through the journey and the tune, the plucking of the electric guitar almost as clear in her head as it would be from a CD player, Elisha's feet stumbled for a second time.

"I hope Neil Young will remember," the line went through her head, "a Southern man don't need him around anyhow." This time her misstep caused her to halt.

Allen, almost walked right into her. The wall of Elisha's backpack came quickly upon him and he came to a complete halt with his hands out.

"Whoa, what's wrong?"

"'A Southern man don't need him around anyhow...'" Elisha whispered.

"What?"

Elisha turned back to Allen, her hand slowly rummaging through her pocket, almost afraid to prove her thought. "Neil Young wrote a song called 'Southern Man,'" she said to a perplexed Allen. "He criticized attitudes in the Southern States. In the song *Sweet Home Alabama*, it talks about how 'ole Neil put her down.'"

"Are you okay, Elisha?"

"Then it says," Elisha brought the GPS in front of her but closed her eyes, not wanting to look at the arrow, "Neil Young should remember a Southern man don't need him around.'" Elisha opened her eyes and read the display screen. She faced Allen, and the arrow they followed now pointed directly back at her. She didn't look at that arrow though.

"I don't get it," Allen said.

"When we left the cabin, we headed north all the time, right?"

"Right. North to Doctor Hadden's site."

Elisha closed her eyes. "So, we should be going south, right? We should be heading south back to the cabin, right?"

"Right..." Allen trailed off, coming around to Elisha's side to see the screen. In the top corner of the GPS display screen sat the letter *N*, with the arrow pointing to the right of the screen. Allen looked up and got his bearings for a second. Elisha turned back around, returning the arrow they followed in their original trajectory.

"We've been heading northeast," Elisha's shaky voice advised before Allen could figure it out for himself.

"What?" he rushed up to her side. "No, no, no, no, no. Madoc said to follow the program, It would take us back to the cabin."

"This isn't the program to go back to the cabin."

"What about program number two. Look at that one. Or number three."

Elisha pressed the menu guide and attempted to call up the second program. After a few moments of fiddling she declared, "There is nothing in the program two file. There's only the one program, and it's taking us northeast."

Allen stepped away, his hands held up in exasperation. He walked in a large circle, puddles splashing, then back over to Elisha. He looked at the GPS again, then walked in his circle once more. He opened his mouth repeatedly, trying to say something, but nothing came out. Parts of sentences, "Madoc said," and "Program one," and "Follow the arrow," squeaked out but no actual statements were made.

"I don't know what we're going to do," Elisha said calmly, her eyes emoting what her voice would not. Allen completed his fourth aimless walk, then turned quickly and rushed up to her side.

"Wait," he blurted out. "Check landmark number two in program one. The uh... uh...waypoint. The second waypoint."

"What?"

"Each program, you follow the arrow to the waypoints. The coordinates to the landmarks. See if you can scroll down to landmark number two."

Elisha looked at the screen, manipulated the cursor, and brought the setting to the next coordinate. The screen flickered for a moment. Then the arrow readjusted, and pointed in the opposite direction from before.

"It wasn't set to take us directly back to the cabin," Allen explained with a sigh. "Tyance set it to go to the spot on the carved map. After that, it was going to take us back to the cabin."

"Right," Elisha gasped, with a lift in her heart. "That's right. We just have to skip the first waypoint, and start following to the second one. That's the one to take us back." Elisha lifted up the GPS, positioned her body until she was facing in the new direction of the arrow. *Sweet Home Alabama,* she thought to herself, for no reason. She had never even been to Alabama before. A few confirming nods from her head, and her feet began to move again. She set forward, now heading south.

"Wait," Allen called out from behind her. She came to a halt, and turned toward Allen, who was still firmly in place.

"What is it?"

"The first waypoint," Allen said softly. "How far away are we from the first waypoint?"

"Allen, I don't think we should—"

"That's what Doctor Hadden was looking for. That's where the petroglyphs pointed to."

"Doctor Hadden is dead," Elisha said sternly. "Whatever it was that got Tyance and Madoc..." She paused with a deep breath. "It got him too. He never left his camp, Allen. He's not there."

"How far?" Allen's voice was still soft. He finally moved his feet and came back up to Elisha. The two stared at each other, then Elisha looked down at the GPS. She fiddled with it, then looked back up.

"Point seven kilometers," she said. "That's seven hundred meters. Just about half a mile."

"That's what Doctor Hadden was looking for," Allen repeated.

"Allen, we're not going—"

"Seven hundred meters," Allen almost whined. "I know he probably didn't go to that spot, but whatever is there is what all of this has been about. We're within seven hundred meters of it. We can't get this close, and not..." He became quiet.

Nothing more was said. A silent debate between the two went on while the rain came down, heavily. The lightning and the thunder subsided, though the constant percussion of rain falling to the ground continued. Elisha stared at Allen, watching the thin rivers of rain run across his face. His tired expression was oblivious to the streams.

"Seven hundred meters," Elisha repeated. She looked back at the GPS direction arrow, once again pointing northeast.

The two walked away from the cabin.

* * * *

This was stupid, almost fully formed in Elisha's mind. Seven hundred meters across uneven, though slightly less tree-crowded terrain took much longer than the same distance would on a clear field. The stumbling, awkward effort of pushing through the woods, so familiar to her now, would have been so much better spent going south. South to the cabin. South to the satellite phone. Instead, they spent the time walking toward the first waypoint on program one on the GPS. Once there, they were nowhere—just as Tyance said; the middle of nowhere. The spot was just like the rest of the forest they saw the last few days, with no interesting features. *This was so stupid.*

The rain relented, not quite gone, but definitely tapering off. The trees' branches were bent down toward the dark ground and puddles. Allen did a walk around, trying to locate signs that, perhaps, Doctor Hadden went there, or even evidence of a burial mound or clearing. Yet, there was nothing—just trees and bushes, rocks sticking out of the ground, and the occasional bird chirping in the distance. Allen brought his hands up to his mouth, cupped in preparation to call out Hadden's name, but thought against it. Hadden wasn't there. Nothing was. He was wrong.

He shot a look of defeat and apology over to Elisha.

This was stupid. The words went through Elisha's mind again after Allen slumped his way over to her and looked down at the GPS. He saw that she had already flicked it over to waypoint number two.

"I'm sorry, Allen," she said.

"*I'm* sorry," he corrected.

"It's not your fault." Elisha wasn't angry with him; in fact, she kind of admired his stupid optimism. It wasn't that Allen himself was stupid to want to go to the location, just far too hopeful. Too hopeful that purpose could be given to this disaster of an expedition.

She looked away for a moment, to take a pause before making the decision to resume their escape from the wilderness. As she looked back, Allen had his hand up, pointing off in the distance, his view cast beyond her. Unexpectedly, he darted off, following his point, puddles of mud and water splashing as he advanced.

Elisha watched as he went over to an area slightly off their direction of travel, ten meters from where she stood. He went toward a large collection of boulders pressing themselves through the ground. She didn't know what Allen saw over there, and couldn't understand why he chose to stand in front of the rubble, looking down at it. With a slight sigh, she followed after, and as she got closer, she saw the blackness at the base of the boulders, the way the light was drawn out into the ground, surrounded by rock. Allen hovered over the entrance to a cave, his body rising and falling heavily.

Elisha dropped the heavy bag from her shoulders and let it fall, then leaned the shotgun beside it. She kneeled down to the hole, about a meter and a half across, watching as the remaining rivers of rain made their way into the descending blackness. Looking at the walls of the cave, Elisha saw the slope downward was gentle and almost tiered. She wouldn't go as far to describe them as steps, but it looked as though a force outside of erosion took the effort to make the descent into the tunnel easier.

"Do you think this might be it?" she asked, peering into the darkness. "Do you think this is what the map told us to look for?"

Allen tapped Elisha on the shoulder, then pointed at the rock above the cave. She followed Allen's finger to the figure carved into the stone. A single figure, a glyph, the shape of a human, almost like a stick man, pulled apart and disjointed. The same shape in the center of the stone spider-web, the same figure Allen described on the back of the copper spider found in Doctor Hadden's burial mound.

"We have to go in," Allen said, dropping his own pack off his back. "We have to look." He, too, went to his knees but he turned his attention to his pack, digging to retrieve a flashlight.

"I don't know Allen…" Elisha stopped herself. *Go look*, she interrupted herself. *He's right. You have to go look. Why else did you come out here?*

"I'll go in then," Allen said. "I won't go in too far. I just want to see where this goes. I won't even go out of your sight. You wait here—"

"No," Elisha broke in, retrieving her own flashlight. "I'll go with you." The two turned their torches into the blackness, the beams of light cutting into the dark, then sucked into it, revealing little more than the walls of the tunnel. "You surprise me, Allen," Elisha said, still looking down the tunnel.

"We can't go back and say we didn't look." Allen gave a feeble, terrified, laugh. "This is the one Doctor Hadden thought was going to be the pinnacle of his career. This could be the equivalent of November 1922 in Egypt. This is everything that ever interested me in archaeology. What if Carter decided that he didn't want to go into the tomb?"

"They say he was cursed from going in that tomb," Elisha gave her own weak laugh, "and that's why he died."

Allen stared at Elisha, torn between surprise and bother. She gave a shrug as if to say sorry. Putting their packs and supplies off to the side of the cave, Allen squatted down beside the hole, and said a brief prayer to himself. Elisha grabbed her shotgun and passed it over to Allen. It never occurred to Elisha that she might handle the weapon better. Allen took it, slid the strap over his shoulder, also not realizing he had no clue how to operate a pump-action weapon outside of what he saw in the movies. He crouched down and waddled into the hole.

Then the two descended into the cave.

The flashlights pointed forward like defensive sabers, they advanced downward, almost crawling sideways into the dimness. The tunnel stayed just slightly less than a meter and a half in diameter, and did not diminish in size as they went down. Elisha kept her beam of light over Allen's shoulder, occasionally glancing back at the gray light of day coming in from the mouth of the cave.

The gentle descent was constant, easing them on their way down. Allen kept one foot forward, squatted low and using his free hand to keep balance as he put one foot out, got a hold, and scooted up to it—always piercing into the darkness with the flashlight. He looked back occasionally, but only for a quick glance, not wanting to take his eyes off of the black ahead in case anything appeared.

Ten, then twenty, then forty, then sixty feet they descended. Elisha thought about turning back, but the farther they went down, the more excited she got. Frightened as well, concerned for sure, but excited. She allowed her light to slip down to the ground underneath her, amazed at how dry it was considering the amount of water pouring in. She saw the tiers of rock were dry, the water from above was drained some other way, out of the tunnel.

Finally Allen realized the tunnel was changing. The beam of his light licked along the edges of the cave as it came to a halt, and blackness continued on past it. He continued his crawl down the tunnel until he reached the dark. Pawing forward with his hand to feel where the floor of the tunnel resumed, he nearly lost his balance as he felt deeper into the air, his fall only being stopped by a sudden grab from Elisha, who took hold of his belt when she realized he was about to topple.

"Allen!" Elisha unintentionally yelped as she took hold and pulled him back.

"Jee-zus," Allen gasped, his flashlight now pointed at the black where he had failed to find any ground. "What the hell? It just goes into nothing. How can it go into nothing? It..." His voice trailed off. When he realized his voice was bouncing back at him from a great distance away, he was in awe. "It's a cavern. It's huge." He felt Elisha come up close behind him and peek over his shoulder. "Careful," he said.

Elisha swung her flashlight all over the darkness ahead of them, but could not catch anything in the beam—no floor, no ceiling, no walls, nothing. The beam of light just faded into the black of the cavern.

"There's a ladder," Allen whispered. While attempting to see how far the cavern went down, he realized the flat rock wall beneath him apparently had a ladder carved into it, intermittent foot holes spaced all the way down from the opening where they sat. Elisha squeezed past Allen, her hand on his shoulder, pulling him away from the edge while at the same time pushing to look past. When both beams crossed their paths of light, the flashlights showed down below, about a dozen meters, there was a floor. Once again Elisha and Allen locked gazes.

Then they descended the ladder. Allen first, swinging his legs over the side of the tunnel's mouth and catching one of the holes. He put his feet carefully onto the first carved rung he found. Slowly he released his weight from the side of the tunnel and allowed the rung to take his full heft.

"Is it strong?" Elisha asked, her hand clamped onto Allen's shoulder.

"It's fine," he answered, surprised. Allen touched the first rung hole by his hand and rubbed it. "I have no idea how they carved it into the stone...It's so smooth. Weird." Allen wrapped the strap of his flashlight tight around his wrist and began to descend. Going down blindly, Allen had to swallow his fear several times. All he made out was the ladder in front of him when Elisha's flashlight, wrapped around her own wrist, swung by up above. Everything else was black. After a few moments of going down the ladder slowly and carefully, he doubted that he saw the floor of the cave in the first place.

Eventually, though, his feet fell clumsily onto the solid ground, his foot pushing down hard to reach the next ladder rung, startling him as it touched surface. "I made it," he said excitedly. He stepped away from the ladder, allowing Elisha to touch bottom.

Turning to face the rest of the cavern, his light continued to slice into endless blackness. Deciding to try a different approach, he directed a pool of light onto the ground, now realizing It was not like the floor of a cave, but rather a flat surface, completely level. It looked almost like it was covered with giant slate tiles.

"Wow," Elisha said, looking at the floor.

"Who the hell did this?" Allen gasped, kneeling down to the ground and touching the smooth surface. "Who the hell lays tile on the floor of a cave?"

"Allen, look at this," Elisha whispered. He lifted his gaze from the floor and glanced over at his friend, who had walked out a few feet from the rock wall. Although she had not been able to find anything other than endless darkness in most directions, Elisha's flashlight had caught a shape a short distance in front of them. Allen came close to Elisha, doubling up their light. Together they made out a railing, over a meter high, stretching its way parallel to the wall of the cave behind them, along into blackness. Vertical struts supported the rail every three meters or so, carved and heavily ornamented. The two advanced to the rail, and Allen went to touch it. He then put his flashlight over it and saw that the cave dropped again on the other side of this railing, and back into blackness again.

"It's made of stone," Elisha said, running her hand along the rail. "Carved stone."

"The cave gets bigger down there," Allen said, running his hand along the smooth cold banister. He felt the indentations and texture in the rock; felt the intricate carvings that covered the banister. "This is incredible." His hand touched a more angular shape as his fingers ran across the rail. Then the railing let off a glow.

"Whoa," Elisha said abruptly. On the railing, at the point where one of the vertical supports was, a small diamond-shaped rock was imbedded into the stone. As Allen's fingers ran across it, the rock emanated an eerie, dull yellow-white glow.

"What the...?"

"How did you do that?"

"I have no idea," Allen said. "I just touched it."

Elisha looked along the railing until she saw another carved baluster, and saw another small angular rock imbedded into the stone above it. She reached out and touched it. It, too, glowed softly. It illuminated the area around them.

"What's making them glow?" Allen asked loudly, his voice echoing around the cavern, startling them both. Allen backed away from the banister.

"Maybe we should get out of here," Elisha said.

"Yeah." Allen nodded.

"Yeah," Elisha repeated, turning back toward the ladder. She turned her flashlight onto the wall, searching the uneven gray surface for the way back to the tunnel.

The beam of light struck the Lochkray in the face, but he didn't flinch, not even when the daylight released her sharp scream. He had quietly come up behind them, taking care not to be heard. This normally simple task had been difficult for him, for the Lochkray was distracted with awe and delight. The beam of light would normally burn his nocturnal eyes but he didn't even notice it. In fact, he wanted more light. *More light.* His own sight allowed him to see around the cavern far better than the daylights could, but he desperately wanted to share it all, even with them. The Lochkray glided toward the two, taking advantage of their shock to hold them for the brief moment required to effortlessly slide the shotgun off of the male's shoulder.

Allen and Elisha, finally realizing what was happening, attempted to create distance between themselves and the bald man, pressing backward until they returned to the railing. Their flashlights never left the form standing with his right hand stretched out in their direction, a look of confidence cracked across his face.

Beside Allen, the tiny rocks that he and Elisha had touched glowed brighter. Allen's gaze wandered from the bald man and darted between the two lights. They grew stronger as this huge man, dressed entirely in black, pointed at them with one hand, while the other held Vance's shotgun firmly like a staff.

As the light became brighter, the Lochkray allowed a smile of astonishment and elation to crawl across his lips. He brought both hands together, still holding the shotgun, held them in front for a brief moment, then spread them away from one another. All along the railing, at every baluster, rocks began to glow—illuminating the entire rail as it stretched off fifty meters in each direction, until the side walls of the cave, previously invisible, were shown.

Encouraged by this, the Lochkray reached his hand up toward the black where the roof of the cavern was hidden. From high above them, light began to shine. The massive vaulted ceiling glowed, as the entire upper limit of the cave came to light. The Lochkray looked about, now able to see the entire cavern.

Cathedral was the first word Allen thought of to describe the scene. The cavern reminded him of the largest cathedral ever—and they were in the choir parapet. The wall running in back of them was stone, the rough wall of a huge cave, but the rest of this giant room was made of bricks, carvings, and pillars. The rib-vaulted roof high above stretched away two hundred meters.

Where Allen expected a lectern and altar to be at the other end of the cave, the room ended abruptly in another massive wall. Arches and pillars running along the entire room, on the level below, created an arcade of alcoves that looked like separate rooms off of the main chamber. The smooth walls around them were covered with roots and moss pushing down from above, somehow having made it through cracks and holes in the ceiling.

Instead of pews, what looked like stone stands, each the size of a billiard table, littered the immense chamber. Each console looked as if it was carved out of a massive boulder, its legs visibly ornate even from the balcony. Some of their tops were flat and smooth, others had ridges and bowls carved into them. Allen could only guess how many tables there were. They were scattered everywhere on the floor below, except for a large area where a circular pool of black water sat. He figured the pool of water was massive enough to hold an entire school bus. A wide walkway extended out from the balcony where they stood, out to hover over where the pool was. This walkway, supported by a series of columns standing in pairs, stretched out into the underground temple, the ornate glowing balustrade running all the way along.

The Lochkray now walked past the two daylights, his hands still held out, his face showing a fascination unfelt by another Lochkray for generations. Every so often he pointed his finger at another spot on the wall and it would light up and glow from within. He pointed at the tables below and they also illuminated as if suddenly plugged into some invisible electrical source. Whole tables came to life, their tops glowing in different colors, some of these appearing to move and swirl, their stone surface becoming liquid.

"Jesus, Allen, look," Elisha gasped, pointing high up at the walls. Allen pulled his gaze off the floor and saw that the roots that took hold along all the walls were starting to move—starting to move as the bald man pointed at them. They undulated like snakes, slinking along the pillars and arches, stretching down to the floor, or pulling back to the ceiling, or both, the walls of the whole room came to life—moving and squirming.

The Lochkray continued along the walkway, recognizing items and pointing at them, infusing them, turning them on after sitting dormant for so long. Organic chemicals came together at his thought, minerals were mixed with alkali on his whim, the room grew bright, acknowledging his presence and command.

He realized that each step he took along the walkway toward the Sovereign's Rostrum—preparing to take his position there—was heavy and clumsy, not like his usual agile gait. He breathed heavily and tried to calm himself. The Lochkray stepped up to the end of the walkway, a platform he knew he should never have been allowed to tread upon. His hand reached forward and touched the rail. Directly below he saw the giant pool of water. He stared at this—stared hard.

Elisha reached out and took Allen's hand as the black pool shone a silvery blue, and then moved. Water flowed along the walls from the tops of the pillars. Four small waterfalls fell to the floor and then ran along prepared trenches to the pool of water which swirled and twisted.

The Lochkray stared into this swirling natatorium below him. Then he looked up at the walls, twisting and moving with water and plants. Then up at the high vaulted ceiling as it glowed down on him approvingly. Then down at his feet, planted so firmly on the edge of the monarch's promenade, standing on the Lochkray prow—the Sovereign's Rostrum. Like a king. Like a god.

Finally the Lochkray turned his attention back toward the two daylights who stood beside one another in wonder and fear. He tossed their weapon over the railing to the chamber below where it clattered mutely under the sounds of the moving waters and roots. A smile slipped across the Lochkray's previously gaping mouth.

A wide smile, a gloriously happy, completely unlike a Lochkray's smile. He opened his mouth to say something, but could not think of what words to put to them. There was apprehension and awe on their visages, to be sure, but they still did not understand what it was they were looking upon. The Lochkray's mind raced to think of what to tell them, of what to say to make them comprehend the wonder they were in and the meaning of it all. To explain to their feeble human understandings that this single room would have more effect on their existence than any other place or event in their feckless history. His smile quivered and shook until he could stand it no longer.

He said the only thing he could manage.

"Kraell'Haatch."

Brian M. H. Goodwin

Part Five
Kraell'haatch

Chapter Twenty-Three

"Is he a Lochkray?" Allen asked.

Elisha looked down at Allen, who had slumped to the ground, his eyes wide in defeat, staring forward pathetically. "I was beginning to think the thing in the forest was one," she answered, Allen still not looking directly at her, "but I think... maybe. I don't know. I think he is."

"Did you see how fast he moved? All I did was stand there. I had the gun, and... It was unbelievable. He just...he was so fast. I had the gun, then he...so fast..."

Elisha stepped back from the doorway. The chamber the two of them were now in was barely three meters square, a closet compared to the cavern It sat beside. A barrier covered the opening to the alcove, a door that grew out of the walls and seal them inside—the thick root-like branches just reached across the aperture, and became like a woven wall, thick and solid.

"And strong," Allen was going on. "So strong. He picked us up like nothing. I don't think my feet even touched the ground."

Elisha walked away from the door and did a circle of the room again, just as she had when the large bald man had first put them in this place. Allen was right, he was fast. The giant man had rushed over to them. He took them by the scruff of the neck, and they were incapable of struggling. Elisha didn't know if it was shock, or if the huge man had somehow been able to confound her, but she hadn't even contested his actions as he guided the two of them, one in each hand, off of the balcony, through the giant chamber, to this room. It just happened, *just happened*. Now, she was already incapable of recalling what had occurred and how it came about. The man made the room come to life, turned to them, and put them in—she hadn't even been capable of looking around while he led them here! The last image she could recall with detail was that awful smile forming those odd words: *Kraell'Haatch*. Everything else was like a dream.

So there they were, alone, locked in a tiny empty room, the only exit sealed off by a thick wall of organic matter. Elisha walked around the space in full, her hand sliding over the closed doorway as she went by it, and then to Allen on the opposite wall.

"Try and think back to the campfire," Elisha said, sitting down on the ground, her head even with Allen's. "When Vance talked, what did he say about the Lochkray?"

"That they were a society of nocturnal beings. Like vampires."

"He said they feed on humans," Elisha said.

"Yeah, drink blood or something."

"Blood is feral," the words came out of Elisha's mouth before they were even in her mind.

"What?"

"Nothing," she replied, shaking off half a memory. "No, he said they fed off your soul. Remember he said they lived in caves, like an underground city?"

"Yeah, that's right."

"It must be like this place. He said their technology was advanced and different from humans'."

"Yeah, he called it cerebral-organic. Organic-mental…or something like that. That's why this cave looks like it's alive, and why he can make the lights come on by just pointing at them. Right? That's how he made that door come down, like out of nowhere—"

"That's how he got us into this room without a fight," Elisha finished. "Vance told that story about the captured priests, and one of them said the Lochkray could fog your mind. Make you have fantasies and hallucinations. I mean, he just came out of nowhere, took away your gun, and led us to this room. We didn't even have a chance to react. It felt like a…like a dream."

"Nightmare," Allen corrected. "This is a nightmare."

"He hypnotizes you, I'll bet. I don't know how, exactly, but I think that's what he does and how he got us in here with so little effort." Elisha closed her eyes, and rested her head on her knees, her arms wrapped tight around her shins. *Don't let him hypnotize you*, she said to herself. *You can't be hypnotized if you don't want to*, the voice of a first-year psychology instructor ran through her mind. *Don't let him.*

"How can he do hypnotism without even talking to us?"

Elisha turned her head, her silent shrug her only answer.

"Do you think Vance made it out?" Allen asked, suddenly raising his head. "Maybe he's already close to the cabin? He can call for help. He had that emergency GPS thing. He could have called for help."

"Maybe," was the unconfident reply.

Allen bowed his head down with a defeated sigh. As he drew his breath back in, his head came back up. "What's that smell?"

Elisha tilted her head upward, nodding it back and forth, at first not knowing what Allen talked about. Then her nose caught it—a slight ammonia-like smell in the air, faint, and yet causing the back of her throat to burn.

"What is that?" Elisha repeated the question.

"It's like a cleanser, or chlorine or something." For a flutter of a moment, Allen believed the bald man was going to kill them by gas. His hand went to his face, the lamest of masks, but before it had time to fully seal around his mouth and nose, the smell subsided.

"I can't smell it now."

The aroma had wafted by so quickly Elisha had not even had time to consider what Allen had. She returned her head to its resting place on her knees, her eyes closed again.

How long has he been with us? she wondered. *He was there when Vance fell over the cliff, he was there at the docks. Did he come up with us in the plane, or was he already here? Something was bothering me before I ever came up to the cabin—was it him I saw?*

A chill shivered over Elisha, causing her to tremble. She saw the man before, seen him at the docks, and knew his face from somewhere—*Do you amuse?*—and knew his voice—*What is it that you seek?*—and knew his touch—*Two hands*—and suspected he had been with her for quite some time. Her stomach quaked in loathing at the idea of that horrible man being within her mind, her dreams, her thoughts. Violating her.

Don't let him hypnotize you, she repeated to herself, with more resolve. Her flutter of loathing quickly shifted into a personal animosity. *When you get the chance,* she went on, *take retribution.*

* * * *

At the edge of the upper level, up against the back wall, the Lochkray stood, naked. The lights were dimmed, the cavern darkened into shadow, illuminated only by the blue glowing, swirling natatorium of water on the lower level. The walls stopped moving, the roots and branches held still, awaiting instruction.

After placing the daylights in a cell on the level below, and having presumed to take on the earliest steps in awakening the ancients' plans, the Lochkray returned to the second level to ready himself. Animation and illumination were little more than tricks, an easy way to confirm that he reached his goal, It truly existed, It was designed and capable of attaining greatness. The full power of Kraell'Haatch took concentration to unleash, however, and strength of mind and focus to start. For whatever reason, Kraell'Haatch was abandoned and lost—uninitiated. Since then, it had grown ready and waited for this moment.

The great cave was silent. The Lochkray stood at the edge of the walkway, staring down the Sovereign's Rostrum. His feet started to move along the cold stone floor toward the end of the walkway once again, this time with concentrated intent.

He allowed each step to hold long enough for the freezing floor to burn his naked foot, then he took another step. He listened intently, trying to catch each voice the cavern whispered. With more effort than it took to distract any daylight, more concentration than to hold prey in a clumsy sanok's illusion, he focused himself on becoming one with the cavern, intertwining his own mind with the living cells all about him, making the cavern an extension of him.

He opened his mind more with each step, letting go of his own body, becoming one with every fleck of being, every particle of life.

He reached the end of the rostrum, his eyes closed tight, his mind a liquid, flowing and searching the living entity that was the cave.

First, he required apparel suitable for this moment. His mind's eye crawled through each section of the chamber, searched for all required substance, located cellules that could become fibers, attained all he required to create.

He reached his hands downward, his fingers separated to their maximum. He breathed deep, and from the ground itself came what he needed. Cellular structures designed by the ancient Lochkray secreted and spun cloth instantly, emerging from between the tiles of the floor. In straps and lengths, they made their way around him, wrapping and draping him in a cloak of white.

The cloth reached over his shoulders, wrapped around his arms, became tight where required, let loose where comfort allowed. When his body was covered, the last straps of fiber stopped climbing from underneath his feet, and the task was complete.

The Lochkray opened his eyes and stared down at the bright garment he made in his mind and formed with his call. Satisfied, most satisfied, he began.

He cast his gaze upward, to the ceiling of the mighty chamber, shaky hands breaking into that gaze. His mind became an extension of those hands, reaching out along his fingers, and feeling far above, within the ceiling itself, to locate what was aging and maturing. His mind's touch caressed what was up there, felt it existed. His eyes closed again, as did his hands, his outstretched fingers drawing into a fist, his mind pulling downward.

Up above, organic apertures furrowed open. All along the ceiling of the chamber, colossal mouths parted, and from these descended clear canisters. Even with his eyes closed, the Lochkray sensed the light that was coming from them, luminescence from the contents held within each of the giant tubes.

It worked, the Lochkray thought as his eyes opened to see the multicolored tubes breaking their way out of the roof. *There they are.*

The satisfied grin the Lochkray suppressed so often broke its way across his visage again. His fingers jumped out from his hands once more, and several of the canisters returned, disappearing into their orifices. Others, though, remained and waited. Up above, root-like conduits crawled across the roof of the chamber. Endless snakes that attached themselves to the canisters still hung down.

Then, one by one, the conduits detached and the canister disappeared into the ceiling again, only to be replaced by another clear canister containing glowing liquid, which emerged from another part of the ceiling. Then conduits and tubes attached to these, and the same thing would happen. The Lochkray nodded at the activity above. Knowing it would still take time to find out if the canisters above yielded their distillation and let him know for sure that all was worth it, the Lochkray turned his attentions to the rest of the chamber.

At first, pointing toward the glowing pool below, he had the natatorium spew forth a wall of water up to his level. Immediately—like a giant jet—the water reached up and stood there, flowing yet solid, splashing upwards and falling back down to its own pool. There it held an odd dike of water as if designed to hold back air.

The Lochkray lowered his hand, and the wall remained. Nodding, satisfied, he pointed to this wall of water and brought it to life. Upon the flowing form, light crawled up from below, and then changed and flicker. Then an image emerged upon the water. Like a mirror enlarged, the Lochkray's own face stared back at him. The Lochkray stared at himself in fascination.

A moment of consideration crossed that face, and then the water began to flicker again. The Lochkray, his eyes closed once more, felt about the room for a source of another image. His mind focused itself until his imagination was like a corridor. A hallway. With portals running along either side. The contents of the rooms behind the doors were completely new and yet still known to him. He thought his way through this hall, and located the proper portal, and reached out blindly for a source of a moving image.

The wall of water spouting upward from the tarn stopped its aimless flickering and took the form of a male, a daylight man, his lower half concealed by a ledge covered with edibles. A raw severed fowl sat in a dish, bowls of dried spices, liquid, and vegetables surrounding it. The daylight flamboyantly combined the bowls, narrating his actions as he went along.

A mixed empathy fell over the Lochkray, watching this man creating a meal for entertainment. He felt affection and pride, knowing his people were able to create this mastery hundreds of years before the daylights ever conceived of their *television*, and now it was able to pick out their ignorant visuals from the air. Invented centuries before daylights were even capable of conceiving them. The Lochkray knew he was of a greater light than those that walked in the day.

Still, sadness was there in his soul for there were no images of Lochkray to put upon the wall before him. He reached out aimlessly with his mind and replaced the cooking daylight with another signal. The wall of water became the clear image of colorful animated pictures, anthropomorphic animals engaged in hyperkinetic motion.

With a twist of the Lochkray's thoughts again, the image became that of a daylight upon a horse, within a desert scheme, riding fast. The Lochkray did not wait long enough to find out what it was it retrieved from. He allowed the water wall to go clear, and fall back into the pool.

He stopped, and allowed his mind to become one with Kraell'Haatch again. He began looking for records. He wandered without moving, searching within the walls, within the liquids, flora, minerals, and chemicals that twisted their way through the cavern. Searched for a chemical imprint somewhere—an archive.

Four. Four archives.

The natatorium's light flickered, and the wall of water rose up again, drawing the illumination up with it. The Lochkray opened his eyes, and looked at the image. For a single moment of confusion, the Lochkray thought the image once again showed him. The face was wrong. It was the Sovereign's Rostrum, but it was another that stood there. Her hands placed firmly onto the railing before her, she stared back at the Lochkray, as if looking at him directly.

"Kro n'tall," she said to someone out of the view of the image, her Lochkray accent pure and perfect. *It is working*, the words meant, *begin a record.*

"Pcii t," the reply came from somewhere off of the screen. *It has started.*

"Pcii t," the Lochkray repeated in his own tongue to the image before him.

"Lim'htah," she said. *Show me the record.*

The liquid went clear again. The Lochkray's eyes closed, and he quickly retrieved the next archive.

"Karim-potay'nyo parg," said a male who took form on the water screen. *Once it has begun, bring the image closer to me.* He stood silent for a moment, then looked below his post. "Paseek." *Rectify the problem.* The image went closer on his face, his dark visage filling the entire field. "Lim'htah."

Again the image went clear. The Lochkray closed his eyes again. When they opened, the female from the first archive was again shown on the rostrum. Now, however, she was flanked by two males; the one from the second archive, and another. She scanned the area below the rostrum, slowly moving her gaze across the area below.

"Kraell'dya'kah bolo," she said slowly, her voice echoing loudly on the archive. *A place in history we now stand, is that which we have sought.* "This task is completed," she went on, speaking to unseen listeners below, " consequential labor has reached fruition. Here, conceived and actualized our foremost destination, we untie ourselves from the fetters of daylights. From this night, Lochkray shall be nourished without constraint. We shall be found as..."

She stopped speaking and turned behind her. In the shadows, the Lochkray saw another form coming along the rostrum. "Pa," she called over her shoulder. *Stop recording.*

The Lochkray stared, puzzled at the suddenly blank screen before him. With the few words the female said, he had grown excited, realizing that his predecessors had completed what they had sought to do. Now, getting better at handling the system, the Lochkray barely had to shift his attention to obtain the fourth and final archive.

"We are under attack," said a new male on the screen, a panic in his eyes invisible to any but another Lochkray. "Cimmerian Knights have arrived upon Kraell'Haatch. Daylights native to this place have joined them and rise against us. The Sovereign has ordered the release of t'lrome and sanok, but overmuch belated. We are overwhelmed. We are defeated. Kraell'Haatch is to be abandoned. This record is last. To those who find this archive, return to the Lochkray the peace we have seen.

"Be damned all those who live in day."

The image went blank, and the Lochkray allowed the water to fall back into the swirling pond below.

* * * *

Outside the room, Allen and Elisha heard muffled sounds, that of movement and occasionally of speaking, the speaking sounding as if it were booming over loudspeakers. For the last little while though, it sounded almost like music. Not quite clear, but definitely the hint of a beat or tune. Unable to make the sounds out, and too defeated to try, they ignored them.

At first, when they finally heard something on the other side of the door, they had crept close to the covered portal, listening carefully, trying to make out any indication of movement. Now, they were routed in their hearts. After an hour of standing by the doors, they had sat down. They hadn't bothered to try and come to grips with their situation. They simply stopped talking or looking at one another.

Elisha's mind tried to formulate a strategy or plan of action but these thoughts never fully materialized. For every time her mind thought of how to confront the predicament, she became resentful. Angry at the place, full of hate for the man who brought them here. The man who raped their minds and brought them here.

Allen, on the other hand, had his focus on the tip of his index finger as it dug pointlessly into the floor of the small chamber. Grains of sand flaked away from the uneven ground, moved out by his digging. In the hour of silence that he spent at this endeavor, he removed enough grains to allow for a divot, the circumference of his finger, less than an eighth-of-an-inch deep. Occasionally he glanced over at Elisha, who sat with her back against the opposite wall, her head buried between her knees.

Allen wondered, *if she's crying what should I do? What should I say? How do I comfort her?* Deciding it best if she kept her head down, and best if he just focused on the tiny divot he created, he drew his eyes away, afraid she would look up. Afraid she would have streams of tears running down her face and he would be left to stumble through words to comfort her. He couldn't comfort anybody. He had none to offer.

"Look," Elisha's head was up, and her finger pointed excitedly at the covered doorway they had entered the small room through. "At the bottom."

Allen turned his heavy head from his digging and glanced at the opening. The tight interwoven covering was still in place over the door; however, along the lower edge by the floor, it had receded. A triangle-shaped opening appeared, each side almost two feet long. Allen scrambled to his feet and went to Elisha's side. A quick check of her cheeks and eyes, which were suddenly alive and excited, held no evidence of tears.

"Why did that happen?" he asked excitedly.

"I don't know. Do you think you could fit through there?"

"Yeah, no problem."

Elisha got down on one knee and stuck her head quickly through the hole in the doorway, then brought it back in. "I think he's listening to music," she said to Allen. Again she quickly stuck her head out the door, this time taking longer to look about the hallway outside before coming back in. "There is music playing. Classical music."

"Can you see him?"

"No. We're in a hallway. I can see part of the main chamber, but I can't see very much. He's not outside the door, though." Allen got down on his knees as well, and stuck his own head through. The hallway on the other side of the aperture went about twenty feet to the right, before opening up into what Allen assumed was the main chamber, down on the lower level, at the other end from where they had entered.

The hall also went to the left, and descended into darkness. Allen continued to crawl forward, out into the hall. He could clearly hear the sounds of an orchestra playing music in the main chamber. No expert in classical music, he still recognized the tune. Pressing his back against the wall, he looked back and watched as Elisha crawled through as well.

"He must have a stereo system or something," Allen whispered to Elisha.

"Which way do you want to go?" she asked, ignoring the comment. "Further down the hall, or back into that main chamber, where he probably is?"

Allen took a moment to glance back and forth between the blackness to his left, and the ominous chamber to his right, even allowing a quick glance back at the opening they just crawled through.

"I can't see anything down the hall," he replied.

"Let's see if we can find out where he is," Elisha decided, shuffling past Allen and going toward the chamber. Before he could protest, she already moved up to the end of the hallway, and was slowly beginning to edge around the corner, still keeping her back against the wall.

"I didn't say I didn't want to take the hall," Allen hissed, coming up beside her, "I just said I couldn't see anything."

"I don't see him," Elisha whispered back, still inching her way around the corner. Taking a deep breath, she turned herself around, and peeked around the corner. "I don't see him," she repeated, moving her head at a slow pace. "I don't see him." Inch by inch, the great chamber revealed itself to her. The giant arched ceiling was alive with the movement of roots and plants that slithered and shifted across the dome, attaching themselves to each other, connecting, then releasing and moving again.

The chamber looked brighter now, effulgent. At first reminding her of giant chandeliers, Elisha realized they were lucid vats containing glowing liquids, descending from the ceiling. The root-like ducts attached to these, and the liquids within bubbled and lowered. Then the roots detached and some of the clear casks retreated back into the ceiling, into the entanglement of life above, only to be replaced by others appearing somewhere else again. No less than half a dozen at a time were visible on the roof. Elisha guessed, as they were so far away, that the vats were almost the size of small cars—huge compared to how they gently emerged and vanished.

"Jeezus, Allen, you have to see this," Elisha whispered back.

"Is he out there?"

"No," she said before she realized that she had not finished her visual sweep of the room. Then her eyes darted about the entire chamber, all about, and she saw no one out there. She squinted her eyes to survey the upper level at the far end of the room, and made out no movement there either. Allen pushed himself up to her side, and cautiously scanned outside the hall too.

"What are those things?" he asked, looking up at the ceiling. "Are they lights?"

"I don't think so. Watch them for a second. Some of them will go back up into the ceiling, and others will come back down. See? See?"

"That's wild." Allen looked around the floor of the vast room and checked the upper level as well. "I don't see him either," he said. "I can see the ladder back up to the tunnel, though. The ladder out."

"There's a flight of stairs on this side, back up on the balcony."

"Then let's get the hell out of here."

While the melody of piano and violins echoed all about them, Elisha and Allen, tucked as hard as they could into the corner of the wall, edged their way toward the far end of the chamber. Periodically they came to an alcove in the wall and paused. With lungs holding hard onto breath, one quickly peeked around the side and into the antechamber to determine if the Lochkray was within. Sometimes tables, like those scattered about the entire floor of the chamber, were held within the alcoves, other times they served as entrances to other hallways descending into darkness. But always empty. The pair moved forward again, darting across whatever retreat in the wall they came across, and then continue toward the staircase that ascended to the giant balcony.

Please be looking down those halls, Allen thought to the Lochkray every time he saw an open doorway. *Stay down there just a little longer.*

Always their gazes moved about the room, checking whatever corners or views not visible before, to ensure the Lochkray was not hiding. Finally, the daunting, endless distance was covered. They reached the bottom of the stairs and froze there. Crouched low to the wall, they continued scanning the room behind them.

"Where the hell did he go?" Elisha asked aloud.

"Let's not worry about it," Allen replied. "I can see the ladder from here. Let's just get going." He looked at the open stairway, perhaps two dozen steps curving up to the balcony, an ornate railing spiraling up with them. Still crouched low, Allen put a foot onto the first step, but was stopped by Elisha when she grabbed his arm and pulled him back down to the floor.

"Wait," she hissed. Unsure what she saw, Allen tucked himself hard against the wall, cowering as low as he could. When Elisha failed to add any further comment, he relaxed slightly.

"What is it?"

"Wait," she repeated. "One of the guns is still up at the entrance of the cave, right?"

"Yes! So, let's get to it now."

"Wait." Elisha paused again. "Think about what Vance said."

"Elisha, not now, for Christ's sake—"

"Wait," she repeated. "He said this place, this Kraell'Haatch, was where the Lochkray launched their attack on humans. Do you remember?"

"I don't think this is a good time to be worrying about what Vance said—"

"If we had listened to Vance in the first place," she snapped, "we wouldn't be here right now." Allen retreated into the wall again.

Elisha closed her eyes and drew in a deep breath. "He said that they used this place to perfect their weapons so they could conquer people. Right? Isn't that something he talked about?"

"Yeah," Allen muttered back, "that's what he said."

"Then maybe," she continued, "we shouldn't just leave this place. We shouldn't leave him alone here, not without leaving something for him." A very slight mischievous smile fluttered on her lips for a moment. *Take retribution*, her thoughts echoed.

"What are you talking about?"

"He's the reason Rob and Tyance are dead," Elisha said in a harsh tone that Allen never heard from her before. "And John Hadden. Vance was right, he had to be. Look at this place. Is it like anything you've ever seen before?"

"Well...no..."

"Go get the gun, Allen. I'll wait here. I'll wait here and stall him in case he finds out we've gotten out. You go get the gun and come back here."

"Oh, Christ, Elisha. I don't think I could shoot him."

"No," she almost yelled, "I don't want you to shoot him! I just want to damage this place a little. Sabotage."

"What the hell are you talking about?"

"Those things." Elisha's index finger was pointed up at the undulating ceiling. "And those." Her finger now panned over the lower level where the multitude of tables sat. "I don't know what makes them work, but I'm guessing they won't like being shot at."

"I don't know. If he catches us...He's really fast; and strong. Did you see the way he picked the two of us up?"

"Faster than a bullet? Stronger than being shot?"

"Well..."

Elisha's hands fell onto Allen's shoulders and took a firm hold there. Looking directly at him, her gaze took hold of his. "If we take off without doing this, he'll be right after us, we won't have a chance. If we damage this place, he won't come after us, he won't be able to. Please, Allen. We need to do this. I don't know what's going on, but I know we can't just leave him here alone without slowing him down a little. Not after everything we've seen."

Allen's gaze made frantic advances across all areas of the chamber. The undulating ceiling, the floor littered with tables, the stairs, the ladder to the tunnel, Elisha, back to the ceiling, and over it all again. *This is nuts, this is nuts*, his mind repeated. Finding his own frenetic vision too dizzying, he closed his eyes. His chest rose and fell with a deep, calming, breath.

"Allen..."

"This is nuts," he said aloud, his eyes open again, this time fixed on his partner.

"Why don't you just come up with me?"

"I need to make sure he doesn't come after you. I'll be right at the bottom of the ladder. Someone has to make sure he doesn't come up behind you before you get to the gun."

"Why don't I stay, and you go get the gun?"

"Because..." Elisha's mouth quivered for a second. "Because I know he won't hurt me. I...I amuse him."

"What?"

"I don't know how I know it," she shook her head rapidly, "but I know it. He finds me entertaining in some way. He won't hurt me. I don't know if he finds you as amusing."

"This is nuts," Allen repeated. "You stay here. I don't know where he's gone to, but if you hear him coming back, start going up the ladder. I'll meet you in the tunnel—"

"Don't worry about me," Elisha interrupted.

"Elisha, he's going to be pissed if we do this." Allen turned toward the stairs and walked up the first few, stopping to look back at the room to see if anyone came to stop him.

Believing the two were still alone, he continued on his way, his back hunched over, his fingers brushing the ground as he kept as close to the stairs as his body would allow, while still permitting rapid advance. Elisha copied Allen's visual check of the room, then his advance up to the balcony of the perverted underground cathedral. Once the stairs came to their summit, the two scurried along the balcony, their eyes always alive across the rest of the chamber.

"Okay," Allen hissed under the sound of the music, his hand touching one of the lower rungs. He turned back to watch Elisha coming up behind. "Okay. Okay." His eyes went across the chamber once again. "Okay. I'm going up. Are you sure you don't just want to get the hell out of here?"

"Just get back as quickly as you can," Elisha replied, tucking herself hard into the corner of the back wall and the balcony's floor. "Get the gun, come back and get me, and we go." Suddenly the plan made a lot less sense to Elisha. A tight feeling in her throat prevented her from swallowing, its discomfort only matched by the pressure in her chest. Allen looked up the ladder, toward the tunnel.

"I'll be right back," he said.

"Go," Elisha shot back, giving him a push. "Just go."

His arms feeling weak, Allen ascended the ladder. Slowly at first—step, grab, pull, step—each action deliberate and matched by a glance down below and then about the empty chamber.

"Go," Elisha repeated with a much harsher, frustrated squeal. The time it would take Allen to retrieve the gun and return would be waited with severe anxiety, and his torpid ascension, she knew, only prolonged the agony.

"Go," Allen repeated to himself.

Elisha watched as his more rapid climb continued, up all the rungs until he reached the dark tunnel against the high rock wall. His top half disappeared into the mouth of the cave, then his feet were pulled in. She watched for a moment, waiting for his head to stick out, and give her a quick wave, to which she would advise him one more time to go. But his head never appeared. He disappeared into the cave and continued on his way to the weapon without ever looking back. After it was obvious that Allen wouldn't give a wave, Elisha turned back to ensure the chamber was still empty except for her.

The Lochkray stood leaning against the railing almost directly opposite of where Elisha stood. He stared at her calmly, draped in a hanging garment of bright white. Elisha brought her fingers to her mouth to catch the scream about to escape. She suppressed the jolted yell only by closing her eyes and turning quickly away from the giant male who somehow moved to that position without being seen or heard. Had her mind thought the moment through, she would have wondered if he had moved to that spot, or if he always stood there, somehow making it so she and Allen could not see him.

Her fists now shoved up to her mouth, knowing she had to look again and terrified for knowing it, she reopened her eyes, and turned toward the Lochkray. Only in the second of frightened retreat she took, the Lochkray had moved. Moved closer. Much closer. Mere centimeters from her own face, the Lochkray's hideous visage tilted slightly to examine Elisha. Again she closed her eyes and turned her head to press into the rock wall. More quickly she reopened her eyes, afraid to lose sight of the man-monster again. This time, he hadn't moved at all.

He stood still, leaning slightly forward, his pale eyes scanning up and down her timorous countenance, peering into her own tear-filled stare. Her breathing was rapid and shallow, her voice missing, unable to call out to Allen. The Lochkray eliminated a few of the precious centimeters that stood between his face and Elisha's. Unable to retreat any further, she pressed her head even harder against the rock wall. He was so close to her that she heard the wet suction sound of his mouth as it opened, his thin lips snapping as they separated. Through his mouth a deep breath was drawn.

Elisha could smell his breath, dank and deep, as it wafted out gently through his lightly yellow teeth. Elisha closed her eyes once more. *"They learned to draw out a living creature's life force,"* the voice of Vance Halverson reminded her. *"Soul."* Her hands now folded over her heart, Elisha waited for whatever the Lochkray would do to her.

"Beautiful," he said.

Elisha opened her eyes and gradually looked back at the Lochkray. His face was still fragile centimeters from her own, but its advance stopped. Her mouth quivered in confusion, unsure what her ears heard. *It spoke. It said...*

"Beautiful," he repeated. This time he raised his finger and held it close to Elisha's face, pointing upward. Then the hand pulled back, as did the Lochkray, distancing himself from Elisha, allowing her to peel away slightly from the rock wall. "The music," the Lochkray continued as he pulled himself up to his full height. "The music is beautiful."

Elisha's mouth continued to quiver as her eyes followed the Lochkray's point upward to where the soft strains of a gentle orchestra washed throughout the room. *The music is beautiful,* she repeated in her thoughts. *The music.* She looked back down at the Lochkray, a faint but rapid nodding gyrating her head.

"Yes," she squeaked out. The Lochkray mimicked her with his own head nodding, only much more slowly and deliberately.

"Yes," he said. "I know it is." He turned away from Elisha, and walked back toward the balustrade, his ivory robe gliding just above the smooth floor, billowing backwards as he walked. Elisha quickly looked back the way Allen went, then returned her gaze to the Lochkray as his hands rested on the railing and leaned forward, looking into the chamber.

"Lochkray make not any music," he called back to her, over his right shoulder. "Paint no images. Write no poetry." He turned around to face her again, his weight leaning back onto the balustrades. "We have words," he continued on, his voice oddly distant. "We have words to describe...the color of air. We have none of arts."

The Lochkray retook his footing and stood up tall. Elisha stayed still against the wall, watching the huge man as his eyes scanned above him, as if searching to find the notes of music as they floated through the air. "None arts," he repeated, even more softly. "Sad. It is the way daylights excel over Lochkray. Inability to articulate your perception of the world leaves you wanting. Your wanting provokes expression. Representation. Imitation. Art. Magnificence motivated by ignorant reticence."

No longer speaking, the Lochkray just stared at Elisha as she stood with her back pressed against the wall, unaware of the amusement he found in the irony of her silence. His thin smile cracked across his face. *Dumbfounded. As all daylights exist.*

"You like music?" Her words almost startled the Lochkray.

"Yes," he said softly. Elisha peeled herself off of the wall, though she stayed close. She allowed a gap between the uneven rock and her own back. The awkward silence the Lochkray had allowed to fall intimidated her only for a moment. *Keep him busy,* she said to herself. *Allen will be back.*

"You like our arts? The arts of...uh, daylights?" she continued on.

The Lochkray's eyes darted about the room, still surprised this one would dare to speak to him. "Yes," he answered, firmer this time.

"I thought you hated people. You are like..." Her voice trailed off, knowing she wanted to stall the Lochkray, and also knowing it had to be measured with how far she could go. How far she could taunt him.

"What?" The Lochkray's brow arched amusedly. "Nosferatu? Lycanthrope? Moloch? Vampire? For you, I give assurance, Lochkray are monsters, not."

"I was told that you...hunt people. That you kill people to..."

"To feed," the Lochkray finished.

"Yes. How can you do that?"

Another awkward silence fell, brought on by Elisha. The Lochkray stared back at her, unsure of the meaning of the question. "We must feed," he finally answered.

"You said you like our arts. You admire us."

"Yes."

Elisha almost gasped in confusion. "How can you kill people you admire? Don't you have any pity?"

The Lochkray cocked his head to the side, still unsure of the question. His eyes scanned all about Elisha.

"Have you pity for cattle slaughtered for aliment?"

"Cattle are not human beings!" Elisha yelled at him.

"Human beings," the Lochkray calmly replied, "are not Lochkray."

* * * *

Allen broke out into the afternoon, the cool fresh air washing over him a relief from the dank claustrophobic dankness within the tunnel. He stepped out and turned about quickly, frantically, looking for their packs. There, leaning near the opening of the cave, was the luggage, and beside the packs, the firearms pointing upward to the sky. He reached out to grab one, then stopped, his hand hovering for a moment.

Two?

Both the shotgun and the .22 rifle leaned together against the rocks. The .22 rifle that belonged to Doctor Hadden, and the shotgun that Vance had shot the moose with...the shotgun Vance gave to Madoc...the shotgun that Allen took into the cave...the shotgun the Lochkray took from him before Allen had a moment to react.

Why would he put the shotgun back out here? Allen's mind allowed for a flutter.

The flashlights, he thought, looking at the two short pipes sitting below the guns. *Those are the flashlights we took down. Why the hell would he...*Allen threw away the thoughts with a frustrated huff and reached out again, to take the weapon back into the cave, but took a moment to hover over the shotgun before his hand changed direction slightly and took up Doctor Hadden's old .22 caliber rifle. It was a little less formidable than Vance's shotgun, yet somehow less questionable. He looked at the shotgun on the ground while he fiddled with the other weapon in his hands in an attempt to find the most practical grasp.

Who cares? Allen thought to himself. *Maybe he just doesn't like guns and flashlights in his magic cave.* Allen took a deep breath, preparing to duck back into the darkness.

Then he paused again.

With a tentative air, he slowly pivoted around to scan the forest behind. Somewhere within the feral parts of his mind, instinct had put forth instructions. *Pause,* it said. *Check. Confirm safety. Proceed.* Like a deer with its tail in the air, Allen investigated the terrain for a moment—searching for movement from the unknown causing him to search. His ears heard no sound, his eyes had caught no movement, and his diminished olfactory perceptions had caught no scent. Animal instinct, constantly ignored by everybody back in the civilized world, took the sum of the lack of sound, sight, and smell, and produced a set of instructions.

Pause.
Check.
Confirm safety.
Proceed.

* * * *

"I don't understand," Elisha said to the Lochkray in pitches far higher than she usually employed. "How can you kill humans to feed? It's...savage."

The Lochkray's face suddenly became long. "Savage?" he repeated, the word apparently stinging him. "Savage? Three thousand a-year, daylights have brought massacre to Lochkray. Killed those who are mine with genocidal passion. We fall back, into night, and you follow. We hide in darkness and you take chase with lights. We seek concord in nightfall, and you bring the assault of day."

The Lochkray became louder. "We feed," his voice boomed. "Yes, Is sure, we have fed on essence of the daylights' mortality since our inception. Is what we are. Is where we find our affection. Our necessity. Why deem the ones who retreat on the acquiescence of their necessities as savage...?" The Lochkray stopped, realizing his voice was loudly echoing through the giant hall. He raised his hand and waved it through the air, the peaceful strains of the music came to a halt, the last chords bouncing off of the chamber's walls.

"Into the night," the Lochkray continued speaking, his voice becoming calm once again. "Into the night, in exile, we exist and hide. In darkness we speak of philosophy beyond your comprehension. Know of disciplines outside your capability. Have attained harmony within our people that daylights shall never accomplish. You dare call us savage? You, who inflicts death on your own. Take profit and pleasure at expense of others. Rape your children. Enslave your weak. Slaughter for advantage—"

"I have never—" Elisha attempted to interrupt.

"But you do!" the Lochkray yelled back before she could even start. "You do! The sum of your worth is only equal to the actions of the whole. How dare you have pretension for the value of your kind, while others act against your beliefs? What have you done to halt the killing, the molestation, the dominance, the violations of the strong over the weak? Lochkray kill not their own. Take no advantage of their own. The sum of our worth is equal to a peace. Theories of knowledge discussed at length. Technologies found and employed without affect or concern for the conditions around. Keeping of our weak in safety. Working as an intact unity for the betterment of all. Is how Lochkray endure and exist. Not savage. Abhor where we find nourishment, for it is you, but dare not to call us uncivilized. It is you who are savage. We consume out of necessity. You do same to yourselves out of ignorance."

"What about this place?" Elisha asked. "I was told this place was meant to create a weapon to destroy all people...daylights. How can you condemn us when this has been made to kill us all?"

"Kill all?" he barked back with an ugly laugh. His head tilted from side to side. "Is the understanding you hold? A weapon to kill all? Kraell'Haatch is not to kill all." The Lochkray shook his head, a smile sharply splitting his face. "What made you give credence to the idea we could not have massacred daylights long before? To believe our retreat from our homelands to this isolated place was for the purpose of creating an implement of war? No. The animal form of daylights is fragile." He stopped and his eyes squinted closed with amusement. "So fragile," he almost whispered. "All it would take is our disease to destroy you all. That capability, we have long had."

"Your disease? What do you mean."

"A plague," he clarified, the irony of the situation too overwhelming for him to stop his explanation. "Plague without symptom. Disease without sickness. Invisible epidemic. Delayed symptom. Gestate without evidence, allowed to spread. Surely you have capability to imagine that? No action to quarantine infected, for there would be no intimation. Only when it permeated into all of daylight kind, affects would commence. Quick dissolution. Death for all infected, within days. Months to manifest, days to holocaust. A common occurrence with life, that disease should take a species. All it would take is delayed manifestation. This ability is familiar to the Lochkray. Familiar for many a long time. We cannot eliminate our source of life—our nourishment. How could you think that we would be so shortsighted as to come here to destroy all that we rely upon?"

Elisha looked about the giant chamber in a stutter. "Then what is this place?"

"A place of new beginning," the Lochkray stated proudly. "A new sunset."

Elisha watched as he turned away from her and moved back to the extended walkway, the fingers of his left hand gently strumming across the pillars of the balustrade as he went. His right hand reached upward and beckoned for her to follow as he glanced back at her. Elisha's eyes darted upward at the tunnel to the outside. Then she followed the Lochkray, cautiously.

"You see," he growled as he walked along. His arms reached upward to the ceiling, and then pulled downward. The undulating organic ceiling shuddered all at once. "See what Lochkray produced on the eve of our expulsion from our new twilight. Not a weapon of destruction, but an aliment of life."

Elisha watched several orifices appear and open up high above. Then, from each of these, the transparent car-sized tubes emerged from behind the vaulted dome above her, their glowing liquid contents filling the giant room with color. Elisha counted at least two dozen as they came down and took a solid position far above. She continued to proceed along the extended walkway to where the Lochkray stood, her head angled backward to watch the activity above. The rootlike pipes she saw going from tube to tube stopped moving, and the ceiling became still.

"*Trah-pallamon*," the Lochkray called out to the room ecstatically. "*Kohm-tayyell pag Traa-kee. Kraell'Haatch.*"

"What are those?" Elisha asked in a whisper, coming up to the Lochkray's side. He gave her a quick smug look over his shoulder, and raised his hand upward again. This time, a single organic pipe allowed one end to detach itself from the ceiling, close to the central tube, and descended toward them. Elisha took a step back as the tube was drawn to them, making its way like a snake slithering through the air.

"Life," the Lochkray replied, catching the living conduit out of the air. He turned back to Elisha, and held the tube under his face. Thin wisps of a subtle bluish smoke puffed their way out of the end of the tube and were immediately drawn into the Lochkray's flared nostrils. "Food," he exhaled in a deep voice, his eyes closed, his body shuddering with elation. "Nourishment. Yielding that what we need to survive."

"But you feed on people."

"No longer," he said quietly, his eyes still shut, savoring the taste of what he consumed. "Lochkray found substitute. Then it was lost. A substitute to the essence of daylights." He opened his eyes again and released the pipe, and allowed it to retract quickly upward. "Kraell'Haatch is a place meant to end days of hunting. After so long, found it is. We shall learn from what our ancestors knew, and we shall require to feed on daylights no more. To find Kraell'Haatch was Lochkray's last hunt."

"B-but..." Elisha stuttered out again, yet came up with nothing more. The two once again stared at each other.

"Go," the Lochkray finally said to her. "Go back to your home. I have no need for you here. You are of more use to me back among your people."

Elisha continued to stare at him without moving.

"Go," the Lochkray repeated.

"What about Tyance and Madoc?" she asked in a dry voice. "Doctor Hadden?

What about that thing, that animal that was attacking us?"

"Your Madoc," the Lochkray shrugged, "brought wound upon the sanok. It is now dead or dying."

"Sanok? What is…it killed them," her voice shrieked.

"No right," the Lochkray yelled back, equally as loud. "You have no right to be here. Sanok was our sentinel, set in motion to hunt those who would invade what is ours. You are the ones who dared come here without legitimacy, without right. Your daylights died at the hand of their own ignorance."

"You let them die. You didn't warn us."

"Obligation did not exist to."

"You *are* a savage."

The Lochkray's hand slapped its way across Elisha's face so fast that she never even saw it. The stinging force sent her down to the ground, the sound of the hit so sharp and swift that she was scarcely even sure she heard it.

"How do you dare?" the Lochkray bellowed, hovering over Elisha with his hand held high in the air to administer another blow to her already reddening face. "We are the enlightened, not you—"

The sudden *snap* made the Lochkray come to a halt, and the smashing from behind made him whirl around. From high above, the bottom of one of the giant tubes shattered on the ground below, its glowing contents falling in a giant wave that splattered across the lower floor of the chamber.

The Lochkray's scream echoed in the chamber, a word unrecognizable to Elisha, shrilly cutting through the sound of the falling glass and liquid. He turned back, to where the shot came from.

At the edge of the tunnel, staring in utter amazement that he actually hit one of the tubes on his first try, Allen sat with the .22 across his lap. He watched the liquid explode onto the tables along the floor below. He brought the weapon up again, hovered with it for a second then brought it down, unconvinced he was able to do all that damage in the first place. If he hadn't seen the man smack Elisha to the ground, he probably never would have.

The Lochkray raised his hands above his head and brought them down fiercely, as if throwing two invisible balls at the opening of the cave. From high above, two tubular pipes, like the one the Lochkray had inhaled sustenance from, followed the Lochkray's direction and shot down at Allen. From her position on the floor, Elisha saw the pipes' attack on Allen, as well as the stunned obliviousness on his face.

"Allen, look out," she screamed at him. The Lochkray turned back at her in a fury and made another open hand to fly across her face.

Allen's eyes darted toward his assaulted friend, then frantically looked around him to identify the cause of her warning. A moment before they came in contact, he saw the tubes as they moved sinuously through the air at him. In a panic, he ducked forward to avoid their advance, but threw himself off balance. He toppled forward and down to the balcony below, landing on the smooth tiles with a violent blow, the .22 clanging down at his side.

"Fuhg," Allen cursed as the right side of his body erupted in pain. He rolled onto his back, and saw the tubes taking blind swipes at where he was sitting, fifteen feet above.

"Allen!" Elisha screamed again.

Through the sharp pain, he reached out and took hold of the rifle again, pushing himself backward and frantically coming to his feet. The Lochkray started to advance on Allen, but stopped when the rifle's muzzle pointed directly at him.

The Lochkray tilted his head to the side and surveyed Allen. A question ran through his Lochkray mind: *Is it capable?* Though thought in a Lochkray's language, Allen read its meaning in the half-bemused look on the huge male's face. Allen knew it would not take a moment for the Lochkray to discern the answer he already knew in his heart. With only the slice of a moment to make a decision, Allen turned his rifle upward again and pressed the trigger twice, again striking one of the huge containers filled with colorful liquid, and again shattering it, causing the liquid to pour downward.

The Lochkray turned and ran to the edge of the balcony's banister with his hands outstretched as if making an attempt to catch the debris and fluid before it fell below.

"*Prasayya*," he shrieked. "*Chay!*"

Perhaps if Allen had realized the meaning of the words, or if he saw how the second canister's contents were furiously mixing with the contents of the first on the chamber's floor, he would not have squeezed the trigger again. However, in ignorance, he aimed at more of the huge tubes in the ceiling and fired again. *Snap.* And again. *Snap.*

Allen stopped firing, realizing that a new rumbling joined the sounds of the crashing glass and liquid—a deep reverberation, building on the level below.

"*Schalee'ch-ptah!*" the Lochkray screamed at the sight before him.

A dark cloud was building around the lower level, like a smoke clinging to the ground rather than rising. It billowed and built, rolling over and over itself, becoming larger, filling in all space on the lower floor. The glow of the natatorium could still be seen seeping through the rounded clouds, but now its color had changed from its bright sapphire to a dull emerald, the contents of the massive tubes mixing together in the water, combining angrily. All across the massive floor, the cloud spread, reaching out in puffs. Flickers of light shot through the smoky fog, like lightning within clouds.

Allen lowered the weapon as Elisha ran up to his side. The Lochkray searched the lower level frantically, his hands beginning to reach to the ceiling to order conduits down to attempt to clean up the mess below but his hand hovered in confused indecision. The dark flashing cloud was visible to Allen now, as it climbed up to the balcony in billowing waves.

"Oh crap," he said to Elisha. "What have I done?"

"We have to get out," she replied anxiously, pulling him by his arm to the ladder carved into the wall. Allen's legs remained rigid as he stared dumbfounded at the rumbling mist's approach.

"You said to shoot them. You said it would slow him down, he wouldn't be able to chase us, you said—"

"Allen, we have to go!" Elisha yelled, all at once realizing too loudly. The Lochkray spun around. Anger exploded across his face, mimicking the explosions of light and smoke behind him.

"*Schalee'ch-ptah*," he hissed at Allen and Elisha.

"Go, go, go," Allen frantically told Elisha with his eyes still locked on the Lochkray.

"*Schalee'ch-ptah*," the Lochkray screeched out again. He knew this daylight could never shoot him, and was convinced its weapon was empty of bullets. Allen raised the gun again, trying to keep him at bay. The Lochkray stepped forward furiously, knowing well that the weapon in the Allen's hands was not a threat, that this boy academic would never have the heart to kill him.

What he underestimated, however, was Allen's frantic nervousness. At the sight of the Lochkray's angry advance, Allen flinched. The weapon wasn't even fully raised, still only held in one hand. Allen flinched. His hands clenched and his finger squeezed around the trigger.

Snap.

The tiny .22 round burst out of the front of the rifle and took its unintentional target fifteen feet away. The spinning, cone-like piece of metal struck the Lochkray's right leg, slightly above the knee. It forced its way past the thin layer of skin and into the muscle and tissue of the Lochkray's thigh, only coming to rest after bouncing off bone and stopping within his leg.

With her hands and feet placed on the lower rungs of the ladder, Elisha watched over her shoulder as the Lochkray's entire face squinted and gravity brought him crashing down to the floor of the balcony.

"Oh, shit, I shot him," Allen yelled.

The Lochkray wrapped his hand over the wound on his leg, his face still tensed in pain. Behind him, Elisha saw the undulating cloud of smoke and light already licking at the edge of the upper level, beginning to seep onto the balcony.

"Come on," she yelled.

Allen tore his gaze off of his wounded enemy and followed after Elisha. The rifle was slung over his shoulder awkwardly as he reached out to the wall and grabbed onto the first rungs. His feet propelled his body after his clamoring hands, as he furiously went up.

He kept his eyes locked above, watching as Elisha climbed the entire distance and disappeared into the tunnel at the ladder's end. Her legs just vanished when her face reappeared, joined by her arm, which reached down to him.

"Come on," she went to repeat, but the last word never fully formed, instead coming out more like an "aw" sound. Allen saw the terror in her face before he felt the hand wrap around his leg.

His foot was pulled off the ladder's rung and his entire body dropped a foot until his full weight was taken on by his hands, which still held tight onto the wall. The Lochkray then reached upward and took hold of the back of Allen's belt, straining Allen's arms as the Lochkray pulled himself upward.

"*Chaar ralee*," the Lochkray hissed, using Allen like the ladder, grabbing onto his shoulder and moving up. Allen looked down into the eyes of the Lochkray, which burned at him. Below, the smoke already fully invaded the balcony, invisible now beneath the blanket of dark haze.

Allen kicked downward at the Lochkray, deliberately trying to strike his leg where the accidental shot went in. The Lochkray winced in pain and the grip on Allen's shoulder released. Allen kicked out until he found a rung within the wall to take his weight.

With the Lochkray's hold now only on the back of his pants, Allen allowed his right hand to release, the strap of the .22 sliding down to his hand. Awkwardly, but with as much strength as he could manage, Allen took the rifle in his hand and frantically swung its stalk down. The butt of the gun connected with the Lochkray's face. Already weakened from the agony in his leg, the Lochkray released his grasp on Allen and fell backward.

Elisha watched the huge male fall into the rising cloud that swallowed him. Allen, however, did not watch as the Lochkray disappeared into the darkness with his arms outstretched and grasping at the empty air. He was too hurried, again pulling and pushing his body up the ladder, drawing himself up to the tunnel, an awkward advance with the rifle still in his hand.

Elisha retreated back into the tunnel as Allen came up to it, his arms reaching over the edge. At first he attempted to toss the rifle up to her, to slide it along the ground as he pulled himself up, but the butt of the gun caught the edge of the tunnel and Allen lost his hold. Had he been more focused, he could have easily caught the weapon before it fell. Instead, he allowed it to drop into the smoke below.

"We have to get the hell out of—" Allen started. With only his torso into the tunnel, his legs still climbing their way out of the chamber, Elisha saw the Lochkray seemingly explode upward, behind him. His huge arms wrapped around Allen's neck and took hold.

He brought his face up to Allen's ear, still cursing in his Lochkray language over the rumbling beneath them. Elisha stared in horror at the Lochkray's face, now melted and distorted. From his furious ruby eyes, his Lochkray blood oozed out like a flood of black tears—the same dark fluid that filled his mouth and poured out of his auricles.

"*Kareem'cha*," the Lochkray gurgled through his poisoned breath. "*Chaar'ralee kay.*"

Terror flooded over Allen as he lost his hold and fell backward into the cloud, the dying Lochkray wrapped hard around him, listening to Elisha's horrified shriek. The cloud enveloped the two, wrapping around Allen's vision, and filling his lungs as he prepared to cry out. The noxious mixture of the organic matter killed Allen quickly. Without coughing, choking, or burning, the cloud seeped into his blood and invaded his being. Unlike the Lochkray, Allen was not able to fight death. It took him hastily. He never felt the thud of the balcony, where the two landed below. His body was numb as it rolled off the Lochkray, oblivious to the night being's frenzied thrashing and screams.

Within the flashing cloud, the Lochkray eventually became as still as Allen. The burning mist that melted his skin and organs invaded all the cells of his being, and he found himself no longer able to resist the fog. He stopped moving, and let his cognizance fade. His vision gone, he allowed his last conscious thought to sweep the tunnel above and feel the mind of Elisha.

He felt her cowering. Felt her terror. Felt her grief—and it amused him.

Chapter Twenty-Four

Tears streaming down her cheeks, Elisha broke out of the cave into the dying moments of the day. The late afternoon sun still had enough strength to cut through the forest's branches and cause her eyes to squint as she emerged from the darkness. She brushed by the luggage as she burst out of the tunnel, tipping it over in a dull thud. Far down in the cave, the advancing cloud that killed Allen had dissipated, slowly feeding upon itself, swirling and panting downward, eating away at the biotic walls, killing the chamber as it abated.

Elisha burst forward, almost ready to run into the woods ahead of her. Instead, her feet faltered and she stopped. She brought her hands to her face and fell backward onto the hard ground, crying. Behind her hands she saw Allen's face, hopeful at the thought of escape and that horridly melted form rising behind him. Like a flashbulb burnt into her eye, the image stayed locked, Allen's last moment. With that horrible tick of time caught in her mind, other thoughts raced. The most prominent of these was simply, *What now?*

She sat there wondering and reliving as her brain attempted to fully comprehend everything which happened. So surreal and without any scale of experience with which to measure the moment, her thoughts swirled and muddled, until her crying was the only thing that made any sense. It was the only thing which felt even remotely familiar.

Then with an abruptness, her head went upward. Her eyes widened and she stopped crying. Somewhere, beyond her full senses, something had set instinct to call upon her—an unseen sound, an unheard sight. Something caused her skin to tingle, and focused her caution to a point.

Just as it had with Allen, somewhere within the feral parts of her mind, instinct had put forth instructions: *Pause*, it said. *Check. Confirm safety. Proceed.* Allen had done it. Had confirmed he saw no threat, and proceeded back down the tunnel to his death. Elisha, however, remained still. Instinct's instructions, unwilling or unable to evolve, repeated the tacit commands:
Check.
Confirm safety.
Check.
Confirm safety.
Check.
Confirm safety.

Elisha allowed the back of her hand to smear away the tears on her cheeks, to clear away the irritation of the droplets' descent along her face. Still, her eyes remained unblinking as they rapidly surveyed the trees about her.

With injuries severe, the sanok's lunge from the woods came so awkwardly It would look comical to an onlooker. It attempted to spring from the woods' darkness, but it underestimated the wound on its right arm. As it went to swiftly stride toward the prey, its own support buckled and it fell forward. Yet sheer determination of the dying animal forced it to continue toward the intruder, sitting so close to the burrow it was compelled to protect from all encroachment.

Elisha screamed and scrambled backward. Even with its ensanguined body and feeble attack, the sanok's jaws advanced and snapped shut onto empty air only a few feet from her before she moved. Her legs kicked frantically, pushing her across the coarse ground. Each centimeter she retreated from the dying sanok, it matched, pulling itself toward her, continuously snapping its mouth open and shut, as if in hope the extra reach of each bite would be just enough to take hold of the prey.

With great strain, Elisha kicked herself to her feet and darted to the cave's entrance. This action excited the sanok, whose snakelike body, spotted with holes from Madoc's .223, twisted in derangement behind it, apparently separated from the determined eyes on the creature's head. It dragged itself forward quicker, focused on reaching the prey. Its gaze locked on the target, and its advance continued, even as Elisha grabbed Vance's shotgun from beside the cave and fumbled with it, at first attempting to put the weapon's stalk under her arm, then placing it awkwardly into the crotch of her shoulder. The creature saw the dark hole in the center of the tube, and saw Elisha's wince as she tensed up on the lever. It continued its wounded advance.

Elisha stared at the weapon in confusion. She had pulled the trigger but nothing happened. Attempting to recall everything she saw her father do with his guns, her shaking hand reached forward to the barrel of the weapon and pulled back hard on the rack. A perfectly good red casing was spat out the weapon's side and fell to the ground as she snapped the rack forward again. Again Elisha raised the weapon up high and pulled the trigger, and again the spongy pull resulted in no shot going off.

The sanok, now right on top of her, having her pinned against the entrance of the cave, brought itself upward, pushing itself to its full height. Even while its arm screamed and its body twisted in agony, the sanok brought itself up to tower over Elisha. To look down on her before it completed its last task. To eliminate this intruder.

Elisha did her best to ignore the form mounting to tower up over her. Her frantic gaze searched the shotgun's frame, trying to remember everything—anything—she knew about guns. A button sat behind and above the trigger on the right side of the weapon. She pushed it in. This caused the button to pop out on the left side of the weapon. Elisha looked at this newly emerged button. It was red. A red button had popped out on the left side of the weapon when she pressed the one on the right.

What had Dad said? her mind asked rapidly. *About the safety? About red?*

The sanok's head slowly descended, a fatigued satisfaction in its simple mind allowing it to accept and enjoy this last moment. This last kill. This last hunt.

It's the safety, Elisha recalled. *Remember? Push the button, out comes red. Red—you're dead. It's what Dad taught you. Remember? Red—you're dead.*

"Red—you're dead," Elisha said to the sanok's teeth. Awkwardly pointing the barrel upward, she pulled down on the trigger. The loud *boom* quickly snapped the sanok's head backward. Elisha screamed at the sudden sound and kick, forcing the weapon out of her fingers and down to the ground.

The sanok stopped when the force hit it. It still stood tall, its teeth bared, ready to drop onto Elisha with all of its strength, but all movement came to a halt. The full blast had exploded out of the weapon and pushed through the fleshy portion of its jaw, under where its tongue would be, through the U of the mandible, and found a way up to its complicated mind, exploding out the top of its head in a fountain of dark blood.

The sanok hovered, its brain shut off. So many vicious kills it made, on animal and man. So many panicked deaths. So many horrific last moments it had inflicted, it didn't realize its own final thoughts would come with such a simple clap of thunder. The animal shuddered in its place, and then melted back down onto itself. Already weakened, the final explosion did the ultimate damage, and snuffed the animal out. Elisha watched it fall to the ground with a heavy thud.

She picked the shotgun back up and placed it into the crook of her shoulder. She aimed the barrel at the still animal laying at her feet. She racked the weapon again, and pulled down on the trigger, wincing as the shot blasted out of the barrel and slammed into the smashed head of the gurgling thing. Elisha awkwardly pulled back on the rack again, steadied the gun, and fired another time, this time into a completely motionless pile. When she pulled back again, the final cartridge fell to the ground. The next time she pulled the trigger, nothing happened.

The last echoes of the weapon's thunder faded away behind the ringing in Elisha's ears. She stood, the weapon weakly falling down to her side until the tip of the tube touched the ground. With a quivering lip, she let go of the firearm and it clattered to her feet.

Elisha weakly sidestepped and backed away from the animal and the gun, until she was able to find a spot where the sanok's blood had not splattered the rocky terrain. She then allowed her legs to quit, fell down, and began to cry again.

* * * *

The sun disappeared behind the trees of the horizon before Elisha raised her head off of the ground, flakes of wood chips and dirt clinging to her tear-streaked cheeks. It was an hour later before she crawled over to the backpacks and went through them, searching for the most essential supplies. An hour after that before she stood up, and faced the direction of the next waypoint on the GPS.

Hours after midnight, she finally stopped walking. Without even looking at the tent, she simply dropped the backpack down and fell on top of it and slept. When dawn broke again, she got up and began to walk again.

Nobody followed her.
Nobody watched her.
Nothing hunted her.

Epilogue

Staff Sergeant Scott Mariglia stared across the commander's desk of the Cochrane detachment of the Ontario Provincial Police. Compared to the other rooms in the functional building, this one was very cozy, with a blue carpet to match the drapes hanging closed over the window. The walls were painted a soothing pastel green, and the swivel chairs were nicely padded. Compared to the practical tile flooring, beige blinds, and office chairs in the rest of the police station, this room was luxurious. So it had to be. There had to be a place of slightly higher decorum in the detachment for its commander to work within. One never knew what level of guest might come through the door to speak with him. With nearly four dozen persons under his command in three different detachment areas, all kinds of public officials, members of the press, and members of the public would visit. The staff sergeant never knew who he would have to speak to.

Today proved that point. He had a guest he would never have imagined would be sitting across from him. A priest. A monsignor from Eastern Europe. It had been three months since that girl flew down with Matt Fanning, her entire party killed. Killed by a vampire, she said. No sooner had one of his constables shown up at the Bush Air office than the ball started rolling. Rolling right out of his control and off to the Criminal Investigations Branch. The staff sergeant found, as always happened with CIB, he went from top of the heap, down to having to scramble to get any kind of information.

Three months later, when all was said and done, it was Mariglia who had to answer the questions. The questions from the press, the families, the public, and anybody wondering which branch of the service was supposed to be billed for which task performed during this fiasco. What a fiasco it had been: five people dead. Four murdered, one suicide.

Thankfully, because it became evident it was a murder-suicide, the press and public lost interest with the case more quickly than if there were charges laid. With the obvious culprit dead, it became little more than a very odd story. Like a clap of thunder, the press loudly cried out about multiple murder in the north country. Then, the thunder just rolled away. No whodunnit. No trial. No sensationalism.

"Belarus," Mariglial said to the priest across from him. "I remember seeing your country's hockey team play in the last winter Olympics."

"It was your country's team who beat them." The old priest smiled, his English phrased perfectly, his accent not befuddling the words' clear meaning.

"Yes," Mariglia laughed. "Sorry about that."

"Two teams compete," the old priest replied, quietly, with a forgiving shrug.

"So," Mariglial decided to depart the pleasantries, "I understand you provided a statement over the phone to one of our officers, back when this investigation was going on."

"Yes. A Detective Beamer. He was most polite and helpful. It was a great shock to learn that our own Mister Halverson came to your country and done such horrible things. Your detective was most considerate. Is why I wanted to come here to meet him. I wish I could have come sooner, but..." Again the old man gave a forgiving shrug of his shoulders.

"Well, I'm afraid that detective is no longer at this detachment. He was only brought in to assist with the investigation. Because it was a murder investigation, we have to bring in help from Region."

"Is a shame. I imagine you can be equally as helpful in explaining to me what your investigation revealed."

"Well," Mariglia started, with a lick of his lips and a clearing of his throat, "it was quite the investigation. Basically this girl, this Elisha King, wanders out of the bush three months ago and says that her group has been killed. When asked who killed them, she says it was a," he shook his head with half a laugh, "...like a... vampire kind of person.

"So we talk to her, she says her university group went out looking for some professor to try and get him to come back to their school—it was some kind of research grant problem between the professor and the university. She says that while they're up there, the group is attacked by some kind of monster controlled by this vampire. The vampire is trying to keep them from finding a huge cave filled with...I don't know, treasure or something. She says she finds this cave and the vampire kills everybody except her. That was the long and short of her story, anyway. So, naturally, we figured she had killed them all."

"Naturally."

"Right. So, she tells us about your guy. The American who worked at your monastery. Vance, uh..."

"Halverson."

"Right. I guess Detective Beamer went over all this with you. Apparently he left your monastery on bad terms or something."

"Something like that." The old priest nodded.

"Right." Mariglia paused for a moment before deciding to continue. "So anyway, your former employee apparently is the one who told them about the vampires. When our officers went up to where all this was supposed to have taken place, what we find is the three other members of the King girl's party, the professor that they went looking for, and your Mister Halverson. All of them dead, just like the girl said. However, from what our investigators determined, they were all killed by...well, as you know, Mister Halverson. It appeared as though he hung himself."

"Appeared?"

"Well, from what I understand the bodies were not in good condition when we got out there. See, that area is heavily populated by bears. Black bears. All of them were...well, they weren't in good condition when our people found them. Mister Halverson's body was found underneath a tree with his belt hanging in it, not far from where the rest of the bodies were found. There was the suicide note."

"And the girl?" the old priest asked. "What of her? How did you know that she was not involved in their deaths?"

"Like I said, we thought she was at first. We interviewed her, multiple times. Even had polygraph come up...uh, like a lie detector, and had her talk to doctors. According to the doctors and the polygraph analyst, she believes what she's telling us. She believes that they were all hunted down by monsters to protect a magic cave."

Mariglia's body shook with a suppressed, humorless, laugh. "We don't know if she was doing drugs up there, or if maybe the bast...uh, your Mister Halverson drugged them, or what happened. She seems to be suffering from some kind of post traumatic stress syndrome or something to that effect. We looked into her story, went exactly to where she told us. Sure enough, the bodies were all there but there was no cave. We even went looking at the archaeological site that the university professor was supposed to have found, and it turned out to be nothing. According to the university, anyway. Just a garbage pile with no artifacts of interest or anything. The sad thing is, it looks like the professor was trying to fake a site for fame, or funding. All of this was for nothing. A hoax."

"Where is the girl now?"

"She was in a hospital for a couple of months. She's out now, living at home under the care of her parents."

"I don't suppose I could speak with her?" the old priest asked.

"No," Mariglia stated simply, "I don't think that would be a good idea. You gotta realize she's been through a lot, and we can't—"

"No need to explain." The old man raised his hand, shaking his head. "I knew your answer before I asked. I don't suppose there is much she could tell me I don't already know." He got to his feet and extended a hand across Bell's desk. "I thank you for your time, Staff Sergeant Mariglia."

"Not a problem at all. I hope you didn't come all the way from Belarus just to speak with me."

"No. We have had poor Mister Halverson's remains interred in the city of Timmins for the last few weeks. Now I am going to escort them back home with me." The old man pursed his lips, hating to lie. "He may have left on bad terms, but the monastery was his home for so long. He has no family, so I will take him back for burial."

"May I ask, what happened to make him leave?"

The old priest pursed his lips again. "As I told your detective, he believed in old stories. Began to believe in the...vampires and monsters. He believed it was true and left. We did not know he was coming here. We never thought he would hurt anybody." The old priest opened his mouth to say something else but the words just hovered.

"Do you know the word Lochkray?" he eventually asked.

"No." Mariglia paused to think. "Wait, uh, yeah. Low-ker-ay. That's what the girl said the vampires were called. That's what he called himself in his suicide note. It was in the report."

The old priest nodded. "Thank you for your time," he repeated. Mariglia escorted the old priest through the front door of the detachment, then returned to his office, shaking his head. *Strange man*, he thought to himself. *No wonder his friend went insane.*

Outside the building, the old priest sat down in the passenger side of a blue four-door Pontiac. The younger priest who sat beside him didn't start the car. The older priest bowed his head down and spoke to himself.

"Forgive me the lies at the expense of your name," the old priest muttered in Russian, his eyes closed. "You are revered by those who know."

"What did you find out?" the younger priest asked.

"What we already assumed," the older replied, lifting his head. "They believe

Mister Halverson to be responsible for all the deaths. They say he left a note."

"What of the girl?"

"They believe her mad."

"So they have been deceived."

The old priest motioned with his hand toward the steering wheel of the car, and the younger priest started the vehicle. He pulled out of the parking lot and turned toward the city of Timmins, where Vance's body was kept.

"They have been deceived," the old priest finally answered, ten minutes later.

* * * *

Elisha King opened her eyes and stared at the ceiling of her bedroom for the longest time. She studied the flowery pink border wrapped around the top of her room. Far too childish for her liking, the remnants of a child's room being kept intact by her overly sentimental parents. Then her eyes came down to her bedside table, where a glass of water sat beside a lamp, equally as juvenile as the border that ran around the top of her room. She looked at the several tiny brown plastic bottles with white plastic lids, the name Elisha KING typed across the white label of each.

She cast a cautious glance over at the closed door, and listened to the sounds on the other side before sitting up in the bed. In the distance she could faintly hear the mildly tinny sound of voices coming from the television in the living room. She brought her hand up to her eyes, and pinched the bridge of her nose between her index finger and thumb.

She stopped telling her story three weeks before. After being interviewed, interrogated, incarcerated, and committed, she was smart enough to realize the truth was never going to be understood. She began doubting herself at times, but then she would comfort herself into believing she knew what she saw, and heard, and felt. No one else would ever believe it. She had grasped that reality a month before.

"Vance Halverson left a letter," she was told by one of the doctors, during a session. "It was found on his remains. Experts have studied it, and it is in his handwriting. I want you to read it."

The photocopy the doctor had was difficult to make out, but with some focus, while one of the orderlies stood behind her and the doctor stared at her from behind his ridiculously thick glasses, she followed the words down the page:

> *I am the Lochkray. Fear me, and do not come into my forest. I have killed these for coming to my country. I will now join them in death so I might kill them again for their intrusion. I leave you a survivor to warn you of my anger. Fear me. I am the Lochkray. I will come back.*

She cried after that. Simply cried. It was then she stopped talking to the doctor. It was then she realized.

Looking about that simple room, at the apathetic woman who stood over her shoulder and the pretentious doctor who sat before her with his hands folded on the table, she realized. Within the helplessness she felt at that moment, she came to the realize she was never going to convince anybody. And, too, the realization she had to get out.

Now, only a week away from her next appointment with the doctor, she just stayed in her room, and never mentioned the Lochkray. Never mentioned how she saw Allen die. Never mentioned Kraell'Haatch, or the monster the Lochkray called sanok. When she said nothing, nobody asked. Nobody cared about her story—which made it easy. She didn't have to come up with a lie to match the "evidence" they found in the backwoods of the north. All she had to do was deny what she said before, what she saw, and perhaps claim amnesia on the rest. That would keep them happy. That would get her out of this house. That would get her off the dizzying medication. That would get her out into the world again.

Because, she needed to get out.

She had work to do.

For another realization came to her, those days lying in her bed, lucid thought peeking through her hazy mind in moments before prescribed dosage was re-administered. While she might deny all the moments to her family, friends, and doctors, she reviewed them over and over in her own mind. Over and over—every word, every sight. Every instruction.

"Kraell'Haatch was not made to kill all," the Lochkray said. *"The animal form of daylights are so fragile,"* he said. *"All it would take is disease to destroy you all. That capability we have had for so long.*

"How could you think that we would be so shortsighted as to come here to destroy all that we rely upon?"

Elisha closed her eyes to suppress her churning emotions.

"Go back to your home. I have no need for you here. You are of more use to me back among your people.

"All it would take is a disease to destroy you all. That capability we have had for so long.

"A plague without symptom. A disease without sickness. An invisible epidemic, one that would gestate without evidence until it had time to spread.

"Only when it had permeated into all of daylight kind, the effects would commence. Months to manifest, days to total holocaust.

"Go back to your home. I have no need for you here. You are of more use to me back among your people.

You are of more use to me back among your people."

Months to manifest. How long did that give her? Elisha wondered. Nowhere near long enough. Nowhere near long enough to spend days laying in her pink childish bedroom, staring at the ceiling, trying to pick clear thoughts out from the haze of prescriptions.

She was infected. The pilot who came to get her was infected. The ten police officers she dealt with were infected. The staff of the hospital in Cochrane, and the psychiatric institute in North Bay. The pretentious doctor. Her parents. Her sister. Her friends. Everybody each one of them met. Every patient in the hospitals, every store clerk they dealt with, their friends, their families, and everybody they talked to. She had to get out. She had to find a Lochkray.meet with them and see if there was a cure.

Please be wrong, she said to herself. *But prepare if you are right.*

* * * *

That night, the Lochkray awoke. Still exhausted from months of manipulation, of twisting the minds of daylights, he realized that he was weak and hungry. The daylight authorities believed the girl insane, and the acolyte of the Cimmerian Knights was responsible for the deaths of all those people. And all the while he felt ill from the contamination at Kraell'Haatch. The contamination that killed Kraell'Haatch. The contamination that destroyed his kind's hopes.

That night, as he woke and recognized his hunger, he also realized the hiding of his failure was complete. Now what remained was to amend the consequences of that failure.

The Lochkray walked out on the city street, his long black overcoat barely skimming over the sidewalk as he went. He scanned the daylights about him as they wandered through his night, oblivious to his watching. He walked past them, apparently dodging their glances like raindrops, and yet just calmly strolling along.

Then he stopped.

His head jerked suddenly toward the other side of the street, his eyes becoming determined slits, his nostrils flaring and inhaling deeply. He found what he wanted, walking along the street with another female friend. He changed his direction and headed across the road.

Twenty-one revolutions around the sun, twelve days from her last time, her virtue unknown. In an age of loose ethics, this quality of prey was a rare find, and upon seeing it, the hunter's dark heart pounded hard. He found her scent among the stench of the city and inhaled it deeply, feeding his appetite, turning its smoldering into a blaze. He followed after the two carefully. Followed them as they wandered through the city, until they came to a club, where pounding music overflowed into the street and enticed them.

One more dance before I start, the Lochkray thought to himself, and followed them in.

About the Author:

Brian M.H. Goodwin is an award winning writer of horror and supernatural fiction, the author of A Fear Unnatural and Last Dance of the Lochkray.

Born in the early 1970's, Brian grew up in the suburbs of Toronto, before leaving home to attend Peterborough's Trent University in 1992, where he obtained a degree in Anthropology.

Following his graduation in 1996, he attended the Ontario Police College, and has become a trained and experienced officer and criminal investigator. Brian has worked in police Detachments throughout the province of Ontario since 1997.

In 2005, his novel *Last Dance of the Lochkray* was first published as an e-book. This book received critical praise, and also took the Electronically Published Internet Connection's EPPIE award for Best Horror novel in 2006.

After a hiatus from writing, in September 2011, his supernatural thriller *A Fear Unnatural* was published by Eternal Press. Following that release, *Last Dance of the Lochkray* has been made available for sale once again, this time from Damnation Books.

Brian currently lives and works in a small community in central Ontario, a loving husband and father of two children. Somewhere between the busy duties of his work, home, and family, he tries to find the time to write, with a desire to entertain with tales of the macabre and supernatural.

Visit him online at:
http://www.brianmhgoodwin.com

Also from Damnation Books:

Ancient Blood: The Amazon
by Bob Nailor & Jack Franklin

eBook ISBN: 9781615727704
Print ISBN: 9781615727711

Dark Fantasy Vampire
Novel of 93,038 words

The Chronicles of Vamazonia

An evil, 500 years in the making, lurks in the jungles of Brazil. Today it wants to be free.

Time has allowed evil to lurk and grow in the jungles of Brazil for over 500 years. Today that evil wants free. What can a young woman do when confronted with the reality of horror? Ana is an anthropologist and so intent on being one with a lost tribe she will do anything, even hunt human prey.

Also from Damnation Books:

The Last Vampire
by Kathryn Meyer Griffith

eBook ISBN: 9781615722075
Print ISBN: 9781615722082

Horror Vampire
Novel of 104,029 words

Author's new revised edition. The earthquakes with their falling ash, the global floods and the devastating fires arrive first. Then the worldwide plague with its stench of death. And as mankind suffers and dies out, vampires, their numbers dwindling, struggle and fight fiercely among themselves to survive in a world where there aren't enough humans to prey and feed upon. As the weeks go by they become fewer, more desperate and more ruthless.

Emma, as the world disintegrates around her, finds herself alone, family all have perished…and fending off an unnatural hunger as she becomes one of the undead. Fighting her unwanted destiny she's determined to resist the bloodlust she feels, the need to kill and feed on humans, of losing her humanity, for as long as she can bear it…but she's so hungry… and the night calls.

Visit Damnation Books online at:

Our Blog—
http://www.damnationbooks.com/blog/

DB Reader's Yahoogroup—
http://groups.yahoo.com/group/DamnationBooks/

Twitter—
http://twitter.com/DamnationBooks

Google+—
https://plus.google.com/u/0/115524941844122973800

Facebook—
https://www.facebook.com/pages/Damnation-Books/80339241586

Goodreads—
http://www.goodreads.com/DamnationBooks

Shelfari—
http://www.shelfari.com/damnationbooks

Library Thing—
http://www.librarything.com/DamnationBooks

HorrorWorld Forums—
http://horrorworld.org/phpBB3/viewforum.php?f=134

CPSIA information can be obtained at www.ICGtesting.com
Printed in the USA
LVOW082059290313

326559LV00003B/57/P